Dedicated to my father, Luciano, who passed away on the morning of October 14th, 2023, after nearly fifteen years battling Parkinson's Disease.

He was a man devoted to his family, who loved numbers and languages, and the free air of the countryside.

A man of few words, a great sense of humour, and an incredible depth of wisdom.

I miss him greatly.

My heart is forever broken.

*Thousand-Year Dream:
Vilkacis*

Copyright © 2012

All Rights Reserved.

Thousand-Year Dream: Vilkacis is a work of fiction. Names, places, and incidents either are products of author's imagination or are used fictitiously. Any resemblance to actual events, locales, or persons, living or dead, is coincidental.

Book cover and artwork by author.

Other Books by Zach S.Z. Murphy:

Cathedral of the Damned

Aberrations

Thousand-Year Dream

Revolution. Progression. Mastery.

Join the journey on Instagram @dream.under.the.light

I. Vade Mecum

I: Vade Mecum

2000 years before the Great Battle of Guard…

Under the waning light of cast-iron lanterns, slick black ink spread across the dry parchment, trailing the path of a time-tested brush. The old writer hurried to preserve his trove of memories from decades long past. A story of comrades-in-arms, shaken fealty on the eve of thralldom and war, and secrets that would threaten the stability of kingdoms. The shadows flickered and shied away from the flames around the antique wooden desk where the cowled writer sat, retelling the tale of the Twelve Knights….

I awoke to the fury of massive steel claws smashing through the earth and rock, shattering the battleground in a blast of earthen debris. With a breath of flame and dark fume pressed angrily through the nostrils of its elegant draconian head, the Sentinel – the last of the ancient drakes – kept its luminous crystal eyes on the remainder of us. Its solemn and booming voice echoed in the monumental hall with sadness and anger, as its majestic wings folded back and twitched anxiously in realization that indeed it was the end.

Its brethren were slain amidst an array of stalagmites, amongst the ruins of their Mountain lair, their blood oozing from the open wounds like molten metal onto earthenware.

Around me, the lord-knights were themselves determined to bring an end to this age-old conflict for the domination of the world. They have come from every corner of Terra Mia, traversed the oceans and unforgiving lands with the vast armies of twelve kingdoms unified solely by a common foe. We have lost too much in the war with the drakes. Whole cities were trampled to ash and memorials; our armies, after decades of unending warfare, now lie scattered dead in the fields as the sacrifice of sons and daughters for the final offensive to liberate mankind from the oppressive chains of our former guardians.

Nobility had given way to despotism; compassion to greed; reason to unbridled rage, until at last Fate had granted this moment of silence between the vestiges of valor and the last shreds of fear.

The lord-knights, nine of them still on their weary feet while three lay dead, spread out to surround the Great Sentinel.

It leaped forth like a shadow cast from sudden light, and cut through the ranks of knights that attempted to corner it. Two of the knights were flung aside in the shuffle, but the rest of us reacted quickly and increased our distance as the drake swept its tail across the ground.

Algernon Vant of Guard, ever seeking to claim eternal glory in his bloodthirst, was tall and regal, an unmatched tactician, but with his tattered robes, pierced armour, and a steaming spear, he appeared demonic. Too far to be affected by the tail-sweep, he threw his weapon into the Sentinel's exposed flank, but with its scales too thick, the weapon splintered uselessly away.

The drake now drew its gaze to him, but the knight from Guard was undaunted. Algernon unsheathed twin swords, and held them invitingly to his sides.

For victory, he rushed fearlessly toward the drake, as the rest of us knights seized the opportunity to ready our longbows and gunpowder arrows and launched an all-out attack. The impact of the chemical-laden arrows against the hard skin of the beast caused the powder to ignite, and in consecutive order, every arrow exploded.

The force impeded the Sentinel's charge toward Algernon, wounding it severely as its boilerplate-like skin was ripped apart. It reared back to cover its hurt side, and Algernon closed the distance he needed to bring his twin swords to bear. With the screech of metal against metal, the blades thrashed across the Sentinel's hide.

With a roar, the drake swung its clawed hand and threw aside Algernon like a mere doll in the hands of an angry child. Algernon flung onto the cavern wall, and lost grip of his swords, but still drew breath.

Once again, we unleashed hellfire arrows onto the drake, and in a haste, it covered itself with its majestic wings. The explosions set off, blanketing the Sentinel in fire and smoke, but as the dark wisps blew away, it spread apart its shield and spat its own fiery attack.

Blue flame blasted into the bowmen, incinerating one into ash, while scattering the rest of us into retreat. It followed this devastation with a roar born from the darkest depths of enmity, inciting a sphere of unseen power throughout the Mountain. Every knight, fallen body, and the Mountain itself shook under the terrible calamity. Nothing remained standing, and the roof of the cavern cracked open, revealing the pale light of a full moon.

The dust, free of the destructive bloom, begun to resettle, dancing gently in the moonlight. There was solace to be sought in this lull, and the Great Sentinel, its fury melted away, waited somberly for the moment to pass.

Ingrena, young warrior-Queen of Magna Carta was among the first to recover, yet she was dazed by the impact, and her ears rang impetuously. Her heater shield was broken, and every muscle ached, but she struggled on. She did not attempt to retrieve her sword, but a vial of the Elixir that was given to her on the eve of her journey.

Glancing at the quiet drake, she felt sorrow for it, even as its luminous eyes bore down on her. She crawled over to me, lifted my head onto her lap, and opening the vial, she poured its liquid onto my lips, then left the last few drops for her own tongue.

I looked up at the drake while holding my ribs tightly, and I knew now, that it cannot co-exist with us in this new world. I reached for my magnificent crossbow, and tightened its string.

Sewell of Gabrialtar shouted for me to ready my arrows, and he stood up with renewed energy while balancing on his fiendish-looking lance. Beside him, Valor Drol of Templari stood up as well, wielding his massive eidolon-shank.

They charged, but the drake unfurled its wings and jumped high into the air – its nostrils wreathing flame with its motion. Having pulled back my crossbow, I quickly inserted my special bolt – its crystal head painstakingly forged from pure fossilized blood of the drakes themselves. I aimed, and released the trigger.

The arrow pierced the Sentinel's right eye, and it screamed in horror at its loss, its flailing body and wings casting shadows in the streaming moonlight. Angered beyond reason, it crashed into the cracked ceiling of the cavern, shattering stone apart and exposing the moonlit night.

It fell to the ground along with the pieces of the Mountain, and it was then when Sewell, Drol, and all empowered knights struck head-on with their swords and spears. Their blades pierced into the core of the beast, and sliced long gashes across its wings, limbs, and belly.

Its screams turned to moans, and with a sigh, the Great Sentinel collapsed. Tears of molten metal – what would become fuel of progress by the will of our engineers and alchemists – trickled from its body and formed streams that joined the draining blood of the other slain drakes.

Alas this chapter ends.

There was no cheer for victory. The long war was over, and the longer road to rebuild the world in humanity's fashion seemed too bitter to savor for the moment. Those knights that still had strength helped those that were struggling, and the dead were counted.

A glint caught the eye of Queen Ingrena, and she stopped to look at it. A small pond had formed where various rivers of the Sentinels' blood met at a depression on the ground. In the midst of the molten pool of liquid metal was something that had solidified under the cool air wafting from above, and also reflected the light from the waxing moon.

One by one, all of us stopped and turned to this light, and together we approached it. The anomaly, appearing like an island in a platinum lake, revealed itself to us. Its shape was jagged, hewn from the numen drakes' native dialect, waiting for the care of a master blacksmith, but it was the Thousand-Year Dream – our token of victory.

Are any of us worthy of it?

None dared take one step further, but it was I, Alexander Mellka, that took it, and it was then that I heard these words like whispers from a ghost:

"Glory may come, but to the spoils you've come to reap, none of you will savour its fruits. We may inherit a world in shambles and ruined by centuries of war, but our people will rebuild. There is still hope. Believe what you may, but there is none in this age or the next that are deemed worthy of a dream."

And so I write this with truth and honour as bestowed upon me by my brothers and sisters-in-arms, my city-state of Floria, and of our creator, Gloriam.

Mellka, now much older and in his last years, sat before the old desk deep within the bowel of the Cathedral in Floria. Surrounded by the soft spill of oil lanterns, he wrote the last pages of his great book, the Vade Mecum.

He continued writing....

The Church, whom I owe my existence, was created long ago under the tutelage of sages to worship something far greater than any on this world or beyond the celestial sphere.

He hesitated, letting the ink drip like tears.

Now that we've shed the chains that bound us to a common Enemy, there is a dangerous stirring amongst the high echelons. There is rampant greed now, wanting of great power, and unyielding control over the masses. Sermons have become cries to war against the fellow man. The sacred cloth of learning and humility have been traded for armour and vanity. What was sacred has become a whisper in empty halls.

I fear an end to the old ways, a corruption of the spirit that founded this benign institution. With my passing, the Church will commit as it will unto the undoing of all. The world is changing, and in the Mountains the cogs of revolution have begun to turn. These people, no longer in the shadow of the Sentinels, will rise inheriting the traits of their former masters. Invention and manipulation of the elements and of politics will be their weapons. Elsewhere, the people stir with industry, and the economy of the future will determine the rise and fall of borders between kingdoms. Beyond all, even to the whim of foresight, from a land born in flame and quenched by the ocean to the East and South, the wings of all free people will sunder apart under the unforgiving thrust of the Vilkacis.

Mellka stared blankly at the flickering light of the lanterns, then continued.

To all hopes I rest in Queen Ingrena, the last guardian of that small device that was left to our keeping by the Great Sentinels themselves. There is a dream to be found, alas who may be worthy of it?

Setting down his writing tool, Mellka gave his words one last glance before closing it. Its blue glass cover was bound heavily, yet seemed so fragile at the same time. He stood up, and grimly wondered at the meaning of the shadows dancing on the walls, terrified of the flames.

He looked up, and felt dwarfed by the immensity of the Sacred Vault. Shelves that housed centuries of knowledge rose taller than a guard tower and stretched into depths farther than the length of the Cathedral itself. Treasures gathered from before the Sentinel War and from all over Terra Mia collected dust under the looming archives. Amongst the trove also rested the tombs of his fellow kinsmen-in-arms, with only two empty sarcophagi left – Queen Ingrena and his own.

Great doors were violently opened, and the determined march of soldiers echoed within the hall. In time, a tall Precept Cardinal and his loyal squad of Iron Sabres entered the Vault.

Mellka remained impartial, he had the foresight to know their purpose, and was resolute to meet whatever end. He turned away from the tombs of his comrades, and faced the Cardinal whose face and head were shrouded by an elaborate silver helm.

"It is indeed providence, my lord, that you should be surveying the spot of your grave on the eve of your death." The Cardinal's voice was hollow and cold, but there was also a thirsting ambition.

"You've made your choice, Precept Pious," Mellka said, recognizing the voice, and looked at the Iron Sabres. They stood proud and fierce behind their armour, the black manes on their crowns wavering impatiently. "And with a slick tongue you've convinced others to this damning cause."

"You've outlived your purpose as the head of this Order," the Cardinal replied. "Industry has begun its toil, and nations are shifting the roles of their leaders. The people are caught in the wind of change, and they must be guided by a strong Church, for we are the unmoving bedrock in this chaotic sea."

"I already heard your speech," Mellka retorted, "and I am not moved. Your motive is noble at a distance, but all you want is my seat and title, and your methods will cause more harm than good."

"If you step down or retire, then who should take my counsel seriously when people can still turn to you? No, my lord, you must die tonight."

"I warn you. Should you commit on this path, you will seal the fates of all other grand masters that succeed me. The Order will be reborn in blood, and this Church will wield no other tool but that of violence and fear."

"This must be done, Great Lord Mellka. You will best serve us now as a martyr, as a saint, to usher the new Faith upon Terra Mia. Your name lives eternal as a hero to humankind."

"Nothing is eternal," Mellka said with conviction.

The Precept Cardinal unsheathed his short sword, and in turn, the Iron Sabres wielded their blades. They set upon a concluding trudge to carefully surround Mellka, their footsteps echoing, and their steel shimmering under the faint light of the lanterns.

"In fire we were born," Mellka said darkly, "in fire we will perish."

In unison, the traitors raised their blades and struck.

Little did Pious know how right his dead lord was, for he only lasted mere months before a member of his guard murdered him to give another Cardinal the seat of papal power in exchange for the covetous red robes.

Over the centuries, under wiser leadership, assassinations were carried out by committee, to ensure some form of stability within the Faithful hierarchy, and to prevent dreaded schisms of the Faith itself. Eventually, a Grand Master had the opportunity to be elected by studious debate, culminating to a clash of bilateral armies, followed by long periods of prosperity and exploitation.

Less than a decade after the Battle of Guard, conflicting ideologies met on the field once more.

At the foot of the snow-capped massifs, in a nameless valley at the southern peninsula not far from the outer regions of Templari, an army of the Faithful waited. The endless winter from the high peaks had set in early, and the first fluttering tufts of snow tumbled on the frozen earth.

The ordained soldiers and priestly horsemen shivered and were anxious, but they remained in strict regimental formation at the behest of Grand Master Vatic, riding at the rear-guard with his most loyal horsemen. He was clad in white robes and tempered armour, with gracious neck and shoulder guards, while his elaborate, gilded helmet was in the care of one of his retainers. His bare face was aged but grim, and he cast his eyes dauntlessly on the plain ahead.

Nearby, on a small knoll overlooking the valley, the host of Precept Cardinals observed as official witnesses to the crucial events that were about unfold. Mounted on their horses with their crimson cloaks, none seemed at ease.

They heard a drone in the wind, emanating from the hills, and it grew closer and louder. The ground begun to tremble, and in time, the terrible sound became clearer. The beating drums of doom, and the brazen chants of thousands on their march to the battlefield.

The rank and file were nervous, and unable to hide his plight any longer, Cardinal Abaster snarled at his lack of power to stop this conflict.

"This is madness," Abaster protested aloud. The other Cardinals heard him, but to no avail in moving their hearts.

"This issue is being settled in the old, civil ways," Cardinal Libra replied impassively, her short black hair shifting in the gathering wind. "Would you have preferred a cloak and dagger instead?"

One of the other Cardinals, Achrone, scoffed. "Our esteemed Grand Master Vatic won his papal position by mischief and deceit, didn't he? Personally, I prefer a swift resolution through these means."

"We are in no position to squander our Knights on this petty battle," Abaster cut back. "The Church is frail, and our Order is ready to break at any moment. We've made too many enemies over the years, and they will see an opportunity to crush us into dust."

"All the more reason to force change, don't you agree?" Achrone said coldly. "Unless the record books are wrong, I believe it was through the machinations of you *and* Grand Master Vatic that our Church has become weak and susceptible."

Abaster's eyes flashed with mixed shame and irritation. "...These are loyal men and women fighting for our Grand Master, because they believe in his strength. They are our tools, and not to be blamed, nor cast in the fire!"

"They're well aware of the choice before them. The weak will be purged."

Abaster was insistent, more rightly since it was his neck on the line. "Do you honestly believe that this northerner, this mere War Bishop from Peregrine's Perch will restore what we've lost?"

"He's fresh blood and charismatic," Libra said. "He has the ability and the fortitude to root out the rot in our midst, and steer our beloved Church back to its founding principles. I, for one, will support him in that cause."

The other Cardinals shared the blatant opinion, but some, like Abaster, not wholeheartedly.

With grim acceptance, he stared down the knoll to Vatic and his regiment. "We exerted some measure of control over the Grand Masters of our time, by our will alone. A fanatical leader, like this Bishop you all favour, will yield to no such manipulations, and he will endanger us all."

From the mist hanging over the valley, the feared Iron Sabres emerged. One legion was followed by another, accompanied by an entire battalion of cavalrymen, and behind them still, the cannoneers.

Orders were shouted, and soldiers stirred to the threat. By the time Vatic retrieved his high-crowned helm and mask from his page and locked it in place, the two opposing legions pulled back their readied longbows and released the red-dyed, steel-tipped arrows.

"Raise your shields!" one of Vatic's field commanders shouted, but the soldiers were unprepared for the sudden onslaught and fumbled in disarray.

The arrows pummeled down like hard rain, whistling through armour, wood, and flesh. Unprotected horses collapsed with their riders, and the soldiers too slow to make ready their shields were spared no mercy.

Vatic's horsemen were amongst the most experienced of the ranks, and were quick to act. They encircled their master and raised their shields together to form a protective shell, at the risk of exposing their bodies to the deadly arrows.

Vatic was spared the pain and death, but at the cost of three of his loyal guards. The core of his army suffered a loss of seventy or more soldiers and mounted troops, either dead or too wounded to stand their ground.

Before the last arrow landed, the Iron Cavalry charged. The hooves of two thousand armoured warhorses shook the ground with such terrifying ferocity that callow bowmen and armed clergymen deserted their posts.

The First Line of defense, comprised of parishioners drafted from the countryside, readied their long pikes nonetheless, yet the oncoming Cavalry were undaunted. With remarkable training and discipline, the charge split in three; the center portion mowed through the First Line, like two raging rivers colliding. The second and third group outflanked the loyalist regiment, and cut through the formation.

It was a violent three-pronged assault. Spears and shields were splintered, and hundreds on both sides lost their lives in the first pass alone. Vatic's position was not assailed, though the Iron Sabres skimmed close to his camp.

The three groups snaked through the regiment and reformed in a well-timed retreat. With their backs exposed, the rear-guard suffered several losses from the retaliation of loyalist crossbowmen until galloping out of firing range.

"Prepare for the second pass! Ready your pikes!" one of the leading retainers near Vatic shouted.

Vatic saw his army fractured, and he heard his officers beckon soldiers back into formation. The losses were surmounting, and he waited for the Iron Cavalry to return, but the second pass that was expected never came. The dooming sound of a horn was blown instead.

To the dismay of Vatic and many of his loyalists, they witnessed the unthinkable. Entire companies of Inquisitor Knights and War Bishops, on foot or on horseback, split away from the flanking regiments, and joined forces with the enemy. They rushed quickly, before anyone nearby understood what was happening.

"Traitors! Traitors!" Vatic could no longer maintain his grace, but no threat of words or sharpened steel swayed the turncoats.

The confusion and betrayal was thick, and it was hopeless, but the battle was not over. The turncoats hurried not only to be past the range of their former comrades' retribution, but from the blast radius of the cannons.

The medium caliber guns were rolled in place and readied. At the signal of the Chief Cannoneer, the two dozen cannons – borrowed from sea-faring warships – spat fire and fume onto the valley. The cacophony was punctuated by craters and the flailing parts of flesh and armour. Those loyalists who were not killed on impact, suffered greatly on the ground from lost limbs and decimating wounds. Those few groups of Knights that remained unscathed were shell-shocked.

It was one of these cannonballs that struck Vatic clean off his mount, and left behind his bent and tarnished crowned helm rolling across the frozen soil and blood-spattered snow.

The war horn sounded again, and the last fusillade echoed through the valley. The Iron Sabres dismounted, joining with those already on foot, and drew their signature swords in near-perfect unison. Together, at the toil and rattle of their heavy plate armours, they marched toward the surviving remainder of the loyalist army, and spared no one, whether they stood their ground, surrendered, or retreated.

The Iron Sabres' fiery-haired leader, the charismatic War Bishop from the North, watched on quietly atop his blanched warhorse. Victory was secured, and looking at the string of worried Cardinals on the knoll overlooking the battle, he was confident they will be starkly reminded of this day once he reentered the Cathedral of the Twelve as the new Grand Master.

II. Highborn

II. Highborn

Under cloudless azure skies the water splashed heavily into the air, and thousands of droplets shimmered like diamonds as sunlight passed through them. Seidon resurfaced with a joyful shout, and with him was Tenshi – her cheerful spirit melding with his.

They danced about each other playfully, stirring gentle ripples in the water; their two-mast schooner, *Journey's Prodigy*, swayed patiently while anchored near a small chain of tropical islands. Much smaller than the *Awakening* in size and firepower, with only two guns stowed aboard, it was fast, highly maneuverable, and able to be manned by a skeleton crew of two. It was their home beyond borders, and it was their tellurian symbol of freedom.

Tenshi wrapped her arms around Seidon and pulled him closer for a kiss – tendrils of translucent water dripping on their hair, clothes, and skin. "There's always a clear sky after the storm."

"Always," Seidon replied softly, then slipped from her arms and swam around her.

He dipped underwater, and Tenshi followed his movement under the carefree waves. Giggling quietly to herself, she reached beneath with her hands and held his cheeks as he rose his head partly out of the water.

Tenshi let her lips touch his again – only slower and more affectionately. They gently swam in a circle without letting go of each other.

Staring into Seidon's brilliant grey eyes, Tenshi felt something heavy tug at her heart. "It's been almost six years," she said sadly.

Seidon sensed her womanly grievance, not quite understanding why she was unable to bear children, whether they were both infertile, and without clear answers, the hope of carrying on the long-standing Harbrid family line was in an uncharted ocean. Still, he loved her no less.

He held her hands, and pressed his lips onto her palm as an offer of comfort. He didn't quite know what to say. "I dreamed a dream not so long ago, and it made us whole. More than enough for any man to have reached in his lifetime."

Wet strands hid her tears, but she managed a smile. "But a family of our own is something we both want. If I can't bear you children, the price of my life may have been too high."

"Don't say that, ever," Seidon said, his tone serious. "You've given me strength; you're my every breath – I could ask for no more from you or this world." He held Tenshi by her waist and hoisted her up into the air, glittering droplets showering around them. "I believe anything's possible when you least expect it. All I can offer you is faith."

Her woe melted away into laughter, and he too melded with her uplifted spirit.

A great shadow crossed them as they reached for a third kiss, and a glorious thrum of engines was heard in the wind. They looked up as a flock of birds scattered away to the arrival of a great beast.

They marveled at the splendid and unusual sight of the first-ever sky galleon flying majestically overhead. It was a warship constructed of wood and plated with lightweight armour scales. Its tall masts held brimming white sails and slender jibs, flowing gracefully in the direction of the wind. A rounded forecastle and a high stern-castle housed deck guns and other deadly armaments, while a pair of funneled smokestacks amidships spewed greyish-green steam from the retro-reef furnace in the warship's bowels. Flanking its port and starboard were two zeppelins strapped close to its lower hull and keel, their innovative construction giving the ship its sole defiance of gravity. At the farthest end of its stern, like an afterthought to tradition, hung a large naval lantern and flag with its feral markings and colours – a wing of swords – revealing the ship to be a flagship of the island-nation of Gabrialtar.

Tenshi was amazed, and Seidon felt like a child again. "It's the Highborn. Ever since they broke away from Chimaera and Guard, the Gabrialtar engineers have been working on this prototype for years, but I never thought I'd see her fly."

The *Highborn* continued across the wide blue sky unimpeded, its sleek prow aimed north-westward toward Floria.

The animating force of celebration riveted throughout the floral city as its people took to the cobbled streets leading to the core of religious amalgam that was the Cathedral of the Divine Twelve, its spires and buttresses now at last reconstructed after the *Awakening* had broken them apart with her cannons nearly a decade before.

A gentle wind that blew over the white-walled villas lifted flower pedals of cream and rosette and deposited them throughout like welcoming rain. The splendid gardens that decorated the porches, the streets, and the rooftops were fresh with spring bloom, and the doves flew with free-will.

Floria's port was busy with activity, its docks filled with hundreds of ships of various sizes and types, hailing from every nation throughout Terra Mia. Ambassadors, their aides and escorts, nobles, industrial moguls, ceremonial guards, pilgrims, sailors, and merchants cluttered the piers on their way to the Cathedral. It was a festivity that had not taken place in nearly a century, and it was a timely opportunity that few would want to miss.

Amongst the dizzying conglomeration of ships was the *Second Awakening* under the command of Admiral Messer, on approach to its assigned harbour. The modernized ship-of-the-line was a testament to Magna Carta's firm foothold on the changes that have gripped the world since the war against the Chimaera and Scarecrow corporate superpowers. Like the sunlight shining against its gold-emblazoned name across the bow, it served now proudly as a royal escort to the king and queen.

Messer stood tall on the bridge, his hands clasped at the small of his back, and his eyes watched Floria's approaching harbour closely. The memory of the last time he set sight upon this port was still fresh on his mind, from Seidon's rescue to the city's inexorable bombardment. He stowed away those thoughts and turned to his second-in-command.

"Captain Semmes, heave to and take in sail," he ordered calmly. "Drop anchor."

"Aye-aye, sir," the veteran captain acknowledged, whose auburn hair and mustache were bleached from his time at sea, and turned to the crew working on deck. "Heave to and take in sails! Anchors aweigh!"

As the *Second Awakening* slowed its advance, and came to a graceful halt beside the harbour, King Ingren and Queen Dalena emerged from below-deck and stepped beside Messer on the bridge. They watched as the crew climbed the rungs and wrapped up the sails with professional ease, while sturdy ropes latched the ship securely against its berth.

"I've ordered the majority of the crew on shore-leave, but I'm retaining a skeleton compliment aboard to make advance preparations for departure. If the wind does not avail us, we'll put our new retro-reef engine to the test." Messer's tone was serious. "I will remain onboard as well."

"You won't be joining us for the ceremony, Admiral?" Ingren asked, knowing the reply. "The appointment of a new grand master of the Church comes rarely once or perhaps twice every generation."

Messer scoffed, but held back his reservations to keep a respectful stance with his king. "Last I remember, I had ordered my old ship's cannons to blast apart the Cathedral's towers, and I'm certain the Church hasn't forgotten that incident. Seidon and Poem haven't dared trespass this province, and I very much doubt this new papal overlord will grant atonement for all my sins."

"I was assured by Church officials and my diplomats that they would not take any action that will break the peaceful relations between the new papacy and my kingdom."

"They will arrest him the moment he steps off the ramp," Dalena said, gesturing to the squads of Inquisitor Knights patrolling the area. Amongst the hive of activity on the pier were clandestine friars that paid close attention to whomever disembarked from the *Second Awakening*. "Diplomacy in grey shades."

Ingren was unimpressed. "You do well to remain a step ahead of whatever situation may arise, Admiral." He glanced at his wife, "The former Admiral of the Fleet was perhaps just as cautious."

Dalena smiled. "The present Admiral's concerns are well-founded. Remember to assign a guard detail at all times."

"Of course, Your Highness," Messer said, and bowed to both. "Enjoy the festivities."

"We will," Ingren said as a contingent of Throne Guards emerged from the ship's barrack station.

The half-cloaked and armoured soldiers marched onto the deck and surrounded their king and queen in a ceremonial shield formation, while the crew – with a stern shout from Captain Semmes – formed perfect parade ranks that created a path from the bridge, down the ramp, and onto the pier.

Messer watched the group disembark with the grace and power that only royalty could muster, then turned away to the stern where the Vast Blue shimmered under a bright sun. He crossed his arms, letting the wind waft gently onto his face and hair, and wondered where his friends and old ventures have gone.

While Floria was the religious center of the known world, Lorica was the heart of history and learning. The town had grown little since the Great Library was founded several centuries ago, but amongst the repertoire of elegant marble houses fashioned in ancient styles were established museums and renowned art galleries holding collections that existed nowhere else on the continent. From the various historical guilds that have been created, also sprung up universities and various academies teaching the arts and sciences of the old and modern worlds. Some colleges were open to all, while others were quite exclusive, and held seats only for the privileged.

It was a quiet town, and had always remained neutral no matter how many armies passed through its streets, regardless of whom was at war.

It was peaceful, Poem thought as he scooped up a large stone and placed it beside another where cement paste had been carefully applied. He licked his dry lips and wiped the sweat of his brow with the back of his hand, then stepped back to view his work.

For a year now, he had spent his time building this small cottage of stone from the local quarry and timber from bountiful chestnut trees atop of a small hill on inherited land overlooking the entire town. Largely completed, he decided to extend one of the walls in hopes to construct another room should the need ever arise in the future.

He scooped up some more cement paste with a palette and smudged it on a part of the unfinished wall, then picked up another large precut stone and settled it in place. He let out an exhausted sigh, then walked over to a bucket of fresh well water and splashed some on his face, hands, and neck after taking a sip.

Wiping his face on his shirt, he realized his beard had been allowed to grow untrimmed for several days as the stubbles scraped across the cloth. He moved over to the edge of the hill where a slight wind blew gently, and let his tense muscles unwind.

It was indeed peaceful to be home, he thought again, and he gazed down at Lorica with a faint smile. The Library stood out above all other buildings like a castle, which with no surprise had been originally a fortress of old long before it was converted by the scholars. He knew his mother was there, conducting her noble affairs as head librarian, and he was content to be within reach of her after all these quiet years.

His dark eyes saddened slightly as he glanced to the small mound of earth and grass where a mighty Chimaeran scimitar was impaled. A ribbon of wildflowers, collected from the nearby grove, was tied to its pommel, and the flowers danced to the wind.

He took a few steps toward it, where his sister Genetha laid in rest, then sat beside it facing out to the town and sky. "Wish you were still here," he said softly. "Berating me for every little thing I do wrong."

He leaned back on the grass, and stared up at the blue sky. He had longed for halcyon days since he was cast out of Chimaera by the Sorcerer Siblings, and after the war, he was granted the solace of putting his restless mind and driven spirit at ease. He hadn't used his powers in many years, and his daggers hung on the mantle over the fireplace – the stains of blood long since washed away.

Yet....

Just as he closed his eyes to nap, his ears prickled at the drone and thrum of a powerful engine. A massive shadow crossed over him and engulfed the hillside. He opened his eyelids, and saw the ventral hull of the *Highborn* passing closely overhead.

He was astonished at the sight: wide sails, double zeppelins, and retro-reef smokestacks in all. It moved quite quickly over the town, its shadow cutting across the buildings like a colossal black sword, even as it stirred hundreds of onlookers from the streets.

Poem sat up alert as his curiosity shook away his fear. He didn't know why he expected an attack, even as the *Highborn* continued to travel westward, but assured himself a return to calm with his best efforts. Recognizing the Gabrialtar flags, he vowed to bring himself up to speed with the current affairs of the world.

Backed by the Throne Guards, and led by the ponytailed Ambassador Daedlus, the King and Queen of Magna Carta were escorted into the Diplomats' Residential Estate on the fringe of Floria's main square. Its lobby was impressive in size and architecture, with tiles and pillars of richly veined marble, recessed velvet curtains, and various master paintings and sculptures decorating the premises. The museum-like splendour was punctuated by a grand double-helix stairway that led to the observation galleries and veranda on the upper floors.

Leaders and representatives from every part of Terra Mia were gathered in clusters here, sampling the finest wines and food catered by their Florian hosts. With formal regard, the noblemen and aristocrats bowed as the Magna Cartan royal delegation passed through.

The Throne Guards, in a ceremonial display of their discipline, stopped in formation, and all but two turned on their heels in perfect parade maneuver and marched outside to their waiting posts on the courtyard.

Their overture impressed the delegates, and received an applause.

Ingren accepted it in kind, but he noticed that Julia was slightly uncomfortable by the bland etiquette. "You're still not used to all these boring formalities."

"I don't think I ever will be," she replied, smiling courteously, and nodding to the marquises and barons she passed.

Ingren smiled, reassuring her with a squeeze of his hand on hers. "You're still my Queen."

"The veranda on the top floor is reserved for us, Your Majesty," Daedlus said. "The Public Declaration ceremony will be starting soon, once the closed-doors initiation rituals have been completed." Though he was far older than Ingren by at least a decade, and retained a proud and regal posture, he still felt humbled by his king. "Several nobles from your court are already present there."

"Thank you, Ambassador Daedlus," Ingren said. "Will we be expecting you there as well?"

"In due time, milord," Daedlus replied. "There are still more receptions to conclude before I'm given leave." He bowed low. " Until then."

Daedlus promptly left to his duties, and now only with two guards as their escorts, Ingren and Dalena marched up the winding stairs to the veranda on the fifth floor.

Julia glanced back at the ambassador, suspicious of him. "I've met nearly all the members of the court's diplomatic corps, and I like him the least."

"Your soldier's instinct," Ingren said. "The esteemed ambassador is more business-driven than actual diplomat. His family owns a very influential guild connected to manufacturing engines and other contraptions that use retro-reef fuel. As such, he's had substantial fiscal connections to the lucrative markets of the former Chimaera Conglomerate and Scarecrow Corporation."

"A double agent or a politician with a conflict of interests. Do you trust him?"

"Only within the sphere of his diplomatic duties, particularly here in Floria, but he's been loyal, and his family contributed greatly to the post-war restoration of the capital."

A pair of butlers opened the large, window-paned doors that led to the spacious veranda where many Magna Cartan nobles enjoyed the view. They were surrounded by exquisite gardens, but none of the greenery obstructed the view of the Cathedral and its main square. The festivities, seen in whole from their vantage point continued, with more people arriving every hour. There were performers and licensed vendors gathering pockets of onlookers, and missionaries wove through the crowds preaching their faith and attracting followers.

Here, so close to the Cathedral, security was unrivaled. Checkpoints were established at every street that intersected the square – like the hub of a massive wheel. The courtyard itself was enforced by a wall of Inquisitor Knights in ceremonial attire, forming a steely circle that prevented anyone from setting a foot inside the courtyard proper. The stairway to the Cathedral's main arched entrance was guarded by more Inquisitor Knights and War Bishops mounted on elegantly dressed horses, their long, decorated spears held ready with their deadly points aimed skyward.

Moving past the formal greetings, Dalena leaned her arms on the lacquered pine railing for a closer look at the crowd. The wind carried flower pedals thrown in the air by the citizens of Floria, and the confetti covered the streets like silky snow. Though it was pleasant, her bright blue eyes narrowed toward the imposing religious seat of the world.

Ingren caught a wisp of her feelings, and stood beside her. He gently clasped his arm around her waist as he looked at the Cathedral too. "It's not easy retaining a diplomatic stance during these times, especially with those who have abused their power openly and shamelessly for centuries."

"Seidon once told me his account of what happened here when they put him on trial," Dalena said grimly. "They were ready to execute him for crimes against their purview, because he chose not to follow their creed."

"The world has changed," Ingren said. "With the Second Industrial Revolution advancing forth at an incredible rate, ideas progress, and so does culture. The Church is forced to adapt to current shifts in society, or risk losing its grip on the masses. The idea of Gloriam is still elusive, but the Twelve Saint Knights still present powerful symbolism because they are heroes – even to this day. They are the scale on which to judge morality, sanctity, and belief. This is a tradition that cannot be changed, and they are willing to protect it by whatever means."

Dalena caught a rosy flower pedal in her palm, and she caressed its silky touch between her thumb and forefinger. "I've spent nearly my whole life serving the Royal Fleet, engaging in one action after the next, I never found time to practice this nonsense. I never had to doubt the Church's principles until the war."

"The Church had publicly admitted its error in siding with General Vant, and vowed to atone for this shame by adapting more... 'open' policies with all nations." Ingren shook his head slightly in disbelief. "Their stance would've been quite different if the armies of Guard had been victorious instead."

"This is the three hundred-seventh Grand Master to be appointed..." Dalena wondered, "Do you know anything about him?"

"He's young, that much I know," Ingren said. "He rose through the ranks rather quickly, and he must be quite charismatic to have been elected over all other contenders. Especially since he was a War Bishop, superseding all his seniors and the Precept Cardinals that were above his station."

There was a sudden collective gasp from the crowd below, and both Ingren and Dalena wondered at the people's reaction when a large shadow crossed the city. They looked up and saw the *Highborn* looming mightily overhead.

Its engine thrumming, the *Highborn* slowed down from its initial momentum and turned about over the open water. It lowered its altitude, and slid across the waves. Its flanking zeppelins rose up several degrees like wings, and at last the ship's keel touched water. Powered by the sails, it ventured forth toward the docks, but did not mingle with the traffic cluttered there. It dropped its anchors, and released some of the air inside the zeppelins.

From the hissing vapor, a rear-hatch mouthed open, and a smaller vessel emerged from the stern.

It was a cutter, light and fast, it swung about its riveted iron and ebony prow and headed toward one of the available piers. Once berthed by the yellow and blue-clad mariners, a ramp telescoped from its main deck onto the dock. Heavy boots clanked in succession on the ramp as a dozen

Gabrialtar Dragoons emerged. They were followed by two muscular officers, and lastly by Titus, their Captain-General.

He was of average height, with chiseled features and fierce black eyes. Along with a long white coat, high boots, and white slacks, he appeared thin and fit. His soldiers were also clad in white uniforms with black trims, but unlike them, he held a flowing, braided ponytail that extended past the small of his back. It swayed as he stepped off the ramp from a draft, along with two black ribbons that were tied near his skull and at the tail's flaming tip.

Paying no heed to the scores of people that watched in amazement, he and his officers reached the head of their soldiers' column and together marched onward toward the Cathedral.

In the Hall of the Tribunal, at the heart of the Cathedral, the Holy Community was in attendance as a new grand master was born through ceremony. The five Cardinals sat on their individual thrones upon the high stage, like judges, while the lesser echelons filled the rows of seats surrounding the central court.

Before the Cardinals, stood in line the Scholars of Cromlech, the Cathedral's official record keepers and conductors of the age-old crowning ritual. In opposition to the other ranks of the Faithful hierarchy, they wore no armour and wielded no weapon, save for the ink brush, scale, and tome.

The attention of all present was on one man, the red-headed War Bishop who orchestrated the fundamental shift in the leadership race, and now stood victorious and unchallenged before his subjects. He listened to the Scholars recite passages from the papal creed, as two chosen Iron Sabres secured the latches of his new armour – first the greaves and arm braces, then with the mail coat and cuirass.

All throughout the ceremony, he kept his keen eyes on the Cardinals.

"You stand before this hall, humble before the might and mystery of Gloriam, a herald to the principles of the Faith, and the undisputed enforcer of the Holy Law. The strength and teachings of the Twelve Saint Knights, who delivered us from chaos into order, are at your command." The head speaker of the Scholars closed the old tome he held, and handed it to the scribe beside him.

The scribe in turn brought the old, leather-bound book to the sworn War Bishop, whom in turn bowed low enough to let his forehead touch the tome.

The head Scholar continued, "This world we love, in life and in death, and we are charged with its keeping, though none outside the Faith may acknowledge it nor accept it. This world stands ever on the edge of peril, and we are the shepherds ever vigilant, until Gloriam descends to grant us leave of Man's moral reins."

Another fellow scribe brought forth a white robe, wrapped and folded with a leather lace. The head Scholar took it, and unfurled the florid papal cloak high against the sunlight streaming from the arched windows, allowing the gold and silver lacing to flourish.

"Do you, nameless son of Eginald, accept this charge?"

"I accept this charge and all this position entails, until the ending of my days," the noble Bishop replied boldly.

The two Iron Sabres took the cloak from the Scholar, and placed it on their grand master, clasping it in place with a majestic cruciform badge symbolizing their Order.

Abaster, seated at the center of the five Cardinals, closed the ritual by stepping forth with the ancient sword of the Church – its cross-guard and pommel fashioned in the sacred shape of the fleur-de-lis. He walked past the Scholars, and presented it with both palms upward to its new owner.

"Take your place at the head of the Order," Abaster said, repressing his buried qualms. "Reveal to us your name."

"I am the Grand Master of the Order of the Faithful, Overlord of the Iron Sabres, Follower of the Twelve... Second of the name, I am Alexander Mellka, The Wroth." the inducted Grand Master's eyes bore through Abaster's soul as he took the sword. "My oath is unbreakable."

Abaster was taken by surprise by the sacred appellation, as by tradition a grand master would choose an enlightened and self-reverent title, yet no one had dared to take the name of the Saint Knight since he had passed into martyrdom. "...Gloriam guide you, Grand Master Mellka," he concluded forcibly.

In unison, all members of the Holy Community bowed to Mellka.

"The world awaits now for your proclamation," the head Scholar said.

Splitting their line formation in two, the Scholars filed out from the Hall through the side doors beside the Cardinals' pulpit, while the rest formed two columns and marched through the main entrance and down the grandiose corridor that led outside.

Mellka stood still as the Knights, Bishops, and Cardinals walked past him with the procession of clerics, monks, and friars, facing Abaster like a determined predator.

Abaster was intimidated, and he wasn't hesitant to leave himself, but Mellka stopped him with a hand solidly placed on the Cardinal's polished cuirass just as their shoulders brushed.

"You thread upon a tightrope, Cardinal Abaster, but there's room for reconciliation," Mellka said, his tone deep and icy. "I know you were closely attached to my predecessor's inner circle, and that you had lamentations about my ascension."

Abaster wanted to protest, but from the backward glances of the other four Cardinals slipping out of the Hall, he knew there was no denying the laid-bare truth. He kept his mouth shut for fear of his life.

"There are many to blame for the fall of the Church in these last decades, some, like Vatic, have met their end, while others like you walk about unmolested by the troubles of mortals." Mellka's fiery hair was a testament to his cold grit. "All can be forgiven, of course. All it requires is that you finish the task you started."

From the Hall's entrance, a dozen Honour Guards strode in and stood on either side of Mellka to formally escort him to the public podium outside. Handpicked from the Iron Sabres corps, each of the tall soldiers stood proud under the weight of a flowing chainmail dress, a tall helm sprouting a bleached horse's mane, and a double-bladed spear whose tips were extoled in the prolific fleur-de-lis.

"Meditate on my forewarning, Cardinal," Mellka said. "Once these rituals are done for the sake of the 'sheep', I will call upon you, and I will put you through the trials that will test both your mettle and loyalty."

Mellka turned and walked out of the Hall in the company of the Honour Guard, leaving Abaster alone to consider his stance in this precarious turn of fortune.

Most of the nobles and diplomats paused in wonder and vague misgivings as Titus proudly waltzed through their midst unescorted by his company of guards, and led to the upper viewing gallery on the kind invitation of Ambassador Daedlus, on the behalf of the Magna Cartan Royal Court.

Titus glanced at the guests with an arrogant air about him, as if he himself deserved their praise, or fear, as some observers might suggest.

Stepping through the elegant glass-paned doors, as if accepting a formal dance, Titus bowed low before his royal peers on the veranda, just as Daedlus introduced him.

"Your Majesty, King Ingren the Third, and Your Highness, Queen Julia," Daedlus addressed in astute formality. "Allow me the privilege to present you Captain-General Titus of Gabrialtar."

Ingren nodded in kind, quietly fascinated by this cultured soldier from the southern island-state. "Thank you, Captain-General, for joining us. We finally have the opportunity to meet you."

"The honour is quite mine, Your Gracious," Titus said, accepting Ingren's proffered hand. "I imagine the view of the Cathedral from up here must be quite splendid."

"Indeed it is," Ingren said, glancing at his wife, who was wary of their new uppity visitor. "I had assumed the Gabrialtar Presidency would send a government official to attend this event."

"Your assumptions are correct," Titus said bluntly as he peered over the balustrade to the grand convocation below. "I am such an official, though my title says different, my functions serve both the civilian and military branches."

"It's questionable when the State is also the Army," Dalena commented, her bluish eyes waiting on his reaction. "Such a concurrence offers a very singular point of view."

"It hasn't been long since Gabrialtar declared its independence from the corporate superpowers, my dear Queen, and its people have chosen to govern themselves." Titus smiled, undaunted by anyone's criticism. "I did not hack my way to this position with a sword, nor was I fortunate enough to marry into royalty, but I was chosen from the rank and file for the greatness of my deeds."

Titus' words were wrapped eloquently, but the sting was there, and Dalena rebuked it. "Selfless deeds go on unrewarded, Captain-General."

"Indeed," he replied. "When I introduced the designs for the first flying machine in history, I asked my nation for nothing more than to be at the helm of the *Highborn* on its maiden voyage. More than what I asked, Gabrialtar gave me their love."

Ingren was impressed, though not at the general's self-admiration. "You were one of the pioneers of Gabrialtar's Industrial Revolution?"

"Not quite a pioneer, my Lord, for that we thank the Corporations." Titus corrected, reveling the attention of those around him. "Under the repression of the Chimaera Conglomerate and of Scarecrow's warmongering, Gabrialtar was reduced from kingdom to a mere province whose resources were bled dry by Templari and Guard, and even your kingdom, for over two centuries. Like many others, I saw fit to guide this impoverished island back to its prosperity by seeing it surpass all other markets."

"A very noble gesture," Daedlus added.

"Thank you, Ambassador."

"I'm sure," Ingren said sternly. "On the matter of commerce, our global supply of retro-reef is being substantially drained at an alarming rate. Nations, like Gabrialtar, who are wholly dependent on this resource will soon be facing an energy crisis unlike any other. To prepare for this, and possibly fuse a mutual solution to this potential disaster, I'm arranging a summit open to all governments, science guilds, and clerics. Your government's participation will be beneficial."

"Gabrialtar will be delighted to attend," Titus accepted in kind, glancing at Dalena. "There are proper venues for debate, but here, let us rejoice in the crowning of a new grand master." He turned to the view of Floria's square. "After all, what are we without a worthy shepherd? Without Faith?"

The cheers of the crowd heightened as the arched doors to the Cathedral opened wide, and Ingren – like all others – looked to see the spectacle.

Dalena stood by her King and husband, but her attention wasn't with him or the ceremony, but to the Captain-General. Beneath the courtesy, the veneer of flair and pride, she felt a deep malice. She had no physical proof of this, but it was her instinct that affirmed it.

* * *

In a clamour of horns, pipes, and drums, the procession of the Faithful marched onto the center stage. The cavalry that initially formed the protective circle split in two groups, allowing a path for the five columns of Inquisitor Knights and War Bishops leading the way for the Cardinals. The columns divided once more, like a flowery blossom, and the stage was made ready for the intimidating Honour Guards as they proceeded to the podium at the head of the stairs.

The Honour Guards opened their formation, and revealed Mellka, inciting a cheer amongst devout followers, the locals, and Floria's guests.

Mellka raised both hands high, and basked in the crowd's glee. He allowed them a few more moments, then stepped forth and took the podium. "There are philosophers who pondered whether we, as a people, have ventured too far and too quickly before our time, leaving behind pieces of our souls." His voice was loud and firm, amplified by the acoustic technologies borne from the shortwave receivers. "How much has each of us lost from the toils of war, and the struggle of rebuilding? In this age, there are no more great leaders of men, nor any valiance left to be found... and yet these same men still accuse this Church of presenting a grave threat to the stability of the world. I say nay."

The crowd all around grew quiet, but Mellka pressed on with his declaration. "The true enemy is not the Church, not Faith, but in the corporate bureaucracy that have meddled in the affairs of cultural and social innovation, sacrificing the well-being of our untarnished spirits for the sake of profit and territorial expansion." He kept his words strong, infusing each syllable with passion. "What truth is there to be found by mining the earth? Have our scientists and engineers pursued knowledge beyond the purview of the Church to seek a connection to Gloriam?"

A potent charisma reverberated from his words, and the crowd was vibrant to his declaration. "Have our authors and artists developed a system of free thinking and expression to ultimately undermine our influence? For we are not without scandals, our stout critics ever attacking the purity of this Order, and truly our power over politics have dwindled. Our values have changed. Hope is splintered. Nothing is held sacred anymore."

Mellka's effective resolve revealed itself to the world like a fervour. "Nearly all of the old nations that were swallowed whole in the era of the Corporate Expansion have turned away from the dying regimes of Chimaera and Scarecrow to become sovereign once more. The economics of the world shift without control as more industry demands more resource, forcing corrupting change in the golden rules of politics. In this chaos, the Church of the Twelve Saint Knights remains unperturbed." He paused, reaffirming his promise. "We are the beacon of stability in this new age, and I vow with my life and unto the crumbling of this Cathedral's foundations that I shall bring this saving light into the darkest corners of this world!"

The crowd roared in jubilation, even members of the Order broke discipline and joined in the cheers. The ferocity of the ovation was not entirely unified, as pockets of people were questioning the ambition of this new fanatical pope.

Amongst the skeptics were Ingren, and most of the attendees in the Diplomats' Residential Estate. The exception was Titus, who applauded as if the Public Declaration had been a critically acclaimed theatrical play.

"Wonderful, absolutely wonderful!" Titus commented, as he watched Mellka and his procession retreat from the podium.

"Not entirely heartwarming," Ingren added, a cold feeling in his gut.

"No," Titus said, glancing at Ingren, "but strong-willed." He bowed, "If you'll excuse me, Your Majesty, I have appointments to keep. Adieu."

He promptly left the veranda, and Ingren wondered about him. He saw that Julia felt uneasy as well, and held her close. "A small snake in the tall grass."

Dalena glanced behind her to the Cathedral. "Or something much worse."

III. Restoration

III. Restoration

The Old Capital of Templari was built on ancient foundations that predated all kingdoms known to the annals of history. It was the birthplace of early legend, of the First Kings, and of the first empire. War and devastation brought about its decay and tumble, but new castles were built upon the old stonework, and Templari was reborn once more and for many times again over the expanse of four millennia.

The introduction of retro-reef as an energy source brought change that forced the monarchy off its old throne, and initiated an elected republic whose interests soon corrupted toward the iron-solidarity of the corporate structure. The Old Capital flourished for a time, and paved the way for modernization and mechanization until greed and war brought an end to prosperity once more.

With the Chimaera Conglomerate decimated, its military might halved, the gears of its industrial expansion dwindled, and much of its provinces were left to fend for themselves. Its Administrate, once members of the upper class, had been replaced by a provisional government chaired by foremen, architects, and engineers whose sole agenda was the restoration of their beloved city under the protective wing of Magna Carta's peacekeepers.

The scars caused by the Sorcerer's Cannon were still vivid, and much of the city's districts were in state of disrepair. The old defensive battlements that once withstood whole armies in the distant past were broken, and the heaviest stones were left where they had fallen. Quarters that had once catered to the nobles have become slums, its fountains and statues of old warriors and luminaries weathered by neglect.

Many have lost their lives when Guard unleashed its power onto Templari years before, and the road to rebuild was long and hard for those lacking hope. Yet their hardship was not left to them alone, as those who caused their misery were also punished by it.

After Guard surrendered and the Armistice was signed, its army was dismantled, and the Scarecrow Executive Circle – which had been purged by General Vant's revolution – was replaced by a Senate. Soldiers were given a choice to either depart service, become a functionary of the new government, or to follow the arduous path of their officers and be condemned to the task of giving back what had been taken in the war.

Vant was amongst many of the upper echelon that were spared no such fortune. He was tried by the victors, and exiled to Templari to mend the destruction he had caused. Guard's military remnants were eager to reclaim their glory despite the Armistice, but were denied propinquity to their former general for fear that their fierce loyalty would encourage a return to arms and rebellion.

The grey eastern wall, where once he had led his troops through the ample breach, Rell Vant now assisted in fortifying its grandeur. With only a handful of the former Strafers at his command and a horde of local volunteers, he led the repairs to the Old Capital. To accommodate his new function, he restructured the Restoration League, honouring a society of tradesmen erstwhile devoted to beautifying the old splendour of the city, before the Chimaera Conglomerate disbanded it in favour of reshuffling their expenditures.

The people of Templari opposed this at first, but Vant made his stance clear to the provisional government and to King Ingren. With their permission, he now devoted all his time and effort to the repairs while adhering to the intricate history that laid buried throughout the city, and to the delicate union of modern architecture.

He had risen to a height once beheld by his ancestors, only to have been defeated just as momentously. The last day of that war had changed him, and he tried hard to forget it by minding his chores. Even as he lifted a heavy fragment of what had been a stone guardian's head from the pile of debris near the wall, where the scaffolding had been set up, he knew he held no grudge against Seidon or anyone else. In fact, he still felt he owed Seidon a great deal, however conflicting that may seem to his ego.

He propped the fragment on the edge of a broken fountain that had long since dried up, and stared at the saddened expression on the vestigial head just as Sucre approached with a pitcher of fresh water.

"Something for your thirst, General?"

Vant grinned at the young lad that had been his stouthearted Captain-of-Arms during the war. "I've been stripped of that title long ago, Sucre, it's about time you let it go."

"I'm still drawing breath, sir," Sucre said as he offered the pitcher to Vant. "I suggest you rest your hopes elsewhere."

Vant glanced past Sucre to a section of the high battlement where a quartet of Magna Cartan peacekeepers were monitoring the perimeter, and his smile faded.

Sucre noticed Vant's faltering glee. "I've gathered some news from the locals... it appears that Titus has resurfaced from obscurity at the head of Gabrialtar''s Partisan Army, and he's also become Aide-de-Camp next to the Presidency itself."

Vant remained quiet, and drank from the pitcher.

"I didn't think Titus had it in him..." Sucre commented, knowing he wasn't going to achieve any conversation with Vant on this topic. He stared at the broken wall, and the many ex-Strafers that worked around it. "We can't go on like this, we're soldiers."

He looked at Vant, "There's unrest, like a tantalizing sword over our heads that can't be seen. How long can this peace last?"

Staring at the fragment he found, Vant felt like Sucre had taken the words out of his mouth. "Ingren's a strong leader, but he alone can't keep the broken pieces of the world together."

Nearby, a group of Templari masons finished their shift and were on their way home, when one of them spotted Vant. He was scrawny, unshaven, and with unkept sun-bleached blond hair, but his anger was virile.

His fellow masons attempted to stop him, but he broke away from them. "You think by restoring this wall, you can make amends with us?! You can spend your whole life renewing the entire city from the ground, but it won't change the fact that you don't deserve this mercy!"

His infuriated shouts quickly garnered the attention of the peacekeepers, and of all the workers in the area. The ex-Strafers were amongst the first to cease their chores and surround their former general in a protective circle.

One of older masons, a foreman, grabbed the angry man by his arm. "Zaffre, let him be–"

Zaffre pulled away in a craze, spittle flying from his mouth. "I lost my family when this bastard aimed that

Cannon at us!" Tears swelled from his reddened eyes. "*I lost my family because of you!*"

Zaffre grabbed a small chunk of stone from the ground and threw it at Vant for all he was worth, and the alerted Strafers around him – including Sucre – used their bodies as a shield.

The rock hit Sucre square on his back, and Zaffre had no second turn as the peacekeepers intercepted him, and dragged him away screaming.

Vant saw the pain Sucre endured for him, and was grateful for his loyalty and of those around him, but his own hope was spent. He held his friend closely to check if he had been deeply wounded.

"I'm alright, sir," Sucre assured with some strain.

"This had to be done," Vant said, dreary of the yoke and disgrace.

Sucre ignored his hurt and stood straighter, even though he felt his spirit bent. "A soldier's death would've been more graceful that this overdrawn humiliation."

With the help of a fellow Strafer, Sucre, along with some of the other former soldiers, walked away. Staring after them, Vant couldn't deny what he had said, but in his heart he knew this had to be.

The great Library of Lorica stood vividly in Poem's dream, outside of which he found himself collecting cases of old books and scrolls from a university caravan. His mother, Anadail, stood amongst other high-ranking librarians at the foot of the stairs, and oversaw the donation of knowledge from the local archival guilds.

Gathering as many books as he could carry in his arms, Poem paused a moment as he recalled a similar memory of his younger days. He saw his younger self a step away, mirroring his reaction. With certain horror, he realized he was reliving that same memory.

Behind him, on the outskirts of the town, an explosion riveted the sky and spilled forth flame and fume. By the time the gunshots were heard, Poem dropped everything he held to the ground in shock.

His father had been part of that skirmish, a victim of a premeditated ambush by the forces of Guard under the upstart Colonel Vant.

Poem remembered now, and he glanced at his stricken mother, who somehow knew what had gone terribly wrong. No matter how hard he willed himself not to carry through this remembrance, Poem ran toward the rising smoke.

His lungs burned, his legs ached, but he didn't stop until he arrived at the aftermath. Chimaeran battlers were dead all around him, sprawled on the field along with the charred remains of their troop carrier. The twisted husks of the motorcycle escorts were also in the flotsam, partly hidden by the dark fumes roiling from spent fuel cells.

Poem's eyes stung and tears welled up. He stumbled through the devastation, and dropped to his knees before his father's mangled body. He sobbed, unable to restrain his anguish, and fell on all fours.

"Why? Why do you continue to haunt my dreams?" His voice was coarse, weakened by sadness, but he still had enough

strength to crawl forward and cradle his father's body in his arms.

The smoke veiled his vision, and drenched in his despair, he looked down once more, but it wasn't his father now, it was his sister, Genetha. He held her tightly, pressing his face onto hers, and he wished so desperately to wake.

Vant stood behind him, his expression cold as he raised his carbine to Poem's back, and fired.

Poem sat up from his bed, its sheets rummaged about his legs, and he screamed. Once the air was spent from his lungs, exhausted beyond his corporeal layer. he tucked his knees to his chest and held his head tightly, as if trying to keep his tormented mind from seeping through his fingers.

His breaths were shallow, and cold sweat permeated his skin. He knew he was alone in his cabin, and no one had heard him. The night outside was dying, and dawn was only a few hours away.

For years he'd dreamed this same dream, and each time it left him cold and withered. So little had changed for him since he was exiled by the Sorcerer Siblings, and even after his adventures with Seidon, he still felt lost.

Living in his hometown and within distance of his mother warmed his heart for a while, but he was fragmented. There were aspects of his life that will never mend with time, and he wandered without personal resolution, conflicted by the ultimatums that had to be.

He wanted something so deceivingly dark, so infernally demented, that he was afraid of what he might become. His frustrations swirled, spinning him in a vicious circle of anger and regret. His whole body shook with enmity, and he needed to unleash it.

Only now did he realize that in his waking tantrum, his two daggers had mysteriously fallen from their perch above the mantle. One had impaled its sharp tip in the floorboard, while the other rested on its side. Both blades glowed eerily with hidden power: the elements of ice and of fire.

Poem watched as a mist gathered into frost on the floor of his cabin, and in reverse, tendrils of flame melted it away. It was a representation of the circle he felt trapped in, but in that circle, he found his only solution.

He stood up from the bed, and retrieved both daggers from the floor. Their powers vanished, dissipating like dust and shards, but he felt the weight of both blades heavier than the last time he had used them. What seemed like an age ago.

Wrapped in her hood and cloak, the Chief Librarian, Anadail, descended the narrow stairway into the deep ancient undercrofts of the Library. She had received complaints from a group of archivists of rumblings from the lower storerooms, even superstitious theorems of spooky hallways from the younger academics, but she knew better. She had been a wife and mother to soldiers, and knew quite intimately of their secret pains. She spotted the warm spill of candlelight on the weathered stones, and soon after the long and somber shadow that she traced quietly back to the penitent form of her troubled son.

Poem was on his knees before the memory of his father, a simple shrine supporting a statuette, a rifle, sword, and flowers. He gingerly cleared away the dust from an honourary tablet bearing a holy inscription and name of Ferdinand

Della'Cor, along with the family's coat-of-arms cast in coloured steel.

Anadail approached him, pulling down her hood, and placed her hands on Poem's slumped shoulders. "You dreamt of them again?"

Poem nodded, using every fiber in his reserve to keep from breaking down in sorrow. "I thought I've come to terms with their deaths, but acceptance has deluded me."

"They loved you dearly."

"They were taken from us," Poem cut in, his muscles tensing with anger. "I never had the chance to make my father proud, or forgive Genetha for abandoning me... and Strafe took them both. He *ripped* them away."

Anadail knelt beside him. "They were both soldiers," she said solemnly, her words showing no real comfort to ease her own grief. "They died bravely, bound to their cause; don't disgrace their valiance with despair."

Poem looked into his mother's eyes, seeing her own grief at losing a husband and a daughter, but also her immense inner strength. "You're my last bastion, you've given me everything." He lowered his gaze, as his thoughts grew darker. "I'm sorry I haven't been a better son to you, a better friend, but I'm no good to you if I can't find my place in this world."

"Poema," she lifted her son's face, and pushed the hair from his tired eyes. "I could ask for no better son, and I owe it to your father to keep you well. I've sheltered you from harm, but I can't hide you from your own demons. What decisions you will make, always bear in mind the past... and the mistakes that were made by your father and sister."

Poem pulled her hand away. "I will never be at peace so long as Strafe still lives."

Anadail was taken aback, not by his vengeful declaration, but by the black fire that burnt in his eyes.

He stood up, driven now by an immutable clash of fate. "Have the heart to forgive me, Mother, after this misery is finally over."

Just as he was about to leave, Anadail took hold of his hand. "Don't feel you've been cornered. You *always* have a choice."

Poem nodded, taking her words to his bosom, and pulled his hand away. "...I finished the cabin, and it's yours to keep or sell. Let it be proof to the angels in heaven that I leave no stone unturned, nor any wood uncut until my task is done."

He left her, and never turned back. Anadail sighed, a mother's onus heavy on her heart, and glanced at her husband's shrine. "I've done what I could, Ferdinand. Look after him in places where I can't follow."

A ship amongst hundreds, *Journey's Prodigy* berthed at Gabrialtar's major port of Sewell's Abide, which was the commercial hub of the Empyrean City, the island's growing capital. While the dockyards served the same purpose as any other port in Terra Mia, what branched from the harbour amazed both Seidon and Tenshi as they disembarked.

An ancient plaza surrounded the docks, with equally grandiose monuments heralding the various paths that can be taken upon arrival. Like spokes of a gargantuan wheel, the cobbled streets were lined with stores and stands, each street a bazaar in its own right. Interwoven between the streets were Georgian residences flourishing with patriotic flags and fountains.

Jutting beyond the buildings was Gabrialtar's political seat, Name's Reclaim. Intricately carved from timeless stone, the massive coliseum stood proud in its majestic splendour. High towers surrounded it, each one reaching godly heights and foreboding, as their heads were crowned by gigantic lanterns that burned brightly.

Unbound by gravity, sky galleons, similar in design to the *Highborn*, hovered protectively over the coliseum.

"It's been a long time," Seidon said as he stepped onto the pier with Tenshi a step behind him. "I must have been eight years old when my father first brought me to Empyrean City."

"I remember too," Tenshi said with a smile. She noticed the sheer number of ships traveling through the waterways was staggering. "Though it feels more crowded than the last time."

Seidon smiled in return, sometimes forgetting that Tenshi had shared all his experiences until she herself was born into flesh and blood. Not only the port, but the plaza was indeed crowded with travelers, local shoppers, and tradesmen. Although in appearance it all seemed like a lawless pirate town, the old island city was strictly under the regulations of the Partisan Army and its law enforcement branch.

More often than none, Seidon spotted groups of khaki-clad patrolmen and their officers scrutinizing the crowd and performing on-the-spot inspections.

"I guess the rumour about Gabrialtar's military build-up is true after all," Seidon commented grimly. He kept his heirloom sword, Ancestral, and his trusty old carbine in check, then took Tenshi by the hand and walked down the pier.

They were approached by the pier's caretaker, a stately middle-aged man who probably dreamed of his better days as a shipwright. He greeted them rather mechanically, and opened his large leather-bound logbook.

"Good day, sir, ma'am," he said. "Your name?"

"Harbrid."

"May I ask your purpose here?"

"We're treasure hunters," Seidon replied. "We're looking for trade."

The caretaker quickly jotted his notes down on the logbook. "I see. For how long you will be staying?"

"Not long," Tenshi said, glancing at Seidon. "A day or two at most, weather permitting."

"I see..." He jotted more notes down, then looked up and adjusted his round reading glasses. "Be forewarned that there are certain areas of the inner capital that are under curfew, which includes Names's Reclaim," gesturing to the towering coliseum in the distance, "and the Honourable Pretor – the nobles' district that is currently undergoing renovations." He closed the book, and held out his hand. "That will be thirty silver for berth and security."

The coins already in hand, Seidon offered the man forty. "Keep the change."

Seidon and Tenshi walked past him, and quickly feeling the added weight in his hand, the caretaker glanced back at them with some astonishment.

Reaching the center of Sewell's Abide, before an impressive stairway that arched like a straining hunter's bow, Seidon and Tenshi came across a massive statue of Sewell Nureador, one of the Twelve Saint Knights. The tall and solemn warrior-tsar stared outward toward the sea, his royal cloak flowing and fluttering with the wind like a flag, as it was embroidered with the intrepid silver wing of Gabrialtar.

Seidon studied the many branching streets and corridors around him, and focused on the avenue that was most crowded. "Optio's Square should be through the main bazaar over there."

Tenshi heard him, but her eyes were on the statue. She stared at the impression of an ancient man, saddened by what remained of his life, a memory cast in bronze, without voice or dream. In sympathy, she touched his foot, just as an airship flew overhead at low altitude.

Seidon led Tenshi by her hand up the stairs and through the busy corridor of the grand bazaar. Shops and kiosks lined both sides of the cobbled street, selling wares and services from all over the world. Tradesmen, sailors, tourists, and local shoppers crowded the bazaar from one end to another. Most were colourful characters of different races and cultures, but even the shadiest of them were kept in check by stiff-lipped patrolmen – their eyes keen to trouble with their rifles slung over their shoulders.

Even with the enforcers around, Seidon knew full well the bazaar was a hub of the underworld. From thieves to gangsters, the fringe society was always attracted to the places where profits were made on a whim and in plenty.

"There's an antique shop over there," Tenshi said, gesturing to a decrepit store displaying a wide variety of old and exotic items behind a pair of dusty display windows.

Before heading inside, Seidon caught sight of a familiar heraldic marking on the sides of some cargo boxes stacked along the wall. A stylized black fire-plumed eagle with a burgeoning tail in the shape of the sword lily, and a thorned crimson rose grasped in its beak.

He paused slightly as Tenshi went inside the shop, a wave of memory returning to him. He glanced around him, searching for a familiar face in the crowd, but recognized none. Over-assumption had gotten him in trouble in the past, so he placed the warning on the back of his mind for the moment.

He went inside, and not too far from where Seidon had stood, an aristocratic man with emerald eyes, an ornate leather vest with delicate copper leafing, and fingers decorated with ruby rings, stepped out of his shadowy corner....

The interior of the antique shop reflected the dusty and rustic aesthetic of the exterior. Old furniture and artwork covered the snug room, and the feeling of a cluttered shipboard storage was further added by rows of wooden shelves filled with artifacts and other old devices. There were clocks, sculptures, coins, plates and bowls, pieces of armour, weapons, even a small caliber cannon amongst a myriad of other antiquities.

Tenshi was easily enamored with the intricate porcelain statues portraying fauna, flora, and humans in pose or repose from the exotic cultures of bygone times, perhaps excavated and sold for profit or traded over the years through Gabrialtar's busy maritime commerce. Seidon, on the other hand, was mesmerized by the assortment of old rifles mounted on the ceiling, so reminiscent to how the blacksmith, Teeven, showed his craftsmanship back in his shop at Coastal Sky.

On that same thought, he spotted a rifle he remembered seeing at the smithy's years ago. A finely engraved trumpet-like barrel extended into a gently curved handle that was patterned with hard wood and pearl-like inlays. A beautiful leather strap hung gracefully from it.

"A flare musket..."

"You know your weapons," the elderly shopkeeper commented from the corner of the room. He was busy cleaning the rust from a pair of gauntlets, and despite his age, he seemed quite alert. The scars on his face and hands revealed a past of violence, but his eyes showed placidity.

"I've seen this exact rifle before at Coastal Sky," Seidon said. "Do you happen to know anyone from there?"

"I'm acquainted with no one from that part of the world," the old man said. "The rifle was given to me in payment of another man's debt, that's as much as I can tell you."

Seidon found that odd, as did Tenshi, but he let it pass. "It's alright, I was just curious."

The old man laid down the gauntlets on his worktable, wiped his hands on his apron, and limped over. He noticed the young couple staring, and smiled. "All men who survive battle walk away with a gift. For some it's glory and plunder, others with caution and wisdom. My oldest wound is compounded by age."

He reached the counter, and leaned against it. "How can I help you folks?"

"We're looking for old maps, anything you might have on Tenaya and the Old Ruins there."

"Treasure hunting?"

"Not exactly," Seidon hesitated. "I once borrowed a map from a blacksmith, and promised to return it when I was done with it, but... well, most adventures never turn out like you expect them to."

The old man grinned, and asked no more questions as he lumbered over to an array of large palettes on the wall. One by one, he pulled them out as he searched for the right one, with each shelf holding a series of spread-out maps, some old enough to crumble at the touch. At last finding the right one, he pulled out the entire tray and placed it on the counter for his clients.

"I have a few here dating from the pre-Corporate years, as you can see, the territorial lines were quite different then."

Tenshi was intrigued. "The map we remember must have been much older than that, going back a few hundred years."

Each sheet was attached to a long wooden stick to handle the map without touching the delicate paper, and the old man carefully flipped the maps over to reveal an even older version beneath. The dry parchment appeared very brittle, but the ink was still well-defined. The language and symbols were archaic, but the overall shape of the continents remained the same.

"This one dates back to the time of the Sorcerers' War," the old man said. "The main theater of that war was at Tenaya, so I think this is what you're looking for."

Seidon was impressed, as he studied the area were the Ruins stood today, but was a sprawling holy city back then. "Teeven's going to love this one."

"Teeven?" The old man recognized the name, but revealed nothing else.

"He's the blacksmith I owe," Seidon said, not certain how to interpret the shopkeeper's reaction. "Are you willing to trade for this?"

The old man nodded, glancing past Seidon's shoulder to see the man with ruby rings staring through the shop window. "...Consider this a gift from one fellow adventurer to another." He rolled the map and tied it with a leather bind, then handed the scroll to Tenshi. "If you have any antiquities of value, I offer good prices."

Although the gesture was kind, Seidon couldn't help but feel indebted, if not suspicious. "We're more than willing to pay in silver."

"Please, don't feel that you're robbing me," the old man assured. "My wares may seem lacking, but I'm not poor. Please accept my gesture without doubt."

"We will," Tenshi said. "Thank you."

The old man glanced again to the window, but the aristocrat was no longer there. "Ah, before you take your leave, may I ask your names? I'm Priamos."

Before he replied, Seidon noticed a black heraldic marking on a wall-mounted plaque behind Priamos that was the same as the brand on the cargo boxes outside. It was partly hidden by a hanging tapestry, but the true proprietor of the shop was now vividly dictated. "Seidon Harbrid. This' my wife, Tenshi."

"A pleasure to meet you both, and please take care. Feel free to stop by whenever you're in town."

Seidon nodded, holding the door open for Tenshi. "Good day, sir, and thank you."

Priamos watched as they left, then were followed a few paces behind by a group of armed elitist thugs: the Squires of Debonair, and the Marquis' mercenary crew. Although he felt compelled to warn the young couple, or alert the patrolmen, he knew best to keep free of the Marquis' business.

Quietly, he went back to finish his restorative work on the gauntlets.

"That man knows Teeven," Seidon said with conviction, as he strolled with Tenshi toward Optio's Square. "Something about that name startled him."

"Could that be how he got the flare gun? Is the blacksmith the man who 'paid his debt'?"

"Maybe," Seidon said. "Though I can't imagine Teeven as a gambler, I don't like to believe in circumstance."

The narrow corridor of the bazaar opened up to a square where a monument and fountain beautified the otherwise questionable reputation of the area. A mermaid carved in stone stood proudly at the center of a blossoming pool of water, with thin jets spraying out in gentle arcs. It was a humble piece of architecture, tarnished by the agents of the underworld who loitered about it. Not far from the square, the road tapered into a short stairway where a large underground tavern, aptly named, *Crook's Corner*, offered beverage, gambling, and red-light pleasures to the stout of heart or corrupt of spirit.

Tenshi tensed upon arriving at Optio's Square, and slowed her pace. "We should turn back."

Seidon agreed quietly, seeing no patrolmen in sight, but rather a group of armed men and women creeping toward them from all sides. On one of the closest knave, he quickly recognized the recurring black logo stitched on the man's right sleeve, while on the other was the crimson rose on its own.

"Squires of Debonair..." Seidon pulled Tenshi behind him, and readied his carbine. "Run back to the ship."

"I'm staying here." Tenshi unsheathed her cutlass, as she shared the same battle experience as Seidon and knew how to handle a weapon.

They were outnumbered and surrounded. The only two pathways out of the square were blocked by mechanized carts and makeshift gates, and locals who were not members of this group of mercenaries were quick to hide inside the surrounding shops and residences.

Seidon pressed his back with Tenshi, trusting her ability to handle her own as the Squires encircled them. "What do you want from us?"

The leading man, a roguish blonde with mixed pieces of armour protecting his shoulders and chest, smirked fiendishly with a scar running through his lower lip. "You're the heretic; the one the Cardinals want brought back to Floria to finish that lavish execution of being burned and shot at the stake."

A young woman beside him, Ophelia, expertly handling a black crossbow nearly half her size, scoffed. "They might be worth something on the hunter's market."

The roguish blonde snickered. "We bring them alive, and we get the reward." His laughter faded to something much more sinister. "We finish the execution here, and the Church will make us saints."

Seidon wrapped his finger tightly around the trigger of his carbine, glancing at a scruffy Squire closing the distance to his left. "Then let us ease your passage to sainthood."

He fired at the encroaching Squire, sending him sprawling back against a pair of his comrades, and fluidly unsheathed Ancestral from its scabbard. In tandem, Tenshi repatriated with her cutlass, wounding two before engaging another.

Seidon kept close to her, slashing a lancer's weapon cleanly in half with Ancestral as the man charged, then fired a volley at a rifleman before he could establish his aim. He swung his great sword again, destroying the weaker blades of two ill-experienced swordsmen. While they backed away in fear, more kept coming with frail courage, but were egged on by their compatriots.

Tenshi was undaunted by the numbers, yet she was wary of the Squires wielding pistols and rifles. She moved swiftly, attacking at close quarters with her cutlass to keep as many bodies between her and the guns as possible. She sliced across the leg of a knave before he could fire, and took the loaded pistol from his hand as he fell. She spun quickly and fired at an archer, smashing his bow, and blinding him with the debris.

Worth only a single shot, she then jabbed the smoking pistol across the jaw of a Squire attempting to grab her from behind. As the man tumbled back, Tenshi was shoved down and left open to the whims of the woman with the large crossbow, but before she was able to release her bolt, Seidon hammered his crystal sword through the weapon. Showing no mercy, he reversed his attack and knocked the startled woman on her rear with the pommel of his sword.

The roguish blonde capitalized in an instant, and thrust his long blade at Seidon, but managed only to cut across the surface of his shoulder and narrowly missing Seidon's neck.

Seidon slapped the blade away, and rushed at the roguish blonde as he backpedaled a few steps to reposition his sword for a second assault. In that moment, a deafening blast carried through the Square and a sparkle of bright red flew across the sky under a trail of smoke.

Everyone paused at the sound and sight of the flare, originating from the antique trumpeted rifle at the hands of the man with ruby rings – the Marquis.

"That's enough, all of you!" he said, a flair of condescension in his voice. 'The flare alerted the law enforcers, so consider your odds and leave!"

The Squires of Debonair, nearly decimated with wounded at the hands of Tenshi and Seidon, grudgingly parted ways, allowing an unobstructed path for the Marquis to approach the duo. A few of the Squires, including the rogue blonde, wanted to finish the fight.

"Leave them, Skein," the Marquis ordered harshly, his green eyes piercing through the other.

Skein, intimidated, lowered both his gaze and his sword. He helped his female companion from the floor, still dazed by Seidon's attack, and retreated with the rest of his gang. He gave Seidon and Tenshi an angry glance, keeping a menacing promise to himself.

With the Squires leaving the premises like a dissipating mist, Seidon and Tenshi maintained their vigilance, even as the Marquis stopped a few feet before them with the smoking flare gun rested at ease in his arm.

The man's brown hair was combed back and slick as his notorious reputation for being both a despot and lady's man. His ruby rings weren't as simple as they seemed from afar, each red stone was fashioned in the delicate shape of a blossomed rose.

Amused by the untrusting poises of Seidon and Tenshi, he offered a cocky half-grin. "It's been a while, cousin."

"It's been over twelve years, Regento," Seidon replied, slowly lowering his sword. "You've been busy."

"Of course... as have you from what I hear." He glanced at Tenshi with an inviting gleam in his eyes. "Allow me to present to your darling the new Marquis of Gabrialtar." With the effects of a gentleman, he took Tenshi's hand and kissed it. "I am Liberthier Regento, Seidon's favourite cousin."

"Hardly," Seidon retorted, pulling Tenshi away from him.

"I know who you are," Tenshi said, surprising Regento.

Regento thought it odd, but his narcissism was cajoled. "Ah, so my reputation precedes me, I'm flattered."

"Since when have you taken over the Squires?" Seidon pressed on, not wanting to trust him.

"Took you a while," Regento teased, "but I figured you'd catch on to the rose. Not that it matters now, but I apologize for their unwelcoming conduct. The young, ugly one, Skein, is a devout churchman, and he saw an opportunity to put himself in the good graces of the new pope."

"From what I remember, you're a devoted opportunist yourself," Tenshi said.

Regento frowned at her verbal attack, but was still amused. "Have we met before? Where has my dear cousin been hiding you all this time?"

Seidon sheathed his sword. "Thanks for calling off your buddies, cousin. We'll see you around." He took Tenshi by the hand, and started walking away, back to the safety of the crowded bazaar.

Regento followed. "You loved me like a brother once, Seidon, must you always judge me by the last thing I did?"

Seidon stopped and glared at him. "My father gave you a chance to make something noble for yourself, out of respect for your parents. You were at the height of your career with Magna Carta's cream of the crop, and you threw it all away for what?"

"The diplomatic corps are for the crestfallen, boring old men, and as far as you know, nobility lies only in blood and not in name. You'd be surprised how cynical and quite judgmental the ever-perfect Royal Court really is. I did what very few had the galls to do."

"And now what do you have? A few ships, a few men, and the crown of scoundrels."

Regento's eyes darkened. "You have no idea."

Seidon gestured to the antique shop they had left. "The shop's yours then? How many people in this city do you have eating out of your filthy hand?" He grimaced at the realization of what he just said. "You already knew we were here."

"It pays to stay a step ahead, as I have many investments to protect – your father taught me that." Regento looked into Seidon's grey eyes. "Do you really hate me that much, cousin? Do you feel betrayed, because I abandoned both the hard life of a pirate adventurer and the ludicrous luxury of a royal diplomat? Would you rather I had become a selfless militarist such as yourself? Not all of us are fortunate with the power to change the course of history, and you did your part very bravely, but your story won't be remembered. You'll remain Ingren's dog, and if the Church has its ways, the Harbrid name will end with you."

"It does pay to stay a step ahead, Regento," Seidon said coldly, "but you're a whole league behind me."

Regento matched his cousin's icy tone. "Whatever you think of me, I don't wish you harm, but I do urge you to stay clear of history's way. Disappear into obscurity like the crew of the Awakening, and let the rest of us say our parts in things to come."

There was something deeper laying in those words, but Seidon was unable to grasp it. Eight armed squads of Gabrialtar enforcers scurried past them toward Optio's Square, and without anything else to be said, Seidon turned and walked away. Tenshi felt the hidden warning from Regento as well, but there was little else to be done. She followed Seidon close behind, and glanced back to see Regento one last time before the Marquis blended easily into the motley crowd.

IV. Circles of Transgression

IV: Circles of Transgression

In one of the Cathedral's great meeting halls, decorated lavishly with beautiful murals, velvet curtains, and gold accents, delegates from every industrialized nation were seated around an elegant table nearly a dozen meters in diameter. The surface of the table was an artistic masterpiece in itself, depicting a scene of war that told its ageless story in a perfect circle. If one were to walk along the circumference, he would witness the stirring of conflict between ancient peoples, the raising of an army, the bloodshed and despair, resolution between kings, then peace and flourishing crops and bounty, and as the artist intended, the story was repeated as the observer returned to the point he started. At the core of the table, unmoved by the transgressions, was the Order of the Faithful's sacred regalia.

Ingren was amongst few that remained standing as the delegation waited for their audience with Grand Master Mellka. It was a formality more than actual functionality, as these meetings were usually short and meant only to express congratulations and personal assurances between the politicians and the religious hierarchy.

He glanced to those seated at the table, some whom he knew well, such as the former fleet admiral, Traiza, who now acted as the Provisional Governor of Templari and the former provinces of the Chimaera Corporation. He was given the job at the behest of the armistice treaty, and Ingren vouched for him as a man of good character that can be trusted not to allow ambition to overrun the need of his people.

Not too far from him was Reich, an ex-Executive, and the head speaker of Guard's reformed political identity. The last war had toppled its corporate leadership and replaced it with elements of the old imperial system, which had successfully kept Guard from crumbling apart at the seams. Although the architects of the reform, helmed by former General Vant, intended to keep the military caste on the highest levels of government with a president for life, the end of the Corporate War and the conditions of the treaty prevented the army from heinously blocking power to civilians.

Other delegates included the Prefect of Lorica, Helmer Galvano of Tinkertown, who had retained his position in a recent election, and the Viceroy of Freya, a city-state and protectorate of Magna Carta known as the 'City of the Arts', which was the undisputed center of theater and music. The mayors of several constituencies, towns, and cities that included Coastal Sky and Floria itself were also present, and lastly was Titus of Gabrialtar.

The odd and overweening Captain-General seemed to be mesmerized by a grand mural portraying the Iron Sabres victorious over a besieged city after a terrible battle. He stared at the details of the scene with child-like wonder, noting the delicate brush strokes with the flair of an artistic connoisseur.

"The work of a master indeed," he commented aloud, directed at no one in particular save himself.

"He does seem quite... energetic," Traiza said as he broke away from the gathering to speak to Ingren. His keen sailor eyes observed Titus, and much like Dalena had surmised, his instincts offered an attention to hidden danger.

"The young Captain-General is more austere than he allows us to see," Ingren said in return.

"Gabrialtar's economic prosperity certainly reflects on this herald from the south." Traiza lowered his voice. "I've confirmed the rumours, and it's true that he was chiefly responsible for Gabrialtar's unprecedented technological bloom. He initiated the Research and Development Branch, and had access not only to vehicle and weapon designs from the war, but also in refining retro-reef fuel for advanced manufacturing applications. Beyond the official records of his rise from master engineer to Aide-de-Camp of the Gabrialtar Presidency, there's little or nothing."

Ingren found that odd. "No family history? No previous military service?"

"Records say that he was born in the City of Guard, but his parents were both citizens of Gabrialtar before it was temporarily annexed by Chimaera. He enlisted in Guard's premier military academy; details after that are sketchy and unreliable. The most recent transcript from Gabrialtar stated that he joined the Island Defense Corps while retaining a rank of major. Beyond that, your guess is as good as mine."

Ingren remembered what he told Julia. "...'A small snake in the tall grass'."

The embellished double doors on one side of the meeting hall were opened by a pair of attendant priests, appearing more as Inquisitor Knights without their armour, than lowly ushers. Like a deity stepping off his high-horse, Mellka entered the room and gazed unforgivingly at the delegation, before tilting his head slightly in greeting.

"Loyal sons and brothers, dearest daughters and sisters, I welcome you," he greeted formally.

The delegates stood up in his presence, and those that were already on their feet moved closer to the table as Mellka circled around and took his reserved seat. Once he was seated, so did the rest, except for Titus, who remained beguiled by the gaudy murals around him. Strangely, as Ingren noted, the delegation seemed to have forgotten him or intentionally ignored him.

"With all due respect, we shall keep this brief and to the point." Mellka spared no frankness in his words, and surprised a few of the guests. "My mandate demands a timed and effective review of the work left undone by my predecessors, and I prefer action over fancy words. Likewise, my esteemed guests, you'd prefer to taste the joys and flavour of this good city than engage in frivolous debate."

"Humph," Titus scoffed quietly on a personal thought, moving to another section of the mural he was studying despite the unfriendly attention of the seated delegation, and Mellka's baleful glance.

"I surmise my Declaration may have been a hard slap in the face for some of you," Mellka continued without heed to Titus' rude behavior, "and to others a sign of hope." His eyes rested on the royal delegate from Magna Carta. "Your thoughts, King Ingren?"

"The world is still reeling from the effects of the Corporate War," Ingren said coolly. "The transition is costly in manpower and resources that only now we realize are becoming scarce. We are on the verge of an energy crisis, and without the firm administration of the corporate regimes, provinces of the old world have taken back their sovereignty, while other parties seek to take advantage of this frail situation."

Mellka knew the accusation was poised toward him. "Do you believe my appointment was spurred by a blood-thirsty agenda?"

"Your methods of purging non-believers attest to that possibility."

"My methods were no different than yours when you organized an allied assault to crush Rell Vant's revolt," Mellka countered calmly. "The slight difference in how we weave our future is that I leave no loose ends. The political power vacuum of Guard and Chimaera has caused municipal and spiritual unrest at proportions you're not ready to accept. My mandate is to restore faith where there is none."

"By stirring fear with fanaticism?" Traiza cut in. "The machinations of the Church's propaganda will not restore hope, but invite more strife."

"You, of all here present, must know how terribly your people continue to suffer," Mellka said. "Templari faced the most casualties, and there is doubt that your great city will ever stand proud again. How many families were torn asunder? Have you not had the heart to make the count, for you lost your male heirs when the walls fell?"

Traiza's throat tightened, and he lowered his gaze. Beside him, shamefully not having known the admiral had lost his sons, Ingren looked at his profile in sympathy.

Mellka pressed on. "It is these days, when misery seems to run rampant, that our souls need restitution. That is what I offer."

The solemn silence was interrupted by Titus' unexpected applause. His action solidified the tension, and invited the entire attention of the delegation. Once he knew all eyes and ears were on him, he ceased his clapping, and approached the table.

"Your performance, my High Eminence, was moving," Titus said with a smile. "You've convinced me that religion is the institution of conscience. Any directive to force compulsion is to take away the value this Church has imposed on the world for over two millennia. I beseech you to save our souls with the same iron will that earned you the mantle of leadership."

Mellka remained aloof, while his two attendant priests tensed with hostility. "Forgive me, Captain-General, but your manners are lacking."

Titus feigned surprise, a slick grin creeping on his lips. "Grand Master, I for one, have shown you the most respect out of all these delegates. They've given you skepticism, and I gave you praise. Surely we are not enemies here, but invited guests of honour."

"Are you here on behalf of your government, or for yourself?" Reich asked the question that was most prominent on everyone's minds.

Titus bowed slightly, an arrogant gesture, but deceivingly humble. "Do not judge me so brashly, Senator, for I'm here for the love of my country."

"The sudden emergence of your country as a world power is a cause for concern," Mellka said. "Your independence and recoup as a self-sustaining nation has given you pride and ambition. It's only a matter of time before your wings of steel spread toward dominion, and history repeats."

For a moment, the air chilled, and Titus seemed to have dropped his gentil charade. "During your proclamation, you boasted your ultimatum, that the world should heed to your flag or what? You will call all faithful men to arms?"

If there was a point where a breach in diplomacy would lead directly to all-out war, this was it, and everyone knew it.

Ingren cleared his throat, offering a distraction, and stood up. "We are all here in agreement that our state of affairs are brittle, and that we stand on perhaps the most significant collective decision of our generation. As such, I, along with Governor Traiza, and many others here, will be holding a summit at Templari to deal with matters of sustainable economy and cooperation. This invitation is open to all leaders of governance and commerce, to all who dream of a mutual alliance between nations to trade resource and ideas, and to prevent catastrophe. Your presence, Grand Master, I hope will provide neutrality."

"This Church shall consider it," Mellka said, and to signal an end to the meeting, the attendant priests opened all doors.

The delegation parted ways, but Mellka remained seated. He glared at Titus, as the man stood where he was while others walked past him.

"May the Twelve guide you in your deliberation," Titus said, almost mockingly, and bowed.

"Gloriam be with you," Mellka said in return, coldly, and watched him leave.

Cardinal Abaster paced across the tiled floor of the antechapel, which had been recently transformed into the new grand master's office. The room was scarcely furbished, but housed the most unusual objects from the Cathedral's collection. Occupying the center of the floor, between the main doors and the papal desk, was an orrery.

Fashioned in sculpted copper and unpolished gold, the old clockwork device offered a unique view of the heavens. Orbs of different sizes representing the sun, planets, and moons orbited around the central sphere of Terra Mia, which slowly spun on its axis. The entire contraption was a complex system of gears, a feat of engineering that sadly few will ever see.

He paused to study it, toying with its mechanisms until the clamour of opening doors startled him.

"Do you feel it's justified to keep knowledge and devices such as that orrery from the public?" Mellka queried as he entered his office.

Abaster turned to face the Grand Master, and bowed ceremoniously. "Scientists have always challenged our power over the masses."

"Then you agree that certain ideas are too dangerous to reveal," Mellka said, "that perhaps certain truths about our origins may bring an end to all things we take for granted." He expected no response from Abaster, and received none.

He walked to his desk, where he revealed a familiar book from its protective velvet covering. "This simple thing…" His finger traced the etched shape of the Thousand-Year Dream. "The dark reason why we are here, written by our First Lord Alexander Mellka, and its original, unaltered story of the Sentinel War and rise of our Church."

He opened it, flipping casually through the pages. "Our martyred Saint Knight noted here that he feared the corruption of the upper ranks, who desperately sought to use this testament to fulfill the needs of the greedy and of political ambitions." He closed it shut. "The truths in this book present a direct threat to the foundation of our Order. The recovery of the Vade Mecum was a principal reason why you arrested Seidon Harbrid, but you did not know it was in his possession until you took him into custody."

Abaster pried his eyes from the blue glass cover of the ancient tome. "We received information from Guard revealing the heretic's whereabouts. It was a surprise that he found the sacred book in Lorica."

"Seidon Harbrid and his accomplices are still at large," Mellka said, not caring for what the Cardinal had to say. "Their penances await, and instead of dirtying your hands, you called for a bounty on their heads."

"The faithful will answer the call, it's just a matter of–"

"Perhaps I was wrong to assume the late Grand Master Vatic was unduly incompetent, and that *you* are solely to blame for the fall of our values in allowing the guilty to go unpunished."

Abaster grimaced, his ire surfacing. "The accused have become heroes of war, and are deemed untouchable by Magna Carta and the provisional governments of Templari and Guard."

"No State is above our sacred law," Mellka stated brashly. "No treaty, and no armistice."

Although he should be intimidated, Abaster still felt superior by his seniority. "We cannot ignore the mountain for the sake of moving a pebble."

"Was that your philosophy when you collaborated with Rell Vant throughout this ordeal?" Mellka interposed without remorse. "You lacked the clairvoyance to see past his scheming, and let him manipulate you and our hallowed institution for his own end."

Abaster tensed, his ego no longer able to withstand the verbal beating. "I protected this Church from him, defended Floria with my life!"

"By haggling the contents of our Sacred Vault to buy off his guarantees!" Mellka shouted in riposte. "His sins are your sins, and justice must be exacted!"

"You promised me a chance at atonement," Abaster said, keeping his voice from trembling. "I assure you that despite Vant's protection as a prisoner of war, he will pay his due."

Mellka was unimpressed. "I don't need your assurances nor your services, Cardinal, to do things properly. But, alas, I keep my promises. You have your chance, now be gone until that duty is settled."

Abaster sucked in his fear, and bowed. The rift between them was wide, and widened still as he left the papal office.

With her personal escort of Throne Guards, Dalena was back in the safety and comfort of the *Second Awakening*. Her duties as queen were tiresome, and she longed to return to the seas where her soul felt more at ease.

She strode past the score of sailors prepping the vessel for its eventual departure, while the steward organized the cargo manifest. She climbed the steps to the bridge, the highest point of the vessel's stern, and looked out to the Vast Blue with longing eyes. At least for a moment she felt at peace, as she sensed that she wasn't alone, and glanced over to see Messer sitting quite comfortably on the balustrade with his back against taut moorings. With a knife, he carved a model ship from a scented piece of exotic wood with the finesse of an expert.

The shape of the model resembled the *Awakening*, whose remains rested at the bottom of the Northern Cross.

"From one captain to another," Messer said, showing her his work, "we all remember our first love."

Dalena was impressed with the remarkable details. "She was a good ship... good crew."

"Aye... the Queen's Glory was a fine ship herself."

Her flagship and her squadron, lost in the Sorcerer Cannon's overture many years ago. It was her last station serving as an admiral before war swept her away to places she'd never dreamed to be. "Do you ever intend to retire?"

"No," Messer said flatly. "I prefer a death at sea, be it in battle or against Nature, than waste away my last years in comfort. I've watched greater men succumb to sickness, and their demise didn't justify their lives. Seidon's father, Athan-Leon, was one man I knew very well, and I miss him."

Dalena remembered the man who had earned special treatment by the royalty of Magna Carta, not through the reputation of the Harbrid lineage, but by personal merit and service.

"For a time I knew King Ingren's uncle, who was the admiral in charge before you," Messer continued, "and he was a thorn to all mercenaries of the sea. He gave me chase once, for nearly three months, and no matter how far we sailed, he'd find us." Messer laughed. "Until one day, both our ships needed berth for re-supply, and we found ourselves face-to-face. Rather than calling out all men to arm themselves to the teeth, we enjoyed a good afternoon with plenty of food and drink, and lots of tall stories. It's rare that enemies find a common place in this world, where nothing else matters except for the respect we have as human beings."

Dalena smiled sadly at the story. "I served with him briefly; he was one of my first tutors, and he always scolded me for being too stern."

Messer sighed. "After he retired, he became landlocked and miserable, and he died far from the sea. I don't want that for myself, and I will fight the tides so long as I have breath."

A commotion stirred at the foot of the boarding ramp, where guards prevented access to the ship to a rugged, unemployed sailor simply demanding for temporary work. Both Dalena and Messer took caution, the latter noticing something familiar about the man: his dark complexion, built frame, and his amputated left arm....

Messer couldn't believe it. He quickly ran across the deck, forced his way past the curious crewmen, and broke through the wall of alerted Marines. He grasped the intruder by his muscular shoulders and smiled. "Bale!"

Bale, his face worn with years of hard life, was overjoyed to see his former commander. He laughed, embracing Messer tightly. "The ghosts of the Vast Blue finally answered my prayers!"

"I thought you perished with the ship," Messer said, still amazed. "I thought I was alone."

"I thought I was dead myself, but the current took me too far from the fleet and I ended up on northern shores." Bale shook his head, his eyes watery. "Since then, I was lost. I traveled from town to town looking for work, or for a familiar face, but..."

"I'm sorry, Bale, if I only I knew. Seidon will be so happy to know you're alive."

"He's grown up."

"He has..." Messer glanced behind him to the guards and to Dalena. "At ease, gentlemen. Bale, please pay your respects to Queen Dalena, I'm sure she'll bend and twist every rule in the Royal Navy to commission you as part of my crew."

Bale bowed respectfully to Dalena. "I could use a place to call home again."

"Let this ship be your home," Dalena said with a gentle smile.

Easily homogenous to Bale's tanned skin, the dark mark of the Squires was tattooed on his forearm, but no one took notice.

On the most luxurious veranda of the Diplomats' Residential Estate, King Ingren, Traiza, and Ambassador Daedlus enjoyed an afternoon tea. They were seated at a limestone table, surrounded by florae, and the festivities still carried on throughout Floria. Somewhere nearby, an orchestra performed, enchanting the air with rich music.

Traiza observed in deep thought, and took a sip from his cup. "Rarely during the year do we celebrate like this back home."

"Templari?" Daedlus politely assumed.

"Archway's Path, where my fleet was stationed," Traiza corrected. "I spent nearly my whole naval career there, and only visited the Old Capital for official reasons. The few instances that I recall, Templari's annual celebrations were renowned for their splendour... but that was a long time ago."

"Her towers will rise tall again," Ingren assured.

"I have confidence of the city's renaissance, but it won't be for another generation or two before her people can truly rejoice like they once had." Traiza looked out to the spires of the Cathedral. "Have you ever walked down the city streets, once lit so brightly with colour and light, and then have that memory brushed away by the sheer misery of the homeless and forlorn? Great manors have become slums, and progress, no matter how steady, only reaches few."

"I've read the official reports on the reconstruction; certainly the Restoration League is performing admirably," Daedlus said, innately insensitive to the matter. "I hear the old defensive wall is already rebuilt."

Traiza nodded absently, still drab on the old memories. "General Strafe is living up to his legend."

Ingren set his finished cup down, stopping the attending servant from refilling it. "How are our prisoners of war?"

"Behaving, to my surprise," Traiza said. "Even after all this time, I half-expect the Strafers to rise up in rebellion. They may be defeated soldiers, but their spirits are far from broken."

Ingren understood why. "Their leader still lives."

"Does that make him more dangerous now than ever before? He should've been executed for his war crimes, but you vetoed that decision."

"If it were my powers alone, I would've agreed with you," Ingren said, "but I couldn't ignore the call to spare him. All his men, from the highest-ranking officers down to lowliest cadet begged to save his life, but it was Seidon whom I listened to. He could've ended it himself, sliced his neck and let history judge, but instead he showed all of us a virtue long forgotten, that its practice still deludes most of us this day."

"A valiant lad," Daedlus commented. "It's a shame the Church still has not forfeited his persecution. I've tried to state his case to the Cardinalate, but the Holy Decree will not relent."

Ingren sat back more comfortably and folded his hands together. "An irony of what religion teaches us about forgiveness."

There was a slight pause, as the lively music from the festivities filled the silence. Daedlus glanced at his pocket watch, and was startled to see the time.

"I'm due for an appointment, if you'll excuse me." He stood up and bowed respectfully to both. "Your Highness, Governor, have a good day."

With the ambassador gone, Traiza was more at ease to speak freely to Ingren. "With all respect to you, I don't believe this summit will hold. No one will be convinced to trade freely for the goodwill of humankind, nor can we force it upon any."

"We have to try," Ingren said, "or all of us are doomed to repeat hostilities against each other, because that's exactly what will happen when one starves while another thrives selfishly. This contest is being preyed on by the underworld, a massive black market driven by desperation, and the Church continues to drive its wedge rather than mend. We can't afford to be lax now, there are too many threats lurking about..." Looking past Traiza, he saw Titus on the streets below, dancing with a group of women in jubilation. "Another war will destroy us all."

Immersed in the festivity, Titus danced without reserve. Flags, flower pedals and silky ribbons shifted around him, and he moved from one woman to another as the orchestra reached its climax. He laughed vainly, feeling incorruptible, and with a broad smile he glanced up at the veranda of the Diplomats' Estate where he was sure Ingren watched.

His eyes narrowed ahead of him, where a double row of Gabrialtar Dragoons cut through the crowd like a knife. The officer at the head of the column ordered the soldiers to halt, then approached him.

"Sergeant," Titus greeted, his mood untarnished, "what news do you bring?"

The sergeant, his face deadly serious, leaned close to Titus' ear and whispered his report.

Titus' smile widened. "Wonderful. Prepare the ship for departure."

V. Point of the Sword

V: Point of the Sword

Journey's Prodigy cut through the waves with adventurous expediency, driven by the will of her captain. Her sails brimmed white and proud, the wind sifting through the Vast Blue pushing the vessel in good favour.

Tenshi was at the helm, keeping the bow steady on course, while Seidon tightened the lines holding the mizzen mast in place. Although the schooner was a small ship in comparison to the ship-of-the-lines or frigates, the vessel still needed a crew to operate efficiently. Two was the absolute minimum, but a few more pairs of strong hands would have shipboard operations running more smoothly.

Seidon lived his whole life at sea, and knew this well, but after having lost the *Awakening* and her crew, he refrained from hiring the extra hands. Even when the schooner was commissioned under his command as a personal gift from Queen Dalena, Seidon refused to have Magna Cartan sailors serve onboard.

Tenshi glanced at him lovingly. She knew why he was hesitant, understood his quiet plight, and stood at his side. Until he was ready to accept the mantle his father had given him, *Journey's Prodigy* was serviced by them two alone.

Finished with his task, Seidon climbed his way to the crow's nest. On the highest point of the ship, he was given an amazingly unobstructed view of the ocean and sky. The wind was at his back, and nothing to slow their voyage. He closed his eyes for a moment, and inhaled the unencumbered air, then reached into his shirt for the locket and chain he kept close to his heart.

Opening the old piece, he looked at the youthful portraits of his mother and father. He had found it years ago, when Ingren had given over ownership of his father's private estate near the serene hillsides of Locked Shields on the outskirts of the Royal Capital to him. It was a treasure with no value, a memory preserved in the inks the artist had used, and it was priceless.

He closed the locket and placed it back under his shirt. Far in the horizon, the peaks of the Mountains appeared from the haze, but from far astern he heard a strange drone that was partly hidden by the rustle of the wind.

He turned to face aft, and searched for the source of the sound once he was certain he heard it. He spotted movement across the water, a streamlined reflection that raced quickly across the surface of the ocean. Looking skyward, he saw the *Highborn* with its bow aimed toward them like a kingfisher intended to snatch its prey out of the water.

"Sky galleon coming at us directly aft!" Seidon shouted to Tenshi, and rushed back down to the deck.

Tenshi searched the sky behind her for the vessel and found it, bearing inexorably at them. It continued to descend the closer it came, and the drone of its engines grew louder. She could see its countless gun ports, all of them opened and at the ready.

"Why are they engaging us?!"

Seidon reached the bridge, and moved past her to prepare the rear-mounted swivel cannon. "Prepare to evade if she fires! She has a wide turning radius, so we have some advantage!"

The cannon was light and its caliber small, but its reloading time was much faster than the heavier guns. Seidon had his reservation on how it would stand against a highly advanced warship in mid-flight, but he hoped he didn't have to release the trigger.

"Keep the Journey steady, Tenshi."

The *Highborn* was well within its firing range, but it held back. It approached at incredible speed, and its size easily overshadowed the two-mast schooner, yet it came as if determined to ram them through. With a slight course correction, the sky galleon swooped past the *Journey's Prodigy*, its momentous draft stirring the sails. Its copper-plated keel sliced across the water, then lifted higher into the air to turn about.

"It's coming back around!" Tenshi warned, her heart racing.

Seidon stood beside her, perplexed by the *Highborn*'s gutsy action. Unable to take any defense, he watched in horror as the ship completed its wide arc and faced them head-on. It was still traveling at high speeds, but its altitude was low enough to brush the surface of the water. From amidships, a man with a long coat and braided ponytail peered at them.

It was Titus, but neither Seidon nor Tenshi recognized him. He leaned as far out as he could, balancing himself on the railing with catlike agility while his hand held on to the rigging at arm's reach. His eyes bore at Seidon, a mysterious grin on his lips.

The two vessels passed each other's port flank in opposite directions, close enough that a man could jump the distance safely. Close enough for Seidon and Tenshi to see the dark colour of Titus' eyes.

The moment lasted a handbreadth, but a moment that left a lasting impression.

The ships sailed on in their respective directions without further incidence. The *Highborn* climbed toward the clouds, and sped leeward to the south whence it came until it was a speck in the horizon. The *Journey's Prodigy*, though shaken by the stirred waves, traversed with the wind toward Coastal Sky.

Templari's civic council was held in the gutted hall of a medieval theater. Where the stage had been long ago, was now a long table where all of the city's district councilors bickered between themselves and the citizens that voted for them. The same problems arose, that of insufficient funding and a constant downward spiral in all facets of commerce, utilities, and other social services that have been lacking.

Most of those that sat on the council were former administrators of the Chimaera Conglomerate, and their bureaucratic habits almost always clashed with the feasibility of affairs. The rest were chief architects, engineers, and foremen. Aside from Traiza and his staff, who were absent here, there were no defined leaders. Any decisions that were reached would still have to pass through Magna Carta's overseers before any action was initiated.

The appointed peacekeepers remained at a distance, scrutinizing the crowd for instigators. Their primary reason for being present was not for the council, but to keep watch on Vant and his Strafers, who were there representing the Restoration League.

Sucre, who sat beside the General, glared at the Magna Cartan soldiers, then leaned closer to Vant. "There will be a summit of all nations sometime this month."

"Where?"

"Right here in the capital," Sucre replied. "Preparations are being made at the new government building across town. Security will be tight."

"Show the glamour, hide the rot," Vant surmised sourly. "This is a rare opportunity for anyone wanting change, be it for the good of all or... for reasons too sinister to grasp."

They paused their conversation as someone in the crowd raised up in protest. "My sector has been without running water for three months!"

"We are aware of the situation in the Drol and Venetian districts," one of the councilors said. "The decontamination process of the pipelines is scheduled to be finished by the end of the week, please be patient."

Another councilor spoke up. "On that note, we are still experiencing a shortage of manpower for the clean-up operations, if there are any volunteers, please consult your district foreman or show up at the work site." He glanced at Vant, and hesitated before he spoke. "The Restoration League is also short on hands to rebuild the former Administrate offices. Carpenters, masons, plumbers, welders, any skilled worker must check with the Magna Carta magistrate before being employed by the League."

The noise of the theater hall had lessened, and unfriendly eyes stared at Vant and his men. The peacekeepers became tense, but the situation passed without incident.

The councilor sighed with relief. "Moving on to the next item on our list..."

"This is an opportunity for us," Sucre said once the unwanted attention was steered away. "This rabble is an example of Traiza's diminishing influence with his people. With all the world leaders present–"

"Quit your plotting. We are no longer soldiers," Vant said sternly. "I've traded the sword for the hammer, and I've accepted it. It's time you do the same."

Sucre was shunned, but he remained stubborn. "With all this talk of change, you are the only one who can make a real difference. You are better than their king," he said, gesturing to the peacekeepers, "and they fear you enough while your wrists are in chains more than they ever have when you led your armies."

"Ingren knows that fear lurks in the most noticeable corners…" Vant looked past Sucre to the venomous scowl of the disgruntled mason, Zaffre, as the man stood up and left in frustration. "Too many want me dead, waiting upon the chance that I should rear up my head, but I will not make the aggressive move."

Sucre tightened his jaw, restraining his bile out of fierce respect for his superior. "If you don't act, sir, someone else will."

Vant seized the Sucre's forearm tightly, and looked at him dead in the eye. "Think of the consequences before you take haste with murderous intent. Swear to me you will not repatriate."

Sucre was terrified by the fierceness of Vant's words. He had wrongly assumed that defeat and over five years of hard labour had weakened the General's spirit, and felt ashamed. "You have my word, sir."

Vant released Sucre's arm. "Keep your mind on the work at hand."

"The meeting's adjourned," one of the older councilors cited. "We'll reconvene at the end of the week."

With the rumblings and murmurs of dissatisfaction, the hall emptied. The peacekeepers organized the traffic, making certain Vant and the Strafers left last. Rather than be goaded by them, Vant retained his dignity by remaining in his seat until there was no one left. Sucre and the others kept taut on alert around him.

They quickly stood as a man approached Vant from the crowd. He was tall and had the air of a trained, professional soldier, but far from it, he was an Inquisitor Knight without his armour. The only hint of his religious affiliation was the cross-like clasp that held his half-cloak – the insignia of the Faithful.

He stopped at a good distance from Vant, who remained calmly on his seat while his soldiers stood. "An old acquaintance wishes to speak to you in private. He waits at Our Lady of Hours, the old church near the eastern wall."

Vant nodded, his eyes locked on the other as if he were ready to snipe him. He carefully noted the subtle red piping stitched along the hem of the Knight's cloak. "Tell the Cardinal I look forward to meeting him again."

The Knight was surprised, but the reaction was only expressed through his eyes, and briefly. He bowed properly, aware of the scrutiny of the Strafers, and quietly dispersed with the crowd.

Sucre was eager for answers as Vant. "What's this about, General?"

Vant finally stood up, his regal manner imposed upon everyone around him. "It seems we have an unexpected guest, let's not keep him waiting."

On the edge of a small bluff that overlooked the skyline of the Old Capital, Poem brought his old warbike to a halt. The engine thrummed and memories stirred, both bitter and sweet, but he didn't suppress them. It's been years since he last stood in its realm, the few days he spent surveying the aftermath of Guard's assault still fresh in his mind.

His thoughts went briefly to his sister Genetha, and how she survived the onslaught only to meet her end in a burst of hatred. Here he was, following the same path.

It was strange to see part of the city tall and glorious, and yet another in ruins. It was there, he knew, that Vant and his Strafers served their punishment, as mild and unjustified as the commuted sentence was. It was also there that he sensed some foreboding danger astir, like old grudges that sought absolution.

Without hesitation, he pulled back on the throttle and raced down the bluff and across the expanse to the eastern city wall.

It was a moonless night, and the streets of the old quarter at the eastern wall were lit scarcely by waning lamps. Most of the buildings were abandoned due to the renovations, others like the church, were empty because there were none to service them.

Our Lady of Hours was the historic birthplace of the last king to grace Templari's throne before the corporate structure razed the monarchy down to nothing. Built from large grey stones, its archways were slender and majestic, but the gothic setting was left to the weather for far too long. It appeared foreboding now, soulless, filled with shadows deep enough to hide usurpers.

It was here where Vant headed, with no weapon to defend himself, except for the unyielding loyalty of Sucre and the Strafers to act as his armour and shield. The Magna Cartan peacekeepers had allowed them some privacy, believing it was an early inspection of the work to be done for the coming morning. Not without distrust, some continued their patrols along the battlements and the watchtowers nearby, and like every other night, a curfew was strictly enforced, or severe consequences were to follow shortly after.

Without fear, Vant approached the tall entrance doors and opened them wide into the interior. The groan of the hinges resounded into the decrepit nave, where two rows of pews lined with thick dust and cobwebs formed a path to the pulpit. Along the walls, saintly statues that once shone with colour, now appeared ashen. The heavy shadows that dominated the nave were partly dispersed by broken stained glass windows and holes in the ceiling where light spilled through.

Up ahead, a cloaked shadow stirred beside the altar as Vant and his group approached – their footsteps echoing.

"It's rare we see men of the Faith at this late hour," Vant said loudly. "I'm sure the reason is benign."

Cardinal Abaster moved under a patch of pale light, and his scowl was illuminated. "It's been too long, General, and you've caused me great grief since those days. The night seemed a proper venue for our reunion."

Two fully armoured Inquisitor Knights with red stripes along their cloaks appeared beside the cardinal, including the messenger from before. Their hands, hidden in gauntlets, rested on the hilts of their blue-flamed swords.

"I applaud your efforts to sneak past the guards, you've certainly lost none of your wile."

Abaster wasn't amused by Vant's antics. "When we first met, I had assumed you had the capacity to keep your promises. You vowed a return to the old tradition, pretended to be a friend of the Order, but you deceived us all."

Vant quickly noticed the frailty of Abaster's nerves, and pressed his advantage. "If I had known you were riding my coat tails in the hopes of advancing your career, I would've taken better precautions."

"You used me!" Abaster let out his resentment without reserve. "Because you lost the war, all my efforts have gone to waste, and I am now treated to a grand master that will just as soon see me hang in the Cathedral's belfry!" He shook his head in disgust. "To think that I let myself be deceived by you... and by deadly rumours that you were in league with the living dead – a Sorcerer worst of all. I should've had the foresight to persecute you while I had the chance."

"Isn't that why you're here, Cardinal?" Vant said. "One last chance at redemption, before the bell tolls?" Vant stepped closer to the pulpit and spread out his arms. "Take it upon your grace to do what none other had the fortitude to do."

"Your head on a pike will bring peace of mind to many, and not just myself."

"Then for once," Vant said coldly, "earn your title by doing this deed for the sake of others, and not for your sorry self."

Abaster grimaced. "You're hoping the scuffle will alert the guards, but you forget that men of the Holy Community do not have need for noisy guns. The edge of a sharp blade will do just fine against unarmed felons."

On cue, the two Knights removed their swords from their sheaths as the Cardinal stepped back into the cloistered shadows. A pair of black-clad riders on equally black horses raced into the church proper, before the doors slammed shut. Hidden assassins, all wearing light armours and hoods the colours of night, emerged from the murk surrounding the pulpit – their jet-like daggers and blackened swords gleaming with sinister intent.

Vant easily recognized the select black-clad friars trained in covert operations. "Insidians…"

"Protect the General!" Sucre ordered, and the Strafers formed a protective circle around their leader. Although they were denied weapons of any kind, they wielded smuggled kitchen knives and makeshift construction tools that doubled as maces and axes.

One of the horsemen charged first, scattering the knit group of Strafers into smaller pockets of resistance. He intended to run through Vant, but missed as a Strafer pushed the General between the benches and took the full brunt of the attack. The soldier was knocked several feet away, his back and shoulder smashing against one of the pews in a shower of dust.

The second horseman committed the next charge, just as Sucre attempted to rally the splintered units back into formation. The mounted Insidian struck down the soldiers in his path, as his horse collected speed and momentum toward Sucre's main position.

Assisted by a small group of Strafers, Vant moved quickly to execute a counterattack. They ran to the farthest end of one of the pews, and applied their combined weights to push it into the path of the second horseman. The bench slid noisily across the floor, and the horse's impetus carried the beast and rider through it. The violent impact brought the horse down and ejected the rider, his body rolling several times across the floor before being stopped by the pulpit.

Sucre seized the fallen rider's lost sword, and prepared for the next cavalry charge, but the horseman stayed back while the black-clad assassins pounced forth. He glanced back to the soldiers around him and to the now-unguarded doors, then looked to the General and the few Strafers that were with him.

Vant knew, just as Sucre, that their situation was grim unless the fight was taken outside.

"Get those doors open!" he ordered Sucre before he heard a bloody gurgle from behind.

One of the Strafers beside him dropped to the ground as an Insidian mercilessly slit his jugular. The assassin redirected his blade, but another Strafer struck him with one of the saintly statuettes. Before the debris settled, more Insidians rushed in, and the rest of the Strafers moved between them and Vant.

In the scuffle, Vant risked looking for any sign of Cardinal Abaster, and surprisingly found him making his exit through the underground catacombs beside the pulpit. His two Knights guarded him, and the last horseman provided reinforcement.

With Sucre and his group fending off the other Insidians while they attempted to pry open the doors, Vant took the initiative on his own. He crouched low to minimize his profile, and quickened his pace through the rows of benches toward the far side of the nave.

The doors were opened with a thunderous roar, the hinges nearly popping, and Sucre took the fight out onto the streets where he hoped the Magna Cartan peacekeepers took notice. The Insidians became fiercer as they hacked down the Strafers, but the soldiers from Guard stood their ground and fought – even if severely wounded.

Sucre, cut across his arm and waist, remained vigilant. He looked to the second group inside the hall where the few unarmed Strafers that protected the General were overrun, but Vant himself was nowhere to be seen.

He turned to the veteran Strafer beside him. "Freyr, alert the sentries! Get the whole of Magna Carta here!"

Freyr, although reluctant to leave his comrades, complied with the order and ran. The horseman inside the church saw this, and spurred his horse to a full-speed gallop to stop the soldier. The horse's hooves, thrashing against the floor, echoed angrily across the nave, and the rider's mad charge momentarily dispersed the fight at the doorway. With his focus driven almost blindly, his blade aimed at the runner, he failed to see Sucre rush at him from the side, and was cut down.

The rider tumbled to the ground, a gash across his flank, and his horse continued its charge without a master at its reins. Sucre spared the Insidian no leniency as he brought down his blade through the man's neck.

In no time, the signal flares lit up the night, and the cacophony of Magna Cartan soldiers stirring awake filled the air.

With the horse and rider gone, Vant slipped into the shadow of the pulpit and down the narrow stairs of the catacomb. Weaponless, he chased through the corridor after the Cardinal and his two guards, determined to vindicate the sacrifice of his dead and wounded soldiers.

The corridor opened up into a musty anteroom, horribly neglected, and filled with decaying vittles. With feeble light pouring from minuscule slots above, he discerned two pathways out: the one that led deeper into the catacombs was blocked by debris, while the other branched somewhere above ground. Carefully approaching the latter, he saw one of the Cardinal's Knights standing at the byway, watching him with his sword drawn.

Vant expected him to attack, but instead the Knight turned away to follow Abaster. Only at the last conceivable moment, did he realize there was more than just the two Knights guarding the clergyman.

Acting on instinct, Vant jabbed his elbow into the murk behind him, and struck the chest of an Insidian who crept there. He moved to deliver his fist, but the hooded assassin angrily shoved him away. The Insidian followed with a second attack, and Vant saw the evil gleam of his curved jet-black dagger.

Vant quickly grabbed whatever he could get his hands on from a wooden slab he accidentally bumped into, and threw it at his assailant. The jar crumbled on impact, and although it did little harm, the dusty distraction gave Vant a chance to tackle the assassin down.

The Insidian, the air knocked from his lungs, promptly jabbed Vant in the stomach. He grabbed the General's shoulder, and turned him over on his back, and the assassin brought the edge of his dagger onto Vant's neck.

Pinned down and surprised he wasn't already dead, Vant now recognized the assassin. It was the mason, Zaffre, his bleached blond hair in contrast with his black hood and ash-like face paint.

"*In the Twelve's names I will kill you*," Zaffre hissed, saliva dripping from his lower lip, as his muscles tensed to deliver the deadly lunge.

A muzzle flash lit the dark, and the blast hit Zaffre square across the torso. He flung off Vant and remained still. Without having achieved his desire for wrath, the young man was dead by the guns of King Ingren's peacekeepers as they swooped in like birds of prey, and swiftly secured the small chamber.

They made certain Zaffre was no longer a threat, then the riflemen turned their guns on Vant, while another armed squad chased after the stragglers.

The narrow underground passage ended nearly a hundred yards outside the city wall, where a company of Insidians on black horses received Cardinal Abaster in his retreat from the altercation. Three spare horses were ready for the Cardinal and his two loyal guards.

One of the Insidians held the horse steady by its reins as Abaster mounted. "Cardinal, the city is on full alert, and all gates are locked shut. The King's soldiers will be swarming this area."

"They're already on our heels," Abaster said sourly as he took the reins. "Seal the passage, then we make haste for Floria."

They were all startled by the sound of a motorcycle's engine as it revved, both vehicle and rider cutting through from their flank and stopping in their midst. Their senses already on alert, the mounted Knights and Insidians encircled the intruder with their weapons drawn, and paused in hesitation as the driver shut off the engine.

"Your attack was too bold, too forward," Poem said darkly, his eyes piercing through Abaster. "You underestimated him."

Abaster studied the familiar face, seeing an opportunity to atone for his earlier failure, and arrogantly approached with his horse. "Gloriam must be testing my resolve tonight; little did I expect the heretic Harbrid's accomplice to confront me so candidly. I salute your courage."

Poem dismounted, untouched by Abaster's vile words. "Vant reveals his weaknesses as a feint to invite dim-witted enemies," he said, his tone harsher. "With his enemies out in the open, he controls the whole battlefield." He laughed unexpectedly, but it sounded tormented. "He played you like a puppet."

Abaster grimaced. "You are in no position to lecture me on the art of war. Abdicate this foolishness by surrendering to the will of the Church."

"How many did you lose? Do you spare them any leniency for failing to carry out your will?"

Abaster felt a few eyes from those around him glance at his direction, but he intended not to give any answers. "Enough of your ranting; you're an infidel. Arrest him!"

A pair of twin blades slipped into Poem's hands as he summoned them from their hidden sheaths within his sleeves. "Tonight's not your night for passing judgement."

With the agility of a cat, Poem lashed backward before any of the Cardinal's minions could dismount. He leaped over one of the horses, and slashed the Insidian clear off his saddle.

"Fools, get him!" Abaster shouted, as he pulled his horse away in terror.

Poem landed on his feet running, and he gave the next horseman no opportunity to face him as he struck both the man and horse with a blast of ice from his dagger. They broke formation and fell with a spray of glass-like shards, accidentally tumbling into another horseman in the consternation.

Poem dodged a poorly coordinated attack from one of the Knights as he brought down his sword, and sprinted past him toward three mounted Insidians who blocked his path to Cardinal Abaster. With a burst of fury, he summoned a spray of fiery embers from his second dagger, and forced the horses into a mad panic. The Insidians lost their control, and fumbled desperately to stay balanced and keep the beasts from throwing them off. Poem slipped through them, his sights on the Precept Cardinal, and readied both his blades to strike him.

Terrified, Abaster accidentally fell off the saddle and hit the ground with a clatter of his cuirass. He expected his head to be lopped off at any moment, but was astonished to see Poem frozen in his tracks. He dropped his blades and raised his arms in surrender, and Abaster was flabbergasted.

The Iron Sabres surrounded them all at spear-point, the bulk of their attention mostly on Poem.

Abaster recognized the leader of the renowned corps by the black chevron on his white half-cloak. "Commander Falchier, bless the Saints you arrived here in time."

Falchier eyed Poem as he approached, then turned to the Cardinal as he got back to his feet. His voice, though masked by his helm, was deep and cold. "We were dispatched by Lord Mellka."

"Good, then he'll be pleased to receive this boon," Abaster said, glaring at Poem.

Falchier's hard gaze never left the Cardinal as he towered over the man. "By the highest orders, you are under arrest for negligence of your duties."

"W-What?"

Falchier swiftly removed his sabre and pointed its sharp tip half an inch from Abaster's jowl. "Resist, and be struck down."

None of the Insidians, nor the Cardinal's personal guards reacted out of hand. Though they were shocked, the papal edict and the might of the Iron Sabres were clear and above question. To Poem, it was a turn of events that he feared in silence.

A journey deeper into the darkness.

VI. Cold Flame

VI. Cold Flame

With the *Journey's Prodigy* safely nestled at Coastal Sky's port, Seidon and Tenshi traveled down the familiar road to the heart of the town's marketplace. Not much had changed: the waters were still clear blue like the morning sky, and the mountain peaks peered from the ghostly haze far in the distance. Merchants sold their wares and services as they've done for generations on end, and although it wasn't as grand or diverse as the bazaar in the Empyrean City, the market was more airy and much safer.

Seidon took two ripe peaches from a local fruit stand, paid the grocer his due, and handed one to Tenshi. The first bite was sweet and refreshing, and Seidon felt a sense of deja vu.

"I wonder what Poem's up to..." he said, partly to himself, as he took another bite. "If he ever got around to finishing that cabin."

"I miss him too," Tenshi comforted, hooking her slender arm around his. "We should ask him to travel with us."

Seidon nodded soberly, the memory of his first encounter with Poem replaced by the more recent encounter with the *Highborn*. The man who commandeered the vessel had looked at him straight in the eye as if an unforeseen destiny was abound, and Seidon was indirectly involved.

"After our visit to the smithy, we should stop by the local embassy. I'm sure Ingren's people should know who that man from the Highborn was."

They walked across the street to the blacksmith's forge; the familiar shop sign hanging over the doorway swayed quietly with the breeze wafting from the sea. Inside, it was quiet and cool, unlike the time Seidon first walked in the shop. The furnace was cold and spent, and the tools hung on the wall unemployed for a period of days, if not weeks or months. The place was practically cleaned out of its wares; the racks of weapons and armours were nearly empty, and the shields that once hung on the ceilings and walls were also gone. A single suit of armour remained in a dark corner by the window, slouched as if dejected, and surrounded by wheels from motorized carriages and heavy industrial machinery that sorely needed maintenance.

Most notably of all, the antique flare musket that was supposed to be displayed near the few spears that remained, was gone. Seidon's suspicions tingled with discomfort, as he feared where the answers led.

Tenshi stood by the suit of armour, saddened by the void of life inside the shop. "Something's terribly wrong... the warmth of a blacksmith's fire reflects his heart."

"And it's cold here," Seidon added quietly, and looked past the counter to the far end of the shop where another door led to the smithy's residence. He approached the door, glancing at the lonely anvil by the furnace, and was about to knock when Tenshi abruptly stopped him.

"It's the same mark we saw at the bazaar, in the antique shop," Tenshi said with warning, her eyes on a plaque fastened to the mantle over the furnace.

It was the black emblem of the Squires of Debonair.

Seidon tightened his jaw, but said nothing. He grasped Tenshi's hand, wanting her support, and mentally preparing himself for the worst, he knocked on the door. After what seemed a long pause, Teeven's wife, Nema, opened the door.

Seidon had no trouble recognizing the kind and humble woman, her face and body still rounded with long hardship.

"Good day, Madam, I was wondering if your husband Teeven's here?"

Nema's lips grew a smile as memory finally served her. "Mister Harbrid, so good to see you again." She glanced at Tenshi. "I see you finally found what you sought those many years back."

Seidon was amazed at her sharp insight. "This is Tenshi."

"A pleasure," Nema said courteously, and stepped aside. "Please come in."

The place was small, but cozy. Nema led them straight to the table where Seidon and Poem once shared breakfast with Teeven, but the once-vibrant blacksmith was not seated there. He laid in a hammock at one end of the room, far from the windows or the fireplace, brooding with a bottle of hard liquor.

"Teeven, you have guests." When her husband grunted with disinterest, Nema's earlier delight faded. "Please forgive him. Business has been slow, and our days have been harder for it. Would you like some tea?"

"Yes, thank you," Tenshi said kindly, glancing at Seidon. "I'll help you."

Reneging her spirit, Nema gladly accepted Tenshi's offer and they moved away to prepare the stove. Seidon approached Teeven, who had yet to notice the arrival of his guests. He held a half-empty bottle of local rum at his belly, while his other hand scratched mindlessly at his scraggly beard. He seemed to stare blankly at the ceiling, deep in thought, or lost in the past.

"What's a sailor to do to get some weapons cleaned up around here?"

Teeven blinked back to reality, and he craned his head slightly to Seidon; his brow furrowed to a frown as he tried to set his eyes to focus. A smile slowly crept to his lips, the warmth of his heart returning and still burning brightly. "Well I'll be damned... Seidon Harbrid." He stood up from the hammock with a bit of drunken struggle, but his glee kept him steady. "It's 'bout time you showed up, my dear lad!" He glanced past him to Tenshi. "Caught yourself a beautiful one, no doubt!"

He embraced Seidon like a bear, and although unexpected, Seidon was glad to renew the man's gusto.

"It's been too long, and I'm sorry for that," Seidon said. "I still owe you so much for your help."

"Rubbish," Teeven dismissed as he sat back down. "You owed me nothin'."

Seidon removed the wooden tube that hung at his belt near his carbine, and popped open its cap. The old map slipped out, and he handed the frail parchment to Teeven. "I couldn't forgive myself for losing the guide you lent me, and I hope this original will make up for it."

Teeven gingerly unrolled the map, and his eyes glazed with warm tears bereft of a man who honed his life to the harshness of fire and steel. "You're a noble man... I wish everyone would look to you as an example. You leave no debt unpaid... unlike me." He placed the map away, and his hand once again grasped the neck of the rum bottle. "I bet you were expecting me to be hammerin' away at the anvil."

Seidon grabbed a stool from nearby and sat down. "There's always a demand for the blacksmith's skills, now that it's not just boats and horses that carry people around. I find it hard to believe you're in drought of work."

"Nay, for a time it was good, but it was all supply and demand," Teeven said, his eyes drawn to the floor. "The one year I had hoped to be spared from the taxes, they were collected far too soon. One sorrow was impounded upon another, and I was unable to keep up. I lost all my contracts to smithies outside of town, and little choice I had left after that."

"You sold your shop, didn't you?" Seidon said seriously, "To the Squires of Debonair."

Teeven looked up, a hardened edge in his eyes. "Those bastards extorted me like rabid hounds on a bone. Not long after the war was over did they buy off the mayor's office, then started feeding off the town's indebted folk... I should have seen it, but it was said and done before I realized it."

"Was it the Marquis that orchestrated this?"

Teeven nodded, his anger lodged in his throat, and tried washing it down with a sip from the bottle. "You sound like you know 'im."

"I ran into the Squires when I visited Empyrean City," Seidon admitted, not wanting to reveal his familial relations. "I found your flare musket in an antique shop owned by a man named Priamos. I saw the same emblem of the Squires in his store as the one that now hangs over your furnace."

"At least the ol' man takes good care of his sundries," Teeven said half-heartedly. "But it's best if you avoid 'em altogether. Without the corporate powers to feed the fuels of commerce, the underworld grows ever stronger in its influence. When thieves are given the power of life and death, then you know the world no longer caters to civility."

"Something else's going on," Seidon said with certainty. "This black market extends deeper than it ever has before."

"Far deeper than you expect, Seidon," Teeven replied darkly. "From Gabrialtar you can retrace the steps all the way to Tinkertown, and back around to every theater of the last war." He hesitated a moment. "There's a lot of cargo being moved through here, although I don't know what's in 'em. I know this because they use my smithy as a waypoint to fool the custom officials at the docks. They have several ships berthed there now, moving things to and fro." He smiled with a sense of personal justification at revealing the secrets to Seidon. "If you haven't lost any of your adventurous cunning, you'd know best where danger lies."

In the vast papal office, Mellka quietly studied the sacred text written in the Vade Mecum. He stood with his back to the doors, a hand calmly placed at the small of his back while the other flipped the page of the book lying on his ornate desk. The grand master's throne was across him, a crossbow on its seat, and two handpicked elitists from the Iron Sabre legions standing on guard at either side of it, but he preferred to be on his feet. It kept him from being lax in his duties, and ready for anything. His example inspired the Iron Sabres greatly, enough that they all vowed allegiance to him over any other in the Church.

He smiled tightly at the thought, but killed it quickly as the thick, gilded doors swung open.

Escorted by his own Knights, their red-stripes significant of their association, Abaster stormed in, undoubtedly infuriated by what recently transpired.

"How dare you order the Iron Sabres after me like I'm some criminal awaiting the court," Abaster declared angrily, but kept his tone steady. "You are a grand master by the blessing of the Precept Cardinals, and it does not require wisdom to relinquish some degree of respect to those that made you."

"I'm a mirror to you, Cardinal. What respect have you shown that I should take notice?" Mellka turned around to face Abaster, immediately forcing the Cardinal's Knights to bow in proper manner, but Abaster remained proud. "I vowed a return to Purity, and offered you a chance to redeem yourself by pitting you against a vociferous adversary. You failed."

"The Insidians were not up to the task," Abaster replied with frustration. "If you hadn't restricted the number of troops under my command, this debacle would've ended with the General's head impaled on the highest steeple in Templari."

"Then you rely on numbers and brute strength to bolster your campaigns," Mellka said. "I was wrong to assume you'd have the fortitude to deal with Rell Vant yourself, but instead of dirtying your hands, you leech on the honour and self-sacrifice of those who actually do the fighting." He glanced at the two Knights. "Does this man deserve your loyalty, my brothers? What has he done for you that demands your continuing servitude?"

Abaster blandly replied for them. "These men have an oath to the Church. It's in their mandate to protect me."

"They're not without souls and thoughts of their own," Mellka countered coolly, and gave a simple nod to the Knights, whom in turn unsheathed their swords and pointed them at the Cardinal.

Abaster was taken aback. "How dare you point those weapons at me?! You've sworn an oath!"

"They've realized, just as I have, how incompetent you are. True loyalty can't be bought or bargained with." Mellka seemed to enjoy Abaster's fall from grace. "Fealty will always be rewarded, and to be fair to a man of your stature, I can be merciful."

On the verge of his doom, Abaster abandoned his pride and begged for his life. "G–Grand Master, please forgive my transgression. Give me another chance to prove my worth; although my task's unfinished, I delivered to you another aggressor of the Order – the malcontent who interfered in the heretic Harbrid's execution. I–"

"He will be dealt with shortly, once Commander Falchier breaks him," Mellka said. "The matter of this hour, is what will become of you." He walked around the papal desk, closing the Vade Mecum in mid-stride, and sat on the throne. "When I served as an acolyte in the Sacred Vaults many years ago, I spent every spare hour exploring the old foundations. I've discovered many things left forgotten, both wonders and trepidations that have laid here before the time of our Church." He let the words sink into Abaster's mind. "In the very bowels of the Cathedral there's a single chamber that once served as a means of isolation for the sinners of the Order. Rumours abound of ghosts and madness within those walls, but also enlightenment. My guards will escort you there."

The two Iron Sabres behind the papal throne moved toward the Cardinal, while the Knights kept their swords steady.

Abaster backed away from them, pointing an accusing finger at Mellka. "You can't do this, I'm a servant of the Faithful!"

"There will be no trial or deliberation for the self-righteous," Mellka said with slight venom in his voice.

The two Iron Sabres hooked Abaster's arms and dragged him toward the doors, but he remained defiant. In a surge of guile, he broke free of the guards' grip, and took hold of a dagger hidden beneath his crimson robes. He sprinted madly toward Mellka, ignoring the Iron Sabres and the two Knights that betrayed him.

His rebellion ended with a bolt from the Grand Master's crossbow, and Abaster's murderous momentum immediately slackened, carrying his lifeless body to the floor. The Cardinal fell hard due to the weight of his cuirass, and the dagger tumbled uselessly away.

Mellka, who stood by the throne, lowered his crossbow. He held no remorse as he calmly sat back down. "A fitting end."

In the twilight after the sun had set, Seidon snuck between the narrow space offered by the large stack of cargo containers prepped on the loading dock. The pier workers continued to transfer the heavy boxes with a vast system of pulleys and raw manpower, while the ships, mostly retrofitted barges, were manned and set to depart at a moment's notice. With the arrival of night, the dock was lit with scattered torches and oil lamps, and gave the place an eerie play of soft light and heavy shadow.

Seidon scurried quietly from one umbra to the next, hoping to get close enough to the ships to determine the content of the cargo. On nearly all the containers so far, the fire-branded mark of the Squires was more than visible, and although this wasn't the hub of the black market, he knew it was definitely the spool.

He pressed his back against one of the stacks closest to the main loading activity, and carefully peeked around the corner. Amidst the myriad of workers struggling to lift a container nearly seven feet wide and twice in length from the pier onto the waiting barge, a hooded man conducted business affairs with a Tinkertown official, evident of his affiliation by the high-cut leather coat with floral designs in copper leaf, and customary spiky hairstyle.

"The sanctions must be lifted," the official stressed, "or the Guild will suffer a complete economic collapse, and my people will fall in ruin. The conditions of the Armistice were unacceptable."

"You were in collusion with the corporations," the hooded man countered. "Tinkertown was the main supplier for weapons and vehicles used in the war. The trade sanctions and limits on your research projects were put there by the victors for safe measure."

"Our society is based on science and engineering, not war. We innovate by necessity as well as experimentation. We can't be held eternally responsible for how our clients choose to utilize our inventions."

"Yes, I've heard your case to King Ingren, but your ideology hasn't convinced him or any other victimized faction to relent the sanctions. Besides, the conditions will last another half-decade, and with the Squires providing a safe shipping route, your precious town can thrive as it always has."

"Don't mock me," the official warned. "Helmer Galvano had asked you to support our claim in good faith, and we only hope you can at least demonstrate that you're indeed a man of action."

"Believe me, Mister Nuria, I don't intend on letting our dear King or his peasant Queen from forgetting whom truly runs his court."

With several shouts of warning, the deck crew scattered in fear as the immense weight of the container forced the pulleys to snap. The box crashed down onto the pier, and splintered open as it smashed several planks.

Seidon felt the aftershock of the collision, and from the billowing dust and startled disarray of the workers, he caught a glimpse of what was inside. It was a large metallic engine cowling covered with intricate designs and burnt copper plates, yet it showed signs of heavy use and weathering.

He paused in disbelief as he realized that it was a piece of the Sorcerer Cannon, apparently dismantled and now under the possession of the Squires. One piece of thousands, enough to re-assemble the cursed machine anywhere in the world.

He watched as the hooded man yelled furiously at the workers, then pulled back his cowl in exasperation. It was Daedlus, nobleman and official ambassador of Magna Carta, a man he'd seen in Ingren's company from time to time.

Seidon had no time to sort his thoughts, as he needed to act fast while the dock reeled in consternation. He slipped out from the shadows and grabbed hold of a torch, then tossed the flaming embers onto whatever he could set ablaze.

Just as he begun to garner unwanted attention, he tossed the torch into the loading bay of the nearest barge and ran.

Chaos ensued as the flames quickly spread, but Seidon was spotted fleeing from the scene by a squad of Squires just arriving to the pier.

Leading the group was Liberthier Regento.

By the time Seidon returned to the smithy, the entire town was astir with commotion. Tenshi and Teeven were already there, watching the flames engulf the distant wharves where the barges were berthed.

Teeven smirked. "You live up to your father's legacy of stirring trouble."

"He had good reasons, and so did I." Seidon said. "The Squires are smuggling pieces of the Sorcerer Cannon from Tinkertown."

Tenshi was startled. "The Cannon? But it was destroyed, wasn't it?"

"I thought it was," Seidon said with dark thoughts. "But like all machines, it could be repaired. With a weapon that powerful, few could resist the temptation. Even Magna Carta's prone to corruption."

"Then it's best you unravel this quickly," Teeven said. "Head for Tinkertown. I'll deal with the Magna Carta embassy, and let 'em know what's going on."

"No, you can't. This black market has spread everywhere, and I'm afraid the embassy has been compromised. This needs to be taken directly to Ingren."

Teeven agreed. "Then you two best be off before unfriendly eyes turn."

Seidon shook Teeven's hand firmly. "Thank you for everything."

"Nothing owed," he said in return, accepting a hug from Tenshi before he watched them leave. "...Be safe."

A blood-stained gauntlet struck Poem in the face, and snapped his head back. He was bruised and bleeding, restrained to the cold stone-laden wall by shackles and unable to defend himself. He kept his gaze on the ecclesiastic warden who dished out his torture, and to Commander Falchier. The Iron Sabre stood across the small dungeon with two of his brethren, arms crossed, and his expressionless mask unwavering.

He waited for Poem to break, to scream out mercy, but he wasn't satisfied.

"You must understand, this Church nor I hold any ire toward you," Falchier said with his deep voice. "Every man has a threshold..." He gave a curt nod to the warden, and the heavy gauntlet struck again. "Lessons in humility are swallowed with bitter wine."

"I believe he's humble enough, Commander," Mellka said as he entered the dungeon unescorted.

Falchier, in tandem with the warden, bowed formally. Poem, too tired to move his aching muscles, glared at the Grand Master through the sweat-covered strands of his hair.

Mellka met his stare as he approached him with a deceptively conceited gait. "What are the charges?"

Falchier straightened his back at full attention. "Aiding and abetting a convicted heretic; wounding and killing several Knights of the Order while escaping arrest; blatant obstruction of justice–"

Poem grimaced. "Those charges have no merit."

"Protected by the kingdom of Magna Carta and its allies..." Mellka said. "In the past, this Church and *its* allies declared war on any State who harboured terrorists. The Holy Law is above all other law, and no king nor general will ever interfere."

"Is this the same excuse you used for that botched expedition to dispatch Vant?"

"Poema Della'Cor," Mellka ignored Poem's riposte, and offered a smile. "Your name has a long history, in fact, you may be a descendant of one of the Saint Knights. Which is intriguing, since you possess unnatural abilities that you obtained from exposure to retro-reef – the fabled Sentinels' blood that I surmise the Sorcerer Siblings experimented with during their blasphemous reign," he said. "Upon reading the Vade Mecum, broadened by many historians and artisans after our First Lord had written it, and long since it vanished from our archives, certain truths have surfaced surrounding the myths of both the Sentinels and the Sorcerers. What we once constituted as wretched and offensive, it now seems widely misunderstood."

"That book doesn't belong to you," Poem said acidly.

"It belongs in the Library's keeping, for all Terra Mia to study... I agree. Unlike others you've had the misfortune of coming across, I do understand the need to spread knowledge where ignorance thirsts. Many would appreciate its beauty and its arcanum, but what few could truly understand the essence of the Vade Mecum? From those few, how many can make a difference?"

"It only takes a few to start a revolution."

Mellka nodded, quietly enjoying this debate. "Don't be so quick in wanting to overthrow this Church if you still don't understand how much of the world leans on it for support. Our ideals have shaped civilization, like the earth guides a river. All else that embroils in war only stir ripples in the water and nothing else."

Poem spat excess blood from his mouth. "I'm not going to deliberate the fine points of moral politics with you, so save your breath on trying to convert me."

"I'm not trying to convert you," Mellka said. "You are fiercely loyal to your principles, and I respect that. You're perhaps ten years younger than I, yet you've endured so much – *that* I can see in your eyes."

"I... I'm tired... of fighting and running..." Poem looked away. "What do you want from me?"

"The same that you want for yourself: restitution." Mellka turned to the warden. "Remove his chains."

Poem was as surprised as the warden, but the latter didn't question the order. Rather unceremoniously, the warden unscrewed the shackles from Poem's wrists and ankles, and too tired and beaten to stand on his own, Poem dropped instantly to his knees.

"All your transgressions against the Church have been pardoned," Mellka declared. "All matters that are left, are between you and Gloriam."

Poem shook his head, and glanced up at Mellka. "Do you expect me to be grateful?"

"Whatever your conscience demands, Della'Cor." With a gesture, Mellka signaled the warden to leave. "You are a hero of the last war, yet heroes only shine on the surface. Beneath the bravery, you wanted to satisfy your demons by sending Rell Vant to the grave with your bare hands."

"I'm not the only one."

"No, but to you alone this means more than personal honour or friendship. It's above vengeance, isn't it? Your hatred extends deeper than any living man here could ever transpire. You know it's wrong, but you persist."

Poem grimaced, part of his frustration directed at Mellka for instigating his emotions. "He ripped apart my family... parts of my soul... and I want them back."

"Acceptance is what you lack," Mellka said. "The part of your soul that you're missing, is faith; the belief in something greater than oneself to dispel all the insecurities of the world."

Poem's unexpected tears washed the dirt and blood from his cheeks, bridled with anger. "*I want him dead...*"

Mellka felt the heat of Poem's fury, yet he bent down beside him and looked him in the eye. "Then I will give you what you want."

Teeven hammered hot steel against the anvil, inciting sparks with each stroke. With the eye of an artist, he forced the malleable metal to the shape of what will become a great sword, then thrust it back into the blazing forge. Over the cacophony of his tools and the cackling flames, he was startled as the door to his blacksmith's shop was kicked open, unsettling the dust, and stirring fell deeds.

He reflexively wielded his hammer as he would an axe, but paused as he recognized the intruders. "Back again, Marquis? There's nothing left to take except for the coal in the furnace."

Regento strode in alongside four Squires, including the temperamental Skein and the crossbow woman, Ophelia. He glanced around the shop briefly as he approached Teeven, undaunted by the blazing heat or the blacksmith's belligerence.

"Rekindled the fires have you?"

"I got work to do," Teeven spat. "Get on with it or get out."

"I'll keep it brief then," Regento said callously. "I know you've played host to someone we both know. I know you let out some secrets, lamented on your misery, and now you've caused us some grief. If you think that your forced service to the Squires have been strenuous, you have no idea of the torment you're about to receive in payment for your lack of... discretion."

One of the Squires attempted to seize Teeven by his muscular shoulder, but the blacksmith tossed him away like a rag doll. His defiance was met by a swift blow across the jaw from Ophelia's giant crossbow, followed by an inconsiderate kick to the solar plexus from Skein.

Regento was remorseless. "Even Priamos knew better than to desist, although his son wasn't so wise." He delayed a moment as the fourth Squire dragged Nema into the shop. "A tragic story really, but with what's at stake here..." He glanced at Teeven's wife. "...some lessons must be taught again."

Although restrained by three Squires, Teeven was enraged like a bull. "Don't you dare touch my wife!"

"Then tell me where Seidon has run off to!" Regento snapped back.

Teeven was trapped in a dilemma. He glanced at his terrified wife, and his heart gripped at his decision. "Heavens above, forgive me... I told 'im there be a haunting in the Old Ruins, and I lent an old map for his treasure huntin'."

Regento offered Teeven a half-grin. "You lie."

On cue, Ophelia re-aimed her crossbow from Teeven to Nema and shot a bolt through the woman's leg. Nema dropped to the floor screaming in pain, and Teeven felt it with every grain of his being. He cursed madly and nearly broke free from the grips of his captors until Skein pounded him on the back of the ear.

Ophelia armed her menacing crossbow once more, and waited on Regento's order.

"This is business," Regento said, slightly annoyed at Nema's wounded sobbing. "In this realm a man will wage war because he's afraid of dying broke. Throw honour out to sea, and do what a good husband must do to keep his wife from further harm."

Teeven felt feverish with frenzy, yet he trembled at the sight of Nema's anguish. He forced his next words like bile through clenched teeth. "Tinkertown... bastards."

Regento nodded quietly in grim satisfaction, and walked away.

With no one to hold back his reins, Skein, appearing devilish from the glow of the forge, struck Teeven repeatedly. His fellow Squires joined him, and as big as the blacksmith was, his body was no match for the unrestrained ferocity of the ruffians.

Nema, with a surge of valor, struggled on her wounded leg to scatter them away from her husband. In the scuffle that ensued, Ophelia's crossbow misfired, and the bolt delivered a killing blow through Nema's chest. She fell heavily on the anvil and scattered the tools, then remained still on the ground, blood pouring from her wounds.

With a hair-raising scream, Teeven cursed and thrashed in blind rage. He felt nothing as he seared his hand reaching for molten-hot sword basking in the forge, and impaled the steaming blade through the gut of the nearest Squire. He directed his tantrum to Ophelia, but never met his mark as Skein delivered his sword across the blacksmith's back.

He landed near Nema, his flaming sword clattering near a pile of oily rags. It wasn't long before the fire spread, and the surviving Squires took their leave of the doomed shop.

VII. Castles of Sand

VII: Castles of Sand

After the debacle at Our Lady of Hours, Vant was confined to his moderate living quarters under temporary house arrest, unallowed prolonged contact with either his men or the local populace. Despite his narrow escape from the clutches of the Insidians, with many of the perpetrators and his brethren wounded or dead, the Magna Cartan magistrate decided best to limit his public visibility. Sucre was given temporary charge of the Restoration League, and was also the only Strafer allowed to visit him without restraint.

The only defenses Vant had should the Order of the Faithful mount another ambush, were a rotating shift of four heavily armed royal infantrymen loaned from the garrison ship anchored off the rocky coast of Templari. Although better equipped than the regular peacekeepers, he doubted their efficiency against determined assassins, or a mob of Templari citizens who sympathized with the Church's bold ideology.

In the modest suite he was imprisoned in, he had no other weapon except his books. Bored, he spent his time studying military history by the fireplace, and relived famous battles of the past described by both the victorious and the defeated. Given this leisure, he was almost grateful that the magistrate didn't lock him up in a damp, rat-infested cellar.

The two royal soldiers stationed at the entrance opened the door, and Vant glanced at his pocket-watch, finding it too early for the changing of the guard. His senses taut, he kept his calm as several imposing Magna Cartan Elites strolled in and stood in formation along all four walls of the suite. In their wake, a squad of ever-impressive Throne Guards formed a narrower circle, acting like a second group of shields for King Ingren and Queen Dalena.

"My first guests of the day." Vant set his book down and stood up accordingly. He made certain to show he wasn't intimidated, nor was he a threat. He lowered his chin slightly in respect. "It's an honour to be visited by royalty."

"Everybody wants you dead, Mister Vant," Ingren said. "And if the Church won't adhere to the treaty and fair treatment of war criminals, then who's to stop anyone else from trying to put an end to your legend?"

"You have few alternatives, Your Majesty," Vant replied. "Lock me up in the deepest dungeon far from civilization, or in the highest tower of your kingdom; or commit me to the guillotine and be done with it."

"Your death won't assure peace," Dalena said. "It would only satisfy the depraved, and undermine the basic tenets that keep us from tearing each other apart."

"Then you're more attuned to the affairs of humankind than I gave you credit for." Vant gestured to the windows. "From here, you can hear the citizens taking to the streets in their support of the Church, and they will just as soon question whether Magna Carta is here as keepers of peace or as occupiers. This is *exactly* what the new Grand Master hoped for."

Ingren finally saw part of the truth unravel. "You're simply a catalyst to garner followers."

"Enough to challenge the throne of the world," Vant concluded. "No great army marching across the fields; he will conquer the people with religion. This you're already aware of, a subject all kings are taught. You're here for something else."

"You're very perceptive," Dalena commented sourly.

"The sword and shield are my brethren, and you've taken them from me," Vant countered. "I depend now on my instincts and intellect alone." He gestured to the seats, "If you may permit...?"

Ingren nodded his consent, and Vant sat down. He rested his elbows on the armrests, laced his fingers together, and waited patiently for the royal pair to pose their questions. Neither one cared for his display of arrogance.

"What do you know of Titus?" Ingren demanded.

There was a brief inculpative silence before Vant finally answered. "He's a former regular born and raised in the City of Guard. He achieved the rank of Major through hardship and dedication, and was one of several Strafer officers under my direct tutelage in the art of tactics and military disciplines."

"He was your protégé," Dalena summarized, glancing at Ingren with admonition.

Vant continued, "He specialized quite proficiently in artillery and amphibious assault, often rotating between ground operations and the Navy. He fought at Tenaya during the opening battles with the Chimaera Vanguard, and he fought at Lorica and the Midwestern provinces during Scarecrow's Border Expansion. He was present on the assault on this city, and fought for the defense of Guard until the end of hostilities. He refused to join the Restoration League and opted for a return to civilian life, at which point he disappeared from public view."

Ingren was disturbed by the man's link to Vant, but it was too early to judge. "Why do you think he joined Gabrialtar?"

"Gabrialtar was the land of his forebears, and it was the first annexed region to break away from the corporate yoke and reclaim its independence. It was a newborn nation in flux, and lucrative opportunities were abound."

"From what I've heard, he established an extensive campaign of governmental and economic reform, and its success granted him access to political elections," Ingren said.

"You don't expect soldiers to adjust so easily in peacetime, no matter how much they long for it." Vant glanced at Dalena. "You understand this most, my Queen. A soldier fights for peace, but once he has it, he doesn't know what to do with it."

Ingren was starting to piece together the puzzle that was the Captain-General of Gabrialtar, but the man's bizarre compulsion was still an enigma. "Was he always this ambitious?"

"Titus was an efficient Strafer, but his cunning had limits." Vant paused, as he too seemed perplexed. "This grandiose display of imagination was very unlike the man I knew to be quite timid. He was the only Strafer who kept silent while all others advocated for me during the trials, and earned the choler of Sucre and my men when he left."

"Defeat must have been quite bitter on his heart," Ingren guessed.

Dalena knew what great violence can do to a soldier once it seeped past the uniform and into the skin. "Bitterness is a state of the mind."

"Never lower your guard," Vant warned, his tone deadly serious. "These are dangerous times when you hope to build great castles out of sand."

Ingren heeded to the warning, which was a surprising gesture for Dalena.

"Don't you want another war?" Dalena accused. "To find an excuse to rally your loyalists and take advantage of the confusion? By now you must've gotten wind of the instability in this city that are wrongly denouncing Governor Traiza's competency, but you're waiting for the right moment to capitalize."

"Only with meaning, do I prefer war," Vant cut back. "You mistake me for a butcher who keeps his knife sharp only to hack and slash."

"Seidon saw some small measure of hope for you," Dalena retorted. "I didn't then, and I don't now."

Vant, with all his boasting to satisfy his amour-propre, said nothing in return. Ingren and Dalena were about to turn and leave, when Vant stood up.

"I have a request, Your Majesty," he said. "I wish to be present at the summit. I can offer you a better perspective on your situation."

"I'm afraid your name alone will provoke the delegates," Ingren replied. "And there's still a matter of trust."

Vant grimaced. "Then at least allow me the freedom to walk the streets. I will take the proper precautions of course."

"You're a target of opportunity without these walls," Dalena said. "What do you hope to accomplish except to instigate a riot?"

"It's a simple request," Vant said coolly. "You and I know that no thickness of stone nor amount of guards will stop my fate."

Ingren took a moment to consider it, and with a reluctant sigh, he nodded.

Onboard the *Highborn*'s luxurious office-quarters, with the clouds whizzing past the viewports, Titus conferred with the Presidency over the shortwave receiver. More advanced than any equipment before it, the shortwave transmission was displayed in saturated colours on a plain white curtain. Projected on the canvas was the talking head of President Gehenna, a stately woman in her late forties wearing a high-collared suit that defined both her feminine curves and unflinching leadership.

"Gabrialtar once opposed the establishment of the corporations," Titus said, seated comfortably on his velvet-cushioned chair, "but the scaled resistance was repulsed, and its treasures annexed – all the island's military downsized to a mere defense regiment. Worst still, the entire incident was excluded from official history."

"You're concerned this 'incident' may happen again?"

"Madam President, you're a scholar by patrimony, you don't need my wisdom." Titus' seductions at her vanity worked like grease on gears. "We've rebuilt our country with bare hands, and we're once again independent. We've amassed a larger and stronger military than ever before, and we have the technology to put our dreams forward."

President Gehenna still had her concerns. "The opposition have reason to be alarmed, Captain-General. We are partly to blame for the worldwide collapse in retro-reef mining and renewal. Industries are shaken by this crisis."

"That's why King Ingren and his starving allies will demand the impossible from your government – from *our* people. Their positions are weakened, and by forcing us to submit to free trade, they will use our stilts for leverage."

"We should not appear inconsiderate or too ambiguous."

"Compassion is given to our neighbors where it may, but our independence is still in its infancy, and we will easily lose our foothold."

Gehenna could argue little to that point. "The Name's Reclaim is shaking with heated debate on our course in international affairs," she said. "Any forward action must be taken with considerable deliberation on the matter of our established relations."

"I don't intend to jeopardize our standing with other nations, Madam President, but neither will I allow us to be taken for granted."

"Your loyalty is noted, Captain-General. You know what's best for our people, act accordingly on our behalf."

"With pleasure," Titus said with a sadistic smile. "I believe the summit will be broadcast on the shortwave for public record; I hope you will closely monitor the progress."

Gehenna terminated her transmission, and Titus casually switched the receiver off. He mulled over a few amusing thoughts, then glanced at the lithe figure in the dark corner of the office.

"We will be arriving shortly," Titus said plainly. "You know your orders."

With an escort of two Marines, Messer strolled along Archway's Path's old harbour alongside Bale, who wore the dress uniform of a royal fleet yeoman. The paths bordering the myriads of military vessels and passenger ships were crowded, some heading for Templari and others shipping out overseas. Most of the vessels stationed here belonged to the former Chimaera – now dubbed the Provisional Naval Squadron due to the treaty – and to Magna Carta, but all the escort vessels for the delegates attending the summit were also moored here.

"I remember boarding the Awakening for the first time here," Bale reminisced, pointing to a part of the dockyard that was reserved for merchant ships. "I knew I was in for something great when we stormed out of here with fresh loot and three custom frigates hot on our arse."

Messer smirked. "Everything happened so fast, I still can't remember how we made it through in one piece."

"Almost one piece," Bale corrected, gesturing to the stump that remained of his left arm. "The frigates made a mess of both crew and ship. Guess it wasn't all bad, I had the biggest share of the loot thanks to the arm."

"You're a truer pirate than I," Messer admitted. He glanced at the tattoo on Bale's right forearm, something he noticed before but didn't question until now. "Since when did you join the Squires?"

Bale tightened his jaw, having hoped the subject would never come up. "I had nothing left after the Awakening sank... I made my contacts through the blacksmith at Coastal Sky, and carried on from there."

"The black market's nothing new," Messer said. "They feed on the desperate, always resorting to the extremes. I imagine your moral compass had been tested now and then."

"I have nor want any part of them," Bale said flatly.

Messer kept it at that, not wanting to press harder. Ahead of them, an officer from the *Second Awakening* came running with a sense of urgency.

He stopped, saluted while catching his breath, and reported. "Sir, you have a priority message waiting."

"The Cannon's being transported in pieces through Coastal Sky, and there's hard evidence it's coming from Tinkertown. I'm en route there right now, so this might be my last message before we pass under the Mountains," Seidon said through the small shortwave screen. "I thought the weapon was dismantled and sent to the smelters after the war."

In the *Second Awakening*'s communication room, Messer and his officers listened to Seidon as he transmitted a message on the shortwave receiver. Bale stood outside the entrance, his back to the wall, and his ears tuned in to the conversation.

"Apparently the task was muddled in the bureaucracy," Messer said sourly. "Do you have any idea where the shipments are heading?"

"No," Seidon said, static flickering through his image. "The Squires have chapters all over the world, and if they're not using it for themselves, then it's going to highest bidder. Everyone's a potential enemy."

"That's a long list," Messer said.

Bale felt tense, not only with the mention of the Squires' involvement, but the depth and extent of the corruption Seidon was unraveling. He shuffled closer to the shortwave receiving cables that ran along the top of the wall, and hesitated.

Seidon glanced away for a moment, then turned back. "Messer, you can't trust anyone. With Regento as the Marquis, he can reach out to the highest levels of government through bribe or extortion, and he has the means to enforce it."

"What are you saying? Who else is involved?"

"Nobody on the King's council can be trusted, Messer–"

"Seidon?"

The transmission was cut as Bale severed one of the cables with his knife, out of view of the startled officers inside the communication room. Cursing himself and filled with guilt, he slowly moved away, as the technicians scurried to reestablish the connection.

"Get him back, now!" Messer ordered.

"Sir, the King must be made aware of this," Captain Semmes urged.

"The summit's started by now," Messer said, as he conceived a plan of action. "He'll have his hands full."

"You don't actually believe the Royal Court's been corrupted? That's inconceivable."

"Is it?" Messer challenged, reprimanding the captain's naivety. "I've known Seidon since he was born, and he certainly wouldn't make any accusations without merit."

Behind the captain, Messer caught a glimpse of Bale's retreating form. He felt a quiver of dread somewhere on the back of his mind, but he didn't dwell on it. He turned back to Semmes. "I want you to go to Templari and inform the King directly. If you can't reach him, then inform Queen Dalena."

"Yes, sir."

The summit was held in the largest conference chamber of the newly constructed Administrate Parliament, reserved for the heads of civilian governance and Chimaera's provisional military office. It was floored with crimson tiles of intricate design, woven like a renowned tapestry, while the walls were adorned with the flags of every nation attending. Each ensign hung like a velvet curtain, one knot tied to the adjacent flag in symbolic unification. The ceiling curved into a geodesic dome with open windows to the sky that flooded the chamber with natural light.

Two long tables, fashioned from polished obsidian, were placed closely together at the center of the chamber to form a uniformly stretched figure-eight. The delegates were seated and in discussion, with the host nation acting as an intermediator at the head of the conference. One ceremonial guard from each nation stood along the walls of the chamber, and at least one assistant or interpreter for each seat.

Traiza sat at the head of the table, and he kept ominously quiet. Beside him was King Ingren, who understood his discomfort, as what they hoped to be a productive dialogue devolved to become a rally point for bickering, particularly for members of Templari's own political parties. More to his surprise and chagrin, two Precept Cardinals from Floria,

Achrone and Libra, were also present, but maintained a grave haughty air of superiority.

There was a single empty seat, reserved at the far opposite end of Traiza and Ingren, and it belonged to Gabrialtar. The absence of a major player had stalled the proceedings, and impatience crept in.

"Perhaps we should go on without Titus," Traiza suggested in a hushed tone. "Everyone's getting restless, and the tension's thicker than the fog after a heavy cannonade."

Ingren nodded, his expression serious. Captain Semmes had recently delivered the ill news, and the information was still hard to digest. He decided to retain what he knew from his few allies at the table, until he was certain of whom to trust.

Traiza prepared himself mentally, and stood up. "Ladies and gentlemen, thank you for your valued attendance, and in sharing the spirit of collaboration. There hasn't been a summit of this nature in at least a century, and like our forefathers many years before, we are brought together because our choices will decide the fates of our sons and grandsons."

Titus strode in, his footsteps echoing noisily, and the hem of his coat trailing in his wake. He waltzed in unescorted by any guard or assistant, and stole all the attention from Traiza. "Forgive me," he said courteously, "but the choices our forefathers made were done in ignorance. If you all studied your history, we suffered the oppression of the corporate era."

Mutters of mixed reactions filled the room, and Traiza glared at the newcomer with no appreciation. He ushered his greeting with restrained contempt. "Glad you could join us, Captain-General."

"It wouldn't make sense to leave an empty seat, would it?" Titus countered, pleasing no one but himself. He pulled his chair back far enough to cross his legs comfortably, and sat down doing so. He assertively propped one arm behind the back of the chair, and casually gestured Traiza to go on with his speech.

Traiza wasn't about to be goaded by his antics, and being a hardliner ex-admiral, he didn't hesitate to attack Titus' reputation. "You've been invited here on a serious matter that affects us all, and you can find no excuse for your tardiness?"

"I was actually touring your delightful city," Titus said calmly, "and it takes time to truly appreciate its beauty. If I had known this summit was about me, I would've come sooner."

This time, some of the delegates laughed, but the majority remained pedantic.

"Since you represent the island-state of Gabrialtar," Traiza said, "then the matter at hand does involve you."

"Ah, and you're referring to the global shortage of retro-reef?" Titus retorted. He looked to Cardinal Libra, who stared at him with displeasure, and winked at her. "Fascinating."

"This energy crisis is threatening to destabilize the fragile post-corporate regimes established after the war, which includes Gabrialtar." Traiza glanced to the others present, and hoped to keep Titus' idiosyncrasies from occupying the focus of the meeting. "Unless we invent a more efficient way to process retro-reef or discover a renewable resource in the next decade, all our progress – from the shortwave to the motorized carrier – will be scuttled."

"The impact on our society sounds much more severe than you let on, Governor," the Viceroy of Freya said.

"We've never faced anything like this before," Traiza replied. "The totality of war has given a taste, but I don't dare imagine the worst-case scenario."

"But we're not talking of an end of our peoples," Senator Reich of Guard, a known skeptic, disputed. "We are resolute, and we will weather such crisis with no loss of life."

"But we *are* talking of an end, in one form or another," Titus intruded. He glanced at the cardinals again. "Perhaps this was foretold by divinity; a ravenous punishment for our belligerence."

"Enough of this underhanded evasion of the point!" Traiza snapped, slamming his hands on the table.

"I don't consider raising these distinctions irrelevant, Governor," Titus said, pleased to have angered Traiza.

"Are you speaking on behalf of your Presidency, or not?"

Ingren placed a hand on Traiza's arm as a warning, and the ex-admiral grudgingly calmed down.

"...Honourable delegates, forgive my temperance." His eyes stared bolts at Titus. "I leave the floor open to discussion."

He sat down, almost gratefully, but no one hurried to state their opinion. For a moment, the proponents either kept quiet or muttered amongst themselves. Unity was fractured, and as fragile as glass.

Ingren stood up, and his presence was a beacon to keep harmony intact. "We have the ability to counter the effects of this crisis by forming an international alliance, and creating a mutual charter between all nations of good will." He gave the room time to assemble their thoughts. "This proposal will be arduous for our generation, but it will keep us from warring with each other over resources. We share what we have now, do away with petty squabbles, and let our brightest minds come together to find an alternative means to fuel our industries. This way we preserve our institutions without stalling progress."

There was a long pause as the delegates considered the proposal, until Cardinal Achrone spoke the lingering question common to most. "Who will regulate this motion?"

"A security council of member states, elected by the free people."

"And who will enforce these laws?" Reich followed up.

"Men and women of conscience," Ingren said simply, narrowly avoiding the political death trap he dangerously threaded upon.

"Nicely said," Titus commented with a grin. "Though, with the unspoken taboo on the minds of all present, I question your motives."

The conference stirred with anticipation, but Ingren was unmoved.

"Please, I'm not here to undermine your unity efforts," Titus defended. "Peace is an old dream, but it's delusive, impossible to attain."

"An ancestor of mine once wrote in her journals that, 'peace cannot be achieved simply, and whether or not we will ever reach there, it's the journey toward it where we take a breath of reprieve.'" Ingren was proud to have recited those words, as they once were said by Queen Ingrena. "As long as we willingly strive toward finding a commonplace, then we will succeed in our aims."

"And what *is* your aim, Your Majesty?" Titus wondered playfully. "To expand your kingdom? What's to keep you from placing sanctions on us, and taking our resources by force? After all, you're a king and you answer to none other."

"How dare you question his character," Traiza defended, "after what this man had done for us all."

"The outcomes of the Corporate War has given Magna Carta complete superiority over the oceans, and over the shape of politics in the old world. In fact, without the King's support, your leadership will falter." Titus held no constraint in his riposte. "Otherwise we'd be here mending the troubles of civil war, instead of steering the phantom reins of selfless collaboration."

Traiza was taken aback, as was the rest of the conference, but had no means to counter the bold accusation. The truth, sadly, wasn't far from realization.

Titus maintained his momentum. "Storied nations like Gabrialtar, Guard, and Templari began as monarchies, but the people cried for democracy – not to be ruled by the actions or inactions of a single man. King Ingren's so-called 'republic with a president for life' is a laughable façade to hide his insatiable ambition and birthright to be master of the world."

No one sitting at the table was able to hide their shock, yet Ingren's rebuke was equally startling.

"As a former Strafer under the tutelage of General Rell Vant, you would know something about pride and ambition."

Titus suddenly stood up. "I am Captain-General Titus of Gabrialtar, Aide-de-Camp to the Presidency, and sworn unto death to defend her realm. We welcome our neighbors like brothers, and we repay the wicked with swift vengeance. This proposal of yours will achieve nothing but to add further strain on developing nations, and on behalf of *my* people... I respectfully decline."

In a grand overture, Titus stormed out of the chamber, and not long after the shock receded he was followed by a few others, including the unimpressed cardinals and their entourage. Any hope Ingren had for an alliance collapsed before it was even born.

He sat back down, his shoulders heavy with burden. "All hopes end here."

In the stately quarters of the regional consulate not far from the Administrate Parliament, Dalena paced anxiously as she spoke to Messer over the shortwave receiver. She dismissed all her handmaidens and was alone in the room, and she preferred it at that despite the rules of entourage that accompanied women of royalty.

"I apologize for the delay in communications," Messer said. "Although my technicians believe it to be a common malfunction, I have reason to be open minded."

"A saboteur?"

"I rather not say at this time, Your Highness." Messer grimaced at his own thoughts, then recollected his bearings. "I haven't been able to reach the Journey's Prodigy. With Tinkertown located deep in the Mountains, the signal loses integrity or gets jammed."

Dalena felt his deep concern, and shared it. "You think they're in danger, Admiral?"

"I don't know. The Squires of Debonair are willing slaves of avarice; they're vindictive, and they will do anything to protect their investments."

"You said the Marquis is related to Seidon," Dalena said. "If he's a man that can be reasoned with, he won't allow harm to come to his own kin."

Messer was doubtful and it showed. "He's a cousin by name, but no Harbrid blood runs through him. Only the most malevolent tyrants can wrench the helm of the black market, and Regento asserted himself quite efficiently."

"...Admiral, I was informed by Captain Semmes that the Sovereign and the Royal Castling have arrived at Archway's Path," Dalena stated. "Arrange for them to escort the King back to his home capital. I want you to take the Second Awakening and aid those who may need it."

Messer nodded. "On your orders, Your Highness. Thank you."

"With my blessings," Dalena said with heart.

With a company of Throne Guards and Chimaeran battlers, Ingren and Traiza strolled along the veranda that lined the exterior of the Parliament. They hovered four stories over the main streets where thousands of residents, activists, and loyalists brought their voice to the summit. They chanted protests against Traiza's governance, and shouted support of the Church's recent action on Vant. Some of the more vulgar voices demanded Vant's quick expulsion from the city or death. Whatever their lamentations, Magna Carta's peacekeepers and local enforcers kept the crowd under control.

Traiza, walking along the banister, peered over the crowd with resentment. "What a contradiction we are, to balance harmony with dissent. Titus shamelessly summarized all our doubts and fears, and the horizon never seemed so bleak." He looked over at Ingren, who had kept quiet since the dissolution of the summit. "I don't believe what he said about you, and I'm sure there are many others who still support our cause."

"The damage is done." Ingren turned to Traiza. "We may yet have a need to return to arms, Governor. I've been informed that remnants of the Sorcerer Cannon we purportedly destroyed at Guard are now being syphoned for profit in the black market."

Traiza stopped abruptly, stunned by news. "This can't be. Whatever survived of that infernal machine was dismantled under our supervision, and sent straight to the furnaces."

Ingren paused himself, and let out a sigh. "I don't understand it myself, but the report is valid."

"Could they have found a second Cannon, or engineered another?"

Ingren shook his head, having no answer. "Captain Harbrid has taken charge of tracking down both the source, and the destination of this weapon. We hope to hear from him soon."

"These are dire times indeed…" Traiza had his guesses, as did Ingren, and nodded sullenly in understanding. "Titus was right about one thing, my governance is weak. From the day I arrived here, I've been at odds with the city councilors, and they'd do anything to expunge me. Without your support, this city will tear itself apart."

"It's your leadership that keeps us in one piece," Ingren said assuredly. "I never doubted your competence, nor ever our friendship."

A split-second glint reflected on the window behind Ingren, and distracted Traiza's attention. He glanced across the street and skyward instinctively. He saw nothing at first, but his sharp eyes narrowed at a slim silhouette on the rooftop of the adjacent edifice, and he had only a heartbeat to react.

He launched himself before Ingren just as a long-barreled rifle shot rang out. The bullet struck the governor through the base of his skull, killing him instantly. His limp body stumbled against Ingren, who caught him as he fell with blood spattered on their uniforms. Like startled hornets, the Throne Guards immediately encircled Ingren with their armoured bodies, while the Chimaeras drew their rifles and searched the surroundings for the attacker.

Hysteria set in and the crowd scattered in panic, but no further attack came. Ingren was on his knees, Traiza's bloody head on his shoulder, and he was speechless. Angry tears rolled down his cheeks, smearing the blood from his chin, and he tried to see past the tall guards for the assassin, but the rooftops were empty.

Hundreds fled in fear, misdirected, concerned only for their safety even as a few unfortunate souls were trampled in the stampede. They whizzed past Vant, who watched on the sidelines with a hood to keep his profile low. He remained still in the chaotic swarm, as he searched the building tops for the sniper. Sucre and several Strafers surrounded him, on edge and concerned for their leader's safety.

"General, it's best if we return to our billets."

Vant ignored Sucre's warning, and turned to face the buildings behind him. He immediately descried the cloaked sniper running across one of the rooftops, and swiftly gave chase – startling his retinue.

Sucre attempted to stop him, but Vant speedily disappeared into the crowd. "No, General...!"

Vant slipped through the flotsam and ruck that choked Templari's streets, and he moved fast, dodging obstacles with driven finesse. No one paid attention to who he was, even as his hood slipped onto his shoulders. To Sucre, his actions appeared reckless, but he knew exactly where he was heading.

The street narrowed and various alleys formed alongside the tightly knit buildings. He moved through one, barely wide enough that the brick-layered walls brushed against his shoulders. The far-stretching corridor eventually opened up, and he reached the bower just as the sniper leaped down from the rusty rungs on the side of the nearby building atop a small shed, then onto the ground.

The lithe figure froze immediately as Vant approached, the long-barreled rifle still slung over the shoulders, but made no move to reach it.

Vant kept his distance, and he showed no fear. "I've removed all your chains, except for one."

The sniper hesitated, then pulled back her cowl. It was Mikaila. "He asks about you from time to time."

Seeing her face after so many years, Vant was humbled. He stared at her fierce blue eyes, and smiled tightly. "...What's his name?"

"Marcus," Mikaila replied lovingly, a few strands of her golden hair slipping past her hood onto her slender neck.

Vant nodded, a slight warmth filling his heart, but he looked at her again with a serious mask. "You've just instigated a march to war. To whom lies your allegiance now?"

"You'll find out soon enough, if you haven't guessed already." Mikaila replaced her cowl, and was about to walk away when Vant grabbed her arm.

"Surrender my son before hostilities break out," Vant demanded. "I won't have you raise him on a battlefield."

Mikaila looked into his eyes, not having been this close to him in a long time. "He's been mine for six years, and I won't give him up."

"You *will*."

Mikaila let silence be her answer, and pulled away. She quickened her pace and vanished through one of the narrow alleys before Sucre and a few of the Strafers reached the bower. They found Vant alone, and ominously quiet.

"Take the General to a secure area," Sucre ordered, prepared to disregard his superior's countermand. "Make sure the others get back to the district before the city's locked down."

Vant said nothing and complied without objection. With his loyal men at his side, he retreated back to his temporary cage.

VIII. Cannon's Rebound

VIII. Cannon's Rebound

The fiery artificial lights of Tinkertown resonated throughout the great cavern like a fading sunrise. It gave an air of intrigue, and an adherence of caution that many secrets were buried beneath the Mountains. Strolling down the central path of the modish city, Seidon questioned whether these secrets needed to stay hidden, or brought to justice.

He walked alongside Tenshi, the ports not far behind them, and were headed for the main facilities where the bureaucrats were stationed. Tall lampposts lined the road, spilling soft orange light onto the surroundings. Most of the residences were built alongside the scores of entangled processing plants, laboratories, factories, refineries and whatever else that was carved and shaped from the cavern's dark inner walls. The air felt bleak, bled of life much like the gut of the Mountain where the city was constructed.

With a fascist ideal toward work ethics, very few of the tall and wiry Tinkerers roamed leisurely. Nearly the entire population were devoted to one trade or another, disciplined in the sciences, with very little given to the arts. What bit was given to self-expression showed only on the intricate leaf designs on their leather engineer's garments, otherwise they all resembled one another in stature and grooming style.

Like any city, despite the domination of the skilled worker castes, a certain measure of administrative structure was necessary. The port needed supervision, the streets needed law enforcers, and stately affairs needed politicians. A few of these Tinkerers were ahead of Seidon and Tenshi, their approach led by a tall man whose hair stood on end by a pair of black safety goggles.

He stopped before the visitors, while his two female Enforcers moved to the flanks, each placing a hand on their respective katanas slung at their waists. "Welcome to Tinkertown. I'm Galvano, Helmer of the Community." He glanced at Seidon, then to Tenshi, and casually stopped them from addressing their identities with a gesture of his hand. "Champions of Magna Carta are known to us. Please, what is your purpose here?"

"We're looking to trade," Tenshi replied in Seidon's place. "We might also be interested in exploring some of your archeological sites."

"I see," Galvano said with his sonorous voice. Being much taller than any present, he retained the appearance of superiority. "Tinkertown is open to trade and to all curious minds. Be aware that most of our coordinators prefer wholesale transactions, and very few deal directly with clients. As for exploring our vast facilities, I recommend a guide."

"Thank you, but we will be fine on our own." Seidon offered a slight bow to the Helmer, who accepted it glumly.

"Very well," Galvano said, turning to leave. "Should you require my services, you may reach me at my office."

"There's one other thing, Helmer," Seidon said. "I was wondering where I may find an official named Nuria. I wish to speak to him on a personal matter."

Galvano showed no reaction, but he raised an eyebrow in incredulity. "If I'm not mistaken, he's away on appointed business. You may contact him through his intermediaries."

"I will do that, thank you once again."

Giving no second thought, Galvano and his Enforcers strode away, as did Seidon and Tenshi. Once they were out of view of each other, Nuria, the same official who conducted affairs with Daedlus at Coastal Sky, moved away from the shadows beneath a nearby building and made his approach to the Helmer.

"It's him," Nuria warned.

Galvano heeded quietly, and gave a curt nod to the Enforcers at his side. They bowed in respect, turned on their heels, and followed the two unwanted guests.

In the Sacred Vault of the Cathedral of the Twelve, the forlorn vestiges of what the Church deemed reverent in the passing of days, were in the care of the Scholars of Cromlech. Relics, tomes, ancient devices, and the remains of the saints and lords rested here.

Walking between the sarcophagi of the Twelve Saint Knights, their human image cast in stone on the heavy lids, Mellka imagined he would one day be worthy of being put to rest beside these legends. Far beyond the achievements of all his predecessors, he was vain enough to order his tomb to be built bigger and more lavish than all else before him.

It was a grim fantasy, but it was his own.

The senior Scholar, accompanied by his apprentice, returned from the far reaches of the chamber carrying a blooming ceramic tray. On it was a small packet bound in extremely old leather.

"What have you found?" Mellka demanded.

The Scholar and the apprentice bowed formally, then the former took the small packet and gingerly unraveled it. "The last surviving vial of the Elixir, milord." He presented the fragile glass vial, its contents long emptied except for the tiniest drop. "It belonged to Our Lord Founder."

"I assumed the late Cardinal had pawned it all away years ago." Mellka held the vial between his thumb and forefinger, and studied it up close. "According to the rumours, this liquid was used to kill the Sorcerer Necrosis... I wonder what it would do to half-druids?" He placed the vial back on the tray. "Can the Elixir be reproduced?"

The Scholar and the apprentice glanced at each other in question, but only the senior had any reply. "The methods the ancients used to make the Elixir have long been lost. According to the official records, many chemists have been employed over the years to study the quantity we had left, but..."

"A mystery it remains," Mellka finished, disappointed. "A single drop will do little to dissect the priestcraft." At the sound of armoured boots, he turned to face Commander Falchier as he entered the Vault.

The tall warrior bowed and promptly delivered his report. "Grand Master, the Exalted Cardinals, Achrone and Libra, send news from Templari: The summit had been dissolved as predicted."

"Humph." Mellka wasn't surprised, but was curious to the details of the report. "What else?"

"Governor Traiza is dead."

The finality of Falchier's cold declaration was enough to send a chill down his spine, but it was one of anticipation, not fear. "Have our Faithful prepare, Commander." He glanced to his side, where Poem stood silently at attention beside the sarcophagi, adorning the attire of an Insidian. "The hour has come for our intervention."

* * *

The system of passageways beneath Tinkertown stretched for miles in every conceivable direction. Some led to the peak of the Mountains, others ran along the expanse of the city, but most reached into the depths of Terra Mia. Over the course of decades, if not centuries, the walls of the corridors were reinforced by steel plating and beams. Track lightning was then added, alongside myriads of piping and cables to accommodate plumbing, fuel, and air supply.

Most of these passageways were empty, making it easier for Seidon and Tenshi to explore the underground without too many prying eyes. They discovered many chambers that had been converted to weapons research and development with full staffs of Tinkerers hard at work with both minds and hands. They passed one of the largest sections so far, containing a massive treaded tank that once belonged to Guard's mighty mechanized cavalry, and it was being dismantled by reverse engineers in a study to redesign its power and mobility.

"Weren't their weapons program restricted by the Armistice?" Tenshi noted.

"They have no other profession," Seidon replied grimly. "And maybe too many starving clients are needing their services for them to ignore."

Seidon turned at a T-junction that led to a heightened area of activity. He spotted an assembly of tall cranes, motorized transports, and a large concentration of engineers with a monolithic hangar just ahead. As the corridor opened up, he was able to see the focus of the activity, and paused in grim shock at what he and Tenshi saw.

The Tinkerers were in the process of dismantling a Sorcerer Cannon down to its bare skeletal frame. Its shell had been removed, analyzed thoroughly, catalogued, and stored away in unmarked containers. The main turret was in the midst of being separated from the body, supported by an array of reinforced cables.

"Then it's not the original Cannon that's being sold for parts," Tenshi said in realization. "They found another."

"To be more precise," Nuria's voice said from behind, "it's our third Cannon discovered so far."

Seidon reached for his carbine, but the two Enforcers drew their katanas quickly and he stayed his hand.

"The first had been destined to be recycled, melted down to its basic constituents, but through careful negotiations, we managed to retrieve what was left." Nuria seemed to enjoy giving the lecture. "We then found two more buried not far from where we found the first. Unfortunately, the new discoveries were in bad state of disrepair, but with a little ingenuity we hope to redesign a modular and more practical translation of the original concept."

"Don't you have any idea what you're doing?" Tenshi said. "These weapons are too dangerous for anyone to possess."

"We deal only with responsible clients looking to defend their way of life by the most efficient means possible," Nuria countered. "The weapon itself is not the point of wrongdoing, it is the intention of the user."

"That reasoning nearly took away your privilege when you took sides with the Corporations," Seidon said acidly. "You're on the brink of destroying everything your people take for granted."

"That's why we can't allow you to leave," Nuria said. "Cooperate, and we will provide you fair treatment in our jails."

The moment the Enforcers stepped forth to arrest them, Seidon rushed shoulder-first into the closest one. She had no room to effectively employ her sword, and caught the full brunt of Seidon's charge onto her torso. The Enforcer, the air knocked from her, stumbled back, and fell.

Her partner reacted in reflex, pointing the tip of her katana to Seidon, but was now completely open to Tenshi as she fluidly unsheathed her cutlass and swung it hard against the track light overhead. It smashed apart in a blinding flash and flurry of sparks, startling both the Enforcers and Nuria.

Seidon shoved the distracted Enforcer onto the frightened official and both fell to the ground, then removed his carbine to pin down any further resistance. He kicked the Enforcer across the face and off Nuria, then planted his heel down on the official to keep him from crawling away.

He grabbed the duplicitous Tinkerer by the collar and pressed the muzzle of his carbine to his cheek. "Are the Squires the ones purchasing the weapon?"

The first dazed Enforcer stirred, but Tenshi kicked away her weapon and held her still at the point of her cutlass.

Nuria stuttered, nerve-wrecked at the sight of the carbine and Seidon's unforgiving demeanor. "T-they're just m-mercenaries... g-guarding the shipping lanes! I'm just a l-liaison, I don't k-know where the parts are headed!"

"Who else's involved?!" Seidon commanded, but Nuria was too nervous to reply coherently.

The guards that were stationed inside the hangar had taken notice of the commotion and were running to meet them. With reluctance at leaving the official that was the key they needed to uncover the trail of black market, he took Tenshi by her hand and escaped.

With the *Second Awakening*'s lines secured, the ramp was lowered onto the loading jetty. Messer and his entourage disembarked, and were immediately intercepted by Galvano and a company of Enforcers. The dock was busy with arrivals and departures, but most of the affairs revolved around a berthed ship nearby.

Messer and his crew immediately felt on edge.

"Admiral, welcome," Galvano greeted a bit too excitedly, which was out of character. "It's been several months since your last visit. Are you in need of resupply?"

"Your town seems to be on a state of alert, Helmer," Messer said, his eyes studying the surroundings. "Is something amiss that we can assist you with?"

"No, there's no need to be concerned, Admiral," Galvano stated rather quickly. He glanced to where Messer was looking, toward one of the berths where two squads of Enforcers were locking down a ship. "There was a minor infraction with one of the traders, and we're impounding the vessel until the dispute is settled legally." He looked past Messer to his alerted crew. "Will you and your crew be staying long? I can arrange for proper accommodations in the city."

"Not long, Helmer," Messer assured. "We have orders to carry through, and I'd like to keep ahead of schedule."

"The wisdom of good leadership," Galvano flattered, and nodded politely.

Messer waited for the committee to leave, then walked farther down the pier for a better view of the ship the Tinkerers were impounding. Once in full sight, he didn't need to read its name to know it was Seidon's schooner, the *Journey's Prodigy*.

"Captain Semmes," he promptly ordered, "mobilize our Marines. Retake the Journey, and secure the port." He readied his musket. "Yeoman Bale and Buccaneer Company are with me."

Armed with the latest rifles, the chasing Tinkertown Enforcers herded Tenshi and Seidon toward the open. They seldom fired to avoid accidentally hitting their own in the tight confines of the passageways. To slow them further, Seidon fired at a wall conduit and spilled heated gas into their midst.

He heard Tenshi gasp ahead of him, and nearly ran into her as they reached the exit grounds. Over two dozen Squires waited for them in a pincer formation, including Skein and Ophelia at the head of the pack. The Enforcers encroached rapidly from behind, and hemmed them in.

Without thinking twice, Seidon reloaded and fired at the closest mercenary. "Keep running!"

Tenshi refused to leave his side. With her cutlass in one hand, and a dagger in the other she fended off the boldest of the Squires, while Seidon unsheathed Ancestral and cut through the line with her in tow.

The Squires and the Tinkertown Enforcers scattered their encirclement as Messer's Marines stormed the area. They unleashed a volley from their bayonet-studded rifles, and pressed on until Seidon and Tenshi were behind their formation where Messer, Bale and a squad of reinforcements waited for them.

"Reminds me of old times," Messer mused, as Tenshi embraced him. "Care to make a hasty retreat?"

"Not yet..." Seidon said, happy to see Messer, but flabbergasted to see Bale alive. He approached him carefully, as if he was a ghost, and placed his hand on the big man's chest to be certain he was real. "Bale?"

Bale smiled sadly. "It's a long story, my friend."

"There's an alehouse in Coastal Sky where the maidens serve you by the barrel," Seidon said with a smirk. "You'll tell me all about it until we pass out."

"The last time we stepped in an alehouse, we ended up on a fishing boat off the coast of Barren Lands," Bale teased. "We stunk of fish for a month."

Seidon reminisced with a brief smirk, then turned back to Messer. "If the Squires are here, so's Regento. We need to find him."

Messer agreed. "My men have control of the port; escape on land is the only way out for the Squires now."

Up high, on an arched bridge between two buildings, a group of Squires rolled in a ship-grade cannon on its wheeled carriage. They pointed straight at the center of the clash, loaded the breech, and armed the trigger. Without much concern for their own comrades, the lead Squire sparked the flame.

The cannon recoiled violently, and in the distance the ground exploded. Fragmented cobblestones, bodies, and grey smoke spilled into the air for a brief moment, then rained back to earth. The shockwave knocked nearly everyone else outside the impact crater off their feet.

With sinister glee, the Squires fired again.

Captain Semmes witnessed the cannonade from his vantage point on the *Second Awakening*'s bridge. Well within range for a swift retaliation before the malefactors could reload, he shouted his orders to the crew. "Decommission that gun, now!"

The forward ordnance hatches swung open, and three swivel cannons sounded with thunder. The arched bridge was blasted consecutively, effectively destroying everything on it.

The sound of the *Second Awakening*'s cannons startled Tenshi from her daze, and she found herself alone and separated from Seidon. A dirty fog hung over the battlefield, and in the confusion, she saw a few dazed Marines continuing their barrage on the enemy. The soldiers appeared and vanished into the grey smoke like phantoms.

She struggled on her fours, her elbows and knees numb, and looked around for her cutlass. It was nowhere to be found, but she managed to retrieve her dagger. She gripped its handle tightly when a large man passed in front of her, but it was Bale – his yeoman uniform ripped and stained with soot.

He helped her up, and allowed her to lean her weight on him. "Are you alright?"

Tenshi nodded, pushing her hair back. "My ears are ringing…" It was then she felt everything was dreadfully wrong.

Skein and a few other Squires emerged from the fog, then Ophelia joined them. "She's ours," she declared.

Incensed, Bale clenched his teeth. "She's worthless to you."

Skein smirked. "Not to the Marquis, whom you owe a great debt. Hand her over like a good Squire you are, and be on your way before your friends get suspicious."

Tenshi pulled away from Bale, her heart afire with his betrayal, but his grip was too strong. "How could you do this? Seidon trusted you! *I* trusted you!"

Bale kept silent, his own heart ripped to shreds with guilt. He was ready to relinquish her to Skein when Tenshi retaliated with her dagger, stabbing it deep into Bale's shoulder. He released her in reflex, but she was caught by the Squires.

Tenshi slugged the first ruffian that touched her, but was outnumbered and overpowered. She continued to struggle until Ophelia swung the hard end of her crossbow across her jaw. They then dragged her away.

Bale grunted as he pulled the dagger from his shoulder, seeing his blood dripping on the blade. He looked past it to Skein, and was tempted to force the knife between the merc's eyes.

"Expect to get paid well, big guy," Skein said. "Half the job's done."

* * *

Seidon had been knocked against the wall of a small building by the blast, which cracked the surface layer of the masonry from the impact, and he sat at its foot, dazed. His head was drooped, and his eyes were closed, but his ears tingled with the consternation around him. There was a moment he thought he heard Tenshi crying out to him. At the sound of her voice, his fingers tightened around the hilt of Ancestral, still in his hand.

A shadow crossed him, as a wounded but opportunistic Squire with a gloriously fuzzy beard closed the distance with a saw-toothed knife in hand. He smiled maniacally, ecstatic by the chance to claim a valued prize, and thrust his blade.

Seidon's eyes snapped open, and caught the glint of steel. He moved his head and torso in an instant, and the knife missed him by an inch – stabbing into the wall. The shock reverberated into the Squires arm, but he had no time to counteract as Seidon delivered the Ancestral's sharp length through the man's body until it peered out the Squire's back.

Regaining a sense of where he was, Seidon then mercilessly kicked the Squire clean off his sword. He got up on his feet, and spotted the Marines regrouping around Messer. More troops arrived from the port, led by a lieutenant, and although the Squires had retreated, some of the Enforcers wanted to continue the fight. Nowhere did he see Tenshi.

He ran to Messer, ignoring the sores across his whole body. "Where's Tenshi?"

"I thought she was with you," Messer said, concerned himself. "She shouldn't have been thrown too far from our position."

A lieutenant approached with a fresh company of armed sailors. "Admiral, the Captain received a petition from

Helmer Galvano to cease hostilities. The order is being carried out now for the Enforcers to stand down."

"Make sure they're disarmed and confined," Messer said. "Send word out to the King that Tinkertown is in breach of our trust, and no longer a neutral state."

"We just received news from Templari, Admiral," the lieutenant said, a bit strained to deliver the message. "There was an assassination attempt on the King... Lord Admiral Traiza was killed in the attack."

Messer was stunned by the news, but there was an immediate task at hand. "...The Marines will assume the role of mediators until they can be relieved by the diplomatic corps. Take temporary command of our forces here, Lieutenant, and establish a garrison." He felt his breath shorten, still in disbelief. "Tell Captain Semmes to prepare the ship for immediate departure."

Seidon, like Messer, was stupefied by the ill news, yet his heart thrummed for Tenshi. When he saw Bale, bleeding from a shoulder wound, he felt a cold weight in his gut. The way the big man walked toward him, hunched as if his spirit was broken in half, and his eyes red with restrained tears, it seemed to Seidon as if something had been wrenched from his hands.

"Bale, are you alright?"

Bale barely had the courage to look at Seidon in the eyes. He nodded dejectedly, as a Marine checked and dressed his knife wound.

Seidon found his behavior odd, and it terrified him. "Where's Tenshi? Was she with you?"

A tear strolled down Bale's cheek, but his face was a frozen mask of self-hatred. "I'm sorry, Seidon, they took her. They were headed for the Old Ruins."

Seidon grimaced tightly, an infallible determination in his grey eyes, and without word or warning, he chased after the retreating Squires.

"Seidon!" Messer knew no reason could stop him from his mad charge, and wanted desperately to follow, but was conflicted with his duty to the King.

Bale, split apart by his own desires, knew what he had to do. "I'll go..." He pushed away the Marine that tended to his shoulder, and borrowed his rifle, then ran after Seidon.

IX. Rise of the Iron Curtain

IX. Rise of the Iron Curtain

The evening sky settled somberly over the Old Capital, as the city mourned the loss of one man. A procession of military officers from Templari, Magna Carta, and Guard followed the horse-drawn carriage that carried Traiza's body to his final resting place in the basilica's sepulcher that was reserved for Templari's respected gentry. Bagpipers and drummers were at the head of the column, and Navy officers were behind the carriage, while Traiza's widow and daughters and all else followed suit. Citizens watched on the sidelines, both fascinated and saddened as ceremonies of this nature rarely occurred.

Despite all manner of protests from acting members of Templari's political factions, and even from his own council, Ingren made certain Traiza was remembered with the utmost honour and deepest respect that he deserved. Not just as an admiral, or governor, but as a friend and staunch ally now long gone.

He walked alongside Julia, the pillar of his life, who held his hand tightly as they marched behind the officers and Traiza's closest family. They were surrounded by Throne Guards and Elites, allowing the public no view of the royal cortege beyond the wall of armours and shields. Ingren knew somewhere in the crowd, either watching from the streets or high on some ledge, Vant also paid his respects.

He allowed him that much, before giving the explicit directive to cut the lenience he had allowed for him and his men.

They passed along the waterfront, and they stopped for a moment. Visible in the distance were the flagships and escorts of Templari and Magna Carta's fleets, including the

Sovereign and Traiza's last command, the *Amaranthine*. Their starboard guns were readied, and with a thunderous roar worthy of remembrance, the cannons sounded thrice – the lights and smoke dissipating into the air.

They continued down the old road into the ancient basilica where the bravest and noblest were laid to rest, and where Traiza's casket was destined. The final eulogy and blessings were given by the resident clergymen, and overseen by the Cardinals Achrone and Libra.

The words and formalities held little comfort to Ingren, a spot of black odium in his heart. He vowed vindication, and his silent promise was sealed with the lowering of Traiza's casket into the crypt....

On a rounded old balcony, high above the heads of the people, Vant, Sucre and a few Strafers watched the military funeral in silence. They were partly hidden by the night, and by naval flags fluttering on the archways and rooftops.

Before the procession entered the basilica, Ingren had glanced up toward Vant, providing a vow that they both knew was loud and clear: What freedom had been given, taken for granted, was now taken away in kind.

"What will happen to us now?" Sucre asked, in tune with Vant's concerns.

"Someone must be blamed for this tragedy," Vant replied. "Wisdom dictates for any man to first look in the obvious places."

* * *

The cavalry of the Iron Sabres, at least two thousand strong, arrived at Templari's oldest principal gate. Golden banners with the Order's crest wavered high above their ranks as they entered the Citadel Hall: a long, narrow gallery of archways that led to the interior courtyard just outside the checkpoint into the city proper.

The royal peacekeepers and Templari police were nervous at the sight of so many armed horsemen, but did nothing to provoke a fight. From the core formation emerged Grand Master Mellka, garbed in full armour, with an escort of Honour Guards.

"We're here on the decree of the people," Mellka announced boldly, "open the gates."

In the magistrate's grand consulate office, both King and Queen waited. While Ingren paced around and Dalena watched him with growing concern, they were kept company by vigilant guards.

The doors opened, and two squads of Elites strode in with Vant and Sucre in their midst. The two guests were ushered to the magistrate's desk, opposite to where Ingren and Dalena stood, and were given no quarter to move elsewhere. All eyes were on them.

Ingren continued his pacing, not bothering to look at the two prisoners of war. "If there's a shred of human decency left in you, Mister Vant, you will answer my questions without evasion. Did you orchestrate the assassination?"

Vant had his suspicions on why he was promptly led here, he had actually been expecting it. "No."

"Did one of your men arrange it?"

"Not to my knowledge," Vant replied. "I can at least vouch for all those currently under me."

Sucre's concerns and confusion dispelled as he realized where the interrogation was headed. "If you're accusing the General of–"

"Sucre," Vant warned mildly, his tone underlining the seriousness of the situation.

Ingren stopped pacing, and finally looked at Vant. "You were there, you witnessed what happened. You took advantage of the leeway I granted you, and of my compassion. You even seemed quite eager to join the summit, as if you somehow knew something was going to happen."

"Your Majesty," Vant said, "if I had any clairvoyance of the incident, I would've acted on it."

Ingren didn't believe it, and it sounded in the coldness of his voice. "Had you known about this conspiracy prior to its execution?"

Vant sighed, saddened that his words no longer carried any weight. "...No."

"In no tiniest of measure were you ever aware of a plot to kill me or Traiza?!" Ingren unleashed a bit of his suppressed edge, and it was startling even to those closest to him.

"My Lord, he had nothing to do with this!" Sucre defended, not caring if he was out of line. "We mourn a hero's death as much as you do!"

Ingren ignored Sucre, his fiery eyes on Vant. He wanted a straight answer, or he would tear down all the walls of the city until he was satisfied.

"Yes," Vant said quietly, surprising even Sucre. "The last war left too many loose strands, and by the way of things beyond your knowledge, you lacked the capacity to tie all the ends properly. I knew I wasn't the only one aware of your limits, and I knew someone would eventually put you to the test. The summit, with friends and foes holding hands, was too perfect an opportunity."

Ingren was distressed by the validity of Vant's admission. "It was a gathering of leaders done in earnest... Traiza deserved a better fate than to be an unwilling host to this 'test'."

"I have nothing left, Your Majesty, except my studies in strategy to keep me from my own madness, and I apologize for not having warned you, because I know you would not have heeded to my counsel, and nothing would've changed." Vant tightened his jaw, keeping his emotions at bay. "Traiza died bravely because he knew your life was worth more than his. He would've preferred a quick death in the heat of battle than waste away in the politician's jungle."

"...Then you know who's behind this?"

"Only guesses..." Vant shook his head slightly. "The stage's been set, but the players won't appear until the music starts."

"It was a political murder," Ingren said, frustrated. "I can't imagine why anyone, even the worst of Traiza's enemies on the provisional council, would commit to such extremes. It achieved nothing."

Vant said nothing, even though he knew the blame fell on his shoulders.

Dalena reinforced the King's presence, her stance as regal as Ingren's. Her blue eyes spared no mercy. "You know who the assassin is."

It wasn't a question, and Vant still said nothing.

"If you want to dispel any doubts we have, you *will* tell us," Dalena stressed.

"...It's one fact I cannot disclose, Your Highness."

Dalena was about to lash out, but Ingren surprisingly grabbed her arm and stopped her. He read something beneath Vant's tone that suggested a different approach. "Guards, allow us some privacy... Mister Sucre, you may tend to your tasks."

Without question, the Throne Guards and Elites turned on their heels and marched out of the chamber. With a nod of assurance from Vant, Sucre also left with them.

"If not for justice, not for vengeance, then by all the values you hold dear, you will tell us," Ingren said.

"It is by the values you also hold dear, that I don't tell you."

"You know what this entails. Why would you keep this from us?"

Vant glanced at Dalena, then back to Ingren. "She's the mother and guardian of my child, and I will do what I can to protect them to the death of all else."

There was something Dalena never heard in his voice before, a deep well of devotion that overrode all sense of self-preservation, and she found herself sympathizing with him. "Her crimes are unforgivable. One way or another, justice will eventually speed her fall."

"I'm already in chains," Vant said. "If she joins me in the gallows, then what guidance can we as parents offer? Neither one of us will allow *anyone* to take our child, nor will we let him be cast in chains with us."

Ingren looked at his wife, to gather strength from her vivid blue eyes, then glanced below her stomach, now slightly swollen, but barely noticeable. In his heart, he understood

Vant fully, but they all stood on the brink of disaster if nothing was done.

"We are destined to clash weapons once more," Ingren said. "In an era where we no longer know who our enemies are, then you have more reason to fear that your child may be caught in the crossfire."

"So do you," Vant countered, no ounce of deception or clever wordplay in his reply.

Sighing, Ingren looked hard into Vant's eyes before he spoke. "Citizens, politicians, and soldiers who hold some grievance at the loss of one their own will want someone to blame. You tell me you're innocent of this crime, and I grudgingly believe you, but you're leaving me little choice."

"Then there's nothing more to moot," Vant said.

Ingren grimaced, knowing there was no breaching the master tactician's walls today. "So be it, Mister Vant... Guards."

The Throne Guards and Elites obediently returned.

"Escort the prisoner back to his suite," Ingren ordered acidly.

Vant bowed slightly, resigned, and allowed the Elites to surround him in formation. As they left, the king's official messenger, Rowen, rushed in. He delivered his news directly to Ingren in a hushed tone, and Vant curiously glanced back over his shoulder as he walked away, certain he'd heard Mellka's name being mentioned.

Dressed in black with an overcoat that matched, Poem slipped through the familiar shadows of the old quarters in

Templari, where the Restoration League concentrated its efforts. Most of the damaged buildings and defensive walls he remembered were now whole, yet the scars – especially those of war-torn families – escaped renovation.

He paused in the umbra of a massive angelic statue adorning a central plaza, half of its wing, face, and arm severely brittle by weather and battle, and observed the ex-Strafers at work. Amongst them were groups of local skilled workers and Magna Cartan soldiers, but nowhere did he see the man he searched for.

Disappointed, he moved away from any potential onlookers, reached an open manhole in an abandoned alley, and climbed down its maw. Once his boots reached the floor of the ancient sewers, he turned to the group of black-clad Insidians that stood ready.

"Move to your positions, and wait for my command. We are the Grand Master's vanguard, let nothing slip through our net."

Within the parliamentary conference chamber, the rivaling political factions and their opinionated res publica quarreled ceaselessly amongst themselves, each idealistic mob desiring to fill the void of leadership left behind by Traiza's parting. They rabidly wanted elections, but moderated on whom should take the temporary role of acting governor. Nobody wanted the job, nor would they trust the mantle on anyone from Magna Carta after the debacle of the summit.

"Call for elections now!" a former Administrator shouted, instilling several others to vocally express their consent.

"It's too soon!" another legislator protested. "We have no official station for counting the polls, and we haven't appointed any mediators for public debates!"

"Royalist!" the former accused, stirring mixed reactions. "Would you rather have some foreign king appoint us another leader?"

"Another royal lapdog!" a second malcontent instigated, further dividing the table.

"Be shamed, all of you, retain some dignity for the dead!"

The doors swung open, and their voices were quickly silenced with the arrival of Grand Master Mellka.

"A great tragedy just passed," he said as he walked to the head of the table where Traiza's empty seat stood out like a broken link in the chain, "and you bicker over trivial things without much rapport toward the people who wait upon you." He looked around the conference, his booming voice demanding full attention. "Waiting upon a decisive plan of action that will deliver them further away from the misery they're ennobled in."

Some of the politicians shifted, as if wanting to protest, but held back to keep face before their peers and the Grand Master.

"I see this provisional council stands without an appeaser. Where's the king whose army now occupies your fief?"

Amongst uncomfortable murmurs of the crowd, one of the older councilors, adorning a dreary and proud mask, spoke in place of the others. "We are gracious of your visit, but why are you here, Grand Master?"

Mellka scoffed as he prowled around the councilors, his beautiful armour rattling faintly with each step. Although his voice was floated at the men in the room, his eyes were focused on a distant thought. "It pains me when I think of what's become of the Old Capital, throne of the world, now delegated to nothing more than scraps of its former glory. Over two thousand years ago, Valor Drol marched to his fate from these halls and achieved what few others ever will. His sainthood was not given to him, he earned it. Both his life and demise will forever serve as a standard every man and woman should follow."

He stopped and faced the politicians. "Your people have suffered enough, yet you allow yourselves to be humiliated by an idle king who celebrates his victory over the backs of your dead. And to be more insulting, permitting your enemies to roam under a royal leash that's much too indulgent. Where's your honour? Your patriotism?"

"Templari hasn't lost any of its virtues, Grand Master," Ingren said as he entered, accompanied by Rowen. "Its foundation had withstood countless calamities, and will continue to do so long after we perish to dust and earth."

Mellka gazed coolly at Ingren. "A strong foundation is shaped with faith, not the principles of foreign leaders."

"You treat me like I've annexed this city for my own, when in fact I'm here to lend a hand in mending the wounds inflicted in the war," Ingren said stoutly. "Remember that it was my home that was the first to be bombarded by the Sorcerer's Cannon, and the last roof tile has yet to be nailed down. The road is long, and too many agitators are still abound, causing nothing but discord."

"I corrected all the mistakes that the Church inflicted before my ascension," Mellka said, "and I've done so with precision and expediency because a man's life is too short to squander on worthless goals. You've done your part, Your Highness, and we are grateful, but it's time you tend to your own affairs in that white castle across the Vast Blue."

"Last I checked, Templari's governed by the will of the people, not by the papacy."

The air in the chamber chilled, and the Templari councilors felt it.

A slight grin tipped the corner of Mellka's lips. "You don't seem to grasp the situation clearly, my dear King. This is where the people declare a reform, where the charter is rewritten under Gloriam and the Twelve Saint Knights as it once was long before warmongering Generals and Sorcerers. Where this Church retakes the seat of government." He glanced at the officials around him. "Just a moment ago you were ready to rip each other to shreds over elections, and I will give it to you before the season's end. I offer neutrality, and a solution to the corruption that had set in behind these walls. Do I have your support?"

The councilors looked to each other with uncertainty, but a few who were faithful wasted no time claiming their support. With steady inclination, the chamber was soon drowned with shouts of approval and legislative yeas, which rose to a roar of applause that caught Ingren off-guard.

"What are they doing?" Rowen said in complete dismay. "They're trading social progress for religious irons." He looked to his king, but saw him completely rigid, as if he had just witnessed the betrayal and murder of all his noble ideals, of yet another friend.

Mellka relished the moment, then feigning modesty, urged the chamber to quiet down with the graceful lifting of his hands. "It all begins here and now, my dear friends, all duties and responsibilities will fall back on the denizens of this nation – *immediately*. The ousting of Magna Carta is at hand."

The parliament's response was brutal. They expected process and debate, but Mellka offered them pragmatism at its finest. They shouted commendations, applauded, and vigorously banged their fists on the table.

Ingren was bereaved by the sudden change of face of the very people he'd helped for so many years, out of kindness and the wealth of his royal coffers, who now raised their voices with the banner of the Church – willingly and without shame. He inhaled deeply, and nodded solemnly.

As the ruckus faded, he spoke. "...By the decree of the people, this king and his kingdom will submit."

"Rightly so, Your Majesty, for you are a herald to peace and justice," Mellka said, enthralled by the smallness of such great a figure. "Order your soldiers to retreat from Templari soil, your sailors to unfold the sails to the westward wind, and do so with dignity."

The *Highborn* was stationed several miles off Archway's Path, far from the clutter of the shipyards and within view of the overall coastline. The Gabrialtar mariners and engineers tended to their chores while the dragoons kept watch, maintaining a state of alert since Traiza's funeral.

Titus strolled casually on the main deck, his hands folded at the small of his back, and observed his crew obediently at work. Beyond their backs, he saw a bit of ocean between him, and the multi-national ships embarked in the usual anchorage traffic. His keen interests laid mostly on the unusual increase of Magna Carta's fleet numbers, and the brimming sails of the *Sovereign* as it cruised toward Templari further south.

"Are we off in a hurry so suddenly, my King?" he whispered wittily to himself. He turned to Mikaila as she approached; she wore the white and black uniform of a high-ranking Dragoon officer. "Lieutenant-Colonel," he greeted. "All things went well?"

She nodded briskly. "All executive powers have been transferred to the Church, and almost immediately the order was given to expel Magna Carta from further responsibility."

Titus nodded. "Little did we give Traiza credit for the importance of his role in these affairs. Little do people realize what's taken for granted until it's gone." He mulled over his last memory of Traiza. "Perhaps I was too harsh on the man. I almost feel guilty for emasculating him."

Mikaila had no comment to add, nor any regret for her actions. "What's our next initiative?"

"Like good-natured envoys, we'll pay our respects to the Grand Master on his most recent conquest." He snickered. "Perhaps even have a tea and some biscuits."

Mikaila wasn't amused by Titus' odd sarcasm, so she kept silent and at full attention. In her mind, she compared him to Vant, and were complete contrasts by far.

"I understand you saw Rell Vant in the streets during your operation," Titus noted nonchalantly, as if reading her thoughts. "Was he faring well in his captivity?"

"From my impression, he hasn't lost any of his fire."

Titus eyed Mikaila sharply. "Hmm, then at least he'll put up a fight when the Order of the Faithful implements its infamous absolution on him and his men."

"...Won't we aid him?"

Titus grinned slyly at her suggestion. "My allegiance is clear. I have no reason to save him or carry on his dead cause, and so to be clear, neither do you. The great dream of Guard is long gone, my dear."

X. Ancestral

X. Ancestral

The Squires of Debonair arrived en masse at the Old Ruins, armed to the teeth and tense after their skirmish with the forces of Magna Carta. Led by Skein and Ophelia, they spread their positions in preparation for a rear-guard reprisal. They dragged Tenshi against her will to the front of the ranks, and threw her to the ground.

Forcibly with them was also Nuria, whom had nothing but complaints for the turn of events since Seidon arrived at Tinkertown's front door. His frustrations were expressed loudly, garnering bitter spite from the Squires.

"This is inexcusable!" he shouted at Skein, whose attempts to ignore the official crumbled to genuine contempt. "We had everything under control until you uneducated ingrates intervened in our affairs!"

"Quit your fretting!" Skein shouted back. "My bloody ears are ringing!"

"I will not! Where's the Marquis?!"

"Right here, Tinkerer," Regento said as he approached, passing through a vine-covered portico that was the vestige of an ancient arcade.

Nuria now redirected his vexations on Regento, much to the relief of Skein and his compatriots. "I demand an explanation for this recklessness!"

"In due time."

Regento noticed Tenshi on the ground, too exhausted from battle and toil, yet she still reserved a fiery inner spirit as she looked up at him with the same resentment Seidon would proffer. Not without a sense of cordiality, he gently lifted her up to her feet.

Tenshi pulled herself away from his grip, gracefully enough not to startle the edgy Squires. She stared at him coldly, offering no words, while he gave her a simple lopsided grin.

Nuria pressed on. "What excuse do you have for jeopardizing our treaty with Magna Carta and its allies? Our discretion had been blatantly compromised because your men act instinctively on raw violence to solve their problems! Our research, our industry, our very reason to exist is over because of your barbaric negligence!"

"Your anger is misplaced," Regento replied, turning to him. "When you decided to work with mercenaries; to deal in the underground market, and to use our smuggling lanes... what did you expect? The Squires acted accordingly when your own people failed to deflect suspicions, so don't lecture me about the inconsistencies in your security. I don't care what happens to your town, so long as you deliver your end of the bargain."

"This is preposterous! After this incident, our ports will be locked down indefinitely!"

"You're a clever one, you'll find a way."

"No," Nuria defied. "This operation is over."

The Tinkertown official spun around and strode away, and Regento let it be for a moment. Glancing at Tenshi, he ambiguously drew his pistol and shot Nuria in the back, sending him sprawling on his face amongst the Ruins. By the time the dead Tinkerer's coat flaps settled down, Regento holstered his weapon back to his belt.

Tenshi's heart gripped with both pity and contempt. "He didn't deserve that."

"No," Regento admitted, "but it had to be done."

"There goes the rest of our payment," Skein expressed, kicking Nuria's body over onto his back. "What now?"

"What we do best," Regento retorted coolly, glancing lustily at Tenshi. "We finish the job."

Bittersweet memories returned to Seidon as he walked past the crumbling pillars of the Old Ruins, what had once been the fortress-city of the Sorcerers. The foundations, ravaged walls, and free-standing archways remained as they had the last time he was here. Time and weather had done their part to dilapidate stone and mortar, chipping away what was left after the Sorcerer's War destroyed whatever else.

He thought of Poem and Vant, and of Necrosis. The enigma that had pointed him the way to the Thousand-Year Dream; the same creature that gave Guard a hand in unearthing the Cannon and igniting a war that would cost thousands of lives. Although Seidon never knew Necrosis' whole story, he knew only that corruption had seeped far beyond the Sorcerer's rotted flesh and bones, and that he was betrayed by all whom he betrayed in turn.

Yet in the Old Ruins, chasing after the knaves that took Tenshi, he felt a resonance of the old Sorcerer. His cold legacy of murder and treachery still lingered, and none more obvious than the fresh blood that soaked the weathered flagstones.

He quickly readied his carbine, while Bale inspected Nuria's body.

"Shot," Bale said simply, and searched the surroundings. "The Squires have gone through here." He tightened his jaw, his guilt surfacing. "Seidon, I..." He stopped short of confessing. "We should go back, call for reinforcements."

"They're still here, Bale... there are lots of places to hide." Seidon peered at the somber statues and friezes that decorated the columns that surrounded them. "You and I are on our own for this one."

He approached the largest column, its crown toppled at its base, and tightened the grip on his carbine. Nothing else seemed amiss, until Regento emerged from the column's umbra.

"This forsaken place has a meaning for you, doesn't it, cousin?"

Seidon aimed his carbine directly at Regento's head, and locked back the hammer. "Where is she?"

"I understand why you love her, and it's more than her beauty." Regento revealed his hands as he stepped into the open, showing he was unarmed. "I might not understand it, but from what I've gathered, her corporeal existence is owed to the Thousand-Year Dream. Imagining the possibilities, was she truly a lost soul that anchored to yours? And considering the legend's ties to the Saint Knights, she could even be the reincarnated Queen of Magna Carta." He scoffed at his own speculations. "I know what you're thinking: What does it all matter now? She's free of you, but still and always your perpetual half. Beautifully poetic."

"Regento," Seidon said, restraining his impulse to beat his cousin senseless, "you said we were like brothers, and brothers who love each other will never let anything come between them." He fired, and struck the head off one of the statues near Regento's left. He re-cocked the hammer. "Prove to me there's still some of the same blood running through your veins."

Regento scowled as he cleared the dust and debris off his left shoulder. "I give you my word that she's safe, but you won't see her until that *something* between us is resolved. Lower your gun, and we'll talk this out like gentlemen."

"You have a confused sense of chivalry." Reluctantly, he lowered his weapon. "What do you want in exchange?"

"Cousin, you know me too well," Regento replied with a grin. "I offer to trade her life for your heirloom sword. A small piece of our family history that I've had my eyes on ever since we were kids. Consider it a symbol of your submission... of our brotherly love."

Seidon grimaced, his hand automatically reaching for Ancestral hanging at his hip. "How can I trust you after all this? You're running guns for warmongers, and worst still, the Cannon?"

"They say never mix business with family, an overused adage, but crudely true. Honesty, a rare virtue, is something I take very seriously in both these worlds." Regento closed the distance between them, making sure Seidon saw the truth in his eyes. "I'll tell you exactly what I want to do with the sword: Firstly, I want it for the rarity of it, and for spite. Lastly, I intend to sell it for big money and some bigger favours."

"You have the *choice* to stop another war from happening, but instead you leech off the bigotry and violence for no greater purpose other than your own."

Regento was untouched. "And you have yet to discover the consequences of your brash actions. The old blacksmith and his peasant wife paid for it with their lives, courtesy of Squires' recklessness. Yet another victim lies here in these Ruins, only several feet away. How many more will you throw in harm's way?"

"...Teeven... No..." To hear he and his wife were murdered, wrenched out Seidon's heart. The Squires were as despicable as their Marquis.

"Do we have a deal?"

Seidon released Ancestral from his belt and roughly handed it – blade, belt, and scabbard – to Regento. "You're nothing to me."

The harsh declaration was inconsequential, as Regento needed only to peek at the tempered crystal blade to be satisfied. "She's waiting for you."

The dust stirred as the Squires revealed themselves, eager for a fight. They dragged Tenshi to the front of their lines and unceremoniously released her, but she managed a few steps before Ophelia smacked her giant crossbow to the back of her legs. Tenshi fell to her knees, hurt, and restrained to counter the brutish assault.

Seidon was ready to charge all of them, but the sight of Bale standing in collusion with the Squires stopped him. He stared at his old comrade in shock, and Regento earnestly felt pity for him.

"Desperation will turn even the hardest resolve," Regento said, backing away from his cousin. "Bale was sent to locate you and bring you out for the bounty, and did so admirably." He felt no remorse, but a profound sense of accomplishment. "I'm keeping my word, Seidon, you and I are through." He glanced at Skein, "As for the Squires, they're hungry and greedy, and want nothing more than to claim their prize. It's out of my hands."

Enraged, Seidon spun in an attempt to bat Regento with his carbine, but the Marquis was out of harm's way and retreating from the Ruins. It was now between him and the mercenaries under Skein's wretched influence.

Skein cackled as he waved his sword to signal the others to spread out. He looked at Bale, who was frozen with self-contempt, and patted him on the back. "Didn't think you had it in you, big boy!" He scowled at Seidon, "But don't worry, your cut is going to be well worth it."

He walked up to Tenshi and pressed the top edge of his sword under her jaw. "You can surrender and take your chances with the Church, or you can both die here!"

Seidon shook with wrath, wanting to unleash it onto the Squires, but at a single glance into Tenshi's hurt eyes, and he lowered his aim with a heavy heart.

Skein laughed with great relief, and glanced at his brethren. "Our impoverished days scratching a living off the side alleys' over!" He glanced at Ophelia, "We can finally settle down and live like royalty!"

Heavy thunder echoed in the near distance, followed by another, like drums of war, ruining the brief festive mood of Skein and the Squires. They searched the air for the source of the noise, and as they looked toward the horizon to the north where the sea is barely visible, the first salvo struck the mercenaries' rear-guard.

Shattered stones and flailing bodies scattered on impact, and knocked all else off their feet with the shockwave. The surviving Squires gathered their balance and wits, and ran in panic as the bombing continued.

Off the coast and into the narrow straits from the Northern Cross, the *Second Awakening*'s guns sent another volley into the Old Ruins. Although the target was far inland, it wasn't out of range of the cannons or Messer's eyes.

Aided by naval binoculars and his subalterns' calculations, the trajectories were relayed to the gunnery officers. With hairline precision worthy of the Magna Cartan Royal Navy, the guns sounded at his order.

"Fire!"

The quakes from the bombardment nearly pushed Seidon to his knees, but he recovered quickly and charged toward Tenshi. Taking advantage of the commotion, he fired his carbine at the nearest Squire, and picked up the mercenary's fallen rapier. Losing no momentum, he stabbed the blade deep into the gut of another Squire – setting off the man's rifle accidentally.

His impetus was suddenly blocked by Bale, who shoved him to the ground. He directed his long, heavy-ended Marine rifle at Seidon, and stilled any further aggression.

"I'm sorry..." Bale's restraint took its toll as warm tears streamed down his cheeks.

"Shoot him!" Skein commanded, frustrated by the overwhelming chaos around him. "He'll be easier to manage once we get out of here!" Seeing Bale's hesitation, he walked up to him and slapped him with the back of his hand. "Snap out of it, and shoot!"

With a burning welt on his cheek, Bale advertently struck his elbow against Skein's collar bone and pushed him back a few feet. He then faced him, easily towering over the other.

Skein grunted, more from surprise than hurt, and quickly lost his temper. "*Bastard!*"

He swung his sword at Bale, but struck only the barrel of his rifle. His next wild attempt missed completely and hit the ground, giving Bale the opportunity to stomp at the blade with his heel and wrenching it out of Skein's hand.

Skein backpedaled, cowering at the brute strength exerted by the one-armed man, but the fight wasn't over. At Ophelia's call, she tossed him her pistol, and he caught it swiftly just as Bale charged toward him.

He fired at point blank, and the force of the blast spun Bale around.

Bale staggered, seeing Seidon running to him. "...Send me back to the sea... where I belong."

In one final act, he turned to Skein and brought down the full might of his rifle's heavy end down on the mercenary's shoulder – splintering the rifle and breaking Skein's collar bone and thorax in a single blow. Both men fell away from each other: Bale landed flat on his back like a defeated titan, and Skein on his side. Unable to breathe, the ruffian asphyxiated to the bitter end.

Seidon slid to a halt beside Bale and hunched over him. He lifted his fallen friend by his shirt, his tears mixed with anguish. *"Don't die on me! Bale! Stay with me!"*

With the Squires retreating from the surgical bombardment, and nothing between her and Seidon, Ophelia reeked for revenge. Abandoning her flight, she prepped her crossbow at Seidon – the barbed-tip of the bolt gleaming with her intent.

"Die–"

Tenshi lunged at Ophelia, and grabbed hold of the crossbow. They struggled until the weapon triggered, sending the bolt straight through Ophelia's skull from under her jaw. All life gone from her body, she collapsed backward in a heap.

Shaken, but her spirit afire, Tenshi approached Seidon and embraced him from behind. She felt his pain, and he welcomed her warmth as he let go of his friend, mourning him for a second time.

XI. March of the Saints

XI. March of the Saints

Once the word of Magna Carta's retreat was spread, citizens took to the streets with divided sentiments. Too many celebrated the departure of the peacekeepers, while small groups who no longer felt safe or stood to lose business, protested at the risk of being targeted as royalists.

The retreat was done tactically, in steps, rather than a wild rush. Once the transition of the law offices were completed, and duties fell solely on the existing Templari troopers, the magistrate's core regiment marched out of Citadel Hall in perfect parade formation, and headed down the road toward Archway's Path where several frigates waited to receive them. The embassy was kept at full staff, and served as a temporary shelter for people wishing asylum and immigration to Magna Carta.

The Throne Guards and the Elites were all that were left, with the former guarding the appointed royalty while the *Sovereign* reached secure waters at Templari's coast, and the latter overseeing the prisoners of war alongside a contingent of royal Marines.

Sucre was tense with uncertainty as the transition passed, but he stayed at Vant's side as they left the suite toward their assigned work schedule for the hour. They were barely halfway across the street when the captain of an approaching squad of Elites ordered them to stop.

Vant glanced around him, concerned, but calm. "Is there a delay, captain?"

"The Queen wishes a word with you," the Elite squad leader said.

Vant instinctively turned around, and saw two more squads of Elites following Queen Dalena as she approached. She wielded her old Navy sword and pistol at her waist, a wise precaution in the twisted turn of events. Somewhere in the distance, a riot had started, and a bonfire spread; the noise of the violence echoed through the veins of the city.

"I was on my way to rejoin my League in the eastern slums," Vant said, as if nothing was amiss. "Sucre and I were hoping to restore the water mains."

"You were supposed to be confined to the suite," Dalena rebuked coldly.

"I needed to stretch out my legs," Vant countered coolly. "Logically, staying in any place too long warrants being made an easy target of opportunity."

Dalena grimaced. "I felt compelled to tell you personally, since Seidon would've done the same... Templari is now governed by the Church, and by unanimous election, they're forcing us out."

"That much we've noticed," Sucre said bitterly.

"We're hoping they will continue to respect the details of the treaty, and in the fair treatment of war prisoners."

"You sound doubtful," Vant noted.

"I won't hide the fact that you and your men will be left defenseless once we leave. It will be up to the resident authorities, and ultimately the heads of the pontificate, that will decide what to do with you."

Vant looked away for a moment, earnestly feeling trapped. "There's no debate, my Queen, they *will* order our immediate executions once the last royal soldier is gone. If there's any way you can provide us with weapons and provisions..." He stopped, realizing the futility of asking. "Well, we've survived one assault with bare knuckles and construction tools, there's no reason we can't survive another."

"Our diplomats will continue to fight for you, if it's the least of what we can do."

"Then send your finest," Vant said, then bowed.

Dalena felt conflicted. No matter who he was, she couldn't send him blindly to his doom, regardless of the repercussions.

"Your Highness," the Elite captain said, "your flagship is waiting to receive you."

She nodded gravely, then suddenly felt her neck tingle with caution. The Elites almost immediately sensed the danger, and encircled her loosely, while Vant and Sucre kept close to the soldiers assigned to their keeping.

All around them, marching in perfect symmetry from the streets and alleys, black-clad Insidians surrounded them. Their focus was on the two unarmed prisoners, but they were wary of the Elites that protected them and the Queen. All kept their gloved hands on the hilts of their obsidian weapons, but none dared launch himself before the order was given.

Fencing everyone closer to each other, the Insidians halted in unison and waited on the command from Poem – the last person on Terra Mia Dalena expected to lead these cold-bred assassins. His coat flaps wavering like a brewing storm, he strode alone from the sea of black soldiers and ventured closer to them.

"Poem...?" Dalena ushered between her lips, shocked.

His haunted eyes seemed to look directly at her as he approached steadily like a predator, but in truth his gaze was past her shoulder to Vant.

Even as Sucre tensed, Vant knew this had to happen, yet he didn't expect it so quickly. He studied the enemy formations, formulating strategies, and paused when he saw Poem – with a brooding, yet driven look in his eyes. The man was gunning for his jugular, and the enmity reeked from Poem like a tangible mesh.

Vant remembered the few words Poem had said to him at the end of the Battle of Guard, when he said that he'd never forgive him.

"Poem, what's the meaning of this? What's wrong with you?" Dalena demanded, but Poem was deaf and blind to her presence and the Elites that protected her.

They had fought and bled together, but Dalena no longer recognized the man who had earned her friendship. She stood her ground between him and Vant without fear.

"This has nothing to do with you," Poem seethed darkly.

Poem lifted his arms slightly from his sides, and his two curved daggers slipped from the wide sleeves onto his firm grips. The Elites immediately armed themselves, bringing up their rifles to bear, but they weren't fast enough for Poem. He struck like a panther, sliding past Dalena and her guards, with his gleaming daggers aimed directly for Vant.

The ex-general rushed forward in quick reflex the moment Poem moved, and instantly grabbed Dalena's sabre from behind her. He pulled it out of its metal sheath and stepped back with legs wide in defensive position – successfully blocking Poem's attack in the nick of time with a resounding clash and flash.

It all happened in a blink of an eye.

Driven toward one ultimate goal, Poem struck again harder and faster, but Vant countered each blow and dealt them in return. Although he kept his tactics completely defensive, Poem's mad rush strained against his impulse to deliver a quick mortal blow.

Sucre attempted to assist Vant by charging onto Poem's blind-side and providing himself as a second target. Poem rebuked him with a swing of his right dagger, and sprayed Sucre with a blast of ice shards. Sucre was thrown back, but quickly got up to resume his fight until the Elites held him back.

"Let go of me!" Sucre shouted as he struggled against the grips of the Elites. "Help him!" His furious pleas bounced off the soldiers, so he turned quickly to Dalena. "Your Highness, please aid him! Do something!"

"My Lady, this is out of our jurisdiction," the Elite captain warned. "Unless they openly threaten you, we cannot act."

"You will," Dalena cut back sharply. "On my order."

Around them, the Insidians stirred as loyal Strafers poured through their ranks with modified construction tools and demolition explosives. Given the initiative, they traded their rudimentary tools with the weapons of the fallen enemies and continued their charge.

Seeing this, Sucre took advantage of the Elites' confusion and escaped from them. "Strafers, protect the General!"

Ignoring the chaos that stirred, Poem threw his body back and swung wide, cutting across the air with his dagger. An arc of flame sprang out toward his target, but only managed to singe the hem of Vant's jacket as he backed away. He followed up with a physical attack, which Vant blocked evenly, and counter-attacked with a sharp head-butt to Poem's chin. As Poem reeled back, Vant thrust his sabre – cutting a gash along Poem's side.

With an infuriated snarl and at close quarters, Poem smacked his elbow across Vant's temple. Placing a bit of distance between them, he swung again with his dagger, only to have it knocked from his hand by the raw impact against Vant's borrowed sword.

Both dagger and sabre fell aside, and before they clattered on the ground, Vant lunged at Poem with his left fist. Poem caught his wrist in time and pulled his arm in, then viciously delivered the second dagger into the ex-general's forearm.

Even as the pain flared through his arm, Vant grinded his teeth and clutched Poem's exposed neck with his free hand. Locked in heated combat, they were unexpectedly hit by a blast from an improvised flaming bottle, and thrown to the ground. They crashed onto each other, but Poem reacted swiftly and pinned Vant onto his back.

Without remorse, Poem removed the dagger from Vant's forearm and pressed its edge against the man's neck.

"End it," Vant grunted. "Finish what your father and sister failed to do."

"There's no end more fitting..." Poem hissed. "But your death won't accomplish anything."

Vant was surprised, and uncertain what to perceive.

"Despite everything," Poem said, conflicted with his emotions, "I know you're the only one who can stop this war. You owe that much before I let you die."

The moment Poem eased the dagger's edge from Vant's neck, he was tackled aside by Sucre. Both men recovered instantly with a roll, but Poem once again overpowered Sucre with his abilities. He summoned the fallen dagger from the ground, and used both blades to create a barrier that shunned Sucre and a few other approaching Strafers off their feet.

Poem gave Vant one last glance before merging with the oncoming horde of Insidians.

Amazed by Poem's sorcerer-like powers and by his new shift of allegiance, Dalena knew what she had to do. As the shockwave from Poem's elemental magic passed through like a wind, she gave the order.

"Cover the prisoners of war, we'll take them back with us!"

The Elites complied without objection, expertly forming a vanguard around Vant, and providing a fire blanket for the Strafers' resistance. The Insidians, although high in numbers, shied away from the barrage and refrained from resuming a full offensive.

"Fall back and regroup!" Sucre ordered, grateful for the late arrival of the Elites. He gathered the Queen's sabre from the ground and rushed to Vant. Putting his arm around his shoulder, he lifted him to his feet.

Steadily, the Queen's Elites and the Strafers pulled back from the zone.

Falchier and his Iron Sabres watched the Insidians maintain their half-hearted assault on the Elite's rear-guard, the Magna Carta Queen and prisoners of war safely out of harm's way. A few foes were killed, as were a dozen or so assassins, but the cost in blood was worth the outcome.

Poem approached him, mind and body exhausted, and a bloody gash at his side.

"You've proven your worth," Falchier said. "You belong with the Faithful."

Poem humbly took the praise. "The irony that I wanted so fervently to avenge my family, only to end up saving Vant from his persecutors."

"There are few times that even the impious deserve mercy."

"Then Lord Mellka won't object to this last-minute deviation of his master stratagem?"

"It is by his design that we allow Magna Carta to escape with the prisoners," Falchier replied. "So our Lord Master can use it as propaganda against the King's ambitions."

Ingren stood in the empty conference chamber of the Administrate Parliament for one last time, a sad gaze on the international flags that still adorned the walls. Rowen and the Throne Guards waited loyally outside the doors, anxious to get under way before the fragile peace sheared at the seams.

"Your vision was resplendent, Your Majesty," Mellka said as he calmly strode in from an adjacent hall connecting the chamber to the offices, "but too far for your grasp."

With his hands clasped at the small of his back, Ingren turned to face the Grand Master. "What I offered here was international cooperation, mutual respect, but this chamber only serves the power-hungry, the amoral, and no one else."

"You address me as if I were your sworn enemy, but by all counts I hold no ill will toward you or your kingdom." Mellka stood face to face with Ingren, inadvertently sizing him up. "Yet I fear what you may become."

"What I may become, Lord Mellka, is a detriment to your religious crusade." Ingren tensed with anger, but restrained it firmly. "Believe your actions to be holy long enough, and soon you'll fantasize that you're a god amongst men."

"Again you misjudge me..." Mellka paced past Ingren, running his fingers lightly across the backs of the chairs around the conference table. "It's of little wonder of your resentment, since the Warrior-Queen of Magna Carta's past is the only Saint Knight whose bones don't lie in her sarcophagus amongst the other eleven."

"The Great Queen rests where she belongs."

Mellka scoffed. "It doesn't require clairvoyance to see where we stand on certain issues, but I warn you of the severe consequences should you take sides against the Church. King or no king, once you offend one man's Faith, he will act with his heart. The most dangerous tool at his disposal."

"I return the courtesy to you," Ingren said. "The Church made a grave mistake before, lest you repeat it again unto the ending of everything you hold sacred."

"For years many have boasted about your diplomatic prowess, but as all things, the edge becomes dull over time." Mellka tightened his jaw, no longer amused. "I believe your flagship is moored, Your Majesty."

"Your Holiness," Ingren bowed his head slightly, as did the Grand Master, and promptly left the room.

The doors thundered open, and as the royal escorts waited for their king, Titus and Mikaila strode in. Both wore formal attires of the Gabrialtar military in high standing, and while Titus had a wily smirk on his face, Mikaila maintained a focused, predatory gaze on Ingren.

Ingren didn't slow his pace, keeping a regal poise, and ignored Titus' false bow of deference. His eyes were fixed on Mikaila, who now wore the white and black uniform of a Lieutenant-Colonel, and whose icy blue eyes bore through him like a condor ready to swoop in for the kill.

They passed each other like two primal winds, and in that moment, Ingren knew who Traiza's killer was – the same woman who was mother to Vant's child.

He paused at the doorway, glanced back at Mikaila, and decided best to leave her crimes unpunished and unspoken for the time being.

The doors closed shut, and Titus bowed low before Grand Master Mellka, who remained at an aloof distance from the arrogant and eccentric Captain-General.

"I bring a message from Her Presidency in the Name's Reclaim, Grand Master," Titus announced cheerfully. "In light of recent events, she – on behalf of the people of Gabrialtar – congratulates you. You have our assurance and our confidence. She invites you and your papal delegation to be guests of honour on our island nation. My vessel, the Highborn, is at your disposal."

Mellka wasn't impressed nor flattered. "I've often noticed that religion is a convenience to politicians. You face a possible international embargo after your bold refusal to share your resources, and now you come to me with love and open arms."

"You have nothing to fear or doubt," Titus said. "Our invitation is sincere, and if the Church accepts, you will find that we share mutual goals."

Mellka still felt reserved, but was nudged by curiosity. "I will consider it, thank you, but relay to your government that

I will not set foot on partisan ground, but on the birthplace of one of the Holy Twelve."

"Wonderful," Titus said cheerfully, clapping his hands with excitement. "The arrangements will be made with the President's scrutiny."

XII. The Unsung

XII. The Unsung

On the seasonally calm waters of the Northern Cross, within reach of the mountain cavern that led to Tinkertown, the *Second Awakening* and *Journey's Prodigy* paid their final respects to a fallen friend.

Wrapped in the flag of Magna Carta, with the solemn hymn of the dearly departed sung by a choir of sailors, Bale's body was relinquished to the sea. Messer, his officers and crew, and Tenshi watched quietly as the body sunk beneath the surface of the gentle waves to join the watery grave of the first *Awakening* and those that died in its service.

With quiet tears, Tenshi moved closer to the balustrade and tossed a stemless white orchid, which landed softly on the water and marked the grave. She looked aside to Seidon, who stood alone on the stern-castle, his anguish bottled, but deeply hurting.

Messer stared at the dancing sparkles of sunlight on the waves. "Take care of them, Martial." Grim with the fresh loss and old wounds, he sighed and gave a curt nod to his subaltern.

Semmes turned to the crew. "Ready sails, stow the anchors!" On his command, the crew mobilized and soon the ship-of-the-line was alive again.

Tenshi was about to join Seidon on the bridge, but Messer held her back. "Leave him be for now."

Tenshi's heart gripped with sympathy for Seidon. "He's hurting."

"We all are..." Messer glanced up as the first topsails fluttered open to the wind. "He blames himself, you know this. When he left his mother to pursue a life at sea, she passed away. When he left the Awakening to find you, his father passed away. When he left to fight the war, he lost his ship and all his friends..." His chest tightened with sympathy. "And now Bale... whose soul was reclaimed. The weight's on my shoulders too."

"He won't lay down his burdens until he finds restitution," Tenshi said, certain of this. "I know how far he will go, and I'm afraid for him."

Seidon approached them, fiercely determined. "I'm taking my schooner back to Gabrialtar. I don't need your crew."

"That ship needs at least five strong hands to run the lines," Messer said. "They're loyal and able, and you will have them."

"Get them off my ship," Seidon cut back, sharper than he intended.

Messer kept firm. "You're gunning for Regento and the Cannon, but you can't do this alone. You have an obligation to the King, Seidon. You've accused Ambassador Daedlus, a member of his Royal Court, of despotism. By law, he can't be simply arrested and cast in iron, he must follow through a formal inquisition where you are the only witness."

Seidon tensed with frustration, but Tenshi's caring touch as she partly embraced him, eased his ire.

Messer pressed on, laying a fatherly hand on Seidon's tense shoulder. "Our friends died bravely for us. Don't spoil their sacrifice with blind hatred."

Seidon's eyes welled up with warm tears, even as he strained to hold them back, but he understood what Messer said. "Messer... they deserved better."

"They do."

Like father and son, they embraced tightly, and Tenshi was heartfelt by their union. She glanced over at the white flower hovering gracefully on the shimmering waves, and noted a drop of water tumbling from one of its pedals like a tear.

En route to Magna Carta, the *Sovereign*, accompanied by His Majesty's Royal Squadron, sailed stalwartly across the Vast Blue. The waves crashed fervently against its keel as it cut through the water, and it was felt hardily in the compartmentalized lower gun deck. Crowded with cannons, the gunnery crew, and their officers, Vant and his Strafers had little room to roam about.

The prisoners of war were stationed along the walls of the deck, sitting on the floor, and doing little to provoke the animosity of the Magna Cartan crew. Vant sat with his Strafers, knees tucked, and his arms rested on them, glad he wasn't in shackles.

Sucre approached unescorted, ducking his head from the low ceiling, and sat beside Vant.

"How many did we lose?" Vant asked, his tone grim.

"Five," Sucre replied. "Cullain, Thomas, Horatio, Miranda, and Squallor."

Vant nodded dolefully. "Their deaths had purpose," he assured, mostly to himself.

Sucre agreed silently, and after a moment, he lowered his voice. "General, I know you chastised me many times before on this matter, but I must persist because you taught me to capitalize on every advantage that comes our way. With proper timing, we have the numbers to commandeer this ship–"

"With what weapons?" Vant challenged sternly.

"With theirs," Sucre insisted passionately.

Vant scoffed angrily. "Engage a ship of trained and experienced royalist sailors with our wits and skin-bare knuckles? This is the King's flagship, the single most fortified vessel in the whole of Terra Mia. It will take a sacrifice in blood before it yields to enemy hands; blood that we no longer have the luxury to spare. Even if we succeed with this reckless charge, how do you expect to run the masts and maintain the rigging with front line soldiers?"

Sucre refrained from arguing the point, as he knew he was at fault. His shoulders slumped slightly, but was still adamant. "With hope, sir, since that's all we have left to fight with."

"Hope died when we lost the war," Vant said coldly.

The finality of Vant's words ended all room for debate, and Sucre relented dejectedly. He glanced at the other Strafers, who so badly needed gratification through honour in battle and duty in protecting their general, and kept quiet. Discipline required objective thinking without emotion, and he found himself desperate.

"...Trust me, Sucre," Vant said.

Slightly surprised by the warmth and sincerity in Vant's tone, Sucre nodded assuredly. "Always, sir. We all do."

A high-ranking officer entered, escorted by a pair of Elites, and the gunnery crew immediately gave way and saluted. He stopped in front of Vant and looked down at him with unforgiving eyes.

"I'm Captain Roderic," he declared gravely. "I'm here to escort you to the Vice-Admiral's quarters. His Majesty demands your presence…" He glared at Sucre. "In private."

Below the *Sovereign*'s stern-castle, the ship master's quarters was spacious and elegantly decorated with exotic carpets, ornate furniture, and tapestries. King Ingren was given the seat of honour, while Vice-Admiral DeCalmas and Ambassador Daedlus took the humbled seats at the side of the rectangular table fashioned from pine and accented with gold leafing. Dalena sat beside her husband, her posture reserved and queenly, but her thoughts were far from the discussion at the table.

"It's unclear how to fathom the Church's political agenda," DeCalmas noted, his veteran years showing in the white streaks in his hair and wrinkles around his eyes. "They've always kept their meddling behind closed doors, choosing sides at a whim, and all the while maintaining a pretense of neutrality. This recent debacle was too bold a move. Something else is astir."

"It's Grand Master Mellka, Vice-Admiral," Daedlus said in a scholarly manner, "he's the instigator of change, however torrent, but also a propagator of good will. You need only to study the finer points of the Holy Law to understand his motives… his intentions for the future." He gestured to Ingren respectfully. "As His Majesty is aware, Templari was at the brink of breaking in half. All of its infrastructure could've been rebuilt in a day, but the rot would still remain. It needed moral guidance, forced or otherwise, over democratic reform. It needed the rigidity of religion to apply the mortar between stones, over any selfless assistance our kingdom offered to rebuild the walls for them."

"Our kingdom did not merit their bile," DeCalmas said, "and now that we've harboured the Strafers, I could only imagine how easily they can turn our allies against us."

"Perhaps it was their intention all along," Ingren said grimly, glancing at Dalena with quiet concern. "A means of churning the storm already over our heads."

"An intriguing theory," Daedlus noted.

"A viciously underhanded tactic is what I would call it, Ambassador," the Vice-Admiral retorted.

Dalena pulled her chair back and stood up. "Excuse me, gentlemen." She turned to Ingren, and lowered her chin. "My King."

All three men stood properly, and with her servant trailing her heels, Dalena left the room. Ingren looked after her, wondering what bothered her, as he sat back down.

DeCalmas checked the time on his pocket watch. "I'm due to return to the bridge. I'll be excused as well." He bowed to Ingren, and nodded to Daedlus, then left.

"Some tea, Your Majesty?" Daedlus offered, still on his feet.

Ingren returned his attention to the table, silently wishing to be alone with Dalena. "Yes, thank you."

Daedlus sat down and waved to his personal assistant, a young man with a scruffy beard, who promptly brought the tray with porcelain cups and kettle. He poured the hot liquid in one of the cups, then wiped the rim with a velvet napkin. Setting it on its saucer, he served it to Ingren.

He prepared a cup for Daedlus, but this time omitted wiping the rim of the cup.

"If I may ask, milord," Daedlus said, "what will you do with our honoured prisoners?"

"...Like all else in this world, things change. Their fates still hang by a thread." He sipped from his cup.

"Hmm..." Daedlus drank a bit of his tea. "If I may be blunt, Your Majesty, it would be a great shame if their heads rolled under the guillotine. Mister Vant still exerts an abundance of charisma over his troops – those with him and those retired from soldiery. Is he more dangerous now than he ever was during the war?"

Ingren frowned at the ambassador's unorthodox observation, setting the cup down and pushing it away. "Those without heritage, so eager to seek purpose in their lives, yielding for someone to motivate them, and if there's a beacon that can incite and direct such fervency for the benefit of all or the delusions of one, then he is more a danger to himself."

Captain Roderic and a pair of Elites entered, escorting Rell Vant into the quarters. Daedlus stood up and greeted the former Guard general openly.

"So glad to finally meet you, sir." Daedlus shook hands with Vant. "I hope the accommodations aren't too rigid?"

"Sufficient," Vant said, instinctively suspicious of the man. "Honoured to be onboard as your guest." He glanced at Ingren, and bowed. "Your Highness."

Ingren nodded in greeting, though his demeanor was serious. "Leave us."

Without question, everyone except Vant bowed to their king in respect and parted. Once the doors closed, the two men faced each other alone – one sat and the other stood with his hands clasped at his back.

"Her name is Mikaila, the woman who bore your son," Ingren said coldly. "She was the one who arranged the assassination of the Sorcerer Siblings; the one who betrayed her own country to you. Her entire history is riddled with the work of a fully pledged hatchet man. From Chimaera, to Guard, and now serving Gabrialtar as a Lieutenant-Colonel of the Dragoons."

Vant exhaled deeply with mixed feelings in his heart. "You will find no woman more cunning than her, and with all her proven skills, I can think of no better mother to protect my progeny."

"Why is she in league with Titus?"

Vant shook his head. "At my best guess, Titus somehow sought her, and convinced her to join. After the war, pregnant and with no one to turn to, an island haven away from the chaotic old world was more than logical to raise a child."

"And rebuild her power base," Ingren added. "Another venue to wage war, to exercise her skills for yet another political agenda. I apologize, Mister Vant, but I can't see her being a worthy mother. What can she possibly teach your son about ethics, but how to remain steady with a rifle?"

Vant tightened his jaw, his unspoken fears spurred by what Ingren said. With certain reserve, he forced the topic aside. "...What will become of me and my men once we reach shore?"

"You will remain a prisoner in the Tower as per terms of your surrender, and I will give your men a choice to either leave on their own accord, or be forced into the working class."

Vant accepted it without argument.

Ingren tapped his fingers on the surface of the table, formulating strategies to an uncertain future. "You knew Titus. You were the one who instructed him in the art of warfare," Ingren said. "If the order is given to implement an embargo on Gabrialtar, are we prepared for their retaliation?"

"He's a Strafer by design," Vant said. "He chose to reveal the Highborn to dispel the speculation of its existence, but also to reveal the secret might at his disposal. It was a message intended for his future enemies and his potential allies, a subtle implementation of awe and fear... The man I knew, and the man he is now are two different people. I can derive what tactics he will use, but how and most importantly *why* he will use them is beyond me."

Ingren nodded gravely. "Thank you for your insight."

Inside Templari's basilica, amidst vaulted ceilings and patterned tiles of veined granite the colours of onyx, azure, and milky white, Poem paid his respects to Traiza. His crypt was at the center of a rotunda amongst the many antechambers inside the basilica, marked in gold inlays on a large black marble slab on the floor.

Aside from a few caretakers and journeymen, he was alone. He stared down at the gold writing, ushering a silent prayer to a fellow patriot. He paused and looked up at the sound of heavy footsteps, and saw Grand Master Mellka in the company of the basilica's abbot and Precept Cardinals Achrone and Libra.

They discussed an issue of churchly affairs until Mellka noticed Poem, and broke away from the group to join him.

Poem bent a knee and bowed low at his presence. "Grand Master."

Mellka accepted the salute with a nod, then glanced at Traiza's gravestone. "There are two types of men on this world: those that realize they have a choice, and those that don't."

Poem wondered at the words, but said nothing.

"I wanted to personally congratulate you on your victory. You made us proud."

Poem frowned. "Victory?"

"Over your demons, Poem," Mellka clarified. "Your nerves, your spirit, the matter that makes who you are – very few men overcome the walls they build for themselves. You carried out my orders, and kept yourself from delivering a killing blow on your greatest adversary."

"I'm comforted knowing his death is merely postponed."

Mellka agreed. "We've been invited by Gabrialtar's government, and I will be traveling aboard their sky vessel. We have a message to spread, more Faithful to call upon, and I want you to join me."

Poem bowed. "It will be my honour."

"And mine."

The Royal Squadron hung back on familiar waters while the flagship and its escorts sailed down the capital's harbour. Thousands of loyal citizens crowded the piers and rooftops, cheering and throwing confetti and flower pedals that rivaled the parades of Floria. The reconstruction of the city after the dastardly bombardment from the Sorcerer's Cannon saw significant progress after half a decade, and paved the way for modernization that rivaled even the City of Guard. The cultural and political differences between Magna Carta and Templari, particularly when it came to trust and cohesion, was the principal reason for Templari's constant delays in its restoration despite the similarities in battle scars and aging infrastructures.

Standing on the *Sovereign*'s quarter deck and watching the celebration, Ingren finally felt at ease. He squeezed Dalena's hand, and kissed her lightly near the lips. "For a short while, we can leave our burdens behind."

"You make it sound so easy," Dalena said, her eyes on the soaring white spires of the castle, and the impressive array of scaffolding around the new towers.

"You've been holding back since we left Templari, Julia," Ingren said as he gently forced her to face him. "Tell me what's bothering you."

"It's Poem. He never struck me as someone who gives his allegiance freely."

"He must have good reason, or at least a misguided one." Ingren brought Dalena closer to him. "The world's changed, no one can be trusted, but we have each other and that's all that matters right now."

Their lips inched closer as the *Sovereign* slowed down and berthed, now close enough for the colourful ribbons and pedals to land on the deck of the ship. They kissed, feeling the warmth of their affection, until Vice-Admiral DeCalmas and Captain Roderic approached.

"We're ready to disembark, Your Majesties," DeCalmas announced after clearing of his throat.

Breaking away with reluctance, Ingren turned to the officers. "Thank you, Vice-Admiral. It's good to be home."

In traditional ceremony, the crew formed ranks to allow the Elites and the Throne Guards to march with the King and Queen within their formation. They paused at the top of the plank for a splendid view of the capital and its people. Doves were released, and the flock scattered to the sky with graceful white wings.

Ingren smiled, hooking Dalena's arm under his, and together they disembarked. The moment he stepped off the plank, the world blurred and spun. He lost his breath, and all his muscles slackened. He collapsed onto the cobbled road, his coat flaps drifting, and the crowd's cheers turned to gasps of shock.

Dalena threw herself beside him and lifted him in her arms, crying out to him in desperation as every soldier in the kingdom surrounded them....

XIII. In Hatred's Company

XIII. In Hatred's Company

The *Highborn* cast its shadow across Empyrean City as it glided toward Gabrialtar's political seat, Name's Reclaim. It passed between the foreboding barbicans, dozens of stories in height, that surrounded the massive coliseum, and through the protective fleet of sky galleons that hovered around it.

It sailed gracefully to the landing station, a wide veranda with overflowing white stairs flanked by two large angelic statues of solid iron with hands reaching for the sky, and came to a halt beside it. Magnetized anchors from its keel at the bow and stern of the ship were released, and instantly latched onto the outstretched hands of the angelic statues. With its berth secured onto the overhang, the side hatch and ramp lowered onto place.

Deck crews and mariners immediately set to work.

"Such tall towers they've built for themselves," Mellka noted with slight distaste at the haughtiness exerted by the architecture and innovation.

Standing beside his master on the forecastle, Poem quietly agreed with the assessment, though being his first visit to the island nation, he was quietly awed by its magnificence. The old adventurous sensation reminded him of his fellowship with Seidon, and allowed himself a moment to wonder how he and Tenshi were doing. He imagined they would be as surprised and disappointed in him as Dalena was.

Titus approached, all too gleefully. "Ah, Grand Master," he eyed Poem with a smirk, "and guests... we're ready to disembark."

Mellka nodded and waved his arm for Titus to lead the way. "With all due haste."

Accompanied by two Honour Guards and Poem, Mellka followed Titus to the ramp and onto the crimson carpet that trailed across the veranda and up the stairs toward one of the many colonnaded entrances to the coliseum. Dragoons and senate officials formed parade ranks on both sides of the walkway, each saluting Titus and Mellka as they passed them.

Mellka stared at the soldiers and nobles, and kept aloof of the ceremony. "Is it safe to assume that Her Presidency will drop these diversions and propose an open alliance?"

Titus kept his smile wide. "Gabrialtar is only interested in preserving its independence, not in expansion or seclusion. If the Church protects us, then in turn we will help the Church should it wishes to... exert its influence on a larger audience."

Mellka suspected as much. "The Church will keep an open mind."

"All in good time, Your Excellency," Titus said as they walked up the flight of stairs. "But first, you will be treated to Gabrialtar's finest opera in the opulent space of the congress chamber itself."

Poem hung back as Mellka, Titus, and their escorts walked past the massive columns into the Name's Reclaim's inner halls. He looked back, and took in the sight of the sky and cityscape around him, then instinctively bore his eyes on a familiar face in the scattered crowd of officers following the reception.

It was Mikaila, unmistakably, and he immediately strode to intercept her as she climbed to the top of the stairs. He grabbed her arm and pulled her away from sight, into the privacy of the column's shadow.

"I remember you," Poem hissed icily. "You betrayed one absolutism for another."

Mikaila was undaunted by Poem's threatening tone nor the troubled look in his eyes. It didn't take her long to recognize him. "The Siblings deserved their fates. I think I did you, and many others, a favour which I'm owed."

"Favour?" Poem strained to keep himself from strangling her lean neck with his bare hands. "You turned your gun on me, my friends..." Poem seized her by the collar and pushed her hard against the column. His seethed his next words through his teeth. "*And my sister.*"

Mikaila didn't resist, and kept her fear in check. "Unlike you, I don't regret anything."

Just as Poem was about to act on his impulse, he heard a child calling out to her mother, and Mikaila broke away from Poem's grip to bend low on her knees and hug her son, Marcus.

Poem stepped back, shocked. He stared at Mikaila and back at the child, and felt conflicted. The child's resemblance to Vant was uncanny, yet his eyes belonged to Mikaila. This much was true as they both looked at him, waiting on his next move.

Unable to carry through his threat, Poem turned and left.

At the core of the Name's Reclaim, the voices of an epic opera carried acoustically throughout the coliseum, decorated in wine-red carpeting, with pillars and podiums carved out of aged oak, and seats arranged in ascending rows of an ancient amphitheater. Finely dressed, the operatic duo standing at the brightly lit center of the main floor alongside the accompanying orchestra gave their finest performance for an esteemed audience of politicians, industrialists, and nobles. High in the presidential booth, Mellka sat in the company of President Gehenna, her stoic Vice-President, and Captain-General Titus.

Mellka was no stranger to music, and was delighted, but his devotion to his duties left little time to meander in the arts. Time was precious, life was short, and there was much to do. To his left, the stately matriarch in her high-collared gown listened patiently, and Mellka suspected this pleasantry wasn't entirely her idea. To his right, as odd a character he was, Titus was openly enamored by the music. Deeply moved by the sounds, the Captain-General quietly followed the words of the song and stirred his hands in perfect synchronization with the maestro.

Sensing Mellka's stare, Titus smiled. "Do you hear the richness of the voices bouncing off the high ceiling, Grand Master? Beautiful... but not quite up to the glorious acoustics of the world-renowned opera halls of Freya."

"I take it you're a usual visitor to the City of the Arts?"

"As often as my charge allows."

A Gabrialtar officer moved past the two Honour Guards flanking the curtained entrance, and approached. He bowed respectfully to the President and the Grand Master, then whispered to Titus' ear, who acknowledged the report.

"If you'll excuse me," Titus stood up, bowed low, and followed the officer out of the booth.

At the midpoint of one of the many hallways of the Name's Reclaim was the marble statue of a founding head of state, surrounded by the same red carpeting and exquisite oak walls as the congress chamber. On his way toward it, Titus encountered Regento as he emerged from behind the statue, carrying with him an object wrapped in tanned leather.

Titus smirked. "My good Marquis, of what do I owe the pleasance of your visit?"

"Business," Regento said simply.

"Then let us skip the formalities." Without looking at the officer who accompanied him, Titus waved the man away.

Once they were in private, Regento presented the leather-bound object. "What you asked for," he uncovered the Ancestral, its blade sheathed. "It's called the Ancestral, heirloom of the Harbrid clan, and the only one of its kind."

Mesmerized, Titus gingerly took the sword in both hands and opened the scabbard slightly to peer at its crystal blade. "I've tried mechanizing the shaping and sharpening techniques, but the material never held cohesion. The crystallized blood of the drakes, rare an ore as can be found, demands the patience and conviction of human hands, not pistons and hydraulics." Seeing his reflection on the Ancestral, he smiled greedily. "To simply admire this masterpiece does no justice."

Regento felt apprehensive with the sword in Titus' possession, but he craved for greater things. "This bargain was secured with a great loss of life from my Squires, and not to mention the bad blood between its owner and myself."

Titus nodded, taking considerable effort to pry his eyes away from his prize. "Nothing was done in vain, Marquis. By tomorrow morning you will have the favour of the Presidency and a place within the order of nobles. Land and title that is owed, are yours."

* * *

Messer, Seidon, and Tenshi were allowed into the King's chamber by the steadfast guards, and found Queen Dalena sitting by the window alone in the living room. She was distraught, her eyes red with drawn tears, and refused the assistance of her maidens with her silence.

In the next room, doctors and servants crowded around Ingren, who laid deathly still on his royal bed, looking pale and withered, but still drew breaths. Rowen stood vigil at the doorway, his arms crossed, and his jaw set tight with repressed disappointment at himself.

Messer bent his knee to Dalena in respect, then stood and strode over to the bedroom. The servants gave him the way, but the doctors continued to contemplate without relent. Seeing Ingren so weak and inanimate, Messer's gut wrenched with shame. He wanted to seek revenge, to find resolution, but could do nothing but stay out of the way of the medical staff. He joined the grim officers that stood at the corner of the room, DeCalmas and many others amongst them.

Seidon grimaced as he felt the hopelessness in the air, and glanced away from the bedroom. "What happened?"

Dalena nearly lost her rigid composure as she finally realized Tenshi and Seidon were there. It took her a moment to gather her voice. "...He... just collapsed..." She lowered her chin with the weight of her anguish. "The doctors think he was poisoned... they don't know what to do."

She broke down in tears, but for the sake of maintaining a queenly composure she tried desperately to hold them back, pressing her fingers to her forehead. Tenshi, gripped by her plight, walked over to her, and comforted the Queen with a sympathetic embrace.

"You're not alone," Tenshi said softly.

Dalena accepted the warmth of the words, something she needed to reinforce her faltering strength. "I know he's strong, he will see this through... as will I."

Seidon approached Dalena, and knelt before her. "Julia, who's to blame? Has anyone come forward?"

Dalena nodded, her stern spirit resurfacing. "I commissioned a formal investigation, and entrusted Rowen with the task. He excluded agents from the Church and any rogue elements from Chimaera. He believes the King was attacked during the voyage home." She paused at the precariousness of the situation. "No one wants to consider even the notion that someone within the royal circle could've committed the crime, and are staunch on blaming the obvious enemies. Rell Vant and his men have been separated and locked up in the Tower dungeons, all of them pending a severe call of retribution by partisans within the court."

Seidon turned serious. "They were prisoners onboard your ship, how could they have had access to the King?"

"...The King met with Vant in private for a short time. Anything could've happened, and Admiral DeCalmas is fiercely committed to force an expedient trial."

"And execution," Tenshi added sourly.

"Vant has nothing to do with this," Seidon said with resolve. "It gains him no foothold, no change of tide. This was an underhanded tactic meant to weaken the King's position... and yours." Seidon lowered his voice, making sure no one else heard him. "I've reason to believe Ambassador Daedlus is in league with the Squires of Debonair. These mercenaries have operated all over the world, and Regento, my worthless cousin, is the Marquis. He's conducting operations from

Gabrialtar, and I don't believe there's any coincidence with the growing hostility between that nation and yours."

Dalena was intrigued, yet it was something she had already realized. "I can't trust the military brass, nor the Royal Court or the diplomatic corps. Many royalists still see me as unfit to wear a crown due to my lineage, and I'm finding myself powerless to act due to Daedlus' influence with the aristocracy. He's considered an industrious patriot, and there's very little to discredit his reputation."

"You're still the Queen," Tenshi said, "and you have your followers. Your orders carry weight regardless of who opposes you."

Dalena needed to hear that to enforce her conviction, though her thoughts were on something else. She leaned closer to Seidon. "There's one other thing, Seidon, something you should be aware of before the pandemonium unfolds. Poem resurfaced in Templari during the evacuation; he was wearing the colours of an Insidian, and bore the sacred cross of the Faithful on his sleeve. He had no other aim but to kill Vant, and he almost succeeded. He was a different man, so much so that I couldn't recognize him as an ally."

The news of his old friend was unexpected, and disturbing. There was much at stake, and Seidon dared only to cross the threshold before him, rather than to fathom Poem's conflicted loyalties. Seidon glanced at Tenshi, then back to Dalena. "We'll stay here by your side for as long as you need us, my Queen."

Daedlus strode along the capital's marina, enjoying the brisk waft of wind from the ocean waves. Ships of various classes and tonnage sailed to and fro, their masts cluttering the horizon. Although the kingdom's capital still reeled from Ingren's untimely collapse earlier, life in the white-walled city resumed at the speed of commerce.

He stopped by an observation point, rimmed by a decorative handrail, and took in the view.

Another man joined him, the simple servant who had prepared the tea for the King onboard the *Sovereign*. With short brown hair and eyes, and not much taller than the average citizen, the man could easily blend in any crowd and instantly lose his pursuers.

Daedlus kept his eyes abroad. "He will live?"

"As you stipulated, yes. Your beloved King will have no voice nor willpower to act until the housekeeping's done."

"I admit," Daedlus thought aloud, "I had my doubts when the Marquis recommended you, but seeing the fruits of your trade, I offer instead my compliments."

The man nodded curtly. "The craft of the poisoner are discriminate, yet honed by time and practice."

"Well earned, Mister Nalth." Daedlus produced a hefty satchel from inside his jacket, and handed it to the man. "The Squires have set up a temporary safe house near the merchant district's loading dock, it's best if you stay there for the night, then make effort to leave the kingdom as soon as humanly possible."

Nalth snuck the bounty inside his coat, and smirked. "I'll simply follow the rose."

Once again strangers, both men parted ways.

XIV. Subversions

XIV. Subversions

Poem paced patiently outside the closed doors of the congress chamber, trailing the beautiful red carpet that decorated the hallway. To his right, master paintings hung on intricate gold frames following the slight curve of the wall. To his left, the wall was opened at intervals, providing a majestic view of Empyrean City, and he stopped to gaze as a sky galleon flew by like an avian guard on a watchtower.

With time and exploration of the buildings and interwoven roads, he began to notice oddities which had escaped him before. There were scarcely any civilians or usual naval traffic, particularly in the bazaar and the port of Sewell's Abide. Scaffolding covered most of the buildings, not designed for renovation, but to provide elevation for myriads of skilled workers in reinforcing doors, windows, and roofs.

Looking closer with an eagle's eye, he spotted various groups of soldiers marching in formation as they patrolled the streets. Guard posts and pillboxes were dotted throughout the city, either implemented to protect the Name's Reclaim or repel an invasion from the sea.

Gabrialtar was mobilizing, and Poem felt a disturbingly familiar chill run down his spine.

The doors opened and Mellka stepped out with his Honour Guards trailing a few steps behind. Poem bowed as he approached, then followed the Grand Master as he continued walking down the hall.

"You seem distressed, Grand Master."

"None at all," Mellka said. "My ears are tired of the babble from the Presidency and her supporters. They put their cultural and economic independence on a high pedestal, flaunting every justification for protecting what is theirs."

"Then what does the Church have to offer that they don't already have?"

"Aside from religious zeal?" Mellka mocked. "Gehenna and her caucus want the blessings of the Church, for us to be their shield for any threat to their realm... and any future ambition. In short, they want us to be their alibi."

Poem grimaced. "If I may ask, what answer did you give them?"

"I opted for a recess. I will not repeat the mistakes the last few grand masters and cardinals have made, but nor will I shun their hand in friendship aside. I will prepare a decent speech to warm their hearts, and open a road for us to return to matters of our own keeping."

Poem glanced outside as the intervals passed, seeing the fleet of sky galleons amass. "There will be a point where no one can be spared of what's to happen next."

The royal warden unlocked the thick, iron door with a hard twist of the cell key, and wrenched it open with a heavy squeal of the hinges. It felt to Seidon like the opening of a heavy gate to a dungeon where a mythical creature resided, but as he stepped inside the rounded room, there was no monster.

Although the tight confines was furnished with a bed, small desk, and chair, Rell Vant chose to sit on the floor rug beneath the archer's window – a thin, vertical slit that provided the clue that the prison was high up in one of the oldest spires of the castle. A sliver of dusty light pierced through, gently warming the old stonework.

Seidon was weaponless, as per rules of visiting the prisoner, and the warden closed the door behind him. He approached the center of the room, and glanced around. "Not quite where you hoped to be when you started on this journey."

Although pensive, Vant smiled faintly, and finally looked at his visitor. "I'm grateful, actually." He gestured to the walls around him. "This particular cell had been home to some of the greatest figures in our history: from the traitorous sister of the Absent King in the time of the Sorcerers; to the Chastised General during the age when this kingdom was split in three... and even my great-grandfather, Alrosa Vant, who defied the Royal Court for a matter of honour when one of the king's nobles insulted him."

Seidon was impressed. "A haven for the scandalous."

Being in the presence of the man who ruined his dreams, and saved him from the hangman's noose, Vant was divided between the shadow of enmity and unfaltering respect. "...I hear Ingren's in a deep coma."

Seidon nodded grimly.

"I can vouch for my men's innocence. Neither one have the skills nor access to the poison that was used."

"I don't believe you were responsible either," Seidon said flatly. "And I will fight to clear your name of this incidence, that I swear."

Vant was taken aback. "I don't deserve your defense, Harbrid, just make sure the lawmakers relieve my soldiers of this conspiracy within their own ranks."

"Then you arrived at the same conclusion I have..." Seidon lowered his tone. "There are traitors in the Royal Court."

Vant nodded. "Consider them purists: The orthodox royalists who will bend tradition for no one, and who'd rather kneel to an empty throne than a crowned pretender. Blood by lineage or blood spilled is their creed."

"The Queen, she's in danger isn't she?" Seidon paced anxiously at the realization. "Will these bastards go that far?"

"To assassinate her? No. They'll risk all or nothing to discredit her, and force her to relinquish. Shame is easily afforded, and there is no measure of the brutality she will face." Vant stood up and approached Seidon. "But in all this, there are men who stand to gain advantage, either as a distraction or something much shrewder."

"The Squires of Debonair," Seidon revealed. "They've been smuggling pieces of the Sorcerer Cannon that was destroyed, and another set that were found at Tinkertown. Although we disrupted the operation at the hub, we still don't know how far the caravan had reached."

Vant paused at the mention of the Cannon. "...Gabrialtar. They must be the high bidder."

"And if this embargo goes along, they might be tempted to fend their borders with extreme impiety."

"A war worse than the last."

"All the more reason to find the culprit who poisoned the King; we need to expose the guilty and prepare for the inevitable." Seidon knocked on the cell door in preparation to leave. "I know you still have eyes and ears in the corners of this world that somehow never escape you. I hope I can depend on you to help me."

The warden opened the door, and just as Seidon was about to step out, Vant grabbed his arm. "Tell Her Majesty, that although her and I will never see eye to eye, I will support her."

Seidon nodded. "We'll speak later, Vant."

"Harbrid."

The warden closed the door shut and locked it firmly, leaving Vant to contemplate on the bits of knowledge he gathered. He turned to the window, deep in thought, and looked out at the world and the many possible futures that it held.

Alone in the King's chamber, Dalena sat on a velvet-padded chair beside her bed-ridden husband, quiet and vigilant. She caressed his hand warmly while she pondered on the wisdom she needed for her next task.

"I need you..." she whispered to him, "though you'd always remind me of my strength, that I'm your pillar... maybe we're truthfully each other's half." She leaned over to him and kissed his hand. "Wake for me, my King, please."

Ingren remained cold and inanimate, with only the subtle heaving of his chest to show he was still alive. Dalena tensed with sorrow, but at the sound of approaching footsteps and the rattle of armour, she cleared away her anguish and hid any weakness from the two Throne Guards that strode in.

They bowed and stood at either side of the doorway as an old baron, Chancellor of the Royal Court, Precidious, stepped forward to offer his respect.

"Queen Dalena, the court seeks an audience," the old man announced.

Dalena nodded as she softly laid Ingren's hand on the bed. She stood up regally and full of power. "Then it's time to quench the restless."

Dukes and marchionesses, magnates and diplomats, all nobles were assembled in the Throne Room. They spoke amongst themselves, wary of their title and lineage, and each shared the anxiety created by recent events.

Ambassador Daedlus was amongst them, listening patiently to the political babble while they all waited for the Queen. Some spoke of the tension between regions, others of declining resources, and some defended the wants and needs of local districts. All of it was boring, and all of it was necessary.

The room quieted as the old Chancellor arrived, and formally summoned the court to session.

"Her Majesty, Queen Dalena," Precidious declared.

Everyone in the room bowed as the Queen approached the throne. She turned to face the nobles, but did not sit. She bore an air of graveness that could not be contested.

"As of this hour, in light of the subversions against my husband, all legislative power has been transferred to me." Dalena gave the court a moment to digest the declaration, her eyes sparing them no leniency. "While an investigation into this crime continues, the King's last orders were clear. He intended to enforce an embargo on the island of Gabrialtar, and to that end I've authorized the Admiralty to execute a joint operation with Guard and Freya to form a multi-national task force. Admirals DeCalmas and Messer have been dispatched to oversee the operation."

The Chancellor seemed slightly disappointed. "It would have been best, Your Majesty, if you consulted with this court before sending out the Fleet."

Dalena glared at the old man. "No need to lecture me on the expenses and bureaucratic minutia that this court so vainly enjoys. The orders were given before the King fell ill, and I'm making certain it's done in proper."

One of the elder magnates brought her conviction to question. "Do we have any leads on the agent who poisoned our beloved King, Your Majesty?"

"None that are definitive for immediate action," she said bluntly, a hint of dark thoughts in her tone. "An attack on our King is the same as an attack on Magna Carta, and I intend to respond with full authority once those responsible are revealed in plain sight."

"There's no certainty who our enemies are," Daedlus warned. "It would be costly if we should confuse the prerogative of preemptive action against an unwitting government with personal revenge."

Dalena wasn't amused by the diplomat's patronizing tone. "I know my priorities, Ambassador Daedlus, and I suggest you know your place."

"But I do, Your Highness," Daedlus challenged openly, inciting some startled reactions from the other court members. "You're empowered by circumstance, not by any measure of merit. With all due sincerity and deepest respect, your experience lies commanding ships-of-the-line, not kingdoms. The political battlefield is far more volatile than you're prepared for."

Dalena grimaced, heeding Seidon's warning of the man. "You speak to me as if we're equals. Your respect is wanting."

"We're not equals," Daedlus implied without reserve, unintimidated. "Despite your crown, you are not of royal blood, whereas I am." He spread his arms around to his ilk. "As are the rest of this court."

The air suddenly chilled as Dalena stepped down and walked toward the arrogant ambassador as if ready to cut through him with her sword. Without warning, she backhanded him across the cheek. The Throne Guards stirred. "You insult me, and you dare discredit me now that our King is absent. I see before me an opportunist coward, speaking treason."

The court waited anxiously for Daedlus' riposte, and he surprised them as he humbly bent low – the welt on his cheek turning deep red.

"Everyone here knows that I am fiercely loyal to the throne, as long as true blood runs there." His notoriety for being staunch surfaced. "You speak of treason, my Queen, but I am simply protecting this kingdom from rash and costly actions done by an inexperienced monarch. I denounce your decision to ensue an embargo on Gabrialtar, as it will inevitably lead to war. You're using the King's ailment as a pretext to yet another chapter of violence."

Before Dalena could counter the political maneuvering, other voices from the court rose up in courage and seconded the ambassador's statement.

"I am forced to agree with the Ambassador, Your Highness," one of the marchionesses said. "We cannot afford another war."

Yet another noble added, "If Gabrialtar refuses to share its resources, even in this crisis, we should not force them or punish them. They're protecting what is theirs, and will do so with arms."

One by one the nobles joined the ruckus of dissent as it spread through the Royal Court, and Dalena stared at them in dismay while the Chancellor feebly attempted to reestablish order. He shouted for an indefinite recess, but no one listened.

She returned her cold gaze on Daedlus, who now seemed pompous in his position. She neared him, and whispered close to his ear. "This is unforgivable."

Daedlus met her icy tone and returned the softly spoken threat. "Your influence has diminished."

In startling realization, Dalena knew he was right. Even if she threw him to the gallows, the rest of the court will denounce her, and she will lose everything. With the masts of order crumbling around her, she promptly turned and left the room, leaving Daedlus proudly gloating in the aristocratic maelstrom.

At the capital's naval yard, a full squadron of modernized ship-of-the-lines and frigates, clad with layers of iron plates, retro-reef engines, and turrets, steadily left their moors toward open water, following the newly-appointed flagship, *Integrum*, commandeered by DeCalmas – his standards fluttering with favourable winds. The *Second Awakening*, with Admiral Messer at its helm, waited for final embarkations while the rear-guard ships attached to his mandate strutted in formation, their sails and royal flags aimed toward the Vast Blue, and ultimately to the Southern Cross.

On one of the piers that served the *Second Awakening*, Seidon watched the amazing military aggregation with mixed dread and anticipation. With the wind as it was, his Captain's coat, which once belonged to his father, wavered and swayed, and revealed the readied arms at his doubled belt.

Tenshi approached him, and hugged him warmly from behind. She rested her cheek on his shoulder, and watched as Messer's skilled sailors took to the masts. "I want to come with you."

"Julia needs you..." Seidon paused as he thought of the grim days ahead both here and abroad. "You're the only one I trust to finish things here."

Tenshi nodded sadly. "Just remember, he's still your family."

"He's nothing," Seidon said venomously. He then sighed, and lowered his chin. "I got to do this, Tenshi, for whatever may come of it. He owes me more than what he took from me." Seeing that the *Second Awakening* was ready to depart, he turned to Tenshi and held her close. "When all else fails, when need drives to desperation, trust Vant."

They kissed fiercely, then parted for the first time in their lives. She watched him hurry toward the ship as it pushed away from its berth, and jumped safely on the boarding ramp. The ship's sails opened wide, and with great majesty, it maneuvered toward the east.

Behind the closed doors of the Gabrialtar congress chamber, Mellka listened as Gehenna attempted her last reprieve to earn the Church's allegiance. Her loyal ADC, Titus, stood nearby and silent, a glimmer of something deadly in his eyes.

The gracefully tall President paced around Mellka with a stately demeanor, fashioning her hands to emphasize her words. "Our autonomy has been retaken. We're thriving and flourishing beyond the measure of what once was in the time of monarchs. We've amassed a larger and stronger military arm than Guard and Templari in their prime; research, development, new technologies and philosophies have sprung forth, all in the pursuit of greatness."

Mellka nodded simply out of gesture, not taken by the repeated cliches of self-grandeur. "Your Aide-de-Camp here has more than lobbied for this nation of yours, and I admit, his boasting was for good reason. From what I've seen, Madam President, I fully understand the need to protect your investments. You have set a precedence for other self-governing nations to behold, and I am most proud for your accomplishments."

"Still you would not support me?"

"Unlike my peers of history past, I intend to enforce the original rule of neutrality in all matters outside the purview of the Order."

Gehenna was not deflected by the brute decision and pressed on. "It was made clear at the conference in Templari that the world is hungry for resources that we have in plenty, and that if we do not give up this treasure that has defined our independence, they will lay siege on our borders and force us to submit." She stepped closer to Mellka, barely a hand's reach away from him. "Without the Church to protect us, we will be coerced into utilizing military science to save our sovereignty. We will enter war because you would have denied us."

"Every man carries his arms by his own accord," Mellka replied with an intended sting toward her gender.

He turned away from the center-stage toward the doors, leaving Gehenna lingering with resentment. She glared at

Titus, then stormed away toward an opposite exit that led to her office. Her aides and Vice-President promptly followed her.

Titus, on the other hand, calmly followed the Grand Master. "There is another thing Her Presidency failed to mention, that perhaps you'd still care to listen before you retreat to your idiosyncrasies."

Just as he reached to open the grandiose doors akin to the ones in the Cathedral, Mellka stopped and glanced at the pompous Captain-General. "For a moment there, it sounded like an overture to a thinly veiled threat."

Titus killed a grin before it touched his lips. "You're fully aware of our advanced technique of refining retro-reef for better distribution and economical solutions that has benefitted us thus far. We are also able to militarize it." Certain he now received Mellka's complete attention, he continued, "We have access to ballistic weapons of mass destruction based on the Sorcerer Cannon design, and we have the capability of delivering these missiles anywhere on the mainland. No ocean and no mountain will slow us down."

Mellka was stunned, and he heard his heart thumping against his chest within the dreaded silence that followed Titus' revelation. Despite his fear, his Faith kept him from running. "Infernal machines and infernal desires, it all leads to one end – a dark and tumultuous end. Haven't you learned the lesson from your former master?"

"I've learned much from the infamy of General Strafe, but he's of no consequence in this discussion. What you should be concerned with is to reconsider your stance with this nation and yours."

"You cannot forge this coalition with force and hope it will last in goodwill."

"I entirely agree, Grand Master," Titus said. "I'll have one of my ships prepared to transport you back to Templari once you're ready to depart. I'm sure you'd want to stay out of harm's way once the sanction fleet arrives on our doorstep."

With that, Titus left, and Mellka was alone in the chamber with the weight of Terra Mia on his shoulders.

XV. The Chorus of War

XV. The Chorus of War

The merchant district of Magna Carta's sprawling capital was a blend of various cultures from all over the world. Surrounded by a busy marina on one side, the market squares, shops, and storehouses, were all pocketed with centuries-old arcades, and punctuated at its borders by minarets adorning navy flags and royal standards.

Hundreds of people lived and worked in the district, some never going far from the docks and scantily ever seeing the royal castle except from afar. Although reminiscent of the bazaar in Gabrialtar, and even the port town of Coastal Sky, the place held its own exoticism and magic.

Tenshi felt it beneath her skin as she traversed the main arcade alongside Rowen, yet the brooding notion of the Queen's plight and of Seidon's departure watered down the excitement. She stayed focused and resorted to her instincts to find the snake that bit Ingren, but with little information to rely on, the poisoner might be walking amongst the crowd and neither her nor Rowen would know.

"Are you sure the logs weren't falsified?" Tenshi asked.

"The Sovereign's crew manifest was verified by Vice-Admiral DeCalmas and his two top officers," Rowen assured. "There were only so many royal aides and yeomen assigned to servicing the King during the voyage, and whoever it was that poisoned him did so during his meal or tea. That list narrows down, and now we're left with a handful."

"It may not have been any of the King's servants, but someone loyal to one of the officers or any of the diplomats who slipped through the screening."

Rowen grimaced. "Believe me, I've sifted through the names of every sailor, soldier, and servant, and I've excluded none as a traitor except for the Queen."

As they took a detour toward the loading docks, Tenshi spotted a familiar black crest on a large barrel, then again on a crate. Her guts twisted to a cold knot as she fathomed the seemingly unlimited extent of the underground's influence. She stopped beside one of the crates and ran her fingers across the blackened engraving on the wooden surface.

Rowen stepped beside her, his hand automatically reaching for his carbine, concerned, and alerted. "What's wrong?"

"The Squires of Debonair," Tenshi said with deep seriousness, as she touched the trademark rose of the Marquis. "If they're here in Magna Carta, then we don't have to look far for the culprit."

The mist that hovered over the water parted at the advent of the imposing allied fleet as they arrived at the mouth of Gabrialtar's inlet. The massive port of Sewell's Abide was directly ahead, with its great statue of the patron Saint Knight facing the ships of Magna Carta, Freya, and Guard with silent courage. Various ships, military and civilian, were now land-locked to their respective berths, and risked a thorough boarding and inspection should any venture into international waters.

From the quarter deck of the *Second Awakening*, Admiral Messer could see the tall towers that surrounded the coliseum of Name's Reclaim, their crowns lit like beacons from lighthouses. Shadowy shapes of fighting ships circled in the sky around the political seat like birds-of-prey of wood and steel waiting for the opportunity to strike.

"Admiral," Captain Semmes called from the stairs leading to the bridge, "the Integrum has signaled its readiness."

Messer turned to starboard where his captain was looking, at the *Integrum* and the Vice-Admiral's banners wafting in the wind. "Signal our acknowledgment, Captain." He strode toward the bridge. "For King and Cause, the blockade of this island begins here and now, gentlemen! Redeploy the fleet!"

Receiving ayes from his officers, the ship's crew geared into action, and in no time the rest of the squadron attached to his command spread out to form blockade lines. In tandem, Vice-Admiral DeCalmas and the allied commanders also followed suit, reforming the embargo network across fifty-plus miles of the sea, effectively strangling the safe passageways into the island's main port.

Once Messer reached the bridge's bulwarks, he looked again at Gabrialtar. "Be safe, Seidon... I still owe your father."

Discovering a discreet nook far from Sewell's Abide and away from prying eyes, Seidon disembarked from the small rowboat and climbed the rock face and foundation stilts of a townhouse built on the outskirts of the bazaar. He carefully maneuvered to the far end of the medium-sized building, and paused as he heard wooden planks crash against the craggy rocks below. He risked a glance beneath his feet, where the rough waves had finally capsized his borrowed rowboat and smashed it to pieces.

Seidon tightened his jaw, knowing he had to find another means to escape the island once his clandestine business was done. He continued his climb, and reached a raggedly old gargoyle that was once used as a talisman for superstitious sailors, and now doubled as a decorative drain during severe floods after rainfall or high tides. Using its gaping jaw and horned head as leverage, he reached the salt-weathered parapet on top of a forgotten ancient wall and jumped down onto the floor of a narrow alley.

Securing his gear and his covertness, he paced ahead toward the entrance of the alley and found himself near Optio's Square where he first encountered his malicious cousin and his band of mercenaries. Strangely enough, at this early hour of day, the place was virtually deserted. He stopped abruptly and pressed his back against the wall as he spotted a troupe of Gabrialtar patrolmen marching past the central fountain.

He peered around the corner as the soldiers moved past, and saw that the infamous *Crook's Corner* was still drudging with its usual clientele of drunkards and despots. Although it seemed like martial law had set in, the bazaar catered to the few courageous venturers and suppliers. Inspired, he covered himself with an old shawl pinched from an unattended laundry drying rack, picked up a discarded barrel over his shoulder and walked into the open.

With little attention drawn to him, he managed to sneak across the Square and onto the bazaar's main road until he reached Priamos' antique shop. He dropped the barrel at the side of the doorway, and strode inside, only to be surprised to find its door unlocked, and the old man working tirelessly on the dusty shelves.

"There's no more trade here, friend," the old man said without bothering to see who it was that barged into his shop. He was devoted on cleaning the rusted firing pin and hammer of a battle-worn musket. "I suggest you save your silver for food and comfort until this plotter's weather clears."

Seidon removed his cloak and looked around suspiciously for any deception, but found none, and approached Priamos. "Do you keep the door open for the Squires?"

Priamos was startled, and at last noticed Seidon with some fear in his eyes. His shock lasted briefly as he set the musket back on the shelf, and sighed as if with a heavy weight. "With little choice, I do. The Squires teased me about what happened to good Teeven and his wife, and I'm sorry. If only I can match his bravery, I'd be free of my shackles too."

Seidon tensed, the loss of his friends still close to heart. "We all have the choice, old man, and some of us realize it sooner than others. For us and for those fallen, I will make my stand here."

"If my bones weren't so brittle, I'd stand with you, but age has defeated my flame and now these relics are my last battlements."

"Where's the Marquis?"

Priamos gulped at the question, and hesitated, but overrode his anxiety with effort. "The man is now a member of the high aristocracy, a thane with his Debonair brethren acting as his personal brigade. If you want to find him, look past the congress on the high hill, to the Honourable Prator where the military barracks and noble housing are standing."

Seidon stared hard at Priamos, then was about to leave when Priamos caught his arm.

"The district is protected heavily at all flanks by guard posts and breastworks," Priamos warned sternly. "It's foolhardy to storm the front gate, and even more foolish to mount the defenses. If I were you, I'd wait until the Marquis finds reason to leave the comfort of his fort."

"If he's a member of the Presidency's circle, he'll have to convene at the Name's Reclaim."

Priamos nodded. "There are many matters of state, but regardless of his newfound station and charge, he's still a mercenary king. Be mindful to remember that." He reached behind one of the shelves nearby, and produced a slick dagger in a decorated sheath built from pearl-like ivory with red-gold rivets. Its handle was wrapped with cream-coloured leather and copper wire, while its flattened pommel was engraved with a crusading knight. "This belonged to my son, who was able to cut past two armigers and scar the Marquis on the neck before he was struck down himself in retribution. He tried to save me from this soulless service, but his defiance only sealed my fate to the Squires." He handed the dagger to Seidon. "Perhaps it will be better use to you in breaking the bonds."

Seidon was touched, gripping the weapon tightly. "It's good to know there are still kind hearts in this world."

"Only a handful left I'm afraid. Godspeed, Sir Harbrid."

"I'll set you free." Putting the shawl back on, he cautiously left the shop and proceeded through the bazaar toward Gabrialtar's military stronghold.

Waiting as one of the airships docked alongside Name's Reclaim's many jutting ports, Grand Master Mellka studied the vast view of the city beyond the colonnade, and the sea of the Southern Cross that laid beyond its coast. The horizon was cluttered with the masts of the allied fleet, clearly under the banner of Magna Carta, and blocked all sea-faring routes to and from the island.

Titus quietly stepped behind him, sharing the same dreadful sight. "They've already denied us port on nearly every corner of the old continent and the royal kingdom. Our trade routes have been severely disrupted, and both entrepreneur and politician are in outrage. Although we've been prepared for some time now, how long can we last under this siege? Perhaps several months or a few years? This is only a glimpse at what you're abandoning us with."

Mellka turned away from the view and faced Titus. "Somehow, Captain-General, I don't believe you're as ill-equipped as you proclaim."

"Nay, your Lordship," Titus admitted confidently. "Our mastery still lies with the clouds and angels."

"With smoke and demons as well," Mellka retorted acidly. He moved away from Titus and headed for the boarding ramp of the waiting airship, where his personal guards and Poem joined him.

Titus watched him go with a slight half-grin. "You claimed neutrality... perhaps you should profess your position with actual diplomacy." He walked away. "Prove to us that your blimpish Faith can truly save us from ourselves."

Poem heard Titus' hidden challenge and expected Mellka to spin with indignation, but the Grand Master remained calm as ice. He glanced back at the portentous monger's retreating back. "I've instructed the commander of your escort to hoist the proper colours once the vessel's ready to undock. The blockade fleet will not fire knowing you're onboard."

"You will not be accompanying me back to Templari, Poem," Mellka said flatly. "Although I'm due to promote the

Old Capital prelate to cardinal, I have need for you here. The situation is too volatile, and we owe our hosts an attempt at negotiation between them and their enemies."

"I will do my best to forestall this embargo," Poem said. "But I tell you now, I will not be able to stop what's inevitable."

Mellka paused at the foot of the ramp. "Just be prepared to choose sides when all talks dissolve."

With those cryptic words, he boarded the sky galleon with his guards, and Poem stepped back as the vessel majestically maneuvered away and set its bow toward the north-eastern sky. The flags unfolded and revealed the insignia of the Order and the papal seal. The sky galleon hovered over the heads of the opposing fleet unmolested, even though their guns, with redesigned mounts, had angled skyward to potentially strike at it.

Poem sighed, peering at the city below, finally left alone to his thoughts. He sensed that he was no longer alone, and glanced to the side to see Mikaila leading a company of Gabrialtar officers. She returned the glance, something hidden and vicious in her eyes, then moved on.

Poem ground his teeth, holding back his impulse to assault her for her part in his sister's murder, and relied on the mandate Mellka had charged him with. There was peace for him to herald between the rivals, an irony that he should present it.

Dalena paced in deep contemplation within the small observation gallery of the Throne Room's antechamber, the scope of the capital and the sea in view. With the paneled doors opened, the white silk curtains wavered gently, made translucent by the sunlight.

Her servants and guards waited inside the antechamber, their collective fealty to her crown and earnest respect for her person unable to break through her stonewalled plight against the King's unbending court. So they remained quiet, yet vigilant, suspecting anyone outside her circle despite their inherited loyalties.

It took Daedlus some convincing, even with Precidious' established leeway, to be allowed in the Queen's presence for a few moments in private. He deflected the ire of her personal staff as he strutted past them, following the old Chancellor onto the gallery.

Precidious bowed before Dalena, then turned back where he came, giving Daedlus a bold look of warning. "She's still the Queen, Ambassador, have care to remember that."

Daedlus idly acknowledged the wisdom of the admonition, but did not necessarily heed to it. He slowly approached the Queen, like a prowler, who still had her back to him.

"You will not bend your knee to me?" Dalena said, stopping the Ambassador in his tracks. "Am I not deserving?"

"Perhaps you misunderstood my intentions," Daedlus said placidly. "You were a fine soldier, a well-respected and decorated Admiral of His Majesty's Royal Squadron, and on those regards you have my admiration."

"So you drew the line when the King placed a crown on my head?" Her analysis was cold and incisive.

"This kingdom survived as long as it did on unbreakable tradition, on a clear and visible distinction of classes," Daedlus retorted. "To blur those lines is to invite anarchy, and smear the proud legacy of our forefathers with the blood of lesser men… and women."

"Will it displease you to know that I carry the King's unborn heir…?" Dalena gently stroke below her stomach, now slightly swollen, then faced the surprised Ambassador with a gaze that speared through the man's soul. "Your voice in this otherwise trivial matter threatens the stability of the upper caste, whether you realize it or not, and in time this dissension will spread all over this nation. Our enemies will then know when and where to strike. I may not be a politician, I admit I have limits, but as a soldier I know how to defend what is precious."

Daedlus' momentary surprise turned to an acidic scowl at her revelation. "What *is* precious? How much control do you believe you possess? You need the court to excise your powers, and you cannot dissolve the court for any contentious reason. Throw me in chains, and you will face a partisans' revolt. You cannot dare to wage your interests against us and hope to win."

"By foolishness or design, you're teetering on the edge of civil war."

"Certain extremes are costly, but effective in the long run. Nations are born when differences are resolved in absolute."

"Then draw the lines here," Dalena cut back as a pair of Throne Guards flanked the Ambassador. "You're confined to your estate under heavy guard until a proper trial can be assembled to deal with your sedition."

Daedlus grinned tightly. "Yet another reason why you do not deserve that crown…*Your Majesty*."

With a silent nod to the guards, Daedlus was taken away, but too proud of himself he pulled free of their grips and walked on his own. Dalena knew it was the beginning of the end, and begged for Ingren to wake. Looking back out to the city, she also knew somewhere there was still a glimmer of hope.

Passing an old archway, Tenshi and Rowen entered the grand souk that dominated the merchants' port. The narrow alleys were crowded with people of all walks of life, providing little subtlety, and they pushed their way through in search for their nameless suspect.

Tenshi led Rowen through the maze, driven by her instinct, and her eyes took in every detail. She slipped between the shoulders of a band of mendicant monks, and immediately spotted the black regalia of the Squires etched on a mosaic of stones that made up one side of a two-storied townhouse. She moved past it into a roofed avenue that led toward the interior courtyard of the market.

She passed another archway into a sunken courtyard with a trio of blooming cherry trees at its center. Three ornate minarets surrounded the courtyard, which served mainly as watch towers, and provided duty for a garrison and local recruiting office. Large candelabra hung from simple lintels that jutted midway from the minarets, providing light throughout the courtyard during late hours.

Rowen noticed a few squads of the King's soldiers marching with eloquent ceremony through the souk, patrolling the streets and hoarding attention. "If I had any palpable notion of how deeply the Squires have embedded their rank-and-file in His Majesty's capital, I'd have the entire local garrison emptied onto these streets."

"The Squires won't risk a direct confrontation," Tenshi said. She paused by the cherry trees to regain her bearings.

"They syphon their scheming through regular businesses that have been bribed or coerced."

"If their operations are compartmentalized," Rowen said, "then we will have a hard time breaching whatever defenses they have established here."

Tenshi nodded, noting the Squires' logo carved obliquely on the bark of the tree beside her. She looked around the courtyard again, and spotted the rose again, this time on the hanging sign of a gin mill. "Like any mercenary guild, they need a rat's nest somewhere."

Rowen followed Tenshi's gaze, and grimaced. "Follow the rose."

The gin mill, fittingly named, *The Rose and Sheath*, was host to a majority of men and women who have either seen rough seas as sailors or the destitute conditions of poor soldiers on battlefields abroad. Most drank away their days and swapped stories, while others gambled with old card games and ancient chess. They cared for little else until Tenshi and Rowen casually entered their haven.

Despite drawing unfriendly gazes, they paced steadily across the room, moving past the many patrons seated at their tables, well-hidden blades and blunderbusses rested within reach.

"Recognize anyone from the Sovereign?" Tenshi asked with restrained calamity, catching a glimpse of the barkeep pouring whiskey from a large stack of liquor barrels in the corner. Carefully observant, she noted that not all the barrels held liquids, and that a faulty plank revealed a spattering of gun powder on the mill's floor.

Rowen studied each man, whose faces were unshaven, scarred, and marred by brutal living. Some wore antiquated chain mail coifs, and almost all wore one form of light armour or another regardless of fashion and practicality. Over at the far end of the room, near the entrance to a storeroom, there was a slight sense of familiarity from a man of average looks and pedigree.

Rowen felt his guts nudge toward Nalth. "Admiral DeCalmas stated in his report that when the King was in council with him and Ambassador Daedlus, there was a servant he didn't recognize from the usual royal retinue. He assumed he was from Daedlus' personal staff, but made no inquiry on an 'otherwise insubstantial matter' as he stated it."

Tenshi deliberately laid her palm around the handle of the clockwork pistol hanging at her side, a late addition to Magna Carta's arsenal, and let her hardened gaze fall on Nalth's inconspicuous countenance. He seemed placid at first, pensive as he slid a finger on the moist rim of his lager, then all suspicion was founded as he suddenly bolted into the storeroom.

At the same time, the patrons stood and brought their weapons to bear on the two strangers.

Tenshi's reflexively dodged behind a table as Rowen kicked it over its side, and she immediately shot the liquor barrels with her readied pistol. The potent alcohol exploded under duress, and caught the mercenaries off-balance. The blast obliterated the bar and surrounding furniture, and gouged out a hole on the side of the building, which undoubtedly startled the local populace and caught the unbridled attention of the Magna Carta patrols.

Before the dust and debris settled, Tenshi moved away from cover and sprinted after Nalth, shouldering a few staggering Squires out of her way, and lodging the butt of her pistol under the chin of the dazed barkeep as he attempted to block access to the storeroom with a rustic hunting rifle.

Rowen, his knightly sword of the Throne Guards drawn, attempted to follow her, but able Squires emerged from the dirt floating in the room and surrounded his position. He shielded a wild attack by a harpooner with his blade, then elbowed the assailant's nose and cracked it open. He then ducked as a rifleman shot and missed, punching a hole through one of the windows, and cut the man low at the Squire's exposed flank and belly.

Rowen again moved back to avoid a determined thrust from a young musketeer's rapier, and the second attempt managed to slice a gash through his sleeve and shoulder. Now at close quarters, Rowen effortlessly countered by grabbing the musketeer's elaborate gorget and pulling the man aside and onto the floor. He followed through with a merciless swing of his sword that severed the musketeer's hand off at the wrist – rapier still in its grip.

Unexpectedly, a lumbering Squire rushed Rowen, and tackled him through the door. Both fell into the courtyard with the door's hinges splintering loudly off the thick wooden paneling. Rowen was pinned by the weight and brawn of the robust Squire, with his sword impaled on the ground and out of reach. Despite the pain on his back and shoulders, he kicked the Squire off him.

The mercenary recovered quickly, and was joined by his brethren out in the open. To their dismay, and at the rattle and clicks of four columns of the King's infantry aiming their guns, the Squires hesitated to pounce.

Rowen returned to his feet, retook his sword, and stood at the head of the Magna Carta contingent beside the regiment commander. He boldly pointed the tip of his sword at the Squires. "In the name of King, arrest them!"

* * *

In full stride, Tenshi caught sight of Nalth as he maneuvered around the boxes, bags, and barrels that cluttered the storeroom. Nominally dark without available windows, there was a sudden breach of light as the poisoner bursted through the backdoor and onto the busy souk avenues. Tenshi was hard at his heels, pushing past a horde of bystanders with graceful agility while Nalth plundered through like a raging bull.

He glanced back, then turned sharply at a shoulder-narrow alley, practically running sideways between buildings until reaching the harbour. He looked frantically at the myriads of ships, some docked while others were casting their sails or firing their engines, and ran toward the closest herd of departing vessels.

Tenshi slipped from the alley, pausing for a split second to track the poisoner's flight, and continued the chase through the fishermen's quarter. Sunlight was scattered by canvases providing temporary shade on the long and wide stretch of pier, and just the same both merchants and shoppers moved out of the way.

Nalth, without stopping his mad race, pulled out his pistol, cocked it and fired back at Tenshi. He missed, even as she side-stepped, and splintered the side of a wooden kiosk. In cool riposte, Tenshi recovered her posture and stood still while she aimed at Nalth as he wove recklessly through the crowd. She fired, and struck a surgical hit at the back of his right leg.

He collapsed and nearly drove through a stand of wares, but with grit and desperate stamina, he limped hurriedly to the boats.

Tenshi resumed the chase, tucking away the gun in favour of the cutlass, and reached close enough to swipe at Nalth before he jumped from the pier onto a small fishing boat. He floundered under the weight of his wounded leg, but did little to slow him. He rushed to the stern and jumped onto another boat, knocking over its rower, then latched on to a hanging chain and climbed the side of a galley.

Tenshi followed a parallel route, running across a perpendicular pier of the fishermen's quarter, all the while keeping her eyes locked on Nalth. She leaped onto a dinghy and strode past its startled occupants and jumped from the bow onto another pier that stretched closer to the galley Nalth boarded. She spotted him running alongside the galley's bulwarks, threatening the sailors out his way, then he suddenly leaped from the vessel onto the pier directly ahead of her.

Grunting as the pain sheared across his body, he spun and continued running. He turned and flew up a flight of stairs that led to a coastal fortification with a watchtower facing the open sea. He burst through the gate, passing between several guards stationed there, and pushed whatever strength he had left climbing the winding staircase to the top of the old tower. Once he reached it and realizing how high above the ground he was – high enough to match the tallest masts of corsairs and schooners as they passed – he knew his options of escape dwindled next to nothing.

"Did you poison the King?!" Tenshi demanded as she positioned herself between him and the only way back down.

Exhausted, but belligerent, he turned to face Tenshi. He reached for a small flask tied on his belt beside the pouch of money, and popped its cork open. With his free hand, he unsheathed a slender stiletto, and poured the flask's oily liquid onto the blade. Tossing the empty flask on the floor and shattering it, he grinned, showing the dripping blade to Tenshi.

He closed the distance and slashed high, but cut only air as Tenshi backpedaled, then swung down and struck her cutlass. He backed away, knowing he was at a disadvantage in reach of arms, and dodged Tenshi's riposte. He delivered a flurry of short lunges, keeping her at bay until she found an opening and swung toward his hip, cutting open the pouch and scattering the money all over the ground.

Growing restless, he pushed hard with a low thrust, but Tenshi moved faster and countered with an upward cut through his armpit. Nalth reeled away, the new wound forcing him to lose the stiletto. He wheezed now, having lost a lot of blood, and the arrival of Rowen and several Magna Carta soldiers helped matters less for him.

"Surrender now!" Rowen ordered, coming up beside Tenshi.

Nalth backed away from them, until he was cornered by the battlements lining the tower. He glanced behind him, then glared at his enemies before him and without hesitation jumped on the crenelation and leaped heroically across the water onto a passing galleon. He caught the pronounced rake of the mainsail with enough force to snap a line, and hung precariously for a moment too long. Unable to heave himself onto the rake, and quickly losing grip to the wind, he slipped. He fell several stories onto the main deck, smashing his skull against the portside rail.

The ship sailed on as the alerted crew surrounded his body, and both Tenshi and Rowen grimly faced the consequences of their failure to capture the poisoner alive.

XVI. Flight of the Vilkacis

XVI. Flight of the Vilkacis

Under white banners of peaceful envoys, the Gabrialtar cutter approached the small artificial islet that rose above the water between the port of Sewell's Abide and the embargo fleet. Floored with massive flagstones and peppered with shambled tower bases, the islet was at some point in distant history the outer fortification of the old Empyrean City, now submerged.

Two other boats were already tethered to the converted marina, guarded by Magna Cartan sailors and infantrymen, while Vice-Admiral DeCalmas and Admiral Messer waited patiently for negotiations to begin. The waves crashed eagerly against the large, sculpted stones and the Gabrialtar cutter as its delegation disembarked. Most were mariners, and only one was a foreign ambassador, though he was the last person Messer expected to lead diplomatic talks.

Like a portent of death in the shadowy outfit of an Insidian, Poem retained none of the piety or humility that once shaped his reliance and comradery in those years past.

"Honoured Admirals," Poem greeted formally, "welcome to the Saint's Foothold, and the sovereignty of Gabrialtar. I am here on behalf of Her Presidency, and on the neutral charter of Grand Master Mellka, to negotiate a cessation of this illegal embargo and arrange a proper venue for discussion."

"You give us assurance that the Church is indeed neutral in this affair?" DeCalmas demanded tactfully, suspicious of Poem regardless of the reply.

Poem nodded. "I give it."

"Very well," DeCalmas said, preferring to be at the bridge of his command ship. "There are terms to be met, mainly cooperation and willingness to submit to free trade of resources vital to international stability."

"Her Presidency will grant debate on this matter, but asks for your fleet to withdraw and reopen the sea routes."

"We will not disperse this embargo until we've seen true commitment to negotiate a truce," DeCalmas replied sternly. "But we will compromise, and pull back our ships three hundred yards to deeper ocean, and allow safe passage to merchant vessels and fishing vessels."

"We will, however," Messer added, "board them should the cargo and crew deem ostensible."

Poem locked eyes with Messer for a moment, then pulled away. "Agreed. I will have Her Presidency contact you by the end of the day to organize an official forum, and be invited as ambassadors of peace to the Name's Reclaim."

"Until then." DeCalmas gave Messer a glance, sensing unfinished business between him and the mediator, then promptly turned and strode back to his boat.

"I never thought I'd question your loyalty," Messer said, breaking the uneasy silence.

"If you want an explanation, I have none to offer."

Messer was repulsed by Poem's cold riposte. "Neither do you offer trust. If these talks break down, I will have no remorse should my cannons settle your last hour."

Poem wasn't deterred. "You are not my enemy."

Before Messer could question him, Poem turned and walked back to the cutter, leaving the Admiral with little choice but leave the Saint's Foothold and whatever old fellowship had existed between them.

* * *

"Outrageous, don't you believe?" Gehenna commented sourly, as the group of officials left her presidential office, which was more a suite, richly decorated and furnished.

Titus, his hands clasped at the small of his back, stopped his pacing before the President's gilded desk. "Our coastal guard have confirmed the sanction fleet's withdrawal; the city's no longer within their cannons' range."

Gehenna tossed down the written reports on her desk, and leaned back on her ornate chair. "Their presence still threaten our economy. I will not have them disrupt our shipping lanes with impromptu inspections."

"I have few suggestions to offer, Madam," Titus said coolly. "While the ocean is restricted, we still have mastery of the air."

"Retrofitting merchant vessels with our military technology will be too costly, and consume an inordinate amount of time and resources," Gehenna said.

"So it leaves us with two options: Either we follow through with the negotiations and ultimately sacrifice all advantages we have, or we break this embargo with entire might of Gabrialtar here and now."

Gehenna was uneasy by the notion of war. "How far do we ride on pride until it destroys the very thing we hold dearest? I was elected to bring proper change to our nation, but nowhere in my string of promises did I ever offer a lurch to all-out violence against our adversaries. If this infraction can be dissolved with peaceful talks, then I will give these Admirals a chance to trade terms until we reach a solution."

Titus approached her desk, rested his fists on the edge, and leaned forward. "This is beyond pride, this is about our right to govern what is ours. They demand us to give them our fuel, our tools, and our treasures so they can satisfy the hungry, but nowhere do I see an end to this problem. We will only be adding ourselves in this vicious circle, chained to obligation, and punished for liberation. I'm your ADC, Madam, and what I offer is the only solution."

"To commit to war?"

"To offer the King and his allies a choice. What better way to demonstrate our resolve by unleashing the Vilkacis? Initiate it at your word, and I will be prepared to launch it."

Gehenna hesitated as she sensed something deep and cold in Titus. She considered all her options, and realized how few they were. "I will make this decision at the absolute end of all diplomacy."

Climbing the last of the rusted rungs, Seidon left behind the ancient underground aqueduct through an open manhole and stepped onto a large field of stone and mortar. He quickly established his milieu and snuck toward the umbra of a defensive wall. A waft of heated air was released from the exhaust vents of a nearby sky galleon as it ascended, forcing him to press back against the palisade he hid against.

Keeping his hand around the handle of his carbine, he gingerly peered around the corner.

Regento, wearing a lavish outfit befitting that of a congressional thane, presented himself on the tarmac with the same infamy and vanity that garnered his reputation. He was amongst a cortege of Squires and support personnel who serviced the airship terminal located at the heart of the Honourable Prator district. There were at least a dozen sky galleons and smaller vessels nested in large berths filled with water, with three more warships being constructed in the dry docks. Surrounding the tarmac were the military barracks, and encircling the legion of Martello towers were the lavish noble housing – castle-mansions in their own right.

Seidon judged against his impulse to charge blindly into their midst, and watched as Regento strode toward one of the smaller vessels which he guessed would ferry the freshly proclaimed Gabrialtar noble to the Name's Reclaim. He calculated the intervals, and decided to maintain his stealth for as long as it gained him an advantage. He let go of the carbine's handle, and wrapped his fingers around the hilt of the fine rapier he borrowed from Magna Carta's weapon caches, then sprinted from the wall to the nearest stack of equipment. Making certain no one's around to observe his movement, he dashed again to the adjacent clutter of mechanical parts, and steadily enclosed on Regento's position.

Seidon waited as his cousin and escorting troupe boarded the ferry, and ran past an array of canvas-covered tool sheds to a parked armoured half-track. Unexpectedly, the vehicle's driver stepped off the cabin, and in the moment the man's eyes widened at the intruder's presence, Seidon rushed him. He unleashed his rapier's ornate hilt and rammed it clean across the driver's temple. The driver was thrown back hard, bouncing head-first off the half-track, then collapsed to the ground unconscious.

"I'm sorry," Seidon whispered into the unfortunate man's ear, as he carefully tied the driver's hands with a belt and hid him beneath the half-track.

Putting aside his guilt for the time being as the ferry's engines spurned to life, Seidon squatted beside the vehicle's front bumper and fixed his eyes on his quarry nearly fifty yards away.

He was about to jump into a mad run until his instinct held him back like a short leash. A platoon of Gabrialtar Dragoons marched between him and the ferry, led and rear-guarded by a quartet of equestrian officers. Seidon held his breath and hoped he showed little of his profile as the soldiers strode past in perfect parade formation.

Up ahead, on wings granted by the zeppelin devices, the ferry had begun to lift off its watery berth.

Anxiety drove his nerves, but he kept still, his knuckles turning white as he gripped the rapier tighter. When the last of the platoon left his view, one of the officers on horseback trailed back and stopped. He looked toward Seidon's direction, hidden in the shadows of the half-track and the clutter, and seemed suspicious. After a second of hesitation, the officer nudged his horse to creep toward the parked half-track.

Seidon's heart raced, especially with the ferry rising up behind the horseman, and charged in a blink of an eye. He grabbed the stricken officer's arm and pulled him unceremoniously off his saddle, then smashed the officer's face with the blunt base of his rapier's hilt. Risking subtlety for dire necessity, Seidon ran like the wind toward the ferry, spotting a dangling line at its keel. He leaped onto the bulwark that surrounded the berth and reached for the line – catching it in time.

He hung against the keel, relinquishing the courage to look down at the ground as the airship lifted higher into the air, then carefully climbed up toward the nearest external emergency hatch nestled next to the side pod cannon. He forced the latch open, seeing no one inside but the unmanned large bore gun, then snuck inside.

Dissension spread through the Royal Court, and previous oaths to uphold the law was left numb. Dalena listened as the nobles squabbled against opposing opinions, some having the audacity to direct their frustrations over Daedlus' house arrest toward her. Rowen and the Throne Guards were taut on alert, and stood close to their Queen, while Precidious frustratingly attempted to call the council to order.

"All voices shall be silent, now!" Precidious demanded. "This is a house of lords, not some flea market auction!"

One of the aristocrats, a bureaucratic man whose family had long served the kingdom's banking institutions, ignored the command, shaking his fist at the Queen. "This is an outrage against Sir Daedlus' arrest! We demand he be released, or our fiefs will unanimously boycott this monarchy!"

"Ambassador Daedlus was arrested on suspicion of treason," the old man explained. "He threatened the Queen. This arrest is legal and not to be questioned, or threatened by petty revolt!"

The frustrated aristocrat stood his ground. "He's a patriot who dared to stand against this warmongering pretender!"

"We are Her Majesty's servants!" Rowen lashed out. "Respect her or be expelled from this court!"

More insults were traded, and Dalena had enough. She stepped forward, past the armoured protection of her guards, and the court surprisingly fell quiet.

"The man who poisoned your King was found, and the mercenary sect that he belonged to uprooted. The culprit is dead by his own fault. He was a hired professional, and paid to commit his crime, but what motives linger behind those who contracted him? Is it to prevent war, or instigate another?" She paused a moment. "Long before I accepted this crown, and more so now, it is my first and solemn duty to protect Magna Carta, and until I'm convinced of your collective loyalty, this court is hereby dissolved indefinitely."

The nobles were flabbergasted, and Dalena left them no room to disagree as she promptly turned and left the chamber. Their discordant tones were cut short as the doors closed shut behind her by the guards.

In the brief privacy, she stopped and reflected on what she'd done, the weight of her actions portending to break her spirit. "Ingren, forgive me..." she whispered, then continued her march down the hallway.

Tenshi waited for her at the end of the corridor, framed by a window-filled veranda. "Your Highness, what will you do with Ambassador Daedlus?"

"He'll stand trial before a jury of his peers, though a firing squad would be more fitting," Dalena said. "He's a zealot who has no qualms dealing with mercenaries to achieve his aims."

"You're convinced he was the one who hired the poisoner."

"The circumstance speaks for itself. Unfortunately, it won't be enough to convince his staunch supporters. Placing him under house arrest only serves to aggravate the gravity of the situation... and I just disbanded the court."

Tenshi was quietly impressed with Dalena's resolve. "Then you only have a short amount of time to justify your actions, and secure an accord with your subjects. My Queen must commit Daedlus to a public trial, for all to see the danger he poses, and once discredited, he should be stripped of his title and imprisoned."

Dalena wished it was that simple. "If found guilty of treason, he will face execution. If absolved, he'll have what he needs to force my abdication, and bring an abrupt end to my King's reign if he never wakes from his slumber. There has been no such thing in over a century."

"Magna Carta will forgive you, Julia, since these are extraordinary times."

"Otherwise," Dalena disclosed, "we must be prepared for civil war."

In the great congress chamber of the Name's Reclaim, the seated political figureheads of Gabrialtar, all tuned to the giant shortwave receiver monitor that hung over them like a godly chandelier. The Admirals of the embargo fleet communicated their terms to the Presidency, while Titus – ever so uppity, calmly paced in a wide circle across the center floor.

Poem was also present during these crucial negotiations, standing near the closed doors with his arms sternly crossed as he listened in place of his Grand Master.

"After agreeing to a restricted no-fly zone and disarming all your high-tonnage military vessels, you will allow free access to a team of international inspectors, formed from engineering corps and geological guilds, to disseminate your retro-reef processing technologies and properly evaluate energy production potential within Gabrialtar territory." DeCalmas allowed a moment for the conditions to be digested. "These conditions have an expiry date, and will be dissolved within one full year. Sovereignty will remain undisputedly yours, and diplomatic and commercial affairs will return to convention."

Gehenna was appalled by the demands, but held back the bile for fear of an uncontrollable crisis. "How is our sovereignty not in dispute with these implacable violations you deem as terms of cooperation?"

"Circumstances of the times have left us with little choice, especially after the murder of Governor Traiza," Messer said. "This strictness of our terms stems primarily from an assassination attempt on our King by an infiltrator whose allegiance is to the Squires of Debonair. A mercenary group who are well-known to operate from your island, and who are supplying your factories with materiel to feed the furnaces of your weapons' development."

"This government does not deal with the dregs of the underworld," Gehenna retorted with offense. "Law and conscience dominates here."

Titus glanced at Regento, who was amongst the throngs of politicians.

"Nonetheless," DeCalmas continued, "we have need for caution, and no need for bloodshed. This fleet is not here on campaign, but a means to resolve this impasse. Please consider these terms."

"Not with the fate of our prosperity in your hands," Gehenna said. "But… in spirit of cooperation, restrictive as it is, I will call for a referendum on this matter, and let the people decide a course of action. In the meantime, I strongly suggest your fleet allow trade routes to re-open fully–"

"If I may, Madam," Titus interrupted with a graceful gesture of his hand, stopping between her and the shortwave monitor. Once he received the assent from Gehenna, he faced the Admiralty. "The proponents of war are already in place, my gracious Admirals, whether you intended or not. You barge onto our doorstep, you demand we hand over the lifeblood of our independence, and accuse us of plotting against your royalty. How else are we, as free people of Terra Mia, to respond?"

"All nations are still healing from the wounds of the last war," DeCalmas said sternly. "What we do here is for the benefit of all, not any single party or individual."

"Goodwill is a disguise for ambition, onto the ruin of us all." Titus looked at all the senators around him. "Should we postpone our destruction with this embargo like a castle siege, until we wither and fade under the oppression of martial foreign policies?"

Most shook their heads, while others pondered grimly.

"Shall we submit?" Titus query was simple, but evoked strong reactions from all present. He waited for the ruckus of discontent to escalate, sounding like a crescendo of a perfect symphony. "Then our last choice must be to retaliate." He turned sharply to the Admirals on the monitor. "Gentlemen, will you or will you not withdraw this blockade?"

Messer sighed, disappointed. "Our orders stand."

Titus kept ominously quiet, then craned his head back to look at Gehenna. She considered gravely what her ADC suggested earlier, and with the common feelings in the chamber pressing her hand, she nodded silently her approval.

Titus, tightly holding back a smile, faced the Admirals once more. "There are no more words to trade, instead we will answer to your fears. Consider what's to come as a demonstration of our resolve."

Amongst the confusion that reverberated through the chamber, Titus curtly gestured for the communications to be severed and strode towards a group of high-ranking officers that included Mikaila. "Launch the Vilkacis," he ordered, and the officers set to motion.

Poem, his sense tingling with dread, watched as one officer activated a lever system that transformed the central floor into a control platform with various screens and switches. Lights and gizmos whirled to life, and a single pedestal rose at the center of the platform to reveal what looked like the blade-less hilt of an ornate silver sabre with a swept handguard and black horn grip with finger indentations.

"Now, Madam President; honoured republicans," Titus declared, "we walk hand in hand to reshape this landscape to our favour."

As the officers set to work, Titus climbed onto platform and picked up the hilt. He held his thumb over the flattened pommel, and without hesitation, pressed it firmly.

One of the great minarets that surrounded Name's Reclaim spurred to life with a thunderous roar, and its surface crumbled away. Beneath the façade, ornamented hydraulic panels geared apart to reveal a missile several stories tall, its tip crowned by the giant lantern whose flame reddened. Steam was released from pressure valves like a beastly sigh, startling those that watched its transformation in horror from the galleries of the coliseum to the streets of the city, and the decks of the embargo ships.

With a luminous flash that outshone the sun for a brief heartbeat, the Vilkacis missile launched into the cloudless sky, and curved elegantly toward the ocean – its smoke trail smearing its wake with grey and black fumes.

Onboard the *Second Awakening*, among all ships in the fleet, Messer and his crew watched as the missile begun its descent. Nothing like it had ever been known in the history of warfare, and few were willing to brave its inauguration.

"All hands haul on the main brace!" Messer ordered, galvanizing the sailors to action. "Lift anchor and loose the sails! Fire up the engines!" He rushed toward the bridge, "Captain Semmes, signal all ships to break formation and run for the horizon now!"

In the heat of the commotion that enveloped the deck, he glanced as the other ships set into panicked retreat. The *Integrum* was already moving with its guns at the ready, and the clear colours of the Vice-Admiral's flagship gave warning to all under its command to flee for dear life.

Despite the incessant naval drills and cumulative years of hard living at sea, nothing prepared these sailors for the power of the Vilkacis. The missile smashed amidst the fleet, and exploded under the waves, churning white foam and superheated steam, stressing, and weaving until the gargantuan bubble fragmented into the shape of a winged drake. The explosive potential magnified threefold, and the shockwave broke the blockade apart before it had a chance to scatter. Ships that were closest to the epicenter splintered in half and were swallowed whole by the tide, while the blast waves easily capsized the remaining vessels that were too slow to flee. The few that were spared rode the storm hard, and withdrew without recourse.

XVII. Call of the Righteous

XVII. Call of the Righteous

The primordial power of the Vilkacis missile dissipated in the distance, and while no dull clouds hung in the sky overhead, warm raindrops fell from the sheer volume of water that was ejected in the explosion.

High above Empyrean City, Seidon was a witness to the new horror borne from the Sorcerer Cannon. As he hid in the gunnery venter of the ferry that brought Regento and his cortege to Name's Reclaim, he now understood the end result of the smuggling ring that brought remnant Cannon parts from Tinkertown to the hands of a rising power that was Gabrialtar. Unlike the Cannon, which needed vast resources of men and equipment to move and operate, these missiles could be launched anywhere and at any time as the triggerman willed it.

The rules of warfare had changed forever on this day, and unfortunately, the combined fleet of Magna Carta, Freya, and Guard had to learn it the hardest way. Peering into the horizon where the fleet used to be, visibility obscured by a light mist caused by the aftermath, he hoped Messer survived this deluge.

Spotting a group of men approaching, Seidon cleared his thoughts and drew out his carbine and rapier. With the congress abruptly adjourned, Liberthier Regento and his Squires were prompted to return, and were unprepared for the assault Seidon had in store for them.

The ferry's starboard gunport swung open, and the side pod cannon fired a volley directly into the group. It struck the wall and exploded, knocking down four of the seven guards that accompanied Regento. By the time the debris and dust settled, Seidon punched past the handful of crewmen working the parked vessel, charged down the loading ramp, and swung his sword across the chest of a dazed Squire, moved past him to another ruffian, and viciously jabbed the pommel against the man's cheek.

He set his sight on Regento, who hung on to the wall for balance, and fervently rushed straight at him. When the last mercenary attempted to defend the Marquis, Seidon fired his carbine and sent the ruffian sprawling back. It gave ample time for Regento to unsheathe his sword, only to have it knocked away from his hand by Seidon's brutal backhand. Backpedaling, Regento reached for his pistol, and managed to fire off a single shot wildly into air before Seidon tackled him against the far wall and held him steady with the rapier's sharp edge to the neck.

"How many people just died by the weapon you just sold to these bastards?!" Seidon ushered angrily. "How many?!"

"Gabrialtar defended itself from aggressors who wouldn't listen to reason," Regento said grimly, wary of the blade pressing against his neck. "But you didn't come here to discuss politics."

Seidon slugged him, and Regento staggered to the ground. The proud Marquis held his bruised face, and wanted to retaliate, but was held still at sword point.

Regento grunted in frustration. "I didn't keep Ancestral for myself, Seidon, I gave it to the Captain-General. He requested it personally."

Seidon recalled the ominous moment when Titus stared at him from the *Highborn* as it zoomed by. "Why?"

"He offered a king's ransom, as you can see. A noble's estate and electoral influence, unofficial supplier of arms and materiel for Gabrialtar's war machine; breathing space for the

Squires to operate. He's truly the master manipulator in this government, and I didn't question why."

With a snarl, Seidon thrust the tip of his rapier closer and nicked Regento's chin. "You're a profit-driven mongrel who at the end of it all... will lose *everything*. There's only one title you deserve, Regento, and there's nothing aristocratic about it."

"Get this over with," Regento spat, annoyed by the bloody gash Seidon incurred on his chin. "Throw our blood ties to the sea."

Seidon stayed his course, and surprised his cousin as he replaced the rapier into its scabbard. Instead he unveiled the beautiful dagger Priamos had given him, lifted Regento to his feet by the collar of his elegant coat, and held the slender blade across the old scar on his cousin's neck where the dagger had once scathed.

"Let's see how far your new title takes us..." Seidon said as a squad of alerted Gabrialtar soldiers arrived, and his grey eyes looked to them with the resolve of a madman.

The fog hung over the water, obscuring the recent devastation, and provided natural cover for the surviving ships of the embargo fleet. Debris and bodies floated around them, and rescue parties on boats attempted to save what few men they could.

Messer considered himself a victim of luck, neither content nor anguished, only grim by the severe losses and the memories of the *Awakening*'s demise that still plagued him. He stood on the quarter deck, beaten by the rough weather the ship sailed through, and stared out from the stern to the silhouettes of broken masts and crumpled hulls that still lingered on the mercy of the calming waves.

He gripped the bulwark's railing with both hands, and lowered his gaze. Such wanton death was sometimes too much to handle for any sane human being.

Semmes, his uniform rumpled and torn from action, maneuvered past the busy hive of crewmen and officers, and approached Messer. He sensed his superior's distress, but maintained his stance. "Admiral?"

"Yes, Captain?"

"We've been unable to establish communications with Magna Carta. Despite moderate damage to the equipment, there's too much interference for a coherent shortwave signal to punch through this weather. The other vessels are also experiencing the same difficulties."

Messer nodded quietly. "How many ships?"

Semmes hesitated as he considered the grimness of the numbers, and reported what he knew. "Seventeen, sir, including ourselves and the Allied command ships. Superficial damage on all vessels, but we should be underway within the hour. The last scout party have reported in with casualties, and they located the Integrum's buoy. All hands lost."

"Seventeen, out of thirty-two…" Messer's hand balled into a fist, fervently wanting to storm into Gabrialtar's harbour and blasting every gun and heart onto the Name's Reclaim to bring it down from its mighty pedestal. With effort, he relinquished the vengeful thought. "Notify all remaining ships to maintain a state of high alert until we clear through. Once we're on friendlier waters, order all vessels to divide and head for safe port. Our highest priority is to send the warning to all allied nations."

* * *

Gehenna gazed at the hazy aftermath beyond the bay, and her spirit was bent with souring doubt. "This is unacceptable." She turned from the loggia and faced Titus. "There is no excuse worth the lives lost today."

"On the contrary, Madam President, we've just consolidated our place in this world. Now is the time to make our advances before our enemies retaliate."

"Advances?" Gehenna was appalled at the notion. "This catastrophe doesn't mark the start of a military campaign, Captain-General, it was supposed to have been a phylactery to ward off insufferable foreign policies."

"It's time to take the reins, Madam," Titus said sternly. "With the political insecurities present out there, we are finally in a position to offer our open palm in friendship or our backhand in reprisal. Your Air Force, your Navy, and your Army are ready. Give the order, and we shall triumph."

"Do we dare change the course of the world...?"

Titus pressed on. "No greater moment has presented itself in the annals of our history."

Gehenna wrestled with her dilemma until she was able to summon the courage to decide. She nodded glumly. "Allow them to supplicate before you roll out the cannons."

Titus bowed eagerly, and was about to take his leave when a commotion distracted the occasion.

With Regento being his unwilling hostage, Seidon encroached toward Titus unimpeded by the guards who surrounded him. With weapons drawn, the anxious guards kept their distance while they followed Seidon through the colonnaded observation gallery.

Titus calmly took a step back and covered Gehenna, who was astounded by the aversion. "I strongly suggest you retire to your office, Your Presidency." He craned his back slightly to Mikaila and a company of Dragoons as they arrived in due haste. "I will attempt to diffuse the situation with dear alacrity."

Mikaila swiftly drew her sniper rifle, cocked it ready and aimed – all in a heartbeat. A split-second later, the Dragoons followed in tandem with their rifles. It was an impressive display of tactful training and skill, but did little to dither Seidon's tenacity and Titus knew it.

"Dragoons, escort the President to safety," Titus ordered.

The elect soldiers promptly divided in two groups, with the rear line forming a human shield around Gehenna and leading her away from the premises. Mikaila and the remainder were steady at the trigger, waiting patiently on orders from the Captain-General.

Seidon stopped several feet away from Titus, his grey eyes fiercely resolute as he pressed the edge of the dagger more tightly against Regento's neck. "You have something that belongs to me."

Titus smiled, slightly raising his arms to show that Ancestral was not on his person. "Hello, Seidon, it's been a long time."

The way the Captain-General greeted him sent a shiver of recollection down Seidon's spine. He frowned in confusion, unable to pin-point exactly what it was about Titus that bothered him. Then unexpectedly, he was thrown in turmoil as Poem swung out of nowhere and forced him apart from Regento with a sliver of fire and ice.

Regento weakly stumbled into the guards, who quickly dragged him after the retreating President. It gave Poem wide aperture as he side-stepped an angry counterattack by Seidon's dagger, then fluidly backed away as Seidon followed the attack with a vicious thrust.

Poem brought his two trusty blades before him, and pushed Seidon back on his heels with a spray of ice. Seidon covered his face with his arm, while he unsheathed the rapier with his free hand, and rushed again at Poem.

Steel met against steel with a thunderous clash, and the deadlock was instantly broken as Seidon smacked his elbow across Poem's head. He traced the melee attack with his rapier, but Poem parried with one of daggers – flash-freezing the rapier's blade and shattering it in pieces on impact.

Poem closed the distance, spun his other dagger around and slugged Seidon in the solar plexus with its blunt end. The air was expelled from Seidon's lungs, and he fell to his knees, giving Poem the victory as he held one of his blades to Seidon's collar bone.

Poem looked up at the impinging soldiers, then glared at Titus. "Tell your soldiers to stay where they are."

Titus held his hand up, and the soldiers stopped their movement. Beside him, Mikaila's finger itched over the trigger.

"I have both on my sights," she said.

"Stand down, Lieutenant-Colonel," Titus replied, his eyes locked on the two men.

Mikaila bit down her morbid desire, and lowered her rifle. The Dragoons followed in unison.

"I'm enforcing my executive powers as a neutral emissary of the Church of the Twelve," Poem announced. "He's in my custody."

"I believe he has committed several serious infractions against this State," Titus said, "and should be tried in proper by our court."

"The Church has higher claims," Poem cut back. "You threaten a schism of our neutrality if you interfere."

Titus smirked to himself, and to everyone's surprise, he agreed. "By all means then, for your Grand Master's sake, let justice be done. My men will assist you in arranging a secured transport for you and your... guest."

Titus turned and left, forcing the guards and Dragoons to withdraw without further question. Mikaila was the last one to leave, trepidations and tribulations in her heart.

Under house arrest and by no means restrained, Daedlus was host to several court nobles and bureaucrats at his mansion. Most were disgruntled by the recent dismissal from the Royal Court, and all shared similar contempt for their Queen.

"My colleagues," Daedlus said as he poured red wine onto a fellow's empty glass, "we have reached the threshold of our tolerance. A democratic tradition that has stood for three centuries since the reformation of the royal regime is now broken."

"All owed to our beloved Dalena," the old man, Precidious, grumbled with sharp sarcasm. "That trollop would not listen to reason, and now it's come to this."

The rest quietly added their similar opinion like a sour taste on their tongues.

"We are obliged to restore the crown onto rightful heirs," Daedlus said. "With the King incapacitated, and an incompetent Queen, I see here an opportunity to bestow power to a steward."

"It was done once in the time of the Warrior-Queen, when she was away in battle," Precidious noted.

"And again when our King Ingren fought Rell Vant," Daedlus added. "I believe you were given the honour."

"For a short time," the old man said, not entirely enticed by the notion. "And if some of you might remember, my term was overseen by a selected consortium of lesser patricians, scholars and town officials."

"The quandary is not persuading them, but enforcing this prerogative without the support of the military." Daedlus paced around the circle of plotters, confident and full of command. "The key to dethrone the warmonger is the element of speed and distraction. We need an uprising outside the castle gates, a riot that will draw the Guards' attention away."

"There are few upstarts in this city," one of the nobles pointed out. "The Queen is loved by a vast majority of the people."

"People don't need to know the whole truth," Daedlus replied. "Lie, bribe, threaten. Tell them that their income will be siphoned to the war machine by simple means of legislation, and they will react. Browbeat foreign nationalists with deportation due to xenophobia, and they will stand for their rights. Once they're stirred, we put our instigators in place and lead them to the castle gates."

Precidious was intrigued with the plan. "We feign a peaceful audience with Her Majesty to discuss formal explanations to the court's dismissal."

"She will have no choice." Daedlus said darkly. "She will either concede to the pressure, or be taken down by brute force."

In his papal office, Mellka stood illuminated by the sunlight that flooded through the stained-glass windows, particularly facing one that depicted an ancient mosaic of the founder and Saint Knight, Alexander Mellka. Past the glass, he noted a flock of seagulls dancing across a serene blue sky peppered with clouds. Few remembered that the Church had maritime roots, as the oceans were a conduit to spread the Faith, hence why the Cathedral was built where it can be seen at sea and at the center of Floria – each spire a lighthouse. Although he hailed from the frigid North, he always enjoyed the salty scent wafting from the coast.

The doors thundered open, and Commander Falchier strode in. He bowed curtly, curious why the Grand Master bathed in the light, but thought nothing else of it. "It's been confirmed by our dioceses in Gabrialtar and Magna Carta, the sanction fleet has been decimated by a new type of weapon."

Mellka nodded bleakly to himself, having been warned by this new threat by the pony-tailed harbinger himself. He slowly turned away from the window, and approached his desk, where the Vade Mecum laid open to the Saint Knight's first-hand testament.

He ran his fingers across the words with deep reverence, and recited a passage. "...'Beyond all, even to the whim of foresight, from a land born in flame and quenched by the ocean to the East and South, the wings of all free people will shatter apart under the unforgiving thrust of the Vilkacis...' *Vilkacis...*" He had often wondered at the allegories behind the scripture, but now he was convinced it was all truth. "In ancient folklore, it was a malicious creature that transformed cursed men. At times, they were regarded as benevolent, who shared the fruits of knowledge and invention, all the while scheming with festering hatred."

Falchier was fascinated, albeit morbidly. "Transformed?"

"Not through flesh, but the soul," Mellka replied. "Like a maddened wolf, it's unable to return to its host, as without the soul... the body is dead. So it wanders until perchance it comes across another, heaping more sorrow and enmity." He closed the book, and faced Falchier. "Our great founder prophesied in detail the perils we have just discovered, and what's to come will not be forgiving to any man, woman, or child. Faith is our only shield now."

"Shall I summon the Order to arms?"

"Have them prepare, but do not let the battalions congregate in the same place. A united front, in this case, will not last." Mellka considered what was to come carefully. "This Church cannot condone Gabrialtar's preemptive actions, but neither will we choose sides. Perhaps we will put into practice a notion Poema Della'Cor had once suggested: remission of sin."

"Do we still trust Della'Cor?"

"That question will be graced on his return."

The decks trembled under the titan rumble of the engines as the *Highborn* lifted from the ground, and Mikaila sensed it under her boots. Accustomed to air travel, her nerves remained solid as she tightened the hem of her uniform and strapped on her gear and weapons in the privacy of her officer's quarters onboard the warship.

Sitting innocently on her bed was Marcus, his blue eyes wide from the wondrous terror of the military ambiance. Her presence consoled him, and likewise he warmed her otherwise ice-cold heart. He resembled so much like his father, except for the colour of the eyes, which he took after her own.

She smiled lovingly, and he took notice and smiled back.

Fastening the last button on her lapel, she knelt before him and gently fixed his hair. "The world's changing again, and we have to fight to protect those we love."

Marcus mimicked his mother, and softly pushed back a strand of hair that hung on her brow.

"Your father will be so proud." Mikaila kissed him on the forehead. "Be brave."

She stood up, and checked her revolver for its load, then slipped it tightly in the holster at her hip. She gave Marcus one last glance, and left the room to carry out her duties.

The might of Gabrialtar's air fleet ascended to the skies en masse; fully armed sky galleons of varying tonnage, carrying troops and armaments in their holds. It was a terrifying amalgam of sails, flags, and zeppelins, and the populace of Empyrean City was witness to the historic occasion.

At the port of Sewell's Abide, support ships still adhering their tradition to the sea, steered their prows from the docks, and trailed the air fleet. Amongst the few vessels that remained, mostly merchant ships and fishing boats, a frigate adorned with the standards of the Faithful was stationed at one of the piers. Sailor monks, armed with sewing needles for patching the canvases, and hatchets for cutting through rigging and lumber, served the vessel, which was their floating monastery and consecrated home, and were prepared to take sail back to Floria, but awaited the arrival of Poem and his prisoner.

Escorted by a pair of Inquisitor Knights, loaned from the local diocese, Poem led a shackled Seidon toward the ship. Both men remained quiet during the procession, not having said a single word since the incident at Name's Reclaim. The latter glanced up at the sky, where the legion of sky galleons scurried to war, and wondered if Titus had chosen the *Highborn* as his flagship.

Poem stopped at the foot of the pier. "You may take your leave, Knights. Send my gratitude to the Bishop."

The Knights bowed, and Poem turned to face Seidon as they parted. They stared at each other, their friendship tried and tested to its limits, and priorities mired by their parts in the grand scheme of things.

Seidon broke the silence. "Still fighting demons?"

"Long before we ever met," Poem replied.

"You've any idea how many of us you're letting down? Wondering if everything we've been through was all a mirage?"

"I'm still your friend, Seidon."

"Are you? You're driven, blinded, and so lost." Seidon wanted to believe that the Poem he knew all those years ago was still here before him, but something had changed. "Do you honestly believe that you just saved me from Gabrialtar's courts?"

"Titus is unpredictable," Poem argued. "He drew you out, knowing you'd come looking to retrieve your heirloom sword. He did not expect me to intervene in whatever plan he had in store for you."

Seidon grimaced. "So instead you're shipping me off to your new pope to answer for my heresy."

"Grand Master Mellka will spare you," Poem said. "I'm certain of it."

"Only if I submit, and become like you."

"I need this, Seidon, and I don't expect you to accept it. There's a corruption of the spirit everywhere I've been, driving a wedge between us all. This calling has given me focus, and a chance to travel along a righteous path."

"Piety doesn't suit your colours, Poem."

"The Church has been cleansed since you were last there, and I believe only the Church can mend this broken world," Poem said. "Now I'm taking you back so you can open your eyes."

"Let him go," Priamos said from behind Poem,

Poem grimaced as he felt the cold barrel of a sawed-off rifle against the small of his back.

"Take off his shackles and let us be," Priamos demanded, privy to the sailor monks manning the ship behind him.

Poem took a step forward in a feint to unshackle his prisoner, then replied to Priamos' threat with a brutal roundhouse elbow to the side of the old shopkeeper's head. Giving Priamos no chance to recover, he ripped the rifle from his hands, grabbed the man by his shirt and threw him down.

Priamos landed unceremoniously, disoriented, and Poem remorselessly threw the rifle aside.

Seidon bent down beside Priamos to check him for injury, then glared at Poem. "When Dalena told me about you, I didn't want to believe her. What have you become, Poem?"

He stood up and confronted him, just as a sky galleon loomed overhead and blotted out the sun.

From the *Highborn*'s upper deck, Titus watched the confrontation between the two old friends with an amused half-grin. He wore a full combat uniform beneath his greatcoat and iron epaulets, with his gun on one side and the Ancestral on the other.

With unmatched finesse, he removed Ancestral from its sheath – its hardened crystal blade shimmering under the sunlight – and tossed the heirloom sword overboard. The blade tumbled end over end, subject to the will of gravity, until it cleanly impaled itself on the ground between Poem and Seidon. Both men were startled, and both looked up at him, though distant they were from each other.

Titus scoffed at his own diverting thought, which he kept to himself, and moved away from the railing as the *Highborn* drew further away from the port.

Seeing the Ancestral shimmering a few feet ahead of him, Seidon set aside his questions about Titus, and kept his impulse at bay as he still was uncertain of Poem's intention.

Poem knew he had the advantage, yet he stepped back and widened his arms as if to surrender. "If you really believe I've lost my way, Seidon, then strike me down. I won't defend myself."

It took Seidon a breath to act. He sprinted for the sword, cut his shackles in half against its edge, then grabbed hold of its hilt and rushed toward Poem. He stopped half an inch short of decapitating his friend, and he finally saw the truth in Poem's haunted eyes.

Seidon pulled away. "Just remember what they always say about fighting dragons."

He turned around to help Priamos to his feet, and with a sidelong glance to Poem, they hurried away from the docks toward the crowded avenues leading to the bazaar.

Poem let them go, resigned to the tendency of his heart. He thought of what Seidon said. "...you become one yourself."

Magna Carta's shattered task force arrived at the capital, the dry docks already filled with vessels needing repair, and the wounded were carried off to the hospitals. Leeway was given to the *Second Awakening*, and a path was cleared for Messer and his officers as they disembarked.

"I want you to personally oversee the repairs to the Fleet, Captain," Messer said to Semmes. "We have little time to act if Gabrialtar commits to an all-out attack on our soil." He turned to another officer, "Instruct the Admiralty and the War Office to gather for an emergency council with Her Majesty now."

"There may be a delay, sir," the sergeant of the escort guard said, his attention focused ahead with the rest of his alerted soldiers.

Messer, in his frenzy to organize things, only now noticed that the road toward the royal castle had become crowded with curious citizens. Further ahead, a large horde of men and women were rioting before the main gates. Infantrymen and calvary protected the castle perimeter zealously, straining to keep the masses in order and far from causing damage or injury.

"What's going on here? Why are they protesting?" Messer demanded, feeling uneasy.

"They claim that the Queen had passed a conscription bill requiring all labourers to commit to military service for two years with the threat of imprisonment or unemployment," the sergeant responded. "Others claim that their annual income had been subsidized and routed toward war funds, leaving them a paltry sum to feed their families. None of this is true."

"There are dissidents amongst them," Messer said. "We need to weed them out before this mob turns to rebellion."

An instigator threw himself onto one of the soldiers guarding the gate, and wrestled with the guard's rifle. The struggle was followed blindly by other enraged protesters, who attempted to force the armed troops into a dangerous bottle neck, but the cavalry strode in and broke up the throng – inciting them to more violence. Bottles, rocks, and fruits were thrown along with vulgarities, until the guns sounded.

It was as if a stampede was unleashed.

"We need to get this rabble under control!" Messer shouted over the cacophony. He grabbed one of his terrified officers by his arm, and pulled him in. "Get the Marines out here! Tell them to lock this place down!"

As the officer rushed back to the docks to carry out the order, Messer turned to the infantrymen guarding him. "Nobody passes through those gates!"

* * *

Vant was deep in his study. He sat by the paltry table scribing down his memoirs in ink, with slivers of sunlight peering through the window slit. Although involved in his writing, his ears prickled to the infernal cacophony outside the walls.

The deadbolts to his cell door unlocked, then a heartbeat later, the warden was thrown against the door – cracking it open on impact. The man dropped to the floor, knocked out cold, and two cowled Insidians stepped over him. They entered like prowling predators, obsidian daggers in hand, gleaming with the same deadly purpose as their eyes.

Vant calmly laid down his writing tool, and stood up to face them. Without provocation, he immediately grabbed hold of his chair and swung it at the closest assailant, then reversed direction and threw it at the other. He turned to the table and tipped it over to its side – scattering everything to the floor. While it provided a temporary obstacle, he heel-kicked one of its legs and snapped it free, giving him a makeshift baton to defend himself.

The first assailant to recover charged at him, and grew more restless as each of his efforts were refuted by Vant's grace and skill with the baton. Each missed thrust and swing was rewarded by a vicious counterattack, severely bruising the Insidian and staggering his momentum.

The second assailant joined the fray, tackling Vant against the far wall. Too close to parry with the baton, Vant speared the man in the abdomen, forcing the air out his lungs, then pushed him away. The first Insidian charged again, this time slicing a gash along Vant's forearm, then kicking him across the legs. As Vant dropped to one knee, the Insidian murderously wrapped his fingers around the ex-general's windpipe.

Vant grabbed hold of the Insidian's wrist and dug his fingers under the skin and muscle to force the zealot to release his grip. Adding to the desperation, he mercilessly beat the baton against the man's arm and head.

Growling and grunting in pain, the Insidian released Vant, but it left the ex-general wide open for the second assailant's attack. He sprinted at him with his dagger ready to stab, but never met his mark as a gunshot rang out and struck the man's back. He stumbled against the overturned table, and writhed in agonizing pain.

The last Insidian reacted to the distraction, and Vant seized the opportunity. He grabbed the writing utensil off the floor – droplets of ink trailing it – and stabbed its tip through the assassin's larynx. Shocked and unable to respond, the Insidian dropped his dagger and reached for his throat, only to be struck unconscious as Vant batted his baton under the man's chin with his entire might.

The Insidian dropped to the floor, and the dust resettled. Vant turned to the doorway to see who had saved him from an untimely demise.

Although Tenshi never met him in person, she knew him as well and as profoundly as Seidon did. "Seidon told me I could trust you," she said as she lowered her smoking handgun.

Surprised by the sweet sound of her voice, Vant paused midway of a verbal riposte, and dropped the baton. He was puzzled at first, but slowly and instinctively he recognized her. Awestruck by her angelic presence, he approached her, and with a slight bow, he gently took her hand, and lightly kissed her knuckles.

"I've waited all these years wondering... and finally I see that Seidon's dreams are of quality. With you, how can any man desire anything else?"

Tenshi smiled politely, pulling her hand away. "You haven't lost your touch, General." Her tone grew serious. "The Queen needs you."

Vant's grin faded, and he turned to the Insidian that was shot in the back, but was still alive. He reached down and grabbed one of the fallen daggers, seized the man by his hair and cowl, and presented the sharp edge of the weapon across the chin.

"Who sent you? That insufferable cardinal?"

The Insidian shook his head, wheezing.

"I will ease your suffering. Tell me."

"A-an associate... of Daedlus... and Marquis..." the Insidian garbled, suffering greatly as blood filled his lungs. "...Bishopric owed the ransom... Wing... swords..." The pain and fear overwhelmed the assassin, who beneath the dark clothes was just a misled human being.

"Gloriam be with you." Vant delivered what he promised, and the Insidian slumped. He let the body go, dropping the dagger beside him.

"Wing of swords?" Tenshi repeated.

"Gabrialtar's symbol of independence," Vant replied, and knew who it was that extorted a favour through intermediaries from the local bishop, but withheld the name. He stepped out of the cell for the first time in what seemed like an eternity, and ushered Tenshi with a gentle gesture of his hand. "Lead the way, milady, there's a Queen to be saved."

*   *   *

Dalena watched the escalating riot from the observation gallery, and felt disheartened with personal failure at allowing this to happen. Nonetheless, she remained steadfast in her position, especially with the crisis that emerged from the Gabrialtar incident, and put her trust in the city and naval garrisons to keep this under control.

The doors to the Throne Room were opened unexpectedly, and several members of the Royal Court strode in, lacking no confidence in their march and determined with hidden deeds. The Throne Guards were immediately suspicious, and encircled the Queen in a protective wall that divided her from the courtiers as she turned away from the gallery to meet them.

None of them, except Precidious, stopped to greet her with a formal bow, and when Dalena spotted Daedlus amongst them, she knew it was his scheming that instigated the partisan revolt.

"Your Highness," the old man said, "in light of the protests, we request an audience to resolve this matter."

Dalena approached them, stepping away from the Throne Guards' armoured protection. "What lies did you spread to twist them against the King?"

"They are shouting at you, madam," Daedlus replied coolly. "Defying your attempt to wrestle all power to yourself."

"Please, Your Highness," Precidious cut in, "we're here peacefully on behalf of the Royal Court and the people. There is much doubt and dissatisfaction concerning your reign, and with this new conflict with Gabrialtar ready to erupt, we feel you must step down as Queen, and retake command of His Majesty's Royal Squadron in defense of this kingdom. We insist to discuss the terms of your dethronement."

"Dethronement?" Dalena was appalled at the unabashed treachery. "And put yourselves in place as stewards?"

"It's not uncommon during times of great duress," Precidious said.

"From nobles to plotters," Dalena retorted in disgust. "Guards, unsheathe your swords."

Without hesitation, the Throne Guards revealed their long blades in unison, and held their arms out to point the sharp tips toward the traitorous nobles. The partisans were surprised and fearful of the swords and moved back, but Daedlus held his ground proudly.

"You don't have a choice," Daedlus said. "The wheels are already in motion to undo what you've done."

"Is this how you love your Queen?!" an invigorated voice called from behind the throne chair as it was overrun by a platoon of Elites. "Is this how you treat my wife?!"

With a hand on Rowen's shoulder for balance, King Ingren the Third stood before the conspirators and soldiers – all humbled by his presence. "Guards, place away your blades," he ordered firmly, and with great reverence, the Guards replaced their swords back in their scabbards.

Dalena, warm tears streaming down her cheeks, ran to her husband and embraced him wholly. Body, mind, and soul, she felt complete again. "I missed you so much..." she whispered into his ear.

"My Julia, I'm here only and always for you..." They kissed, and for a while, all the troubles of the world dissipated.

As lips parted, the monarchs understood their places, and returned to royal etiquette.

Ingren moved away from Dalena, his expression hardened, and climbed down the steps to meet his former royal courtiers face to face. All bent their knees to him, with unknowing dread and embarrassment, and they expected a brute reprisal from him. Daedlus wanted to flee, but his bravado faltered, and he submitted.

Ingren's cold ire was focused on the ambassador. "This was all a ruse to give Gabrialtar a reason to declare war, to fill that emptiness of greed leftover from the fall of the corporate regimes… and indeed the wheels are turning."

Too ashamed, Daedlus kept his gaze to the floor. "I–I'm just a pawn in this game, Your Majesty. What I've done, I have done in service to my kingdom. I have not broken my oath–"

"You have broken more than words, Ambassador Daedlus," Ingren cut back sharply, glaring at the rest of the penitent malcontents, including Precidious. "Tell me truthfully, did you all consider your spouses and children when you pursued this unprincipled affair?"

No one replied, as their sins were splayed open, and Ingren spared no quarter. "You've all disgraced yourselves, your nation, and all you hold dear. Your titles, your estates, everything you traitors took for granted by the generosity of this Crown shall be returned to this Crown to pay for the damages you've done to my kingdom."

Precidious, the oldest and longest serving member of the court was shaken to his core. He collapsed on both his knees, looking to the Queen for forgiveness, but Ingren was merciless in his reproach.

"How many were hurt by your schemes? How many lie dead in the streets?" Ingren demanded, then stared at the repentant Chancellor. "You were raised by my father from humble beginnings because he believed you to be moderate and loyal, and you've shattered that trust with your moral ambivalence."

Every member of the conspiracy dropped on both knees with heads drooped, Daedlus being the last of them to surrender fully. Ingren gave a nod to Rowen, who in turn drew his sword, and gave the order.

"Rifles at the ready!"

The Throne Guards stood aside, as the Elites armed and pointed their rifles at the Royal Court. They waited unflinchingly for the next command.

"There will be no trial. By established laws, treason demands a heavy price," Ingren declared. "All of you stand, and face your judgment." Terror gripped the courage of all of them, but Ingren lost his compassion when they threatened his Queen. "Stand!"

Those that accepted their punishment stood, and helped the others to their feet. They cowered before the muzzles of the Elites, as Rowen raised his sword to commit the King's order.

Caressing her unborn child, Dalena asked herself what sort of future was possible beyond this crossroad, and refused to allow her King to become yet another monster.

To the surprise of everyone in the room, she stepped between the guns and the men and women who had demanded her abdication. "Forgive them, my King."

Ingren was amazed at his wife, and humbly admitted in the privacy of his heart, that he wouldn't have forgiven himself for carrying out this execution. So he stood with her, and Rowen quietly signaled the Elites to stand down.

Ingren grasped Julia's hand tightly, and faced the courtiers. "Your Queen forgives you, for she is and always will be my better half."

Dalena's noble gesture instantly earned everyone's respect and admiration, breaking through even Daedlus' rigid skin. All approached her, even Ingren, Rowen, and the soldiers, and all bent a knee before her.

"Are you finally ready to lead this world?" Vant asked as he entered the chamber, unarmed and brazen.

The reaction of the Elites and the Throne Guards were reflexive. They simultaneously drew their rifles and swords and pointed them at Vant, quickly rearranging their formations to give him no space to assail or escape.

Then, to everyone's mixed relief and surprise, Tenshi appeared behind Vant, and stood fearlessly at his side.

Vant bent a knee, and kept his eyes locked on Ingren and Dalena. "I, Rell Vant of Guard, am ready to serve you, this kingdom, to whatever end."

XVIII. Brinkmanship

XVIII. Brinkmanship

Titus stood in the city of Guard's old amphitheater, its arched dome open to the sky, and the seats filled with nervous senators. He was in the company of several Gabrialtar officers and diplomats, and all waited for Senator Reich to decide.

A shadow crossed the skylight above them, and Reich glanced up to see the black iron keel of one of the sky galleons travel past – one of countless armed vessels coveting the sky over the city. He looked down at the string of written papers that constituted a formal treaty between Guard and Gabrialtar, and signed it. The signature felt heavy with liability, but he had little choice, and once finished he passed it on to the next senator to sign.

Titus grinned with satisfaction. "Reparations for your lost vessels and crew during your misconceived blockade will be paid in full as per addendum. I'm glad, Senators, that you've opted for the way of peace."

Reich kept his frustration in deep reserve. "We no longer have a standing army to defy yours, Captain-General."

"Shame." Titus heedlessly took the treaty papers and handed them over to one of the diplomats, then strode away with most of his military cortege.

Stepping outside into the heart of the ringed city, meshed between antiquated architectural designs and future-centric engineering, he took a breath of the familiar air and reminisced of his days here. He walked across the plaza where the Sorcerer Cannon once stood, where he was joined by Mikaila and a contingent of Gabrialtar Dragoons, and noted places where the scars of war were still visible as reminders or as negligence of the contractors to renovate.

Here and there were small craters gouged from the sides of buildings and the ground where the cannonball bombardment struck, compounded with blast marks from gunfire and explosions that the rain has yet to wash away.

"The City of Guard is no longer a threat," Titus announced to his officers, "and the list of Magna Carta's allies has adamantly shortened. I've appointed Colonel Ahcoss as gestapo chief, and assuredly he and his staff will manage things here while we depart for Floria."

"A messenger was sent from the office of the Grand Master," Mikaila reported. "The Order of the Faithful have presented an open invitation to us."

"Considering the Church now also represents the interests of Templari and its surrounding principalities, this meeting with the Grand Master can prove to be fruitful."

"I doubt they will commit to war. Can we use their neutrality to our advantage?"

"All in due time," Titus said with a smirk, proud of the fleet hovering overhead. "Let the strings play their part, and the sonata will come to together."

Poem was led into the Hall of the Tribunal by Commander Falchier, where Mellka was in discussion with the Cardinals on a heated matter. The dialogue ended abruptly as Poem walked to the middle of the room, and after subsequent bows of respect toward the Grand Master, the crimson-robed Cardinals parted.

"I prayed for your safe return," Mellka said.

Poem lowered his gaze humbly as Mellka faced him. "Titus' forces are coming here."

"On the invitation of our Holy Community, yes," Mellka replied. "Nearly all the eastern nations have resigned to a truce of non-aggression with Gabrialtar, and none have the military or economic strength to act otherwise. Only Magna Carta and this Church stand to provide a detriment to the oncoming storm."

"I... failed to keep the peace between these nations."

"What could you have done against such overwhelming odds? No one can stop the tide of fate."

Poem felt something disturbing stir, and he looked up at the Grand Master. "What do you intend to do when Titus gets here?"

"What we must do. I will support his cause, declaring a crusade against the infidels. Here's an ample opportunity to cast aside all non-believers, and bring all else in line with the articles of our Faith. The alternative is to submit, and that I will not do. Rather to wield the spear beside my enemy than bend the knee at his heel."

"What?!" Poem's appalled outburst startled Falchier, who immediately seized Poem by the arm to keep him from advancing on the Grand Master. "You can't choose sides!"

"*You* have chosen, haven't you? Your heart's afire with the need to fight alongside your friends." Mellka was unamused, and had expected it. "Yes, I know about the heretic, this Seidon you're so fond of. The monks who brought you here have broken their vow of silence to reveal your disloyalty."

"I tried to convince him you were a forgiving leader, that the Church was a symbol of unity... but he didn't believe me." Poem angrily pulled his arm away from Falchier's grip. "I have no quarrel to give; I did what was right."

"Yet what seemed right was not necessarily just." Mellka shook his head disappointedly. "I misjudged your willingness to serve this Order. I thought I understood your spirit, and had firmly believed you've proven your worth, but alas I'm an imperfect being in a far more imperfect world."

"Then ask yourself if what you're doing is for the sake of all people, or for the single-minded vision you've concocted for yourself."

Mellka scoffed. "Do not propose to question my reasoning. You bound yourself to this Church, and you wear the cloth of shadow. You are beneath me."

Poem wasn't swayed. "You claimed you will never repeat the mistakes of your forebears, and here you are taking sides on an unjust war! You're a hypocrite!"

"It's a matter of perspective, and I'm afraid yours is clouded."

Two squads of Iron Sabres entered the room, and pointed their blades at Poem.

"What punishment befits the disowned brainchild of madmen who dubbed themselves the Sorcerer Siblings?" Mellka tantalized. "Beneath us there's a chamber for sinners that was conjugated for the last man who defied me. Ponder what you've done, meditate on your regrets... for the rest of your years."

Before Poem could let his rage flow, the Iron Sabres clutched his arms and roped him. He thrashed and screamed, as they snatched his daggers, but was knocked unconscious by a fisted, gauntlet-laden blow to the back of his head and carried away past the Arsenal, far beneath the Sacred Vault, and into the depths of the catacombs once reserved for the Church's wealthiest patrons.

Poem was brusquely thrown into a claustrophobic sepulcher, and the heavy stone door locked shut behind him. The place was dark and damp, and felt far more ancient than the Cathedral itself. He recovered from the ground, his head throbbing from the thump, fumbled around the murk for a sense of bearing until his eyes adjusted to dim pinpricks of reflected candlelight.

The dilapidated walls wore scores of inscriptions and designs, including a large mandala that featured the allegorical numen drake encircling itself in an attempt to bite its tail. He passed his fingers across the agone cryptograms with certain deference and intrigue, until he bumped against an old desk – scattering a stack of dusty tomes off its surface.

Beyond the decayed creaking of dust and splinters from the wooden furniture, Poem heard a heavy sigh of exasperation. A desiccated hand reached toward a lamp hung low on the wall, and turned its flame higher, washing the sepulcher in an eerie orange glow.

Poem took a step back in recoil, not quite trusting his eyes.

Huddled in the corner was Abaster, his sickly pale body draped by his Cardinal robes that no longer held its once bright crimson. His limbs were deathly thin, his eyes and cheeks sunken, and barely had the strength to look up at Poem.

"Are you my angel?" Abaster hushed weakly, his starved body making his cuirass look oversized. "I was dead for a time… I was not saved. Have you come to kill me at last?"

The dry rasps of desperation nearly exhausted the former clergyman, and Poem noticed now that Abaster clutched tightly at his chest, where a black crossbow bolt stuck out from his chest.

"No one here had the decency to release you from your torment?" Poem took a breath of courage to approach Abaster. "How is it you still live?"

Abaster now recognized Poem as he got closer, and attempted to laugh, only to cough severely. "Because of you... he feared you, he wanted to find your weakness. Weren't you there when he asked what became of the Elixir? I heard him from these walls, and his chemists told me." He took a few hardened breaths. "He left me with this bolt, fed me a few drops, and returned me to life. What life? A half-life, barely."

Poem grimaced at the torture Mellka had allowed on this pitiful man, and was convinced the Grand Master was no better than Vant or Titus. Men who twist and shape the world at their whim, caring less for those who suffered by their choices. "Live long enough, Cardinal, and you shall have your revenge."

"What use to me is wrath...? I learned its sour taste when I chased the General, only to trip on my own pride." Abaster wanted to cry, but had no moisture left in his bloodshot eyes. "It serves nothing but itself."

Poem understood plainly, but it made little difference if he was to be left forgotten in the bowel of the Cathedral. "Is there a way out?"

"Only through me, if you'd dare." Abaster's eyes looked to Poem fiercely, even though his body limped as if the invisible ropes that held him slackened. "I will forgive you."

Poem despised the feeling he felt, a mix of pathos and remorse. "You can live, regain your strength," he urged.

"Please," Abaster pleaded, and with surprising brevity, he summoned what was left of his inner spirit and ripped the sharp bolt from his chest. He shakily held the bolt toward

Poem while blood and thick fluids stained his armour and robes.

Poem took the bolt, sensing its deadly shaft and point by its weight, and with great reserve on his part, he moved behind the Cardinal. With a sense of relief, Abaster lowered his chin, exposing the nape of neck, and gave Poem full disclosure to end his pitiful existence quickly and without pain.

Poem hesitated. He knew where to strike, and had dished death countless times in battle, yet this was an errand of mercy, not survival or even vengeance. He restrained his apprehension, and buried all other feelings, then delivered the killing stroke.

Abaster fell forward quietly, and remained still forever, leaving Poem alone to discover a means of escape.

He felt a cool breeze against his skin, and Poem strained in the murk to find its source. When at last he found it, at the spot on the wall where Abaster had rested his back, he realized that the Cardinal meant what he said literally about a way out. With his release, a narrow cavity was revealed. It was barely large enough to fit a grown man trimmed of a belly, and extended deeper underground.

To where it led, Poem didn't know, but regardless he took the lamp from its bracket and started his way down, pausing for a moment to quietly thank Abaster.

Although his legs still felt numb from his long poison-induced sleep, Ingren was more than glad to be up and about surveying the repairs and refitting on several warships. He was closely followed by a retinue of Elites led by Rowen, and accompanied by his top military officers that included Messer. Dalena was at his side, holding his hand warmly, and ever serving as his upwelling of strength.

He boarded the *Second Awakening*, to which a path was cut for him by the crew on a strict order from Captain Semmes, who supervised the bolstering of the ship's defenses. Stepping onto the main deck, Ingren looked beyond the forest of workers, ropes, and masts, to where his Royal Fleet kept vigilance on sovereign waters while floating batteries served as hastily improvised anti-air artillery.

"If they use these missiles again, our ships have no chance," Ingren said, still awed by the report of the new weapon Gabrialtar had unleashed in his absence. He turned to his generals and admirals, gently letting go of his wife's hand. "The old strategies of the battlefield no longer apply."

"Neither do old allegiances," Messer added sourly, punctuating the recent news of Guard's truce with Gabrialtar.

"All the reason to believe this offensive push will be taken to the beachhead," Catherano said, a veteran Field Marshall since the days Ingren's father ruled. "And I doubt they will bargain a pact with us."

"They are motivated by their independence," Vant said, surprising many who had no idea he was amongst them. "If we take this fight to their soil with a preemptive counterattack, they will have no choice but to revert their advance. Their new weapon will lose its main tactical purpose."

Ingren glanced at Vant, who was dressed in a robe and cowl to protect him from vindictive eyes, even though most of the King's retinue regarded him with no less disdain. "Let the diplomats have their turn."

Vant stood amidst the Elites' formation enclosure, trapped, and protected, yet his charismatic presence stood at equal level to Ingren. "Your diplomats will all be refuted. Your Field Marshall is correct in predicting that Titus will be marching here, and will do so when all your preparations to meet him lag behind."

"If they do, Your Highness," Catherano said gravely, "then our forces are ill-equipped to repel them. Our bombard towers and the Navy's batteries were designed to hammer ships off our coast, not wheedle them from the sky."

"Changes are being made as we speak," Dalena assured. "Although Guard and Templari are no longer allied, they have freely loaned us their best mechanicians, and are redesigning our turret mounts and rifled ammunition to fire at higher angles, further range, and at a much faster rate."

"We will need every edge, my Queen," Ingren said. "Perhaps the recusant Tinkerers may want to willingly assist us, and gain them some reprieve from their penance."

"I have confidence the new elected Helmer will have an open mind," she replied. "Despite their collusion with the Squires of Debonair, they're capitalists not sabre-rattlers."

"Modernizing our defenses is our top priority." Ingren looked at the hardened retinue. "When do we expect the Enemy forces to approach?"

"Like all war machines, an army needs supplies," Vant patronizingly stated as a matter of fact, much to the chagrin of the military officers. "An occupation force that strays too far from its supply wagon is forced to withdraw, or take from the lands they conquer. An attack on this continent from anywhere across the Vast Blue will draw the supply lines thin. If Titus is to commit to the first assault, he will not aim directly at the capital, but first establish a base of operations."

"He will try to commandeer one of our ports to the south," Messer guessed.

"Freya, to be exact." Vant was doubtlessly confident. "A commonwealth nation still loyal to the King, a hub of commercial activity, and the center of art and music. Titus, if he's still the same man I served with, is an ardent follower of opera."

Ingren nodded in understanding. "Freya houses the oldest and most prestigious opera hall in the world, amongst other galleries of fine arts. Would he dare scorch it to gain a foothold in my kingdom?"

"There are lengths some men will cross," Vant replied, speaking from experience. "I believe Admiral Messer can attest to the extremities of Gabrialtar's drive."

"So then we act," Ingren said. "Admiral Messer, take charge of the Squadron and attempt to disrupt the Gabrialtar maritime supply lines and trade routes. Harass them by whatever means, and as a former buccaneer, your guerilla tactics will prove very useful."

"Aye, Your Majesty," Messer replied with excitement rising in his chest. "A few ships will suffice; I suggest we hold back the rest of the fleet should we need to mount a direct offensive."

"At your discretion, Admiral," Ingren said, then turned to the other military officers. "Marshall Catherano," Ingren addressed as the Admiralty left to carry out their orders. "Call all our regiments to action, we have a kingdom to defend."

"Yes, my King, at once."

Now apart from the scrutiny of the military officers, as Catherano and the generals mustered eagerly to their duties, Vant made his request. "With your permission, King Ingren,

I want my men released and pardoned. They have better use on the field. If anyone should stop Titus from gaining a foothold, it should be me."

"What do you intend to accomplish with so few men?" Dalena asked the same question that was on Ingren's mind.

"Only the impossible," Vant replied confidently.

Ingren thought it through, measuring trust carefully. "Against the advice of many, I will release you and your loyal soldiers to the cause. Gather your former army if they're still willing, and I will summon volunteers from what's left of our allied forces to reinforce your offensive."

"Trust is frail," Dalena said. "A detachment of Elites will also accompany you. Your newfound fealty will be kept under scrutiny."

Vant grimaced, but accepted it. "I don't intend to break my word."

"Seidon and Tenshi have vouched for you more than once," Dalena said. "You are in their debt, and they are in our trust."

Vant was truly grateful, and nodded. "Then I promise to cast away your doubts, Majesties."

"Something's changed in you, General Vant," Ingren said, "but I ask: Are you doing this for yourself? For those that have remained at your side in renown and in disgrace? Or for something much more profound?"

"One and all, my King," Vant answered.

Ingren nodded, and looked over to his wife. "My dear Queen, will you draw up the official decree and assist General Vant in reforming his army?"

"I will," Dalena assured, and with an escort of guards and soldiers accompanied Vant back to the castle.

The encumbrance of his kingship, compounded by his exhausted bones in convalescence, was taking its toll on Ingren, and Rowen noted it keenly. He approached carefully, and lent his shoulder for his King to lean on.

"Shall we return to the castle, my King?" Rowen suggested. "The doctors were very explicit about your need for sustenance and rest."

"Not yet, my good friend," Ingren said, seeing the crowds around the shipyards salute and cheer him warmly as they passed. "My people need me to strengthen their resolve, and I need them to strengthen mine."

"Of course." Rowen was about to let Ingren go, but the King held him tightly.

"Thank you, Rowen," Ingren said sincerely, "for staying by your Queen's side when it seemed the whole world was falling apart. I couldn't ask for a better friend... and that's why I have submitted your candidacy to the judiciaries for consideration to be my next Chancellor."

Rowen was surprised, and his humility showed. "I don't deserve such position."

"You'll still be watching my back, Rowen, and you do deserve it."

Rowed bowed to his King. "Be it a lowly messenger, captain of the Throne Guards, or Chancellor of your court, I will serve my King and Queen to the end of my days."

Ingren grasped Rowen's shoulder as brothers would. "Don't ever change."

* * *

Amidst hundreds of the King's battalions engaged in formation maneuvers on the vast fields outside the white defensive walls of the capital, with the royal spires rising in the distance, Tenshi watched and waited patiently. She was alone, even as soldiers marched by her, and she persevered her fears for Seidon alone.

The artillery regiments sounded with their cannons, targeting hot air balloons, as engineers attempted to modify the weapons to shoot higher and faster in preparation for the sky galleons. Despite the acrid smoke and cacophony, Tenshi kept her eyes ahead to the horizon, hoping with silent prayers that Seidon fared well and was on his way back to her.

Her entire existence was owed to him, and she yearned with every twine of her being to go out and find him, but her duty to Magna Carta kept her feet where they were. The notion tore her apart, yet strengthened her fierce desire.

Queen Dalena approached with a pair of Throne Guards flanking her, and joined Tenshi at her side. "He'll find his way back."

"I should've never let him go," Tenshi said, suddenly regretting the bitterness. "From the moment I awoke in Seidon's dreams, sensing everything he is and so much more, I knew I was anchored to him forever. We grew up together, yet we were both so different. Now that I'm flesh and bone... it's so easy to feel timid and alone."

Dalena knew exactly how she felt, yet could never imagine the magic of Tenshi's existence. "This war is tearing all of us apart, stirring old grudges and testing the limits of fellowship. We need every hand we can trust to set things right again."

Tenshi glanced beside her to Dalena. "What will you have me do?"

"Be at Vant's side," Dalena said flatly. "Make sure he stays in line."

Dressed in monk robes they had forcibly borrowed, Seidon and Priamos discreetly paid the boatman and disembarked from the scow onto the jetty, whose stonework led up to Floria's main port. The Cathedral stood luminous in the sunlight, and foreboding in its stature. With hundreds of Inquisitor Knights patrolling, amongst other members of the Faithful hierarchy, and the indifferent attitudes of the locals, subtlety was a thin disguise. Nonetheless, they walked toward the heart of the town, brisk with religious enthusiasm and surrounded by magnificent gardens.

"We're here, thanks to you," Priamos said, pulling back his hood and taking a breath of free air. "The Squires have their hands full with bloody noses., and won't dream of chasing an old man across the globe when they have other scars to patch."

"Don't stay in Floria too long, Priamos, war's spreading like a plague."

"I won't. You've given me a chance to start anew, and I won't squander it."

Seidon was a bit unnerved by the Inquisitor Knights treading along the cobbled streets, preferring to keep his cowl up, but he smirked at Priamos' glee. "Most of us don't get that chance in a lifetime."

"You're one of few people I've ever known to give everyone the benefit of the doubt. I hope you can find this friend of yours and prove it to him."

"Poem knows," Seidon said. "If he's here, I'll find him."

"Then be off." Priamos patted Seidon's shoulder. "I'm proud to have met you."

"Likewise, old man." Seidon reached into his cloak and pulled out the ornate dagger that once belonged to Priamos' son. "Poem snuck this in my boot when he arrested me... I return this to you. It served me well, but it belongs in your hands. Maybe it can help you rebuild your shop."

Priamos held his son's blade once more in his hands, and tears threatened to well up in his eyes. He clutched it to his chest. "A mark of our victory."

"Have courage," Seidon said as he pulled away, offering a warm smile.

Priamos smiled in return, and sadly watched Seidon walk away, heading toward the Cathedral. "Godspeed, Sir Harbrid."

A shadow cut across the town, and the thrum of powerful engines was heard in the wind. The *Highborn* arrived overhead, and slowed its momentum and descent. It was unaccompanied by its fleet, and its weaponry stowed....

Titus' footsteps echoed in the grand waiting vestibule of the Cathedral as he toured the premises. The floor tiles were massive, fashioned from veined marble, and the walls were lined with arched alcoves. In each recess stood a limestone statue of a former pontiff, whose base was written the name and date of reign in gold leafing. The sculpted faces and postures seemed venerable, almost saintly, but Titus knew each had accorded their own heap of failings.

The vestibule, which also served as a public space for weekly sermons, had a dozen doors leading to other parts of the edifice, and were each guarded by Inquisitor Knights. Unarmoured, except for their white robes and their staves, they maintained a placid vigilance.

One of the doors swung open, and Grand Master Mellka stepped through. Titus gave him a sidelong glance, then continued his tour of the vestibule's artwork.

Mellka approached him, keeping his reservations about the man tightly capped. "The Holy Community is grateful that you have accepted our invitation, Captain-General."

Titus casually passed his finger along one of the statues to check the dust accumulated on its surface, and was mildly surprised it had none. "I'm here because the Presidency ordered me to, Your Lordship, and I'm rather curious how you will approach this situation without breaking your exalted neutrality."

Mellka wasn't moved by Titus' imperiousness. "To what end are you carrying this war?"

"Until I feel the infractions on my homeland have been vindicated," Titus said simply, masking something much darker beneath his words. "To see the Royal Capital in ruins, and the western countryside burning... madness is art onto itself."

"The Kingdom of Magna Carta account to one-third of our believers, and have been truly steadfast to the Church. I will not see them come to harm by your machinations."

"Ah, and so we arrive at the crux of this causerie," Titus said, exaggerating his hand gestures. "Are we so concerned with churchgoers now? Have you counted heads and noticed the numbers have dwindled since you've taken office?"

"Don't mock me," Mellka warned. "Few weapons can stop the Faithful from rising up."

"As I understand it, a couple of your Faithful made another attempt on Rell Vant's life, and now the Magna Carta bishopric is under scrutiny of the King."

"These errant believers were influenced by corrupt members of the Royal Court, and themselves led astray by empty promises from you."

Titus giggled to himself. "Please, Grand Master, we are steering from my purpose here. Whatever you have to offer, be it toward the same end as mine."

"There's a lesson to be learned about retaining too much pride," Mellka rebuked. "Perhaps I should take this matter of ours directly to your superiors."

Titus' half-grin appeared more sinister with the crazed glaze of his eyes. "Do as you wish, Grand Master. If we're through chatting frivolously, I will return to my campaign. When the dust settles, and all the fires have been snuffed, then perhaps you and I can come to more... ineluctable terms."

With a casual nod of salute, Titus spun on his heels and strode away. Mellka fumed, never having been treated with such disrespect, and he glared at Titus' retreating figure with deep animosity.

From one of the doors closest to the Grand Master, Commander Falchier stepped out, his own hard gaze at the Captain-General. "We have the means in place to subdue him and his vessel, if you give the word."

"No, I will not tamper with the fate already in store for this mongrel." Mellka drew away pensively, "Perhaps Poem was right in his view, though narrow... I misjudged him too harshly."

Falchier wasn't as quick to forgive. "He found a way out of the sepulcher, through a breach. I've sent two of my best after him."

"There is no way out, as I'm sure the dear Cardinal must have informed before his release. I'm certain His Eminence will remember his suffering in the next life."

Falchier kept silent.

Mellka glanced at one of the papal statues, that of Vatic, his tragic predecessor. "...The Church will endure without him. Let Poem discover the harsh truths on his own."

XIX. Truths

XIX. Truths

The craggy path to the underworld seemed to extend deeper and narrower as Poem descended, with only a waning lantern held aloft to light his way. Shadows danced at him like distorted faces, and the air was stale. Few men had to courage to traverse the darkness, but Poem kept his feet moving until he finally stepped through the slitted end of the passageway onto a grotto.

Crystalline stalagmites and stalactites surrounded a trickling pond that was eerily illuminated by his lantern's flame. Elsewhere there were man-made pergolas in a severe state of disrepair, its masonry crumbling from age. No exit presented itself, except the source of water, and when Poem approached it for closer inspection, his lantern snuffed out.

In the complete darkness of the small cave, Poem was unable to take a step in any direction, and fumbled blindly to relight the lantern, but to no avail.

On one of the pergolas, flowers of ethereal light blossomed, as if waking after a long winter, and a lone figure appeared sitting by the archway. He had a pale appearance, with weathered robes and rusted armour, and kept his gaze down as if heavy with thoughts.

Poem took a moment to adjust to what he saw, bearing nothing except the lantern as a means of defense. He took a few careful steps toward the apparition, then stopped short as the pallid man reared his head to glance at him.

"Do you know me?"

"You're... you're the Saint Knight." Poem was astonished, recognizing the man from countless works of historical art scattered throughout the world, and especially within the

Cathedral's halls. Yet he was unprepared for the striking light of strength in the eyes, nor the weight of command in his voice.

"Saint? Humph..." Alexander Mellka balked at the reverent title, and looked away pensively. "What mockery of the word."

"Whose body lies in your crypt?"

"Empty, much like the hearts of many." He bore his gaze at Poem once more. "Who leads the Church now?"

"A militant who fashions his name after yours," Poem responded humbly, and reflected on his own position. "I wanted to believe in his cause to reform, to mend broken promises, but I was misled by my own desires."

"We all share the same fault," Alexander comforted, "but it takes the most profound of experiences to admit it. Some of us follow so blindly, desperate to seek clarity of our purpose in this life that we moor ourselves to the benefactor whose voice is strongest enough to lead us without resorting to our own will. If one is not careful to measure his steps, he will fall."

Poem felt his shoulders slacken with unseen affliction. "Have I fallen that far?"

The flowers on the pergola withered and faded, and the light that illuminated the saintly Knight vanished. The dark lasted briefly, as another pergola blossomed with heavenly flora, but this time the figure that appeared near the archway was that of Genetha – his long-dead sister.

She was in full armour, as she was when she commanded the Chimaeras against the military arm of Guard, and her unforgiving stare bore through Poem like a knife through an old wound.

Poem's knees buckled with anguish, and he was confused. "Genetha?" He glanced around the grotto for the trickster, but saw no one else. "What's going on?"

"Why did you turn your back on us?" Genetha demanded furiously. "You betrayed your kinsmen!"

"No!" Poem reeled back as horrifying memories of his time in the Sorcerer Siblings' underground laboratory flushed before him like a tidal wave. He saw himself back in one of the containment cylinders, stripped of all humanity, and enduring countless days of merciless experimentations under the tutelage of Sefire and Moth.

Genetha placed a hand on his shoulder; her grip was firm, but cold. "You do this for the benefit of the Chimaera Conglomerate, and of all people under its banner. You are a true patriot."

Poem slapped her hand away and took a step back. "You volunteered me to the Siblings! Your own brother! You sent me away to become a monster!"

"We were soldiers, Poem," Genetha berated harshly, "and duty was something you neglected when you ran away!"

Tears flowed from ardor, but Poem's heart wrenched with sadness. "Would it have been better if I died in that laboratory? Did you lose all love for me when I was gone?"

Genetha's bellicosity once again melted away, and she closed the distance between her and Poem. Although her hands were masked with heavy gauntlets, she gently caressed Poem's cheeks and cleared away the tears. "Little brother... don't grieve for me. I don't deserve it after what I've done. I never forgave myself, and I do love you... but, I was never good at showing it, not with words nor feeling."

"You left me too soon, before I had the chance to..." Poem ushered with strain, his throat tight with emotion. "I... I forgave you long ago."

"We never did finish what we meant to say – what needed to be said." Genetha smiled warmly, and kissed him on the forehead. "Take care of our mother, little brother."

She faded along with the light from the blossoms, and Poem tried to cling desperately to her, but was left only with a memory. He cried out in agony, and dropped to his knees, the lantern clattering away from him.

His chin lowered against his chest as he furiously tried to keep himself from sobbing, and with a long sigh, he recovered himself. He wiped away his tears with a hand, and stayed where he was.

Another pergola awakened, and the light was sucked away by a strange shadow hovering over the ground. When Poem's senses tingled at the strangeness, he noted with certain horror at the unmistakable silhouette of Necrosis' rotted, legless body.

A pair of crimson points of light shimmered within its eye sockets, and the sinister death grin sent a cold shiver through Poem's spine. He struggled desperately to find the lantern.

"Do not fear death needlessly," Necrosis sepulchral voice echoed into the cave, "for there is far worse."

Recovering the fallen lantern, Poem rose up in defiance and threw the lantern at Necrosis' silhouette, where it smashed apart against the pergola. With its impact, Necrosis vanished, and a godly light filled the depth of the nearby pond.

From it, a massive, clawed mauler emerged and clamped its sharp talons into the ground. The second set of claws followed, and an ancient drake heaved itself from the water. Its skin was dark and surreal, its head sleek and scarred, and the glowing blue orbs that were its eyes intensely fixed on Poem.

"I sensed the blood of my kind flowing through your veins," the creature boomed eerily. Its voice regurgitated from its large pharynx, but sounded from all around the grotto. *"I tested you, and you are true. I do not fear you, so neither should you fear me."*

Poem found himself speechless, as the mere presence of a Great Sentinel was unfathomable. He dropped to one knee, and was mortified.

By its physical behavior, the Sentinel appeared amused. *"Are you perplexed by my existence?"*

"The last few of your kind were destroyed by the Saint Knights..." Poem tried to convince himself of the well-known historical fact, but found himself on blatant doubt.

"Indeed they were, and I was to die alongside them if it weren't for the pity of the few." The drake heaved closer to Poem. *"They nurtured me, but the rift borne from the toils of war kept any friendship from fermenting. They hid me here, beneath these foundations, a living irony of what priests preach humanity through this world."*

"Why didn't you escape when you regained your health?"

"I hold the last memories of my kind, and I protect the origin of all that you know. This is my last abode."

Poem felt remorse. "Alone, after all this time?"

"*Loneliness is a fleeting thought between dreams, but I bear it with purpose. You, little brother, need not to shoulder such burden at such young an age.*"

"You were the one who showed me…" Poem gestured to the pergolas, "…these ghosts?"

"*Rather, you showed me. You needed to tighten certain knots that have loosened over time.*"

Poem smirked, although sadly. "…Thank you."

The drake bowed its massive head in return.

The moment was broken by a pair of astonished gasps from behind, and Poem turned to see two Iron Sabres wielding torches and swords, stunned by what they saw.

The drake reared back instinctively, and prepared to spread its wings. Its scaled tail snaked into place and twitched anxiously.

Poem stood between the drake and the Iron Sabres. "Lay down your arms, this creature means us no harm!"

"Blasphemer!" one of them shouted while pointing his sabre accusingly, his voice reflecting his dread. "Our Lord gave you his love and shelter, and you consort with a demon?! You die here, and now!"

Words were futile, and Poem was ready to confront them to the end. Without his daggers, he was unable to channel his powers, and he had no other weapons at his disposal except melee tactics. As the two enraged soldiers charged, he raised his arms to his side in sync to the drake's extension of its wings.

The first Iron Sabre to reach Poem, swung his sword high while he ran, and was three steps away from completing his delivery when the drake's muscular talons crushed him to the ground. The brute force of the impact disturbed several stalagmites, and pushed back the last attacker.

Poem retrieved the fallen sword in mid-flight and engaged the second terror-stricken Iron Sabre. He fluidly parried the weak attack, knocked the blade from the soldier's hand, then shouldered him back against a pergola. The brittle masonry crumbled against the Iron Sabre, distracting him for an instant, and was unable to dodge Poem's thrust.

With the bloody blade peering through the soldier's back, Poem let go of the hilt, and the armoured body collapsed by the pond.

He turned to the dragon, who heaved heavily after ages of inaction. "Does the Grand Master know you're here?"

The Sentinel relaxed its guard, and faced Poem. "*As an acolyte, he spent many years exploring the Vault and its many hidden chambers, and when he gained his title, he pursued the darker and deeper corners of the Cathedral. He stumbled upon this grotto by chance, and I tested him. Here he found his inspiration to take the reins of not only his destiny, but that of all followers of his Church. He possesses many virtues, but none that impressed me, and so I let him pass.*"

Poem glanced down at the bodies of the Iron Sabres. "More will follow these men, because of me."

"*An army can slip through that breach, but they will not see me. You came here seeking to escape, and for your companionship, I will show you the way.*" The Sentinel reared back, and pointed to where the pond met the wall of the grotto. "*Swim against the current, and it will lead you to the old aqueducts. From there, your destiny lies with your friends.*"

Poem was curious by what the dragon had said, but did not question it. "If there's a way I can repay you, I will."

"*Find your station in this life, little brother,*" the Sentinel mused, and bowed its head in return. "*Be at peace.*"

The Sentinel crawled back into the pond, and vanished beneath its gentle surface. The eerie glow started to fade, and Poem rushed into the water while the diminishing light still provided a direction. He submerged, seeing nothing beneath except a clear path, and swam against the stream into the narrow cavity toward the surface.

Two more sky galleons arrived, and hovered over Floria like titans on wings. The ships were escorts to the *Highborn*, which was still berthed off the coast, waiting for its unofficial ambassador to return.

The townspeople were nervous, and so were the soldiers and preachers of the Faith. War Bishops rounded up their assigned companies of Inquisitor Knights, and gathered in defensive formations around the Cathedral. An entire cavalry regiment was also unleashed from the Order's garrison, and formed the advanced guard for whatever may befall the town.

The heightened security left few unchecked routes for Seidon to travel unnoticed, and he still found himself confined within the port's outskirts. The Cathedral was in sight, its spires stabbing up at the sky toward the ventral sides of the sky galleons above, but was nowhere near accessible.

He stayed near an ancient aqueduct that ran alongside the port's longest pier. It still channeled water from the ocean, which was processed and carried by an equally old osmosis mill by the waterfront. Its arches provided some cover, and Seidon hoped that it somehow led to a hidden entrance inside the Cathedral proper.

He stopped as he heard and saw a rusted metal grate being pushed aside, where it splashed against the watery runoff from the aqueduct. Taking a stance, he prepared to unsheathe Ancestral from its new scabbard hidden beneath his monk robe.

Poem, drenched and exhausted, crawled out of the gutter, and Seidon rushed to help him to his feet. Both were equally surprised at each other.

"We keep running into each other in the oddest places," Seidon said with a smirk.

Poem couldn't help but smile too. "You came after me, didn't you?" He brushed his wet hair from the front of his face. "You're too stalwart to let me go on a bad note."

Seidon gave Poem a friendly slap on his arm, which resulted in a wet smack. "You're just as stubborn as I am, Poem." He noticed something different about Poem, no longer seeing the sinister guise in his eyes, but renewed fire. "What happened to you?"

Poem glanced at the hole he crawled out of, and wasn't sure how to answer. "It's safe to say a few perspectives have changed."

"Halt!" an equestrian Knight ordered from behind.

The alarming shout was followed by innumerable quads of hooves as the Faithful cavalry formed up on their position. Spears were pointed, and crossbows locked back giving Poem and Seidon no option to escape on foot.

Seidon drew out Ancestral and held it ready before him with both hands, while Poem took his friend's carbine from the hip holster and aimed straight at the company leader.

The War Bishop at the head of the cavalry column, confident of the numbers at his side, was undaunted.

"Surrender lawfully, or treason and heresy will be the least of your damning crimes..." His pomp started to fade as his eyes looked past the two outlaws. "What..?"

Seidon risked a glance behind him, and was dismayed as a platoon of Gabrialtar Dragoons charged in perfect formation from the docked cutters on the pier. They formed a standard battle division, eight men deep and three times as long, with the first line dropping to a knee. All aimed their long-barreled rifles, and waited on the order of Mikaila.

Poem and Seidon stood with their backs to each other, trapped between the two opposing throngs, but while Mikaila had her sniper rifle aimed at them, the rest of the Dragoons had their weapons pointed at the cavalry.

Overhead, the two sky galleons hovered into flanking positions, and their cannons were primed.

"We are taking these prisoners," Mikaila said, her vicious edge punctuated in her words.

The War Bishop was as confused as the rest of the Knights, and it showed in their handling of both weapon and horse. "B-But... these men are under our jurisdiction! They committed crimes on our sacred soil, and will be–!"

"We have our orders," Mikaila cut off, as Titus walked beside her with an arrogant grin on his lips. "We will extricate these prisoners with your cooperation, or by whatever means necessary."

The War Bishop hesitated, and turned to nervously discuss the matter with his subordinates. The situation was volatile, but it was obvious that Holy Law was not impervious to firepower.

Poem knew it, and lowered his carbine. "There's no way we're going to get out of this one."

"Have hope..." Even to Seidon, the words sounded hollow, but he refused to lower his blade. He stared directly at Titus, desperately wanting answers, even if he had to cut through him.

A messenger on horseback bolted from the Cathedral with all the speed his steed could muster. The young acolyte was given a path by the cavalry, and he rode beside the War Bishop. Frenzied hushes were exchanged, and from the Bishop's disheartened reaction, it was obvious the standoff was about to be resolved.

The Bishop pulled on his horse's reins to face the Gabrialtar concourse, and wavered for a few moments before making his promulgation. "...In the name of peace, the Grand Master decrees that these men are your captives by amendment." The Bishop felt he was tasting ash on his tongue. "We... withdraw."

The cavalry reluctantly lowered their spears and crossbows, and followed the lead of the War Bishop in a staggered but calm retreat. Past them, standing in one of the Cathedral's verandas, was Mellka, and Poem locked eyes with him. A thousand thoughts fluttered before the Grand Master turned his back.

Poem turned to face Titus and his soldiers. "There's a strategy in trading one evil for another..." He dropped the carbine in surrender.

Seidon's tenacity kept his jaw clenched, and with a heavy breath, he stabbed his heirloom sword into the ground.

Titus fearlessly approached them as the Dragoons mobilized to shackle the prisoners. "Somehow I knew this will return to me." He clutched the Ancestral's hilt, his eyes on Seidon, and rived it out. "How small the world truly is when looking from above."

He snickered, resting the flat end of the sword against his shoulder as he turned away and walked back to the cutters. "Throw them in the brig."

Standing in the middle of a grassy knoll overlooking the martial fields several miles outside the Freya, Vant took a moment to appreciate his freedom. He wore the uniform of a brigadier general: a dark blue coat with gold lace and epaulets; maroon collar, cuffs, and lapels, with white trousers. The colours befitted a leader of an irregular army.

Down on the field, a few regiments prepared for the march to battle. Most were former Strafers, whose ranks, and titles Vant forced to reinstate as a condition to his commitment, while the remainder were volunteer soldiers from Magna Carta's frontier corps, allied mercenaries, and militant citizens of Freya who've taken to the cause. It was a rag-tag band that will do little else but push a thorn on the side of Titus' war machine, and despite the doubts and respites of many, Vant was confident of victory.

Tenshi, liaison commander of the Elite detachment and wearing a red shortcoat as part of her battle dress, joined Vant at his side. "The Viceroy agreed to your plan, although it took the seal of the King to convince him."

"It's often the generals who move the chess pieces," Vant said, partly to himself, and turned to her. "Because I owe Captain Harbrid an unpayable debt, I cannot put you in harm's way. Your prowess with steel will be no match against cannons from a galleon."

"This contest will be decided by whoever outwits the other," Tenshi chided. "Outgunned and outnumbered, you're still determined to fight for the King, and I plan to help you even the odds."

Vant smirked slightly, chastised, but impressed. "Well phrased, milady, and I am truly honoured to serve with you. But I wonder what the Queen has asked of you should I turn my coat and join the enemy?"

"You have too much conceit for that," Tenshi said, undaunted. "I told the Queen that you value your honour over any other temptation."

"Almost any other, and thank you." He looked past Tenshi to Sucre and a few other officers approaching.

"The Gabrialtar sky fleet has just been spotted off the coast," Sucre reported.

"Mobilize the troops," Vant ordered.

XX. Endearing Plight

XX. Endearing Plight

In the *Highborn*'s bowels, Seidon stared in wonder through the small porthole in his cell as the heavens moved along with the sky galleon's onward travel. Other ships trailed alongside, sails and flags wavering as the keels cut through the clouds.

Poem was in the cell beside him, separated by iron bars, and sat on the floor of the brig uninspired by air travel. "Men were never meant to fly alongside the birds and angels."

"Only on borrowed wings," Seidon said. "At least the view is amazing."

"Yeah, makes you almost forget about the iron bars," Poem humored sarcastically, knocking his fingers between the barrier for emphasis.

Seidon chuckled, and glanced over at his friend. "Don't tell me you've lost your sense of adventure."

"No, not yet," Poem said with a smirk, inwardly glad their friendship passed the rendering toils thrown at them. "Any idea where we're headed?"

"From the orientation of the sun, we're crossing the Vast Blue to the west, and further south."

"They're planning to invade."

Seidon nodded grimly, and sat down by the cell barrier. "...What happened to you in Floria?"

Poem sighed. "I was looking for retribution, a venue for my troubles."

"What did you find instead?"

Poem reminisced his encounter with the Sentinel. "A greater purpose."

Seidon accepted the vague answer silently, then noticed movement from the corner of his eye. Hiding behind an array of pipes and a small stack of equipment crates, a small hand gripped the corner of a box, and an innocent blue eye peered back at Seidon and Poem.

Seidon moved closer to the bars. "Hey little lad, don't be afraid. Come out from there."

After a moment of hesitation, Marcus quietly moved away from his hiding place. Poem immediately recognized him, but kept quiet.

Seidon smiled warmly, and revealed an open palm in peace. "Hello there, what's your name? I'm Seidon, this here, is my friend Poem."

Marcus glanced at Poem, then looked back at Seidon, a few strands of hazel hair falling on his brow. He gingerly approached the cell, and shook Seidon's hand. "Marcus."

"Marcus... a strong name. Why were you hiding?"

Marcus shrugged, and tugged at the iron bars with impeccant curiosity.

"I don't think your parents would want you here, Marcus, you might get in trouble."

"Marcus Vant," Poem announced flatly, startling Seidon.

"Vant?" Seidon gave the child a second look, and no longer questioned the truth. "Is this...?"

"He's our son," Mikaila confirmed as she walked behind Marcus, and placed her hands lovingly on his little shoulders.

"What's a child doing on a warship?" Poem reprimanded coldly.

"He's safer here than anywhere else, or in anyone's care," Mikaila stung in return.

Seidon was astounded, but despite the old grudge he held with Mikaila, he couldn't bear any ill-will toward her son. "Poem's right, and you know it. If this fleet's marching to an invasion of Magna Carta, there's no judging soldier from civilian from the ground looking up. Guns have no prejudice."

Mikaila quietly admitted it, but her stance remained staunch. "I bore him, and raised him alone all these years. I fear for him, but I trust no one... I never wished for him to grow up on a battlefield, and I still don't."

"And neither does his father," Seidon said.

Mikaila sighed with an old regret. "He doesn't know his father."

Poem saw the motherly conviction in Mikaila, and understood her motives more clearly. "You want us to take him to Vant, don't you?"

"It's a promise he made me keep..." Mikaila looked at both with determination. "We will be reaching Freya shortly. I will release you if you swear to me you will take Marcus to his father."

Poem scoffed. "How can you trust us? How can we trust *you*?"

"A mother's intuition," Mikaila said firmly, leaving no room for doubt.

"Will you turn yourself in to answer for your crimes?" Seidon asked, knowing the answer.

She knew he was testing her resolve. "I have neither regret nor remorse to spare. I have only my skills, and my son."

Seidon stared at Marcus, enraptured by his blue eyes, and more so by the child's gentle smile. "We'll take him to Vant. We'll protect him with our lives."

Mikaila was relieved, although slightly surprised. There was something in Seidon that she found herself believing in, and finally understood why Vant stopped her from sniping him during that fateful battle years ago. "...Thank you," she said sadly, as the gravity of her decision now dawned on her.

With the keys in hand, she opened the locks to the cells and allowed Poem and Seidon to step out. They did so with care, half-expecting an ambush, but there was none.

"We're ready when you are," Seidon said, knowing how Mikaila felt departing with the greatest love in her heart.

She bent down to meet Marcus, and pushed aside the hair from his eyes. "These are your friends now, Marcus, they'll bring you to your father."

Marcus caressed her cheek. "Will you come too?"

Tears threatened to well up, but she held steadfast and hugged him tightly. "In a little while... but look in your heart and I'll always be with you."

Gabrialtar sky corsairs scouted the countryside outside Freya's city limits, hovering measuredly like birds-of-prey. Their vantage point gave them perfect visibility, especially at lower altitudes, and there was little to hide whole armies in camp or on the move.

For that precaution, Vant stationed his troops and artillery inside the scattered townhouses and barns available to them. He watched the enemy scout ships circle the sky from the window of a villa, and noted the immensity of the fleet occupying the city some distance away.

He turned to Sucre, who was amongst other Strafers eager for battle. "For old glory, bring swift victory."

"Good hunting, General." Sucre saluted proudly, and wasted no time calling his team to action with a brief but resolute gesture of his hand.

A commonwealth nation with blood ties to the Kingdom of Magna Carta, Freya was an ancient coastal city built atop and around hillsides with great amphitheaters, arenas, and picturesque assembly halls. Roads were narrow and sinuous, with priggish housings packed tightly along the routes, but its inheriting beauty was the magnificent edifice that stood at the crown of a hill closest to the sea.

The opera hall, the oldest and most prestigious in the world, was the chosen meeting place for Titus and the Viceroy, on the unarguable request of the former.

On the formidable baroque stage, amongst the throng of empty seats that surrounded it, the Viceroy and his cohorts approached the Captain-General, who kept the Ancestral in its original scabbard fitted on a leather belt frog at his hip.

The Viceroy bowed a few feet before Titus. "We secede control of this city to you, without condition."

One of the cohorts nervously handed the signed papers to Titus, but was taken by one of the white-clad officers. Titus, disinterested by the affair, glanced over at the massive orchestra pit, and was amazed.

"This' truly the City of the Arts," Titus said in earnest awe. "I'm standing in the same place as all the magnificent masters of the romantic eras long gone, shaping the sound of the strings, the brass, and percussion while beautiful voices echo into the audience..." He turned excitedly to the Viceroy, startling him. "Why should this meager capitulation be marked with dreary discontent? Let us celebrate!" He opened his arms wide to encompass the whole of the hall as he approached the terrified Viceroy. "Engage your best musicians, your finest artists, let us paint the sky with fireworks as we sing to the classic masterpieces of our time!"

Having little choice on the matter, the Viceroy nodded fearfully. "I'll have my staff make the arrangements immediately, sir. Although the director and his troupe will demand time to rehearse."

"This is life, there are no rehearsals." Titus bowed to the Viceroy. "Now go."

The confused Viceroy and his cohorts rushed away, gladdened to be released despite the burden entailed on them.

Titus laughed and clapped his hands immodestly as he studied the architectural beauty of the opera hall, ever more eager for the festivities to begin.

"Ensure that our occupational forces cooperate with the law enforcement precincts," he commanded to one of the officers. "Give the commissioner leeway in deciding the strictness of control." As the instructed officer left, Titus turned to another. "Put the curfew in place immediately. Whoever will not be attending the celebrations are to be confined to their estates."

Two more officers parted to their duties, and Titus turned to the last. "Contact the Presidency, and update them on our current situation. Tell her that Freya will serve as an excellent secondary base of operations, and we are proceeding to the next staging point at launching an attack on the Royal Capital."

"Yes, sir," the officer saluted and left promptly, leaving the Captain-General alone in the hall.

Titus took a long, deep breath, closing his eyes to the triumphant moment when all felt firmly in his absolute grasp. His imagination was free to reign unimpeded, and in his mind, his ears tingled with the fusion of musical instruments in epic crescendos. Ghostly apparitions of musicians in traditional finery materialized in the orchestra pit and played to the Captain-General's grandiose tune.

He twirled and swayed on his feet, waving his arms as he moved to the sound of the symphony, and smiled as he envisioned the seats filled with engaged spectators applauding his masterful efforts. He felt he was a renowned thespian, an unforgettable maestro, and he dramatically emphasized his words with theatrical gestures.

"Although my dreams can never be fulfilled, I take the dreams of all to myself," he expressed. "Even unto the ending of the world, I will summon the sky and the stars upon the earth!"

Behind him, from the curtains, Mikaila walked in, and saw him perform like a terpsichore in a hall empty of music and people. She slowed her pace, a dreadful cold feeling in her gut, and was uncertain how to approach.

Titus stopped abruptly with his back to her, as if nothing had transpired. He glanced over his shoulder at Mikaila with sinister eyes. "You let them go?"

Mikaila nodded, unable to escape the fear she suddenly felt. "They're following an unobstructed route out of the city."

"Good. If all goes well, they will lead us to the hidden army King Ingren has prepared for us."

Despite the fervent aura of imminent battle, Vant somehow found the time to appreciate a moment's rest and drink tea. He sat on a quaint, roasted maple chair borrowed from a nearby townhouse, by a small and ornate wrought-iron table under an old pear tree whose flowery branches provided both shade and cover.

He was unaccompanied, and this unnerved his loyal Strafers enough to demand Tenshi to intervene. She gave the last instructions to the Elite platoon under her command, then proceeded across the sun-laden field from the townhouse to the old tree where Vant relaxed under a warm summer breeze and azure sky.

"The flavour of this part of the world is sweet and quite placid; I understand why King Ingren wants to defend her." Vant took a sip from the porcelain cup, pausing as in the distance, a retro-reef train spewed steam into the air as it traversed on mighty iron wheels across the tracks that connected Freya to Magna Carta, then glanced over at Tenshi with a grin. "Would you care to join me?"

"Your soldiers are restless," Tenshi responded, without rude intention. "They are so concerned that you're out here in plain sight of Gabrialtar spotters, that they're a hair away from disobeying your orders to leave you be, and drag you back inside."

Vant smirked at his soldiers' endearing plight. "Let this be a lesson of patience to my good friends, and at the very least some pleasure in the little good things." He patted the time-weathered bark of the tree beside him. "This tree is providing me with some decent protection."

"I think that's going to be of little comfort to your men."

Vant shrugged. "You don't seem overly concerned."

"You have your ways, and I respect that." A stray thought crossed Tenshi's mind. "I know for a fact that Seidon had, for the longest time, admired your unwavering composure during the heat of combat – before, during, and after. I share that admiration too."

Vant was earnestly flattered. "Thank you. It's good to hear things like that, as they're rare and precious…" His eyes wandered past Tenshi, to a young boy with striking blue eyes. Calmly, the child moved past Tenshi and approached him, holding on his small lips a warm and innocent aura of curiosity.

Although this was a first encounter, Vant felt every pore of his skin flare with an overwhelming sense of recognition. He placed down his teacup, eyes fixed on the boy, and leaned forward with certain anticipation.

Tenshi was fascinated by this young child, who much resembled Vant, and wondered where he had strayed from. She turned around, and saw two familiar figures approaching from the vineyard and her heart jumped with startling joy. She abandoned all else and sprinted toward Seidon, who caught her in a loving embrace that spun them both around in circles. With laughter and high spirits as Seidon kept her off her feet, they kissed fiercely.

Several paces away was Poem, who carried a dark cloud at the sight of his nemesis sitting under the verdant shade ahead, about to be introduced to his first and only progeny. His brooding mood lightened as Tenshi came to him, and hugged him like a long, lost friend who had been found again.

"It's good to see you again," Tenshi said, and gave him a kiss on the cheek.

Poem welcomed the warmth of both a woman and a friend. "It's been quite a journey..." His smile faded as Seidon parted from their company and approached Vant.

Seidon stood behind Marcus, not wanting to be between him and his father. "I guess a little hope helped set you free."

Vant nodded, still mesmerized by the young boy. "Care to introduce me to your young friend, Captain Harbrid?"

"By all means, General Vant." Seidon laid a hand on Marcus' little shoulder. "This is your son."

For the first time in his life, Vant was reverently humbled, as nothing matched the feeling in his heart at this one moment. He slid off his chair and rested his knees on the grass just to meet his son face to face for the first time. "So we finally meet, Marcus."

Marcus was a bit shy, but unafraid. He gently caressed Vant's cheek. "You look like me."

Vant smiled, fatherly tears waiting to be wept, and embraced his son with everything that he was. "There are no words, my son... that can grace how I feel right now." He laughed at his own elation, and kissed Marcus on the forehead. "With you at my side, I will be forever victorious."

He glanced up at Seidon, as Tenshi wrapped her arm around his and rested her head on his shoulder. "I am, now and always, grateful for your kindness... Seidon."

Seidon nodded, understanding. "Mikaila put her trust in us, and her greatest treasure she rests on you."

Vant paused at what Seidon had said, and only now noticed Poem. He stood far away from them, as if a barrier was implacably rooted between them. Whether he was a threat was uncertain, but for the Strafers who recognized him from the scuffle in the Templari incident, he was an enemy.

They stormed onto the field and surrounded Poem at gunpoint and by point of the sword, but Poem remained unmoved and dauntless. Seidon wanted to rush to his friend's aid, yet Tenshi held him back, leaving it to Vant to resolve this precarious impasse.

"Poem's not your enemy!" Seidon defended resolutely.

"I am his," Vant countered coolly, as he stood up. "Strafers, stand down."

Despite their collective dismay, the soldiers unwittingly lowered their weapons and backed away.

"For the time being, Titus is my enemy," Poem said, meaning his words, and walked past the nervous Strafers toward the townhouse.

Vant exhaled heavily, not realizing he had held a breath. He looked down at Marcus, who adoringly looked up at him with wonder. "Now, with all dark things past, Marcus, you and I have a lot of catching up to do."

Sucre and his Strafers huddled on the tops of twin belfries that stood on the fringes of Freya's port, where a good portion of the Gabrialtar fleet was docked for repairs and resupply. Security was at its peak, with entire regiments disembarking to occupy the city in full force, but their arrival was still novel, and the soldiers were unaccustomed to the layout of their new base of operations.

Sucre and his men knew Freya as if they had been born and raised there, and every nook and cranny of the City of the Arts was theirs to exploit. They remained silent and stayed close to the shadows of the crenelation as they watched one of the numerous corsairs that Gabrialtar employed to watchdog the sky over the city.

One in particular, the *Crossbow*, was stationed near the civilian marina, which was cluttered with yachts and other small boats. Its sleek black hull swept back into a pair of armoured zeppelins that gave it the ability of flight, and its single deck of gun ports was painted in subdued gold, which gave it a far more intimidating appearance than its design intended it to be.

The vessel was in the midst of flight preparations, and with the release of anchors, the engines thrummed to life. Within moments, the corsair lifted gracefully into the air – water spilling away from its keel. It pointed its bow toward the inner city, and steadily climbed altitude as it passed between the twin belfries.

Aside from a handful of crew members hoisting the sails, there were only a few guards keeping watch on the main deck, and they walked their assigned routes idly and without expectation.

The corsair was quickly outflanked by a web of grappling hooks that swung out with precision and caught on the gunwales. With the zeppelins' masses covering them, the Strafers climbed the sides of the ship, some taking advantage of the rungs that were used for technicians to inspect the keel and its zeppelin supports.

The Strafers paused just under the sight of a patrol, then as he neared their position, Sucre swiftly snatched the man by his jaw, twisted his neck back and tossed him overboard. The poor guard crashed against the roof of a passing building, and remained still.

Sucre and the Strafers had no remorse as they stormed onto the deck like a pack of hungry wolves, and divided into three teams. One secured the deck, while the second rushed below to take control of engineering. The third, led by Sucre, took the stern-castle where the pilothouse was located.

For the sake of surprise, no guns were used as they slaughtered the trio of armed watchmen in the pilothouse, leaving only the commander and sublieutenant alive for questioning on ship operations. They forced both officers on their knees, and stripped them of their weapons.

The commander resisted, and broke free of the Strafer's grip and was about to fire his service pistol before meeting his end at the thrust of Sucre's sword.

Sucre, his sabre's edge bloodied, motioned the rest of his assigned team to keep moving. "Secure the castle, and the gun deck. Allow them a chance to surrender or dump them overboard." As the Strafers fanned out, he turned to the cringing sublieutenant and the two remaining Strafers that kept her. "Teach us how to fly."

The lights were dimmed inside the old opera house, drawing the attention of all spectators to the illuminated stage. Decorated with magnificence to appear of an age long lost, the costumed actors blended with the setting and unleashed their voices onto the acoustics of the architecture around them. The orchestra in their pit, dressed in their fineries, accompanied the actors with equal splendour.

Titus captured every single moment from his reserved seat of honour, and was absorbed by the opera with unmatched fanaticism. He was in the company of the Viceroy, amongst other high nobles, along with some of Gabrialtar's top officers. Around him were invited guests, afficionados and residents of the upper caste, who swallowed down their fear of reprisal and pretended to enjoy the artful ceremony.

The performance by the main soprano reached its peak, and Titus couldn't help but applaud her. The interruption was slight, and in solicitude, all others in the audience joined the Captain-General's ovation.

"Truly masterful," Titus said to no one in particular, but those who heard him simply nodded in agreement.

An officer entered the hall by one of the far doors, and strode down one of the aisles to approach the Captain-General. He saluted briskly, and bent low to whisper to his superior's ear.

"I apologize for the interruption, sir," the officer said, "but you strictly requested to be informed of any development–"

Titus stopped the man with a sharp hand gesture, his attention still on the stage. "The King's army had been found in hiding after all?"

"Not quite, sir. We still have no information on the size of the enemy contingent camped outside Freya, but we can confirm who we suspect to be its commander... General Rell Vant."

Titus' ears were piqued, although only for a heartbeat. "Fire with fire... I commend King Ingren's thinking."

"Orders?"

Titus waited until the opera reached yet another peak. "Let the esteemed General commit the first act. Once he reveals to us the strength and numbers of his task force, we will counter accordingly." He waved the officer away, and leaned toward the anxious Viceroy. "This composition is phenomenal, Viceroy. I'll be hard-pressed to request an encore."

The afternoon was at its end, and clouds blotted the sky. The battalions were on the march, and both soldiers and artillery filtered through the fields at a quickened pace. Vant remained with a rear-guard, watching the advance with scrutiny and with his hands at the small of his back, while Marcus mimicked his father beside him.

Vant took notice and grinned, patting his son warmly. "The stance of a good leader reflects the strength of his army. You already own such great potential."

He sensed Seidon and Tenshi approaching, and so did Marcus, who turned and rushed to greet them.

"His mother sent him to me..." Vant said to Seidon, a hint of regret in his tone. "She let you bring him to me."

Seidon felt something cold twist at his gut. "Poem and I were captured at Floria, but once we arrived here, she offered to release us on this one condition."

Vant grimaced. "Titus anticipated an armed reprisal, not knowing we're in hiding. He allowed you to leave unharmed, so you could lead him to us... or at the very least, reveal to him that we are here. A mother's good intention was merely a frontage for the catalyst." He lovingly brushed Marcus' hair. "This campaign will be pushed ahead, before Titus has a chance to prepare, but a battlefield is no place for children." He glanced at Tenshi, saddened by his decision. "I must beg of you a single favour... I can protect him far better knowing he's in the King's custody."

Tenshi glanced at Seidon, and both knew this was a request that had to be given despite all else. "The Elites will remain here, and I will transfer command to Seidon."

Vant nodded, although half-heartedly as he truly did not wish to see his son go. "Two of my best men have volunteered to accompany you. Please make both the King and Queen understand the situation."

"They will," Tenshi promised.

Vant looked down at Marcus, and sighed. "Tenshi will be taking you to the Royal Capital; King Ingren and Queen Dalena wish to see you."

"What about you?" Marcus wondered.

"I have a battle to fight," Vant said, sparing no sweet lies for his son. "A war to win, so all of us can live in peace."

Marcus didn't quite understand his father's reason, but accepted it. He dotingly embraced his father, who bent a knee to meet him.

Vant never wanted to let go, but he had no choice. How cruel of Mikaila to give him so short a time with this child on the eve of battle, but seldom life was fair. "Keep me close to your little heart, Marcus. You are forever in mine, and your mother's." Whether it was a moment too long or too short, he broke away, stood up, and allowed his son to grasp Tenshi's hand. He gave her a knowing nod, then turned and joined his battalion on the move.

Seidon knew in some way how Marcus must be feeling, and grasped the child's shoulder assuredly. "Be strong for your father; look after Tenshi for me."

Given a nod from Marcus, Seidon met eyes with Tenshi, both knowing all too well the will to endure these heart-wrenching moments. Terrible deeds were to come, and Seidon joined Vant in his march.

XXI. Ageless Wrath

XXI. Ageless Wrath

On the outskirts of Freya, a company of Gabrialtar regular troops in typical parade formation patrolled one of the main roads in the vicinity of an oratory. Due to the curfew in effect, the streets were empty of bystanders, while the most stubborn were forced into their homes.

Across from the oratory was a large orchard of plum trees on the verge of blossoming, and odd shadows moved under the foliage, upsetting the gentle pedals from their perches.

The company captain paused as he noticed the disturbance, and the rest of his troops were similarly alerted, but before they could take a step to investigate, gunfire sounded. Bullets whizzed past them, wounding two soldiers before the rest scattered in defense.

"It's coming from the trees!" the company captain shouted as he drew his revolver. "Return fire!"

The disoriented troops made a collective effort to provide a fire blanket, utilizing their limited repeater guns to their technological advantage. Bullets tore at the orchard, splintering branches and maiming a Strafer, before the heavy artillery rolled into place.

The thunder of a howitzer firing was enough to startle the Gabrialtar troops, and cleaved their courage asunder as a crater was gouged from the street were they stood. A second volley struck the company captain, and sent the rest retreating into the oratory. There they set up a temporary mainstay, firing from the broken windows and the busted doorway while the alarm was sounded across the rest of the city.

Vant oversaw the attack behind the artillery regiment, fearless of the noise and crossfire as he studied the architecture of the small chapel. He pointed at a high section of the arched roof. "Bombard the bell tower, bring it down!"

The order was replied with honed calibration of the turrets by the cannoneers, and subsequent release of the ordnance. The bell tower was hit severely by the cannonade, the fury and ruckus eventually weakened its integrity, and sent it tumbling down. The heavy debris crashed into the roof, simultaneously eroding the buttresses, and imploded. Thick, grey dust billowed from the destruction, and quieted the defiant Gabrialtar troops that were too unfortunate to escape.

The few that survived were arrested with brute force by Vant's vanguard.

Above, a corsair in mid-maneuvers spotted them, and its guns locked into place in retaliation. Several volleys were fired, smashing into the ground – the shockwaves uprooting trees and breaking the rebel formation.

It was unaware of a second corsair approaching from astern, and with its weapons aimed below, it was unable to respond to the attack on its hindquarters. The rogue corsair's cannonade was relentless and brutal, tearing away entire chunks of the Gabrialtar vessel's hull until a violent explosion breached its engine section and burned the flanking zeppelins from within.

The flaming corsair dove out of control, and slammed across the terrain until all that remained were charred debris and specks of flame. The *Crossbow* circled over the carnage, then hovered over Vant's ground forces and assumed battle formation.

"Forward!" Vant ordered, and his battalions thundered ahead, just as an explosion rocketed debris in the distance.

Seidon and the Elites retreated hastily as the fiery cloud enveloped one of the parked supply vessels at the docks, and dared to watch the onboard ammunition caches detonate, decimating anything that stood within its several-kilometer radius. The blast damaged wayside buildings and nearby sky galleons, not to mention the casualties amongst Gabrialtar soldiers and mariners. He hoped that the civilians were warned ahead of time by secret communiques coursed by the Viceroy's trusted administration, and that few or none were hurt by what was deemed a necessary evil.

If it was Vant's strategy to shake the nerves of the enemy, then this explosion certainly succeeded in that regard. With the entire occupation force and accompanying sky fleet now alerted, the numbers and guns were drawn against them.

The windows of the opera hall rattled, and few shattered from the eruption outside, complimenting the tremors that passed through the walls and floor. It was followed by a mass evacuation that was chaotic at best, but Titus wasn't bothered, only intrigued as musical instruments, theatrical props, artists, and spectators trampled over each other. It sounded like dissonant chords onto itself.

While the Viceroy and his haughty retinue escaped to the safety of the bomb shelters, Titus' soldiers and officers congregated around him, delivering in haste their adrenalin-induced reports, and requesting immediate action. Titus remained seated until Mikaila arrived with an escort of Dragoons.

"The city's breached," Mikaila stated. "We've lost contact with several ground patrols on the outskirts, and that last explosion destroyed a supply caravan. We have at least three other vessels severely damaged, and two corsairs missing."

Titus nodded, idly concerned. "Get the dead and wounded to the medical ships, then instruct the air fleet to take to the skies. The naval support squadron is also to withdraw immediately. Scuttle whatever can't leave port."

"Won't we offer an effective response, sir?" Colonel Reginald, one of the few high ranking infantry officers, demanded.

"Assemble the troops we have already stationed in the city, and mount a pronged attack on the rebels' front. Once you've halted their advance, regroup to the main anchorage, and hold fort there."

Colonel Reginald considered it with uncertainty. "We will lose precious initiative if we withdraw from a successful counterattack. They will take the city without much effort."

"They can take it, Colonel," Titus said pompously, "but with a paltry force, they will not be able to hold it. Urban warfare is a messy ordeal, and right now, we have mastery of the air, and I plan to take full advantage of the fact."

"Understood, sir." With Reginald's departure, the majority of the officers left in a hurry

The building shook from bombardment by encroaching cannons, and it was apparent that time was of the essence.

"The Highborn's waiting, Captain-General," Mikaila said. "The corridor has been secured, but we must leave immediately."

Titus agreed, stopping to regard the opera hall emptied of its residents, and stood up. "Lead the way."

Trapped at a narrow T-junction by heavy fire directed from a legion of Gabrialtar troopers defending one of the access ways to the anchorage, the Magna Cartans took severe casualties in their citadel-like position. One of soldiers, covering one of his own from the corner of a side street, was struck on the shoulder and went down.

Seidon rushed to him, dragging the wounded soldier back from the enemy crossfire. He picked up the rifle and leaned out, shooting several rounds before Poem unexpectedly pulled him back just as bullets tore apart the corner of the building he used as cover.

"We need an upper hand," Seidon said, panting.

"They're holding down their position too well," Poem replied, observing the deployment of the enemy contingent. "They have the numbers to overrun us, but I think they're covering a mass retreat."

"Then we just keep pushing," Seidon said. "Straight into the water if we need to."

Poem nodded in agreement, tossing away the spent rifle in hand. "I'm sure Vant and his Strafers already reached the port by now; we'll have this enemy group trapped in a pincer."

Without a serviceable gun and his daggers appropriated by Mellka's guards, he searched a fallen Gabrialtar soldier for weapons, and retrieved an ivory and copper-cast revolver with spare ammo clips. He found another similar revolver nearby, and picked it up as well.

Wielding both guns in hand as if they were his blades, Poem strode past Seidon to join the frontline assault. "Keep pushing forward!"

"Bring up the artillery!" Vant ordered fervently. "Take those ships down!"

The main road that led to the hub of Freya's main port was barricaded, but it did little to deter the Strafers' advance as it also provided cover. The artillery was rolled in, and in due time, the howitzers sounded.

The Gabrialtar fleet launched away in a frenzy, the mass of zeppelins and sails covering the sky like scattered rain clouds. The brave soldiers that remained behind mounted an effective defense with their automatic weapons, using short bursts to conserve ammo and kept the Strafers at bay.

The cannonade damaged the ships as they ascended, but lacked the destructive yield to ground them. Vant keenly noted this, and glanced up at Sucre's commandeered corsair as it joined the fray.

"Major Freyr," Vant called to his veteran Strafer, "launch a flare. Signal Sucre to move behind our line."

As the flare was sent, Vant instinctively glanced to the side. Away from the main exodus of sky ships was a single galleon, heavily guarded on all sides, waiting for the motor cage to arrive with its VIP's. The enemy position was being checked by the Strafers' left wing, but wasn't enough to compromise the armoured zone.

Vant drew away from the forward column, and proceeded to the left wing. He now distinctly recognized the galleon as the *Highborn*, and knew who it was that the ship waited for. He hurried his steps, and was joined by his guardian Strafers.

"Concentrate firepower on the left flank!" he ordered his troops, and they complied with swift execution. "Seventh Column, swing around the enemy arc and outflank them! Lieutenant Argolla, with me!"

The left wing erupted with heavy fighting, and Vant brazenly stormed through the crossfire with his squad. They cut through the outer defense, knocking down and killing the Gabrialtar guards, just as the wheeled transport arrived with an escort of warbikes.

Dragoons immediately formed a perimeter around the vehicle, and opened fire to stall the Strafers, who reflexively dove for cover and returned fire. Less than a yard from the ramp that led to the towering *Highborn*, they were in danger of being surrounded.

With bullets ricocheting off the thick-plated armour, Titus and Mikaila stepped out of the transport and were shielded by more troops as they hurried to the ramp. One of the soldiers was hit, and fell to the ground, only to be followed by more casualties, as Vant's Seventh Column arrived on their unprotected flank – reinforced by Seidon's Elites.

Mikaila broke away from Titus, and immediately directed the Dragoons to cover all angles of attack. The move was costly, but it was achieved.

With Seidon and the Seventh on one side, and Argolla's Strafers on the other, Titus was cornered. The only way to escape was up the ramp, and to the *Highborn*, whose guns and engines awoke.

Vant had only this one opportunity to strike at Titus as he escaped, and took it while the Dragoons were trapped in the momentary confusion of reestablishing their formation. He primed his pistol and sprinted toward Titus. The Strafers covered him, surgically razing down any Gabrialtar soldier in Vant's path.

His mad rush was disrupted by the escort squad of warbikes, as they overtook him from behind and crossed in between him and Titus. One of the bikers zipped close to Vant, tripping the general, but Vant recovered with an expert roll.

Titus stopped midway up the ramp, his shield of soldiers faltering as bullets converged on his position, and stared down at the rogue general with a grin. He dared him to keep coming.

Vant stood up slowly as the warbikes revved in challenge, and he glanced past them to Titus, just as they charged. He stood his ground as the bikers faced the crossfire from the Strafers, until the last pair were ready to mow him down.

He fired, hitting the engine of the rightmost warbike, which caused it to swerve violently onto its side and roll across the ground. In the space of a heartbeat, he aimed at the last rider and shot him off the saddle with a single volley. The warbike stumbled on its front wheel, and skipped into the air – narrowly missing Vant's left shoulder by a handbreadth.

The crash of rider and machine was violent, but Vant pursued his objective undaunted. He switched hands with the pistol, and drew out his sabre – driven to cut down Titus were he stood.

Titus, no longer covered by his minions, felt no need to run or defend himself. He stood there, waiting, with a knowing smile that sent shivers to any who observed. His arrogance was founded when Mikaila landed onto the middle of the ramp between him and Vant, with her sniper rifle locked and ready.

Vant halted his assault, enraged. "Shoot or get out of the way!"

"Fall back!" Mikaila insisted, her aim unwavering.

Vant was too close to Titus to omit the chance to strike him, and time was crucial, as behind him the Dragoons were on retreat and alerted mariners poured from the galleon. He had but one choice to make.

"I will cut through you, Mikaila!" Vant charged, and swung his sabre even as she refused to pull the trigger. At the last possible second, he missed – the wind of his furious motion brushing a few strands of her blond hair. With an angry grunt, he pulled back in haste with his Strafers covering him.

Mikaila was left untouched, and Titus unscathed. The former let go of a longing breath, and she retreated up the *Highborn*'s ramp with the stragglers.

Titus' conniving smile grew darker. "Now the tables turn." He swung around, the hem of his coat trailing, and boarded the galleon as it begun its titan ascent.

He reached for the swept hilt detonator that he kept on his side opposite to the Ancestral, and ruthlessly thumbed its switch.

Across the Vast Blue and the ravening sky, at the heart of Empyrean City, another tower shook away its foundations and gave birth to a second Vilkacis missile. The fiery spawn rudely awoke the whole city, and heeded to its majestic and terrifying flight.

It arched across the sky, its trail of smoke splitting the celestial sphere in half as it careened toward its destination.

The Gabrialtar fleet pulled away from Freya's airspace, and gathered in a crescent formation. Once the *Highborn* joined the ranks at the spearpoint of the armada, the fleet pounced forth, while its naval support ships maneuvered toward deeper currents.

The few ground troops that were left behind attempted a desperate attempt to join the withdrawal with boats, and hoped to reach the larger vessels before unfriendly guns stopped them.

Something dreadful was amiss, and Vant knew it. He still fumed over his foiled attempt to strike a swift victory, but he knew better than to dwell on such blunders.

"They gave the city back without much of a fight," Seidon commented as he and Poem joined Vant. "Something's not right."

Poem felt tense in Vant's presence, but he kept focused. He glanced up at the fleeing sky ships. "By the looks of it, the fleet's heading north to Magna Carta."

"This occupation was either a feint, or a masterful parry," Vant surmised calmly. He turned to Argolla. "Double-back to the fields; send word to the auxiliary battalion to begin marching back to the capital. We will follow them once we tally our losses and regroup."

One of the *Crossbow*'s cannons sounded urgently, and everyone glanced up at hovering corsair. Sucre and his crew were on the main deck, pressingly pointing out at the eastern horizon. Their exasperated yells were too muffled by the winds and noise of battle, but imperative.

Those on the ground, without the mercy of higher perspective, looked out to the sky from the openness of the anchorage and witnessed a brilliant star glimmering with sinister intent, and was fast approaching.

"No..." Poem reacted for all in disbelief. "He launched another missile."

"All troops to the trenches!" Vant furiously ordered. "Find shelter below ground now! Artillery units, track its trajectory!"

The order was repeated by his officers along the entire extent of the regiment, and soldiers were immediately on the move. Above them, the *Crossbow* climbed altitude and moved away in due haste.

Freyr and his gunnery company, courageous enough to keep to their task while all others withdrew, swiftly calculated the blazing star's trajectory with basic navy tools that revealed to them its position in the azimuth and meridian. With their numbers taken, they theorized the multitude of possibilities while on the run.

Freyr was the first to reach Vant on the way to the old opera hall. "General, it will either hit the city outskirts, or land directly in the fields!"

"Then it's too late to send the warning," Vant said. "Take shelter and welcome fate."

Tenshi led Marcus up the grand stairs to the carpeted landing where King Ingren and Queen Dalena received them. The two Strafers who escorted them followed a few steps behind, whom were themselves watched very keenly by the Throne Guards.

"Your Majesties, this is Marcus," Tenshi formally introduced, having no need to mention whose family the boy belonged to.

Ingren bowed regally to Marcus, and the child imitated him. "Welcome to Magna Carta, young master. You're a noble guest in this castle, what is ours is yours."

Dalena smiled, noting the child's familiar traits. "There's no doubt in my heart now, I understand what General Vant fights for." She extended her hand, while the other rested on her growing belly. "Come, let us show you where you will be staying."

Marcus hesitated, and instead stayed close to Tenshi.

"Have no worry about your parents, Marcus," Tenshi comforted, understanding the child with her womanly instincts. "We will protect you until they return – we promise."

Marcus considered her words, then bravely took Dalena's hand. They were about to leave when a sudden light pierced from the large window beside them.

They all turned to the window, and watched as a massive explosion lit up the horizon and briefly cast night into eerie day. The second Vilkacis had been unleashed, and war blazed in the distance.

Fear seeped into the pores of everyone who witnessed the event, and not a word was spoken.

Tenshi, her heart out to Seidon, stepped closer to the window as the light faded, and pressed a hand on the pane. Her whimpers were soft, but it was felt. "...Seidon..."

XXII. End of Heroes

XXII. End of Heroes

The *Second Awakening* and her battle group encircled a damaged Gabrialtar freighter as it sank beneath the waves. The survivors were rounded up from their lifeboats, and thrown to the brig as prisoners of war.

They weren't far from the coast when a brilliant burst of light erupted in the far distance, pushing aside the clouds, then faded into the zenith. The event hardly went unnoticed.

Messer and his officers were in the midst of debriefing the recent guerilla victory when the communications officer came running.

"All ships are to return to the capital immediately," the panting officer reported. "Freya has been bombarded, and the enemy fleet is moving north."

Messer fell into the urgency of the dismal situation. "We'll suspend operations for the time being. All bows hard about at full sail, and run out the guns."

Vant and Seidon surveyed the aftermath of the explosion, which due to the accurate prediction calculated by Freyr and his artillery crew, landed in the fields outside the city. The impact crater was several miles wide, and scorched everything around it. Nothing was left green or in blossom, and what trees were left of the orchard were burnt beyond recognition.

The outskirts of the city of Freya was also touched by the tremors of the blast, and moderately damaged the streets and buildings, but they were not beyond repair. The irreplaceable were in lives lost during this heinous altercation, and many soldiers perished out in the fields.

"We're at a little more than half-strength," Seidon said, as the *Crossbow* landed in a large lake a few yards away. "It won't be enough to stop Titus from reaching the King's gates."

"It will have to be," Vant replied, as he spotted the retro-reef train. What was once a sight to behold was derailed, its violent departure from the broken tracks marked by a long gash across the ground. "We'll leave behind the allied detachment under the Viceroy's command for relief efforts... Freya will need them. I've ordered what's left of our artillery units to wheel around and render a line behind the Gabrialtar forces. I will transfer my flag to our borrowed corsair, and with the wind on our backs, we will be hard at their heels."

Within the *Highborn*'s epicurean office-quarters, Titus conferred with the Presidency over the shortwave receiver. The display was washed in saturated colours, and Gehenna's projection appeared rather bleak despite her stately appearance.

"There are boundaries for conduct in wartime," she scorned, "and you've overstepped them blatantly and without remorse. You're abusing your punitive powers, Captain-General."

"And I will answer for them before a military tribunal, if I must, *once* this mission is over," Titus said with increasing frustration. "Freya remains largely intact. My true target was to weaken the enemy host marching back to the Royal Capital. It was achieved with great finesse, I might add."

"There are many who are starting to question your liberations on this campaign."

"How is it expected of me to lead your army when I don't have your confidence, Madam President?"

"You may be losing perspective, Captain-General," she said, losing none of her hardness. "This simple matter of protecting our sovereignty has escalated to something perverse... something too reminiscent of the expansionist agitations committed upon us by the corporations. The international community – our recent allies and trading partners – have taken notice. And I will have none of it."

Titus snickered, but there was no mirth to be found in his tone. "I intended to decorate your esteemed congress chamber with the flags of the vanquished, and make Gabrialtar the greatest superpower of this forsaken age. Your anointed posturing heeds to the fear of the inevitable political death of your mandate, but there are far, *far* worse things than death... Madam President."

"Enough!" Gehenna was infuriated. "You will begin peace negotiations with the commonwealth nations, now! Or I will order the fleet to return to Gabrialtar with your wrists bound! Is that understood?!"

"I apologize, Madam President," Titus said with false humility, as he removed his pistol and pointed it behind him to the shortwave projector. "Your transmission is faltering."

He fired a volley, destroying the projector and brusquely ending the conference.

A pair of soldiers rushed into his office, alerted with weapons drawn, but their concern was casually dismissed by Titus.

"The shortwave receiver's damaged," he said calmly. "Have it replaced immediately."

Rowen directed civilians to the underground shelters via the vast tunnel system built during the founding of the Royal Capital. The tunnels had been largely neglected except during violent maritime storms, but since the Battle of Guard, these underground passages were renovated and reinforced to house the majority of the city's population along with provisions and infirmaries to outlast a siege for months.

Casualties from the frontlines that were unable to be patched and sent back were to be brought in the largest open area of the city's undercroft, transformed with sleeping tents and operating salons in a makeshift field hospital.

Tenshi helped unload caches of medical supplies being siphoned by a chain of reserve soldiers and civilian volunteers from stores above ground, stacking them carefully against the wall for the surgeons and nurses to organize. She had desperately wanted to return to Freya with the Strafers that had accompanied her, but greater responsibilities were unexpectedly heaped upon her.

She looked over at little Marcus carrying woolen blankets to the nurses as they prepared the cots, surprising those he helped with his innate strength and unburdened kindness. Traits that were imparted in secret by his parents, or perhaps imbedded in the grain and unspoiled by ambition as most children were.

"Milady," Rowen interrupted, pulling her aside from the work chain and allowing another willing volunteer to take her place.

"Has everyone settled in?"

"Almost everyone," Rowen said, keeping a watchful eye on Marcus as Tenshi did. "Aside from the garrison policing units and the dock workers, there shouldn't be too many stragglers left in the city."

"I can gather up a team and go door to door."

"No, milady, that's my task," Rowen said. "Vant's son is your charge, and there's no one here his life can be trusted with. I believe you can also serve the Queen in the war room; it'll be safest there. Although I wish we could spare him the coming violence; no child should witness such horrors."

Marcus gave Tenshi an innocent smile that was affectionately reciprocated in turn. "The sounds of battle may terrify him," Tenshi said, "but he'll weather such storms, and become stronger for it."

Tenshi turned to Rowen and squeezed his forearm. "Good luck to you, Rowen."

Rowen lowered his chin in deep respect. "And to you, Lady Tenshi. We'll see each other at the end of this."

The King's Royal Army assembled outside the defensive walls of the capital, all armed with long-range hunting rifles added to the standard armaments. Regular infantry, Elites, and specialized sniper units were ready and in formation, while the rest consisted of artillery divisions. Thousands of cannons were organized along purpose-built trenches for safe transport of personnel and ammunition, and reinforced by pillboxes and hastily redesigned bombard towers.

All eyes were on the darkening sky for the arrival of the Gabrialtar fleet, and Marshal Catherano was growing restless.

Officers mulled about him with equal anxiousness, some running to and fro with orders to their respective commands, but all gave way to their King as he approached the headquarters.

"Your Majesty." Catherano bowed briskly, as he reviewed the battle map laid out on a table. "Our scouts have spotted the sky fleet just outside the Locked Shields, and the cannoneer companies stationed on the mountain range have started harassing the enemy ships at their flanks. The distraction is buying us a handful of precious minutes to finalize preparations."

"Any word from Freya?"

"None, sire."

Ingren nodded grimly. "We'll assume the worst. Raise the guns and stand fast; I want that fleet stopped before it reaches the first rampart."

"I strongly recommend that you take refuge at your castle's strongroom, Your Highness. This may be a battle more trying than any other we've faced."

"All the more reason to be here," Ingren said, glancing up just as a glimmer appeared under a passing cloud. "They're finally here." In moments, the dark specks became full-fledged warships. "Now we end this."

As evening fell, the overture of weapon fire that was traded between the ground forces and the sky fleet was overwhelming, drafting acrid fumes from the recoils onto the battlefield like a morning fog. Keels, blimps, and sails were riddled with bullets from riflemen, and tortured by the cannonade. Although shipboard guns ripped the ground beneath them – tossing bodies aside with reckless abandon – the battle was fierce, and casualties were suffered immediately.

One of the cruisers' zeppelins blew out, sending the vessel in an uncontrolled spin until it eventually smashed onto the countryside. Another sky vessel, its main deck aflame from an incendiary barrage, crashed headlong into a pair of bombard towers before crumbling under its weight. Onboard munitions sparked and exploded, causing further ruin on unprotected infantry and servicemen.

Despite the heavy resistance, a few sky galleons broke through the lines. The *Highborn* was amongst the first to trespass over the capital, and was mercilessly pelted by rooftop snipers. In response, it launched cluster bombs from its bays that burst into hundreds of smaller projectiles that rained down on the city. In resemblance of a spectacular meteor shower, the cluster bombs set buildings ablaze and wreaked chaos on the streets.

It was as much a weapon of fear as it was tactical, and it was exactly as Titus intended. He watched as the fires lit the young night from the safety of the galleon's pilothouse, and was determined to raze the capital to ashes.

"Target the castle," he ordered indifferently, "bring down those beautiful towers." He walked out onto the main deck with a coterie of Dragoons, wanting to witness the attack firsthand.

The *Highborn*'s forward guns unleashed a barrage onto the tallest spire, and tore away at the masonry until its crown teetered and fell apart in a cloud of dust and debris. The guns continued to ravage the remainder of the tower until a corsair cut across its path, and unhinged its own firepower on the larger vessel.

The *Highborn* broke off its assault on the castle, and maneuvered to its portside to face the rogue corsair. Its identifying flags were missing, but from the hull markings, it was the *Crossbow*.

Titus could only guess who was at the helm as he balanced himself from the rattle of the impacts, and held on to the railing as both ships exchanged broadsides.

On the ground, Ingren led the onrush back to the castle grounds, and witnessed the carnage in the sky above. His uniform was torn and dirty from fumes and spattered blood, but his nerves were taut as steel as he traversed past the large remains of the targeted tower blocking the main avenue to the courtyard.

There he encountered a group of battered cannoneers assigned to protect the castle. "Target the flagship's stern! Hit it with the flares!"

The cannoneers quickly adjusted their weapons, angling the turrets sharply, and delivered the packages with resounding thunder.

The *Highborn* was hit hard from beneath by the massive flares, bouncing its superstructure steeply to one side, and tossing a few of its deck crew overboard – Titus amongst them. They fell a short distance onto the sparsely colonnaded rooftop of the old castle keep, landing on their sides, while an unfortunate mariner hit the battlement and tumbled from the edge.

The wounded galleon veered hard to starboard and retreated out of the firing range of the King's cannons, returning some of its own wrath along its route that gouged craters from the courtyard and punched through buildings that were caught in the crossfire.

"Come about!" Sucre ordered in the midst of activity on the *Crossbow*'s bridge. "Give chase!"

"Belay that," Vant countered, his gaze on the rooftop where Titus had fallen. "Take us closer to the keep."

Sucre wanted to contest the order, but the general was determined. "As you will it, General. Helm, brings us to the closest tier of the castle keep."

"All able hands, follow me!" Vant unsheathed his sabre, and led the Strafers out onto the boarding ramp just as it swung down with a heavy thud – the corsair barely at a standstill.

He was accompanied by Seidon and Poem, and they charged across the flagstone rooftop toward Titus.

The Captain-General was dazed, but he immediately recoiled as he saw the aggressors coming at him. He unsheathed the Ancestral, its blade gleaming with the firelight of the burning capital around them, and was joined by a Dragoon who had survived the fall.

The marksman fired from his sniper rifle, hitting two Strafers, before he was himself struck. He stumbled beside another dazed Dragoon, who was spared no leniency as the Strafers battered him with several wild rounds.

Titus knew he was cornered, as he slowly moved back, but fought with brevity as the driven Strafers rushed his position. He dispatched the first man with two swings, severing the soldier's sword, then cut a deadly gash across the torso. The ease of the Ancestral's physical prowess gave him confidence, and wielded it against a second Strafer – thrashing him as if he were wheat under a scythe.

The other Strafers withdrew, backing away from Titus, and flanking Vant. Seidon and Poem continued the assault, the latter firing his double revolvers in an attempt to dislodge Titus, but the Captain-General was superbly swift and outmaneuvered the battery – suffering a single bullet scrape to his leg.

Before having the chance to recover, Titus clashed with the flat side of the heirloom sword against Seidon's blade as he delivered a brusque haymaker. Titus backpedaled, then thrust forth, but missed and exposed himself to the full brunt of Seidon's backhand.

Poem committed another assault at Titus' flank, using the hard end of the revolvers as blunt clubs. Titus parried with Ancestral, still disoriented, and retreated as far away from them before reaching the edge of the keep. He strode toward one of the columns, which carried the royal flag on a spear-tipped pole at the top, and used the Ancestral to slice through the pillar's waist with a single swing. The deafening howl of stone being cut was followed by its grand collapse, creating a small barrier between him and his sworn enemies.

Titus laughed maniacally as the grey dust settled, and the torn royal flag crumpled to the ground beneath the debris. He stepped on its insignia, and faced his adversaries – to Vant in particular. "Here we rebuild our dreams of conquest, General!" he shouted with gusto, gesturing widely to the warring sky galleons. "This was a mere idea during the time of the Sorcerers; an ambitious flash of inspiration drawn by your engineers in the Corporate War! *I* have surpassed you!"

"A hateful testimony from a Strafer I once knew," Vant said as he and his Strafers joined Poem and Seidon at their side. "The intelligent optimism of a proud officer with a promising career has soured and rotted over the years. What you escaped from Guard will find you again in Gabrialtar."

"My love is only for Gabrialtar now, General," Titus said darkly. "I've adopted her as my new home, where I've tethered my soul and restarted life anew... and I will fight to protect her even if all else must be destroyed. This loyalty, this patriotism, I learned from you." He glanced at Seidon with eyes that reflected the flames around them. "You, I have no grudge, for long ago you gave me an insight worth a lifetime."

"What are we waiting for, Vant?" Poem said viciously. "Order your men to finish this!"

"You've learned the hard way about misplacing your faith," Titus retorted, his eyes on Poem. "For what you are worth, it would only take a simple push to turn you into what you hate most."

"Something's not right about him..." Seidon said, partly to himself, his instincts overriding rationality. "Who are you?!"

Titus grinned. "Always the first to realize the nub of these little affairs."

"Poem's right, enough of this." Vant raised his pistol and aimed it at Titus. "Strafers, take aim!"

All Strafers immediately raised their rifles, and locked their barrels on Titus.

Titus was arrogantly humbled. "Ah, an execution worthy of a soldier."

A heavy thrum of engines filled the air, and a single bullet zoomed from out of nowhere to hit Vant's pistol right out of his grip.

The *Highborn* returned, having encircled the perimeter after suffering damage to its ventral side, and hovered mightily behind Titus. Positioned along its portside railing was Mikaila and several Dragoons, all with their sniper rifles drawn and ready. Coupled with the galleon's primed port cannons, there was nothing stopping Titus from climbing the zeppelin's support rungs.

He stepped onto the deck, confidently placing away the Ancestral in its scabbard, and stood beside Mikaila. He gave her a sidelong glance, knowing her beautiful eyes were locked onto Vant, not with intent, but the temperateness of love. He grinned rather evilly. "For centuries, I have walked the path of choler and enmity that would make the delusory angels in heaven break apart in sheer terror. Let it be brought to an end here and now at last."

In a flurry of speed, Titus struck Mikaila, and pinned her to her knees in one sweeping motion. He held her own rifle between her shoulder blades, and paid no heed to the confused reactions of the Dragoons around them. She was herself stunned, but felt the fear and truth deep inside her.

Titus pulled back the hammer on the rifle, and smiled. "Irony, it seems, did not escape you." He fired at point blank, and she collapsed near the edge of the deck railing. Without much regard, he tossed the rifle away, and kicked her body off the side of the ship.

All watched, but none with more horror than Vant, as Mikaila's body crumpled onto the rooftop and laid still.

Titus gazed down, reveling in Vant's fresh misery. "Did you not hear the words ushered on my last breath?! I have survived death once before, my dear General, and I survived once more on the eve of your betrayal!"

"Necrosis..." Vant said, still numbed by Mikaila's death, that the realization was cold to his senses.

"Let us not fret, my friends, the days of sorcery are gone." Titus revealed the hilt-like Vilkacis detonator. "Herein lies the weapon of gods."

"Strafers – *FIRE!*" Vant howled with deep rage, his throat and lungs burning.

The Strafers unleashed their assault, spattering the *Highborn*'s bulwark with bullets. The Dragoons were the first to suffer the brunt of the attack, but a few responded and fired back. Titus ducked and withdrew with haste, as the galleon moved away from the keep and climbed altitude.

"Back to the *Crossbow!*" Seidon ordered, and led the Strafers to a retreat of their own across the rooftop.

Vant remained still, his steps moving toward Mikaila.

"War's not over, Vant," Poem said, stopping the anguished General with his words alone. He then followed after Seidon and the others.

Vant gave Poem a sidelong glance, but deep in his heart, what needed to be done came into focus. He forced his feet to move toward the corsair, and once he was aboard, the vessel quickly ascended after the *Highborn*. He held the ropes tight as the wind and speed pushed him, and dared to look at Mikaila one last time.

"Now there's a son... without a mother..." His sadness was profound, but he kept it close to his heart.

Seidon, standing a few feet behind him along with Poem, felt Vant's pain. He wanted to say something to comfort him, but held back.

Poem, unlike Seidon, tried hard to keep his sympathy in check. "Is it true then? Is it the old Sorcerer?"

Vant nodded joylessly, his back still to them. "...Titus was one of the Strafers present when Mikaila used an armour-piercing bullet imbued with the Elixir that I obtained from the Church... Necrosis was too clever even on his death throes, and I should've realized his last words were in fact a spell in completion."

"...He anchored his soul to Titus?" Poem said, uncertain.

"Like Tenshi," Scidon responded grimly. "He said I had inspired him."

"Then let us make this pact, that one of us will send Necrosis back to the tomb where we found him." Vant's resolve was brutally cunning. "Drive the *Highborn* to the sea, let him be buried with the rest of his fleet."

The intensity of the surface-to-air assault on the sky fleet was overwhelming, and with their flagship wounded, the Gabrialtar fleet syphoned away from the capital toward the reaches of the coast. There they were met by the entire naval might of Magna Carta, from first-rate ships-of-the-line to frigates, iron-clad cruisers, and floating batteries, upgraded from their harsh battles of the Corporate War, the King's ships covered nearly the whole horizon of the Vast Blue.

Cannonfire was traded, and havoc ensued. Along the port, high-powered harpoon emplacements swiveled about and targeted a galleon that flew low for a strafing run across the town. The claw-like harpoons lodged into the zeppelins and lower hull, with each impact bouncing the vessel. Reversing its engines, the galleon tugged one of the emplacements off its base, but the severe pressure on the support struts tore one of its zeppelins apart. Losing flight, chunks of hull from the doomed vessel fell away as it careened into a pier, then smashed headlong into the water.

At the helm of the *Second Awakening,* Messer watched as yet another sky galleon succumbed to the merciless barrage from the King's Navy. Fire spit from breaches all over its superstructure, then tumbled from the sky entirely ablaze. The royalist defenders were not spared similar fates, as the sky ships still retained mastery of the proverbial high ground.

Howitzers that were designed initially for trench warfare were now equipped on the castles of the naval cavalry, manned by experienced ground crew, and pounded on the Gabrialtar fleet with relative efficiency. While rounds were fired by the hundreds, with a fraction striking their intended targets, it was enough to provide an effective resistance.

"Coordinate our efforts with the Redoubtable and the Ingrena," Messer ordered to one of the attending officers. "The more of these ships we take down, the better the chances they will flee."

"Admiral!" Semmes called from his observation post, tracking a vessel with a scope alongside another officer. "The Highborn is retreating from the capital! She's attempting to rejoin her fleet!"

Messer searched the sky past the bowsprit, and saw the wounded beast in a firefight with a smaller vessel. "Identify that corsair."

It took a moment for Semmes to recognize its markings. "The ship's flying with the King's standards, sir. It must be General Vant."

"The only one foolhardy enough," Messer said.

In the fortified war room deep in the heart of the royal castle, Tenshi held Marcus close as tremors from the battle outside reverberated throughout the capital. They were encircled by large tables with detailed outlays of the entire continent, particularly the capital city and its surroundings. Officers and technicians constantly updated the current positions and statuses of every force in play, from infantry regiments to ships, and consulted with superior officers within the milieu and out on the field.

Shortwave receiver displays also coveted the walls and central conference boards, their bluish spill adding to the grave atmosphere of the place.

Queen Dalena was the backbone of order in the middle of all this, truly justifying her title and experience, and acted as a proxy for the King as she conferred with President Gehenna through one of the displays.

"There are no terms," Dalena said harshly. "This attack on our kingdom is unjustified."

"...I entirely agree," Gehenna obliged humbly, the inconveniency of her decisions now felt in full force. "Certain measures to protect our resources were taken too far."

"The last war left us with nearly a quarter of a million dead on every side that was involved," Dalena stated, losing none of her abrasiveness. "It left us with an unavoidable energy crisis, and now this..." She allowed Gehenna to digest the ramifications of inter-continental war. "Have you ever considered the lasting impression we will leave on this world after this battle is said and done?"

"There is no excuse, nor any informal apology I can give. I was defending my home, as you are now defending yours." Gehenna replied. "Oblique policies on the part of all governments have been hampered with mistrust, and we've arrived to this. Perhaps all we can do now, before more lives are taken, is to call a cease-fire."

"That's all I ask, Madam President, and I hope against all hopes that in this respite, we can find a commonplace."

Gehenna nodded. "My wish is with yours, Queen Dalena."

The transmission ended between them, just as another tremor passed through the walls, and Dalena sighed as if the conversation had taken all her strength and more. Now the fate of the battle rested with the leaders of the nascent island-nation a thousand miles away.

Titus stood on the open observation deck situated above the *Highborn*'s pilothouse, both hands rested on the forward security railing. The intense battle that surrounded him – explosive clouds from missed mortars, guns firing, ships and men colliding in hellish conflict – were all drowned out by the orchestral music in his mind.

His eyes were closed, and his thoughts were in concord, until a nearby blast shook the galleon with a teeth-jarring shudder.

He opened his eyes as he took on an angry mask, and the cacophony of war rushed back to his senses. Behind him were his officers in desperate need of solutions.

"There is no retreat until I order it, Commodore," Titus said. "We destroy their navy, then tighten the noose on the capital."

"Our casualties are mounting, sir," the dissident sky fleet commodore defended. "This action will leave us crippled even if we score a decisive victory. This fleet will be ineffective in holding the royal stronghold."

"I have no intention of holding it. The orders stand."

Disgruntled, but obedient, the commodore rushed back to the pilothouse, leaving Titus with Colonel Reginald to contend with.

The colonel seemed hesitant, sizing the Captain-General in a new, darker light. "Sir, the Dragoons demand an explanation."

"They *demand*...?" Titus challenged the threat, and would have summarily ordered the colonel and the Dragoons thrown overboard if it weren't for their tactical usefulness. "She was a traitor, Colonel."

Reginald found the excuse hard to swallow. "But she was valiant in your defense, a model soldier for our sniper corps. If she was at fault, then she should have been tried in a military court–"

"She was an unemployed, masterless ronin when she came to us, and a turncoat who was pregnant with Rell Vant's child. The recruiters bent all the rules to keep her in the roster, giving her a rank, for she was a valuable asset, and she knew no other profession. I won't deny her talents, for she raised the Dragoons to proper form. The only shame was that her motherhood was cut short." Titus paused in retrospect. "Do you honestly believe that she would have killed the father of her child to protect me?"

When the colonel didn't answer, Titus knew this debate was over. "Contact Vilkacis Control, and instruct them to reset coordinates for the Royal Capital."

Just as the colonel was about to turn and leave, the *Highborn* pitched sharply from a collision against its port. Panic erupted amongst the deck crew, and Titus regained his balance in time to see the determined bow of the renegade corsair trailing them tightly astern.

Titus smirked. "Do you wish to dance, General? Then let us up the ante."

On the *Crossbow*, Vant pushed the ship and its crew harder. The galleon was a stone throw's away, and he could almost see the white of Titus' eyes from his place on the command deck astern.

"The engines are starting to buckle, General!" Sucre reported over the noise of battle. "Our engineers are doing their best to keep the furnaces going, but we risk explosion!"

"We're at their flank, give them full broadsides!" Vant ordered. "Get all available sharpshooters on the deck and start firing – no one stops until I give the order!"

"Starboard bow has taken severe structural damage," Seidon warned as he oversaw activity from the pilothouse. "The hull plating's peeling back, and the ship's timbers are falling apart at the seams!"

Vant ignored the admonition. "Fire!"

The cannonade erupted at near point-blank range, shredding hulls as if the cladding and boards were consisted of paper. Smalls fires swelled from breaches on both ships, yet the bombardment failed to cease. One of the *Highborn*'s masts snapped from its base and tumbled over onto the corsair, entangling itself with the enemy sails and mortally locking both ships together.

Stray shards of steel and wooden splinters caused casualties on the exposed decks, with a blunt projectile wounding the *Crossbow*'s pilot. Vant gallantly took charge, and pivoted the control wheel in a frenzy to ram the corsair once more against the galleon. Both ships banked violently, and with the irreparable damage to the zeppelins, they lost altitude and swayed toward the sea.

They split the waves ferociously, and were afloat amongst the amalgam of His Majesty's Fleet. The Gabrialtar ships plummeted to the aid of their flagship like birds-of-prey swooping down on the surface of the water, in a hurried attempt to join the fray. The waters were so cluttered with ships, gunfire, and smoke from the discharges, that vessels were far more likely to collide onto themselves. Boarding parties were quickly arranged, and the fighting progressed to infantry warfare with riflemen sniping each other across short distances.

Vant, unlike the corsair, was unshaken. He picked up a scattergun and led the way out of the mangled bridge. "Storm the enemy vessel with everything we have – don't give them a chance to organize!"

The decks were strewn with bodies and debris, while all around them was sheer chaos. Vant in mid-stride paused to assess their overall position, and let Sucre and the rest of the Strafers charge past him. Nearby, Seidon, rifle in one hand, and an axe in the other, called the Elites to action.

The *Crossbow* and the *Highborn* were caught in the crossfire between the defenders and the invaders, charging into the ocean with churning doggedness to surround their crippled flagship. Behind Vant, the situation grew worse as concentrated fire tore down a Gabrialtar battleship during its descent, and it fell hard onto a derelict, mast-less cruiser just a hundred yards off the *Crossbow*'s port flank.

The massive explosion sent a shockwave that pushed ships and men for miles around, spraying debris with equal force and pelting everything around the flash point. It tore apart what remained of sails and funnels, and punctured through wooden and metal-plated hulls, maiming unprotected men.

Vant was struck by a sharp object no larger than a pellet, which pierced through his back and exited his upper chest. His breath was kicked out of him, and his hand reached to his wound, but the shock of the hit kept him from feeling the pain. Blood stained his uniform, and he staggered.

He fell back, onto the arms of Seidon, who caught him just before hitting the deck.

"*Sucre!*" Seidon shouted in deep desperation, and caught the notice and appall of all those around them.

Sucre abandoned all else and rushed to them. He wasted no time ripping open Vant's jacket and checking the bleeding wound. "This doesn't look good." More Strafers surrounded them, while the pall of battle pursued relentlessly. "We need a medic–" He grabbed the arm of one of the Strafers nearby. "Find Hailey, get her here now!"

Seidon held back the inevitable, refusing to accept it, and aware of how this affected the morale of the troops around them. "Sucre, we got to get him below."

Sucre sensed the faltering spirits of his soldiers, as his own teetered on the edge. He nodded to Seidon, then looked to the most senior officer surrounding them. "Argolla, send word to Major Freyr if he's still on his feet; take the fight to their ship, and spare no one."

Lieutenant Argolla rushed to carry out the grisly command, and with a handful Strafers covering them, they carried Vant down the narrow stairwell and passageway, past the frantic gun crews to the orlop deck. Normally staffed by a surgeon and deckhands, the place was dim and used hastily for storage, but the Strafers rigged a few lanterns and set them around the area. They placed Vant carefully on the operating table, scattering the random items that were left behind by the Gabrialtar crew before they were remanded to Freya's security forces.

"Marcus..." Vant whispered feverishly. "...Marcus..."

Sucre was unnerved, and his emotions were left unchecked. "Where's the medic?!"

Seidon felt the same way, but he kept by Vant's side and set a folded blanket under his head to make him more comfortable. It was all or nothing, and everyone here knew that.

Bloodied and battered, Hailey was hastily escorted in, and she immediately set aside her confusion to treat Vant. She turned to the Strafer that brought her, "Put pressure on his chest wound!" She noticed blood from the backside, and feared the worse, as she wiped the entry wound and probed for the extent of internal damage. The effort tossed Vant into a guttural fit, and threatened to aggravate the situation. "Hold him still!"

Seidon, Sucre, and the Strafers held Vant down to the table. Hailey removed her jacket and shoved it under Vant's back, then rummaged through the cabinets for alcohol and salves, but it was obvious from her shaking hands that the situation was hopeless. The blood loss was too much.

"Tell me you can keep him alive," Sucre said, a threatening edge in his tone.

Hailey was uncertain how to answer, but the lack of response was enough said.

"Captain-of-Arms..." Vant said, his voice eerily quiet, yet full of presence and demanding attention.

Sucre was crestfallen. "Yes, General."

"Last orders..." Vant strained willfully. "Victory... to the last man."

Angry tears welled up in his eyes, but Sucre understood the order. "We will make you proud, sir."

Vant, his eyes half-closed, smiled weakly. "...I am proud." Surrounded by his loyal Strafers, he felt at peace, yet there was one among them that he considered a true equal. "Seidon... is the war over?"

Seidon glanced at the others, none of them used to seeing their storied leader detached from reality, then looked back at Vant. "There's one last task, and we can't fail."

Vant lifted his bloodied hand, and Seidon took it firmly. "My son..."

"I'll take him as my own," Seidon comforted with a lump of emotion in his throat. "I will make him remember you with all the love and joy you had given him."

Vant grinned, washed with a relief from all the burdens that few would ever endure, until all life faded from him. He died quietly on the table, surrounded by those who loved him truly.

There was a culmination of silence, but it was broken by gunfire and flak outside the timbered walls of the orlop deck.

"Victory to the last man." Sucre swore on those words entirely, then he and the Strafers straightened their backs and saluted their General before charging valiantly into battle.

Seidon stood up, the vow he made with Vant and Poem remembered unrefutably, and his own will quickened.

Poem directed the Elites on the main deck, the tangled mast serving as a rickety conduit to the *Highborn*. "Take the initiative! Board her or be boarded!" As the soldiers rushed past him, he spotted Seidon emerging from below the weather deck behind the onrush of emotional Strafers. "You alright? Where's Vant?"

Seidon didn't need to answer, and he gripped the handle of his axe tightly. "We have a promise to keep."

The *Highborn* was at an awkward slant, but Titus maneuvered through her corridors with rabid eagerness, stepping over the crumpled bodies of mariners and that of the commodore without so much a pause in his stride. A gash on his forehead let down a trickle of blood, and he ignored it as he bursted into his office-quarters – its furniture strewn about by the crash.

Colonel Reginald was by the glitching shortwave receiver, limping on a broken leg, and looked at the Captain-General as if resigned. "It's over. A truce has been verbally signed."

Titus scowled. "It means nothing," he spat bitterly, and pushed the colonel aside to face Gehenna on the flickering screen. "How dare you send your diplomats before the guns have been stalled?"

Gehenna was not intimidated. "Order all ships to cease fire and withdraw immediately."

"Triumphant, I will not. You would have me fed to the royal dogs to save face."

"Then be relieved of your command. I'm transmitting this order to all captains of the fleet."

"No!" Titus bursted in a frenzy, startling the bewildered colonel. "I will see Magna Carta in ruins!" He unsheathed the

Vilkacis detonator and angrily smashed its trigger-pommel on the tabletop beside him.

The click sounded empty, and Titus, fuming, regarded the hilt-like device with disgust the same way he glared at Gehenna.

"Your mastery over the ballistic missiles have been overridden," Gehenna stated with cold satisfaction. "As is any hope of escaping your trial."

Titus cackled, glancing away for a moment. "How quickly we forget whose credits are due... the sky ships, the refineries, the machine guns... all of it. Who was it that designed the Vilkacis to begin with?"

The terror in Gehenna's eyes were only a window to the horror Titus was about to unleash on her. Coldly, he twisted the detonator's handle, and smashed the trigger again on the tabletop. Only this time, the reaction was carried across the Vast Blue....

One of the remaining minarets that surrounded the Name's Reclaim thrummed and glowed eerily. Fumes and fiery spouts emerged from it, as if a caged demon was struggling to escape. The people of Empyrean City watched in uncertainty as the core of the missile exploded, releasing a sphere of destruction that shred apart the tower, spread to demolish a section of the Name's Reclaim, and parts of the taller buildings in the vicinity.

Two sky ships were also caught in the blast, and fell from their perches in flames.

* * *

Gehenna's image was interrupted with static, and Titus mightily tossed the detonator aside. Removing the Ancestral from its sheath, he turned to Colonel Reginald, who was unable to comprehend what just occurred. Titus killed the officer in one fell swing, then mercilessly stepped over the macabre mess to meet all else who stood in his way.

He marched past frenzied crewmen struggling to keep the galleon afloat, then onto the battered deck where soldiers fought each other using whatever weapon was at their disposal. Beyond them, fleets appeared as phantoms in the heavy fog.

He stood in the eye of the cyclone, and glanced up at the sky, and although it was cluttered with broken stays and ripped sails, he managed to peek through the azure heavens. "How quaint we've become over the ages..."

Sucre spotted him after delivering a lethal blow on an enemy mariner, and assailed the Captain-General in an instant. Titus was ready, and parried the first attack, then side-stepped the follow-up thrust.

"Such fervour," Titus mused as he countered Sucre's mad lunges. "Are we longing for what's been lost?"

Sucre's last swing broke his sabre's blade in half, but he never flinched as he drew out a pistol and pulled the trigger at point-blank. Titus reacted faster and smacked the barrel upward just as the muzzle loaded, igniting a bright spark that shunned Sucre against the nearby mast and to the floor in recoil.

Titus snarled, his face and uniform stained with carbon-scoring, but otherwise suffering no sore. The moment he took a step toward the downed Strafer, Seidon blind-sided him with a ruthless tackle, then swung down with his axe. Titus rolled out of the way, and returned to his feet, only to duck and sprint for the cover of crates as Poem riddled his path with bullets from his double revolvers.

Taking in the surroundings, Titus swung the crystal blade and cut the knot that held one of the sails in place. The canvas unfolded uncontrollably over Poem, and crashed on the spot as he moved out of the way. The action afforded Titus the time to move away from cover and engage Seidon.

Knowing the lethality of his heirloom sword, Seidon avoided parrying and backpedaled away from Titus' attacks. When an opening presented itself, he struck back, and ripped a gash off Titus' flank. Titus retaliated, closing the distance as Seidon attempted to back away, and destroyed the axe's sturdy handle with an angry slash, the tip of Ancestral cutting across Seidon's chest in the process.

The wound was superficial, and it left Seidon defenseless as Titus stabbed the Ancestral into his upper left leg. Seidon yelped in pain and bristle, and delivered a nasty backhanded uppercut in return.

Titus dropped back, pulling Ancestral with him, then felt the full brunt of Poem's onslaught as he summoned a blast of cold ice – using his revolver as a medium - that threw the Captain-General back. More annoyed than hurt, Titus assaulted with the pommel of his sword, and struck Poem on the chin – splitting it. He then cut high, pivoting the blade at an awkward angle due to lack of proper distance, and sliced Poem's shoulder, causing him to involuntarily drop one of his handguns.

Poem, hurt and angry, fired a round from his remaining revolver, which Titus' amazingly blocked with the flat end of the Ancestral before grabbing Poem's gun hand and twisting it away from his person. Poem countered by locking his arm around Titus' sword arm and kept him from using it.

Both men struggled desperately, until Sucre reared up behind Titus and stabbed his broken sabre through the Captain-General's right shoulder blade.

Titus was stunned at first, glancing down at the sharp stump of the severed blade jutting out of his chest, but he remained steadfast. He shoved Poem to his knees, then backhanded Sucre behind him. Ahead, Seidon limped into view holding one of Poem's revolvers in hand, and fired a single volley. The bullet ripped through the gullet, and Titus was left speechless as he reached to grasp his neck with a free hand.

Poem let go of everything, and swiftly pried the Ancestral off Titus' weakened grip. He swung the blade around in a perfect revolution, and stabbed it clean through Titus' torso. A silence seemed to fill the void, as blood dripped from ugly gashes, and vibrant life became a feeble wisp.

Poem put a hand on Titus' chest, and pushed him gently off the crystal blade. Titus dropped heavily onto his back – deadweight and expired before he touched the ground.

"Sleep Necrosis," Seidon said as he stood over the foe that now was no mightier than any fallen soldier. "Join your brethren in the hereafter... in amity."

One by one, the guns fell silent, as the orders for truce spread across both warring fleets, and flags were lowered in need for accord.

Exhausted, but no longer lost, Poem handed the Ancestral to his friend, and Seidon gladly took the heirloom sword back in hands. Both men were glad they lived through this hellish battle, and embraced.

XXIII. Second Awakening

XXIII. Second Awakening

In the aftermath of the Vilkacis explosion, in a world in need of reparation and reconciliation, the Name's Reclaim was left partly in shambles, with a large section of its outer walls and supports obliterated by the shockwave. The reservists and fire brigade organized a search and rescue for survivors, while the engineer corps and local masonry guilds quickly moved to shore up the damaged edifice.

Gehenna was found alive under a collapsed archway, and was rushed to the field clinic to be tended by the army surgeons, as were several other officials and civilians. There were dozens of casualties, and many were still missing under the rubble in and around Name's Reclaim and in the borough below.

Regento had been on his way to a docked transport when the spire blew, and was pinned under a small pillar that folded inward as the transport sheared away from its berth. Though his escorts were killed in the mayhem, he survived, yet was helpless and too far from the search crews for anyone to hear his cries for help. The rescue efforts carried into the night, with the air wafting from the ocean exceedingly cold, but soon dawn broke free of the dark clouds.

He heard a rustling and shuffling of men nearby, and quickly reached out with his ringed hand. "Help me! I'm trapped here!"

There was a pause, as the men deliberated in muffled tones, then the debris that covered Regento was carefully shifted away. It was a trio of rough-hewn Squires that took advantage of the confusion by looting the few valuables strewn about the Name's Reclaim, as well having no misgivings on robbing the dead and wounded.

Regento recognized the stragglers from Skein's ill-fated group. "Quickly now, get me out of this damn bind."

The ruffians looked at each other, neither of them having any compulsion to give aid. Although what they lacked in moral capacity, they compensated with weary avarice and bitterness.

"You drove the Squires to ruin," the oldest of the ruffians grunted. "Lady Fortune must owe you a favour."

"Quit fretting, and grab my hand," Regento snapped.

The old Squire snorted, stealing a sly glance at his comrades before firmly grasping Regento's outstretched hand. "We're though with you," he said, and filched the ruby rings from Regento's fingers. "You're no Marquis of ours."

Swindled by these braggarts, and with no hope of being pulled free of the pillar that was crushing him, Regento lost his nerve. "Bastards!" he cursed toward the retreating Squires. "I'll gut you all!"

He yelled out his frustration, and tried to crawl and scratch himself out of his predicament, but to no avail. The last wisps of night had faded, and the traces of sunlight appeared frozen along the eastern horizon, stretching out time to what seemed an endless slog. He had nearly wore out his throat with his shouting when a hooded figure crossed over him, and with great effort saved him from the crushing weight of the broken pillar.

Regento now felt the shearing pain across his whole back, and knew his right leg was too mangled to bear his weight, as his rescuer lifted him up.

"My leg's broken," Regento protested.

"A lot of things are broken in this world," the hooded figure said, as he wrapped Regento's arm around his shoulders. "Not everything can mend."

Regento thought it strange, limping heavily while leaning on this stranger's strength, but said nothing of it. The pain was intense, and dehydration took its toll on his bearing and alertness. He allowed his rescuer to lead him away from the rubble, but after a time, he noticed they had moved past the search teams, and far from Name's Reclaim.

"Where are you taking me? We passed the field hospital back there…"

The hooded figure held on tight, and kept walking the dazed Regento down toward the old aqueducts beneath the governmental pavilion where several small, secluded jetties stuck out toward the sea and the rising sun.

"I'm taking you where I last saw my son."

Regento tried to pull himself away, but was too weak to resist.

"He enjoyed fishing here, especially in the early hours, and he would always bring breakfast home." The hood fell away, and it was Priamos. "His grandfather taught him; I was too busy with the shop."

They reached one of the jetties, cluttered with old barrels and abandoned rigging. There was no wind, and it was quiet despite the rolling of the waves, as sunlight washed over the sea.

"This is where you left him to bleed out."

"Let me go, old man," Regento threatened in desperation.

"My son refused to join your Squires, to be bullied and coerced by you and your ilk, and you murdered him for his courage." Priamos effortlessly stabbed Regento through the back, and through the Marquis' heart with his son's dagger. "Tell me what were his last words? I... can't remember what were mine when I saw him last."

Priamos unceremoniously dumped Regento on the pile of rigging, ignoring the wheezing and moaning coming from Regento's mouth as blood seeped out his mortal wound. "All the wealth you stole, Liberthier Regento, and not a single shilling could save you now."

Regento's breathing turned shallow, the gurgling of blood that filled his lungs lessening until he passed on with eyes open and staring into the nothingness, while Priamos looked out to the new dawn.

"All those good people you hurt can rest now." Priamos walked away, assured of his terrible deeds, and having found a glimmer of peace for himself.

General Rell Vant and Mikaila were buried in the War Memorial of Magna Carta's capital, side by side, as they would've have been in life during peaceful times. The ceremony was kept simple and amongst those who knew and respected him, as despite his sacrifice for greater purpose, old sins were still far from forgiven.

The Strafers, now commanded by Sucre as part of the King's Guard Legion, fulfilled the departure of their greatest general with solemnity and unswerving loyalty that transformed into love and inspiration. Seidon stood with them, alongside Marcus and Tenshi, a family by happenstance and strengthened with resolve.

Paying their respects in silence, King Ingren and Queen Dalena, prominent and firm, kept close to each other with hands firmly gripped in the company of Throne Guards, Chancellor Rowen, Admiral Messer, Marshal Catherano, other military officers, scholars, nobles, and nearly the entire Elite Brigade.

They all watched as Marcus, red and white roses in hand, moved away from the procession and placed the flowers on his parents' graves; red for his mother, and white for his father. He stood there, seeming too young to grasp the gravity of his loss, but within him was a profound and cultured soul that understood his parents were forever gone.

Seidon moved beside him. "I was a little older than you when my mother passed away; it's a grief that you'll carry for the rest of your life. But with that grief you carry their love, their wisdom, and all the good things to pass on to others. Your parents died as they lived, in the end trying to make the world a better place for you."

Marcus, without needing to say anything, deeply proud of his parents' sacrifice, held Seidon's hand tightly.

Touched by the moment, Ingren looked at Julia with unconditional love and smiled warmly, his hand reaching to caress her swelling womb and to his heir.

In turn, safe and stout by his side, she placed her hand on his.

The closure was marked by the salute of guns that echoed into the air, and through the distant walls of the capital city being rebuilt once more.

* * *

At Templari, in the conference chamber of the Administrate Parliament, the representatives of free nations sat in open discussion on the behest of Grand Master Mellka. He oversaw the meeting quietly, pondering the aftermath of recent events, as the ambassadors attempted to find common ground despite the devastation felt across the known world.

Weeks had passed since Gabrialtar and Magna Carta laid down their arms, so blood was still fresh, and it took all his efforts and those of the Cardinalate to render this gathering possible. Above the accusations, the mistrust, the anger, and the grief, there was something incorruptible in the human spirit that brought them all here. The faintest hope for a lasting peace, and the perseverance to pick up the bits of our lives, and move on.

Mellka stood up, garnering the attention of all present. "Differences will always drive a wedge between us, but we are blessed with the choice to act against injustice. Are we driven by instinct? Or desire? How often do we let our ambitions go unchecked?" He contemplated on his remarks, as did the others. "Somewhere in this war and the last, we lost sight of the fundamentals that separate us from beasts. We've become the dragons we hated and feared... but even dragons dream of the unattainable." He glanced at all men and women at the conference. "Our civilization lies on the edge of obsolescence... reflections of our souls. How do we rebuild?"

"On a foundation of faith," a familiar voice replied.

All looked to Poem as he entered, and Mellka took the answer of his former disciple to heart. He sheltered no grudge, felt no pity, but offered forgiveness in silence.

"On a foundation of faith," Mellka repeated with renewed spirit, "all towers that have fallen can be crowned again. Faith, not on any institution or ideology, but in each other."

The *Journey's Prodigy* sailed through the Vast Blue with impetus and grace borne from its sleek lines and brilliant sails. Its soul was solidified by its captain, Seidon, who passed on his knowledge of the seas to Marcus Vant Harbrid by teaching him to steer on the pilot wheel.

Tenshi was handling the mizzen mast with the wind hard at their backs, and her heart warmed at the wish that was granted to her. She watched lovingly as Seidon became a father, carrying the will and compassion of the Harbrid generations, the charismatic resolve of Rell Vant, and his own adventurous spirit onto Marcus' curious world.

The lesson brought a smile on the child's lips, a reward in itself after a tumultuous campaign from one corner of the world to the next.

The horizon was open to them, and with glorious caerulean skies overhead, they sailed free and to all the mysteries life awaited.

Seidon

Poem

King Ingren

Captain Semmes

Chancellor Precidious

Precept Cardinal Achrone

Precept Cardinal Libra

Mellkan Honour Guard

Sailor Monk

Grand Master Vatic

Tinkertown Enforcer

President Gehenna

Lt. Colonel Mikaila

Gabrialtar Officer

Gabrialtar Dragoon

Captain-of-Arms
Sucre

Anadail Della'Cor

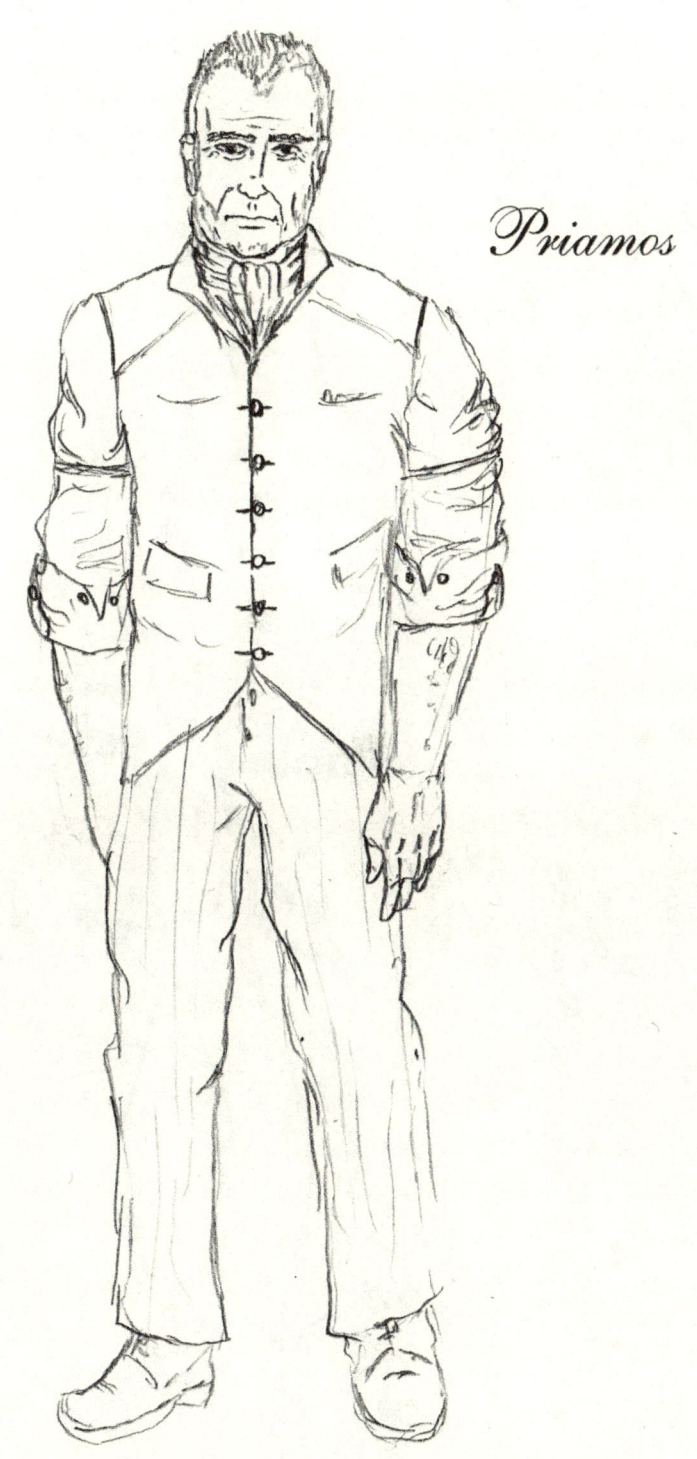

Priamos

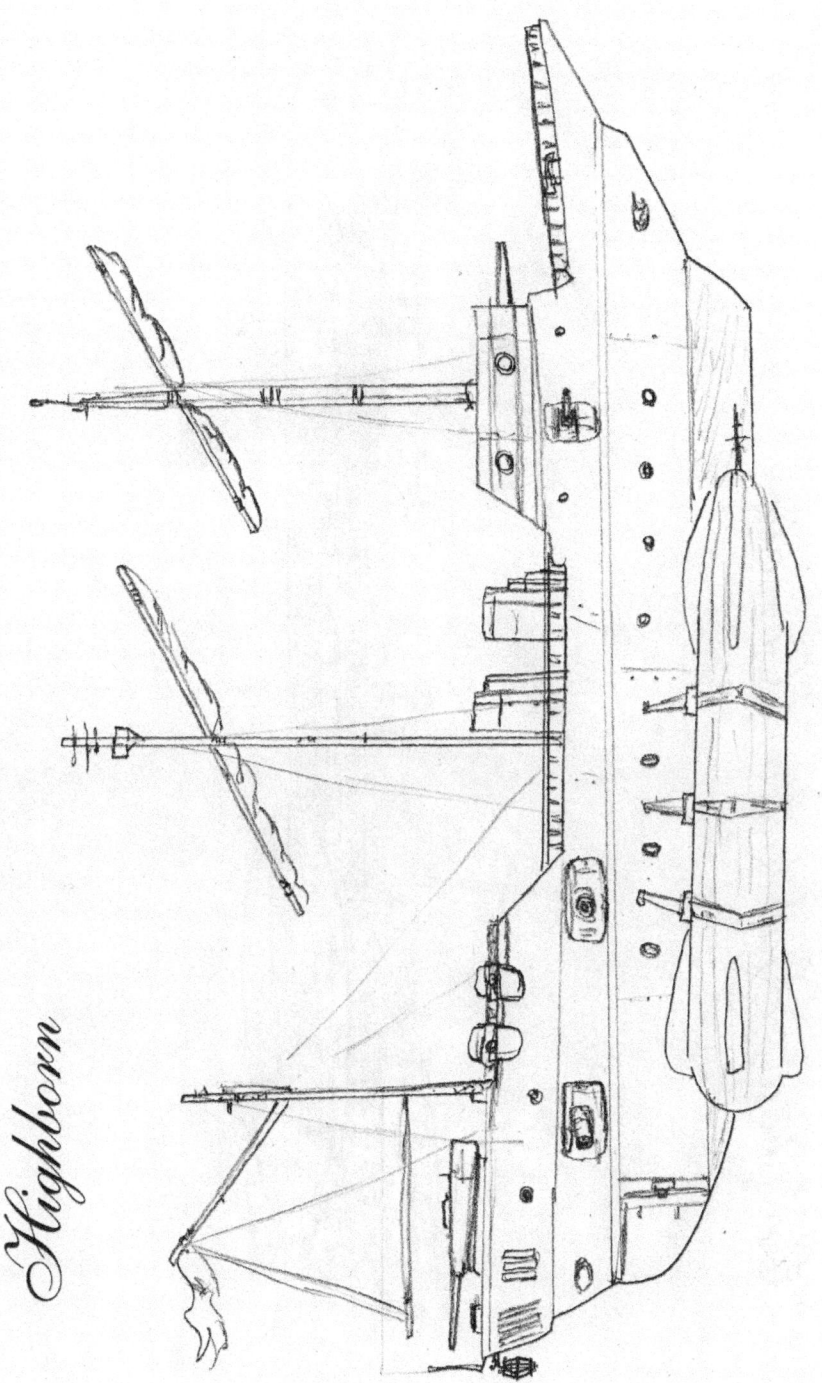

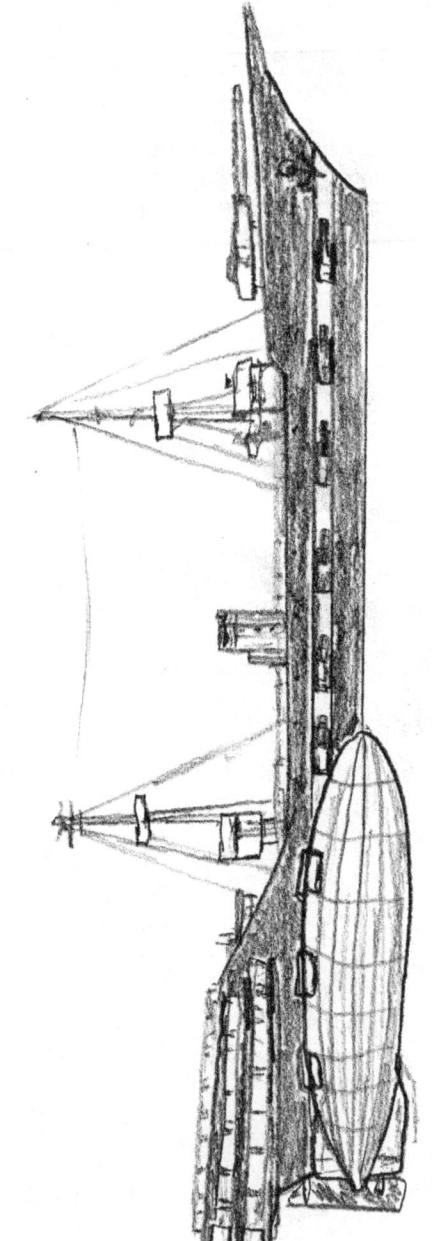

Crossbow, Gabrialtar Corsair

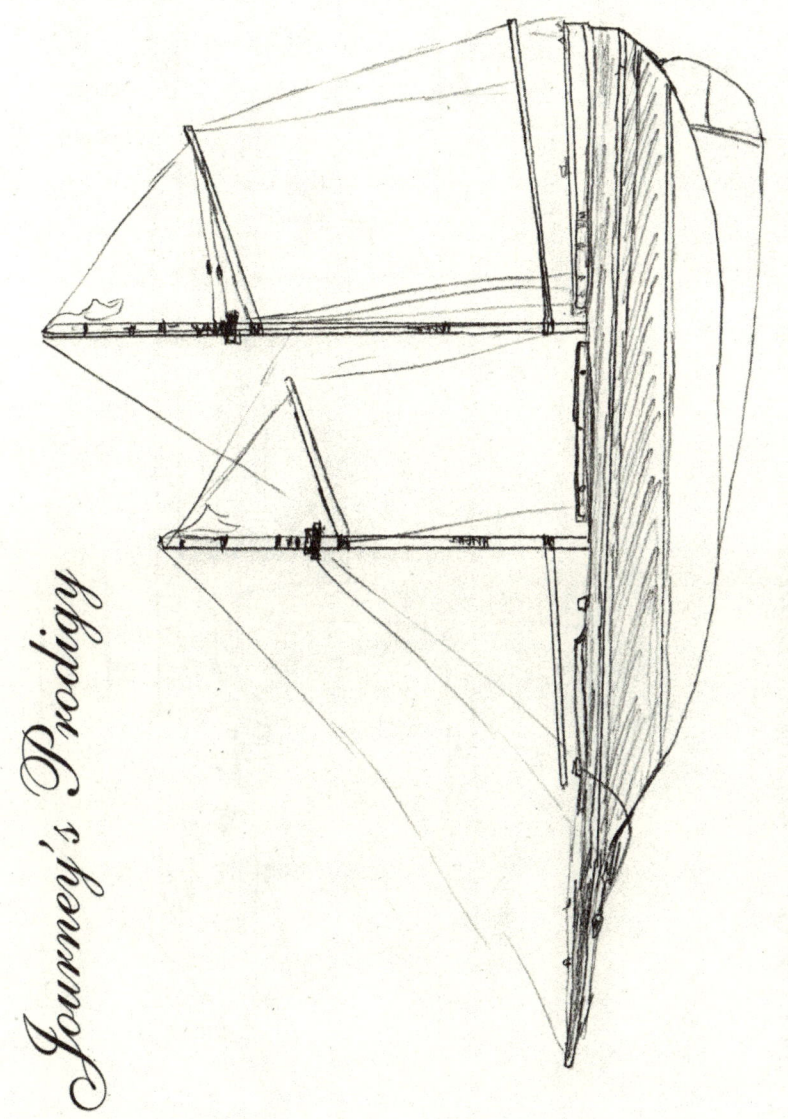

Journey's Prodigy

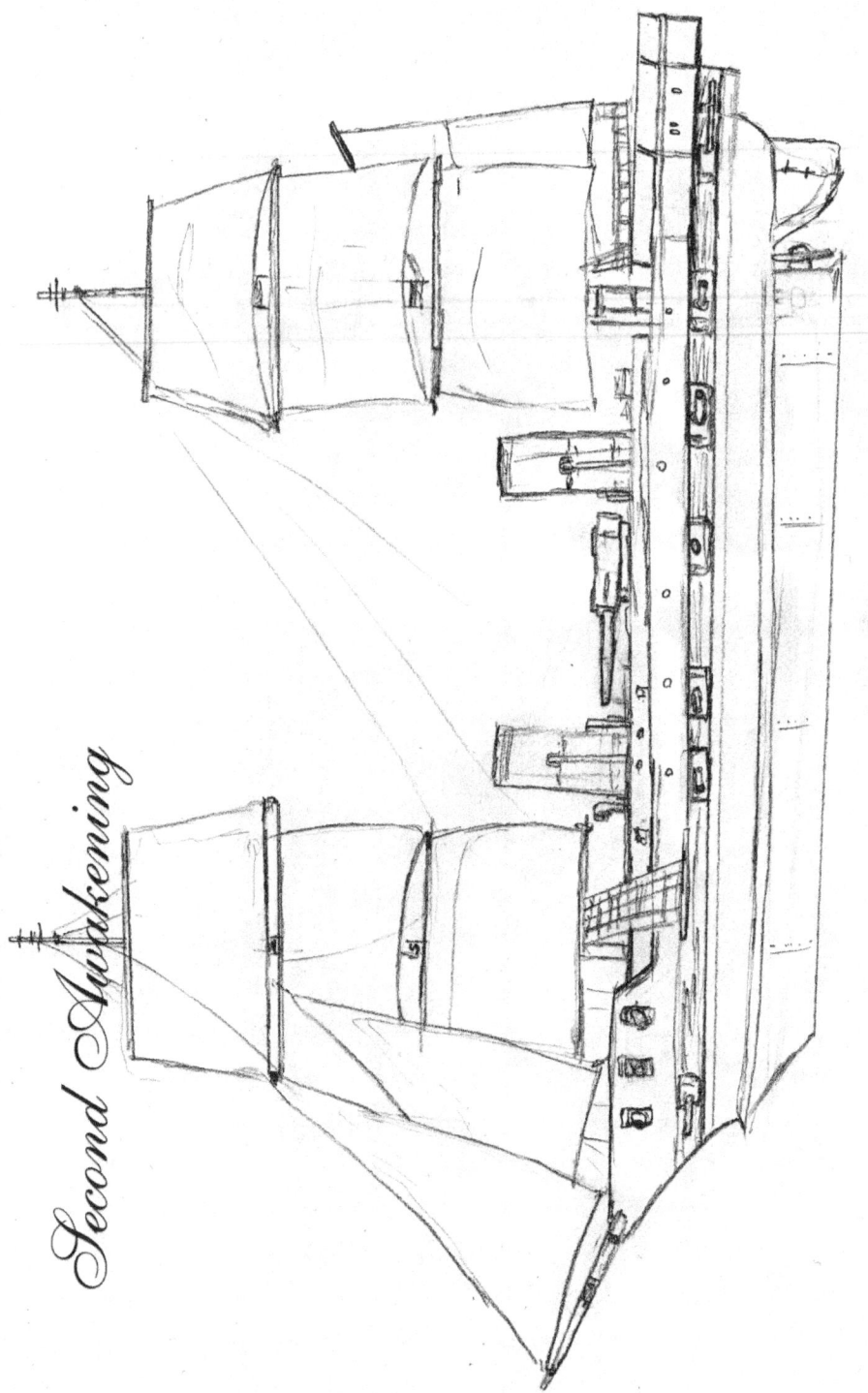

Sea of the Southern Cross

Saint's Foothold

Sewell's Abide

Empyrean City

Gabrialtar

The journey ends....

Made in United States
North Haven, CT
02 June 2024

53135264R00289